Lawrence Scott is from Trinidad and Tobago. His novel *Aelred's Sin* (1998) was awarded a Commonwealth Writers' Prize, Best Book in Canada and the Caribbean, 1999. His first novel *Witchbroom* (1992) was shortlisted for a Commonwealth Writers' Prize (1993), Best First Book. This was followed by *Ballad for the New World* (1994), which included the Tom Gallon award-winning short story 'The House of Funerals' (1995). His novel *Night Calypso* (2004) was also shortlisted for a Commonwealth Writers' Prize, Best Book Award, longlisted for the International IMPAC Dublin Literary Award (2006), and translated into French as *Calypso de Nuit* (2005). It was the One Book, One Community choice in 2005 by the National Library of Trinidad and Tobago. His most recent publication is as editor of *Golconda: Our Voices Our Lives*, an anthology of histories and other stories and poems from the sugar-belt of Trinidad (UTT Press, 2009). Over the years, he has combined teaching with writing. He lives in London and Port of Spain.

For more information visit: www.lawrencescott.co.uk

Praise for *Light Falling on Bamboo*

'In this intimate, compassionate portrait of nineteenth-century Trinidad, Lawrence Scott presents a gripping tale of a world darkened by its secrets and exposed by its art'

EARL LOVELACE

'As little is known about Cazabon's life, Scott has considerable freedom to flesh out and explore the moral implications of his art and relationships. The novel is written in a magnificent prose style that matches the art it describes'

BERNARDINE EVARISTO, *Guardian*

'Lawrence Scott deftly paints a portrait of a man deeply split on every level...While in theory *Light Falling on Bamboo* is the fictionalised account of one man's life, Scott captures so much more. This novel shows us the dark "truth of an age" in a small corner of the New World, once dependent on slave labour. Scott doesn't judge. He shows us a world full of prejudice and social injustice, and we feel uncomfortable throughout. And also, like Cazabon, we fall in love numerous times with this complicated world. Scott, born on a sugar estate, knows this society intimately and paints this world with skill and grace'

MONIQUE ROFFEY, *Independent*

'Cazabon himself is quietly subversive: though his landscapes were commissioned by white landowners, he included dignified representations of those working the land, and in so doing teased out "the honest truth" of post-emancipation Trinidad. Scott does likewise in this beautifully subtle and sensitive novel, which conjures a convincing fictional portrait of a nineteenth-century Trinidadian painter'   DAVID EVANS, *Financial Times*

'This mighty book is saturated in the colour and shadow of paintings and the racial and class issues revealed within and beyond them. An eye opening and impressively composed read'

PAUL SIMON, *Morning Star*

'Scott's historical novel transports us to post-emancipation Trinidad, a country shaking off its violent legacy and simmering with local passions'

JOANNE HARRIS, *Vogue* Books Round Up 2012

'Scott's latest novel is nothing less than remarkable, blending in ambitious detail the real life of one of Trinidad's founding artistic figures, with a fictional account of what his most personal moments might have resembled....The reader leans towards believing, rather than discrediting, the artistic licences that Scott himself has taken – what emerges is the study of a complex, haunted figure'

SHIVANEE RAMLOCHAN, *Trinidad Sunday Guardian*

For Jenny and Marjorie

&

Special thanks
to Geoffrey Maclean

My inexact and blurred biography
Is like his painting, that is fiction's treason,

To deny fact, alter topography
to its own map; he too had his reason

for being false to France. Conspirators, spies,
are what all artists are, changing the truth;

as much a traitor in his comrades' eyes
as the brisk officer; his work was proof.

Tiepolo's Hound
DEREK WALCOTT

But now they had another problem: it was not
how to keep people in captivity. It was how to
set people at liberty.

Salt
EARL LOVELACE

IN A SMALL CORNER OF THE WORLD

Trinidad, 1800 ...

A republic of free people had been a dream, a noble aspiration. It had fired the minds of these sons and daughters of Africa and France. They had been referred to as mules, and worse, despised for the mixed blood flowing in their veins; the colour of their skins. They had been admired for their beauty. It was like the sheen of leather, or like the rumps of horses; this beauty desired in their women but despised in their men.

They had been told to beg for their freedom. *Let them know their place with the blacks of their race. Let them not sit this side of the ferry from San Fernando to Port of Spain. Let them sit apart. Sit at the back of the church. Let them not go abroad at night in the streets without carrying lanterns. Let them not carry sticks. Let them be beaten, knowing that their race, no better than the niggers, can only labour and produce under the whip.*

These foolish laws of the English were dismissed in 1829. At last, they were Free Mulattoes! Learned men of medicine and law, men of letters, moneyed men and women on sugar estates, those with wealth and those without, tasted freedom but not equality with the whites in their councils.

And all the while, the greater freedom had still to be taken by those who were enslaved. They continued to riot. They burned down the fields and planters' houses. Trades collapsed. In 1834, Emancipation! The big disappointment! They had to continue to slave for six more years. No, be apprentices. *Point de six ans!* they shouted. Not six years more! In 1838, at last, Freedom! 'Chattel slavery is now wage slavery' was their cry when that freedom came. Not much had changed. Eventually, they abandoned the estates to work for themselves; to squat, buy and resettle the land, while others, who had arrived on that fateful dawn in 1845 from Calcutta, as indentured, laboured where they had spilled their blood.

The washerwomen under the bamboos were singing by the river, *Doudou ou abandonnée mwe?*

BOOK ONE

1848

I

Rose Debonne Cazabon spoke in a whisper, hardly being heard, unless one of her daughters pressed her ear to her mouth and deciphered her puzzled cry: '*Maman . . .?*' Her full red lips were now a thin grey line, disappearing when she did not speak. '*Maman . . . veni!*'

'She's calling on her own mother to come and meet her and take her to Paradise.' Rose Clotilde, her younger daughter, turned and spoke to the family, standing and kneeling at the side of the bed. She leaned closer to hear her mother better, kissing her sunken cheeks that used to be smooth and rouged. Her green eyes were large in her seemingly shrunken head, her silvering hair pulled back tightly from her brow.

All the time, the click of rosary beads was mixed with the murmur of prayers: *Notre Père . . . Je vous salu Marie plein de grace . . .*; holy waves breaking upon the shore of death, antiphons for her departure.

Magdeleine Alexandrine, her eldest daughter, led the women in the prayers. These were women whom her mother's family had brought with them from Guadeloupe as enslaved; they were free women now, who had come to witness their madam's passing. They kneeled outside on the gallery, blocking the stairs, perspiring with the heat, saying their prayers in -their patois, *Salu Marie plein de grace . . .* accompanied by the rhythm of the Yoruba chants which was creeping into the swaying of their bodies.

Michel Jean, her youngest son, stood to the side of the proceedings looking in. He was astonished at a world that he used to forget and then wake up to in nightmares, crying out, '*Maman*.' Now he again remembered the prayers, the chant, and found his feet shuffling to the rhythm of the African women. He lost himself in that trance.

He is at St Edmund's, the time he misses his mother the most, just thirteen, sick for home, in the dormitory of the English boarding school with the snow falling outside the window and silently covering all the fields and the roof of the college chapel. Far away, in the distance, across a field of white moonlight, he remembers seeing a single, yellow light burning.

She is at her dressing table poised for her toilette. Then she stands in her peignoir before the open window, the muslin falling loosely about her. Beneath the white cloud is the shadow of her brown nakedness.

Josie is brushing her hair, a fire in her hands with the dying sun, as she collects his mother's hair in her arms, her arms full of crinkling tresses, tresses of Africa and France.

He pictures his mother with her beautiful hair arranged on top of her head, or tied with a rich Madras, Martiniquan style. It is morning and she sweeps it up the nape of her neck into a chignon. Then it is evening and she cradles it in a snood studded with pearls. This is when the families visit to drink punches on the veranda and dine beneath the chandeliers lit with candles. He is curled up on the chaise-longue. He waits to hear her descent from the top of the stairs. He hears the tread of her soft shoes and the train of her satins falling upon each step, slipping over the pitch-pine floor. He imagines it is the sound of water flowing over stones into a river-pool. It becomes a kind of mild thunder.

He hears his mother's voice: 'Take care, girl.' It is Josie descending the stairs, helping his mother with her gown. Josie smiles at him. He and Josie are in attendance.

Where was Josie now? He could not see her among the women with their prayers told upon their rosary beads. His mind sped to the jumbie beads they played with as children. Josie had had a bracelet of jumbie beads, black and red. He had not seen her since his visit from Paris in 1840. He thought she would have been here to welcome him after all this time. He turned towards his mother's bed. She will not last long, he thought.

When he first started painting women he painted Josie. She had been his ideal of female beauty, his empress. He had made her his Josephine Beauharnais. Every painting of a washerwoman began as Josie. He remembered his own words: 'I'll paint the washerwomen as if they're empresses.'

Leaving the island, and returning intermittently, had created it in his mind as a place of remembrance. Seeing his mother's diminished beauty now, her dying body upon the bed, it comforted him to leave the room and enter the past in his mind. This pilgrimage takes him down the avenue of *palmistes* into the green air of their splendour against an indigo sky. They take him to the ravine below the Corynth house near the Cipero River. He and Josie are swimming there with her mother, Ernestine. Their black arms are cradling him and bathing his brown skin with green water.

At first, he and Josie had grown like brother and sister, playing together as children in the yard. He thought he had glimpsed her on the veranda among another group of women who had just arrived from Corynth, on the long journey from the Naparimas. They must have taken the steamer from San Fernando. He went towards her. 'Josie.' When the woman turned around it was not Josie.

'*Excusez moi*,' he apologized.

The woman smiled. '*Je m'appelle Celine.*'

'*Ah, excusez moi.* Do you know Josie? You see Josie?'

'Josie? Josephine? Ma Ernestine's daughter? *Non.*'

The yard was filling up. The drums for the wake had started. Their rhythm anticipated the death. He could not see Josie anywhere. He noticed how his sisters followed his every move with their eyes, raised between their prayers for his mother's departing soul.

He stayed with the past. 'Jeansie, Josie, *mes enfants*!' His mother is calling them in from the backyard where they are hiding among the sheets hanging in the breeze, where he plays hide-and-seek with Josie, smacked in the face by the wet sheets.

'Is a white woman he marry, you know.' Michel Jean heard the whispered gossip of the old women from Guadeloupe: 'Is *béké*, *oui*!' They passed on the gossip between their prayers, between the *Salu Marie plein de grace*.

'They say she's a white woman. He leave she behind in Fwance.' The young woman, her head tied with white cloth, did not realize he was standing behind her. 'He's the last one, *oui*. Is she *bébé*, she little darling!'

The women she was talking to raised their eyes in prayer to take a good look at him. 'Look him, nuh,' one old woman whispered. 'A right gentleman, as them English does say now. Is only them English in the place now, *oui*, girl, taking over everything.'

How would he be able to bring Louise to this country to suffer this gossip? He had forgotten what his small island was like.

He decided to ignore their banter. He continued to look for Josie. Why was she not here to meet him? There was no knowing what his sisters, or even Joseph, his brother, might have told her.

Michel Jean felt again the longing and loss, anticipation and disappointment, arrival and departure, which had shaped his life with his mother. Theirs had been a relationship of correspondence; billets-doux, expressing their passion for each other. He had once found in 1840 on his return from Paris that she had kept all his letters from St Edmund's and from the Ecole des Beaux-Arts tied with ribbon in neat bundles at the top of her linen press. When he read them they read like an autobiography of regret which he had attempted to assuage with fantasies of assurance. He wondered what she had believed. He felt ashamed of himself at times. '*Maman*, I can tell you that there is nowhere else to live but Pigalle with its *cafés-chantants*.'

François Cazabon, his father, had now entered the room. He had just arrived from San Fernando. They acknowledged each other formally. '*Mon père.*'

'*Mon fils.*'

They kissed each other on the cheeks.

There was *Papa*, the figure he carried in his mind, tall in his white linen suit; *that handsome man*, his mother used to say, *he think he can have everything for nothing.* For Michel Jean it was his brown skin which still startled him; lighter brown than his own and, when he was not in his linens, but in his khakis for the cane fields, his sunburned arms were then burned darker brown. Michel Jean watched him now, his nose with the slightest flare of Africa, the Frenchman's nose, from that grandfather and great-grandfather before him, the planter Frenchman in Martinique, who made baby with the black woman in his kitchen. Michel Jean's feelings were now, as always, of attraction and repulsion, fear and at the same time a desire for his father's approval.

'We must meet and talk,' his father said. 'Your mother will soon be gone.'

Michel Jean nodded. '*Oui.*' His reply almost inaudible. He then turned his attention to his brother. His father had arrived with his brother, Joseph. '*Mon frère.*'

Joseph had met him at the wharf off the steamer earlier in the day with his wife, Jeanne. He had arrived back, just in time, was how Joseph had put it earlier. 'She still with us, boy. She waiting for you, I think.' His sincerity was flawed by his tone of cynicism and jealousy of his mother's special affection for him. He remembered that coldness he had always felt from Jeanne and his brother. Joseph was immediately talking about the will and how little cash there was and how they would have to wait for the right moment to sell land. 'It would be better to leave things in my hands as our sisters have. They leave me to manage their affairs,' he had said. Michel Jean had felt unable to respond right away. With very little business sense himself, he felt that he needed advice.

*

He had, throughout his childhood, come to understand that his mother had transferred her passion for her husband onto him, her last child, since she had taken him as a baby to live with her when she had left her husband's house. That separation had shaped their lives. She gestured to him now to approach her bedside. 'My darling. You reach. I going soon. Don't forget me.'

He smiled, encouraging her in the last breath of her life, the last moments of her existence, the last departure and farewell.

'It would be nice if you could make another visit and I would be here to welcome you.'

'I know.'

'Your wife? Have you brought her to see your old mother?' She raised her head a little from the pillow, exuding the scent of vetiver in the draught of her movement, trying to look over his shoulder to where she presumed she might see the woman who was to replace her in his life. He explained that he had had to leave Louise and the children in Paris.

'But she coming, eh? They coming, *oui*?'

'*Oui, oui*, she coming. She wish she could've come. She and the children.' He said this more to comfort her than to set out his plans. How was he to organize their arrival?

Rose Debonne Cazabon surveyed the room with a last glance at her small universe. Then she noticed that François Cazabon had come to stand with his children to witness her going. There was him with Joseph and her two daughters. Michel Jean noticed her recognize them and then turn again towards him. The family witnessed what they had always thought was an indulgent relationship between their mother and their younger brother. Michel Jean noticed them turn towards each other. It was a huddle he remembered well.

Sometimes when Michel Jean thought of his father, it was as if he had never existed. He had to strain for childhood memories of him, those that were pleasant and were without that paradox of fear and attraction. Once he had taken him riding around the estate at Corynth. He was still a small boy and his father had sat him in front of him. He remembered his excitement being held there between his father's sunburned arms, which were holding the reins of the horse. But then he remembered his panic and screams of fear to be put down. That was when his father used his whip on the rump of his horse. He had been a disappointment to his father. Yes, he would have to deal with him without his mother's protection.

His father came towards him and then turned away when he realized he was still in conversation with his mother.

His brother, the sugar planter, continued to watch. His sisters patted their cheeks, wiping away tears with their kerchiefs.

His mother sank back to her rest, gesturing to Michel Jean again, to come closer. 'Keep true to her, your wife. And you have children now, eh?'

He realized that she was sinking fast, alert one moment, vague another. He nodded. 'A little girl of four and a boy of three.' His mother's asking for his children as she lay dying filled his eyes with tears.

She smiled. He could see that her every gesture was an effort.

He made his effort. 'Rose Alexandrine and Louis Michel.' Saying their names brought them to the bedside; Rosie his jewel, and his little boy.

'*Oui, oui.*' She was telling him that she remembered the family names, the mantras of ancestry that had been passed on to her grandchildren.

His mind sped to Paris along avenues of poplars, across a river with bridges. He saw Saint-Germain-des-Prés, the meadow with the plane trees and the lindens that grew on what he called his little savannah, *la petite savanne*. He and Louise had courted there. They had sheltered under the trees and clung to each other. The children had been christened in the parish church. He could see Louise, with Rose Alexandrine; Louis Michel still in his perambulator. They were an ocean away. They were a fortnightly packet-steamer away, one that would bring Louise's letters to him.

His mother pointed to an envelope on the table beside her bed. He picked it up. She took it from him and pressed it against his chest, not only the place of his heart, but where she also imagined his soul to reside. These were gestures and thoughts from childhood.

'Something extra for the children,' she managed to say, hardly able to open her lips.

'*Merci bien.*' He guessed it was money. Then he noticed her looking up over his shoulder to see how his father, his sisters and brother were reacting to this secretive disbursement of the family fortune. He followed her eyes and met theirs. The shuffling of Joseph's feet and the brisk rearrangement of his sisters' bombazine skirts told him that they were irritated. His father had long reconciled himself to this state of affairs, as he put it to himself and his family. He had once announced at the dinner table: 'Your brother is your mother's child.' That was the night that Uncle St Luce had teased his father and said, 'This one, François, was an immaculate conception, eh, *oui*!' He was careful to be out of earshot of Rose Debonne Cazabon at the time.

Louise's first letter had arrived in advance of his return. Ernestine brought it to him, as if to remind him of his responsibilities. 'Jeansie, *mon garçon*. All this time we miss you.' Then, after embracing him, 'Is your wife. She must be telling you not to forget she. Josie collect it from the packet.'

'Ernestine. So long.' She was like another mother; part of the household for as long as he could remember. At first he did not understand her. Then, taking the letter, he ignored her words and instead inquired after Josie. 'Where Josie? How come Josie not here?'

'She somewhere,' Ernestine said, dismissing his anxiety. Then she added, 'Why you ent bring your wife? And you have a wife now. No need for all this *commesse* here with Josie, you know. Too much confusion, boy.'

He recalled how Ernestine could upbraid him.

Michel Jean went off to the bedroom that had always been his. He shut the door behind him. There, away from the prayers of the women with the rosary beads encrusting their knuckles, the room getting more and more filled up with his mother's friends and retainers, he opened Louise's letter.

Mon chéri, I miss you. We all miss you. The streets are more peaceful, though the barricades are still there. I have stayed on in the little room off the studio on the rue Blanche that Theo has kindly confirmed I can have for as long as there's need. He refuses to accept any rent. You must not worry about money. Theo and the others at Le Morceau will give me work any time. I've left notices at other studios. Theo's such a good man. Rosie is a darling, my companion. She asks for her *papa*. I must not alarm you concerning Louis. He frets so much and keeps me awake half the night. I do wonder about the mite. He's not like Rosie at this age. Sometimes, when I look into his eyes, I feel that he does not recognize me. But then he will suddenly throw his little arms around my neck and kiss me on the cheek. Like he has just returned from somewhere far away. He does not talk, not yet. If things get bad again in the city we may have to go to Vire where my mother and father want me to be while you're away. I'll miss you there, darling, our little place on the coast at Luc-sur-Mer. Our home is so empty without you. This morning when I woke I thought I heard you in the studio. But then I knew there would be no one there. I love you . . .

Unable to continue, Michel Jean folded the pages of his wife's letter and put it into the pocket of his jacket to continue reading it later. He saw her running along the beach at Luc-sur-Mer. He felt their embrace, her young body cleaving to him. How rapidly as lovers they had become parents. Then his passion had to make room for the care of their children. He must send her some money. He thought of his mother's gift for the children. He would send her that to start with. He remembered that strange look of Louis Michel's, his at times expressionless stare.

He had left Louise with such great responsibilities. Thankfully, she had Rosie. His little girl would have to grow quickly to be her companion. They seemed so far away. The island was another world.

He recalled again the young woman who appeared that first morning in the sunlit studio situated off the Mouffetard; a small, cheap place which was near the Ecole des Beaux-Arts. He had never before experienced nude figure drawing. That was not something Mr Reinagle had ever recommended in Port of Spain. Louise's beauty had captured him. After her first sitting, she had said she would happily come again. She admired his drawing. She was staying with an aunt, she told him. She needed to work. He thought now how he must get back to Paris as soon as was practical after his mother's affairs got settled. He hoped Joseph would be efficient with the will.

He re-entered his mother's room. Her dying overtook all his other preoccupations. His sisters were kneeling at the bedside. His father and Joseph stood at the foot of the bed like sentinels. Josie was still not there.

The servants had shut the jalousies and the bright, yellow light seeped through the cracks to fall in torn ribbons upon the floor. The drums outside had subsided. The prayers were a murmur. He stood among the familiar pieces of mahogany furniture, his mother's dressing table and her press. He stared at her struggling with her shallow gasps for air. The palms out on the balcony were stirred by the hot wind, disturbing the stillness of the room with their lilt and rustle. How much longer could his mother linger? he asked himself.

He whispered to a young girl, who was changing the water in the glass on his mother's bedside table. 'Where's Josie?' Still, he could not understand her absence. She did not answer and moved away, looking at him nervously, as if she had been told to beware of him, he thought.

He noticed that a huge mottled moth had alighted on one of the slats of the jalousies, keeping so still that he doubted its reality.

Was it alive? He stared at its brown shades with a hint of blue on its wings. Then he noticed its almost imperceptible pulse.

As the women came and went from the room, he continued to look out for Josie. She was not among the kneeling figures, their heads bound in white cotton, bowed in prayer. The prayers and the stuffiness of the atmosphere began to feel oppressive. There was hardly room to move. Old Father Maingot entered to begin the anointing of his mother, performing the last sacrament of Extreme Unction. It was so long since he had been part of this world, part of her faith. He stood and watched, finding it impossible to join in with the supplicating prayers.

As Father Maingot completed the blessing, his mother gestured to Michel Jean to come nearer, pulling at his sleeve as he kneeled by her side. Beneath the smell of the priest's oils, he smelled the odour of her ailing body, the intimations of her imminent death. She raised herself on her pillows. She was alert. She spoke even more strongly than before. 'And you have work to do, darling, painting to paint, an island to give to the world, a people whose dignity you must be proud of when you place them in their own world. Don't forget where you've come from. Don't forget the ideas of freedom that have carried us this far. Don't forget the republic we seek in this corner of the world.'

Michel Jean had not before heard his mother express so explicitly her thoughts about what his painting might be and become. Where in her dying had she found all those words? She was as eloquent as Jean Jaillet railing against the English Governor Woodford, or Jean Baptiste Philippe in his treatise, *Free Mulatto*, addressing Earl Bathurst on behalf of his free-coloured compatriots, championing their rights. He was not himself so explicit about his work. He answered her. '*Oui, Maman*, don't worry yourself.'

She continued, unabated. Rose Clotilde leaned forward to quieten her. She put her hand on her brother's shoulder to pull him away. His mother was having none of it. She continued to speak to her son. 'The money is there. There's still money there,' she enunciated clearly, looking over his shoulder at his father, the girls and Joseph. 'Don't let them cheat you out of your inheritance because you're not an overseer on a sugarcane estate. There's more to a republic than sugar and cocoa. Watch out for those who going with the English.' With her eyes, she pointed to his father and brother. He turned to look at them. Their eyes told him to come away and leave the dying woman, not encourage her in her delusions.

It was the voice he remembered of the young mother pushing him out into the world, to leave the island: first to go to school in England, and then, after those years when he had come back to her, to return to Paris, to become a painter.

'More, much more, *mon chéri*, if we're to be a people, a free people. There's much more to a republic. There's more to liberty than labour in the fields. Ideas . . . beauty,' she said now. Her voice faded and she closed her eyes.

The family were all ears and eyes. Joseph had opened the will earlier, an anxious executor, a law unto himself, anticipating his mother's death. Michel Jean had guessed this, talking in the carriage on their way from the wharf. As Joseph went on about the will, Michel Jean had distracted himself as the carriage trundled through the narrow streets of Port of Spain, avoiding the naked children, the beggars and the *marchandes*. The town was swirling around him, the many different languages tingling in his ears with a warm familiarity. They had made their way with difficulty along Almond Walk from King's Wharf, leaving the lighthouse on its mole near Fort San Andres. He had inhaled the reek of the sea. All along the street under the almond trees was the Spanish music of the Venezuelans playing their pianos. Home could also startle him with so many surprises. 'Look, see the coolies from Calcutta. Our only hope now!' Joseph had smiled a smile he did not quite understand. 'The new labour.' He had left his questions for later. Instead, he had allowed memories to seduce his mind, to shut out Joseph's voice, Jeanne's babbling tongue. He could almost taste the molasses on the corner. He thirsted for a coconut water. There was that memory of ginger on a *mamzelle*'s tongue. He noticed the light on the water and on the surrounding hills changing all the time from lemon to subdued white, plain greys and blues, the piercing fire of the sun lighting up the greens and ochres. He longed to paint. That morning, at dawn, up on deck he had sketched the mountains coming through the Boca Grande between Bolivar's continent and the island.

Looking at his father, he could see now that he had decided to stay out of the deliberations because of the earlier separation that had split the family. Michel Jean sensed they did not want him arguing for another interpretation of his mother's wishes. He had distanced himself in the past from these family feuds and dramas by his absence. But now his arrival had revived them.

Michel Jean started to think that his mother's death would never come. He went out onto the veranda for a cigarette. There was a sudden downpour, the clouds breaking over the Maraval hills adding to the tumult of prayers, which had begun again in the room. He had to be there for his mother's last breath, but he still had to find Josie. As he inhaled the sweet taste of his tobacco, he sat back and watched the water dripping from the fern baskets and running down the drain. Thunder rumbled intermittently in the hills around the town. The gulf had disappeared. A stench from the swamp was hanging in the damp air.

Still he could not see Josie. Why was she keeping away? He lit another cigarette. She must be here. He wanted to go and look for her in the yard. But he could not risk his mother passing away in his absence. He could see his sisters noticing his agitation. Rose Clotilde came out onto the balcony to call him into the room. He would not ask her for Josie. The family had always seen Josie as a problem. How was he going to cope with all those complications again? He brushed the cigarette ash off his sleeve and returned to his mother's room.

Light and shadow, light and shadow, phrases in his mind were the sound of the horses' clip-clop hooves on the hard ground out on the street below the balcony. It was an insistent repetition as he knelt at his mother's bedside holding her hand. Behind him, the family went in and out of the room. Muted conversations between his brother and his sisters and their father drifted in, interrupting the decades of the rosary, which were repeated by aunts and uncles who had recently arrived. He noticed Uncle St Luce with his white wife, Margaret. Clifford, her family name, came back to him. They were sugar planters in the south. Michel Jean heard his mother's words again: 'There is still money . . . don't let them cheat you of your inheritance because you're not an overseer on a sugarcane estate.'

His father's firm hand on his shoulder drew him up from his kneeling position into the realization that his mother's hand was already cold in the palm of his own. 'Michel, she's gone, son.' He heard the unaccustomed affection in his father's voice. He drew him aside. 'You must meet me in town when I come from San Fernando on a Thursday. I go by Mr Schoener on the wharf for estate supplies. Meet me then. There are things you must know about this place if you are going to stay any length of time. You not alone, and don't mind your brother. Till later.' He embraced Michel Jean and then said, as he left the room, 'I'm not involved with your mother's will; your brother, as you know, is the sole executor. St Luce will help you.'

'*Oui, Papa.*' It was so long since he had addressed his father in that way. His voice was again almost inaudible as he watched his father leave the room. He would have to learn to speak to him.

His mother had left as imperceptibly as the light had changed in the room. He could now hear the rain on the shingles, and a wind down from the hills had blown the veranda door shut. He went out onto the balcony above the street to smoke another cigarette. Below, in the yard, all who had congregated were sheltering from the rain, wailing for their lost madam, chanting: 'Take the long road to Canaan . . .' The wake had begun. The drumming was now at its most intense. Already he could see some of the young fellas setting up boxes and dealing out their cards. The evening had arrived, and the flambeaux were being lit. He watched a young woman rolling a wick out of cloth and inserting it into a bottle and lighting it. It would be a night of drumming, dancing, rum, black coffee and soda biscuits.

Then he saw her. She was moving about the yard, serving the guests. It definitely was her this time, her face lit by the flame of the flambeau. She was a woman of thirty-five, his age. He called out to her. 'Josie!'

She looked up. At first, she did not realize who had called her. Then she recognized him. 'Jeansie!' Catching herself, she called again, 'Master Michel, I coming.' Her spirit was in that urgent assertion. He waited for her at the top of the stairs.

It was as if everyone was coming off the streets to congregate in the yard. The news of the death was now abroad. The woman town-crier was announcing the death and the coming funeral. '*Messieurs et Madames* . . .' She stood outside the gate with the beauty of the *zanno cylindre* in her ears, *grain d'or* around her neck, waving her stiff *canlandey* handkerchief proclaiming: '*Madame Rose Debonne Cazabon est morte.*' She was resplendent with her large earrings, necklace and madras cloth. Heavy, warm rain was now flooding the yard. Michel Jean stood, choked by his mother's final departure. He inhaled his tobacco deeply, awaiting Josie's arrival from downstairs, breathing in the last sighs of his mother which had lingered beyond her living and were now mixed with the scent of the ylang-ylang in the garden below. He inhaled the salted air and licked the taste of his tears. The rain cooled the air and comforted him where he stood waiting for Josie. What was keeping her now? The downpour of buckets had become the light drizzle of needles, to the leaking *drip drip* from the guttering under the shingles into the drains.

'Josie.' His first inclination was to embrace her and kiss her on her mouth. He could not help himself. She moved towards him, then held back.

'Not here.' She squeezed his hand. 'Later. Jeansie, boy. You reach. I hear you reach. I must tidy the room now.' But she could not resist wiping the tears for his mother from his eyes. 'Jeansie, boy.'

No sooner had he found her than she was disappearing into the business of her service. Josie had made herself indispensable in the household. That was how she remained connected to the family, how she survived. He had not found her because she had been lost in making all the arrangements, in keeping the household running.

When he returned to his mother's bedroom, Doctor Lange had just entered and was instructing the women how to lay out his mother's body so that the family could take their leave.

Josie came in to remove the soiled commode. He could now look at her. She was older. They were both older. With tears in her eyes for her madam, mixed with the joy of seeing him, she smiled. He could still see the girl in her, the young woman she had been in 1840. He had not seen her for eight years. She had not flown the house with Emancipation. She had waited instead for a position, soon she thought, to be vacated by her own mother. But what now, with her madam gone? She stopped a moment as she passed to squeeze his hand. 'Josie,' he whispered.

'Master Michel.' Her formality gave the lie to their intimacy since childhood. Josie knew things about him no one else quite knew.

'Josie.'

'Jeansie, later.'

They could say no more now. His sisters had their eyes on everything. He saw their eyebrows rise, their eyes meet. He noticed them glance away. Their fingers folded linen and secreted away the details of his mother's life into the drawers of her dressing table and the shelves of her mahogany press. This room was not a place for him to stay now.

Josie whispered, looking up at him, 'Come and see me, eh? Later.'

He moved his lips, but no words came. She smiled and left the room with her load.

Josie was still here. Her presence suddenly, for an instant, gave him hope as he glimpsed the women turning his mother's body, washing her limbs. He was breathless now at her departure, fearful at her absence. The light had turned her linen to malarial yellow. She had grown so old with her illness, he imagined her bones to be as cold as the clasps he now saw on the coffin brought in by Mr de Montbrun. The fresh scent of cedar defied the scent of death for a moment. The women laid his mother's body out in the dress she had worn for her daughter Rose Clotilde's marriage; lilac trimmed with tulle and black lace. Michel Jean made a breathless whisper, but no words came as he tried to recite the prayer: *Requiem aeternam dona eis, Domine.* Eternity? How could time be like that?

Outside, the casuarinas were whispering like the women moving around the bed. The sibilance disturbed him. He noticed the shape of his mother's head in the fold of the pillow. There was the scent of the cuscus grass her dress had been hung in. The women entwined her fingers with her crystal rosary beads that caught the light like the jewels at her neck and those which hung from her pierced ears. The women left when they were finished. He was alone with her for a minute before the others were ushered back into the room.

All that he wanted to say and think and feel disappeared in the promise of visiting Josie that night downstairs, in the thought of laying his head between her breasts in the darkness, as he used to in order to forget. He kneeled to the floor to pick up a cotton pad that the women had let drop. It had been soaked in his mother's eau de Cologne, then laid across her forehead to cool her in the heat. He buried his face in it and inhaled her. He tucked it into his pocket. Would he ever be allowed to forget the full weight of the past?

His departure from the island when he was young, and then again when he first went to Paris, meant that he had always felt this need to re-create how it had been with Josie; the very touch of things. He felt that it was his nature. It was what had nurtured him. Could it be any different? But it scared him now, troubled him, as he planned to bring his wife and children to be part of this world.

*

On getting out of bed the following morning, the day of his mother's funeral, Michel Jean stood alone on the balcony outside his bedroom, looking down into the street. Port of Spain – his Belle des Antilles, his Puerto de los Hispanioles, his Port d'Espagne – began to fill him with that old longing for its surrounding hills, its harbour, its pink stone buildings, its shingled roofs. He longed to walk the streets again, the English Governor Woodford's grid which had slowly grown since the fire of 1808, and which had anglicized the Spanish port, subdued the French town, changing the delightfully named rue des Trois Chandelles, which his mother had loved, to Duncan Street, La Place to George Street and rue de'Herrara to Henry Street. He must get down to Corbeaux Town, the old Coburg Town, a pun on its name because of the vultures, the turkey buzzards, which hovered and pecked at the carrion of rotting fish on the waterfront. He had liked, in his twenties, to wander Corbeaux Town to find the subjects for his early portraits. He thought of those Sunday afternoon flirtations, taking a pirogue out onto the water with a pretty *mamzelle* in her best Madras, hidden beneath her parasol, promising to make her famous by his portraiture if she would give him just one kiss.

There was a knock at the door. When Josie entered the room with coffee, she said, 'I waiting for you. All night I waiting. Is grief? Is grief, or the wife you have in Fwance now? You give your heart away and Josie get nothing. All these years now and Josie get nothing.' She had always liked to tease him.

'Josie, keep your voice down. I lay down last night and sleep. I ent wake, girl.'

'Keep my voice down? What is this I hearing? Is so you talking to me now?'

'How you vex so early in the morning? Eh? How you vex? Come, nuh.' He reached out to pull her into the bed with him once she had rested the coffee on the bedside table. She resisted. He wanted to pretend that things could be like they used to be. But he knew they could not be so, and that was the real reason he had not gone to her room last night.

'You not shame, Master Michel? Is no madam I sure that you going and make me with that wife you have in Fwance now. Maybe is two wife you want, one here and one over there.'

'Josie, come, nuh, girl, what mad thoughts you have? Is Jeansie. Is the same Jeansie from long time. You don't remember, Josie and Jeansie? Is so everybody calling we.' He grabbed hold of her, responding with his own teasing.

'Look, cover up your nakedness. Imagine my mother catch me in here with you. Or, your brother and sisters. You know they all over this house, every minute, like sugar ants, fingers going through everything like something they lose. For truth, is more like *corbeaux*, who see something dead and come to feed on it.'

'Josie, take it easy, girl, take it easy.'

'Take it easy? Is eight years, Jeansie, that you away. I is a big woman now. I ent know if you properly know what it is going on here now that your mother, madam, let me not lose my respect, pass away. I ent sure you understand, otherwise I ent think you go lie down there like you is Napoleon, Emperor of Fwance yourself and tell me to take it easy. Is not you in charge here now, you know. Is Master Joseph. Is Mistress Magdeleine and Mistress Rose. Is them who in charge and already this morning tell my mother, my mother who in this house longer than them, that she have to find another work. Is what work Mama doing now, for truth. As if she must find work at all. You can imagine your mother telling my mother, Ernestine, that, eh, Jeansie? So don't come with your freshness now. You should've bring your freshness in the night when I waiting for you, downstairs.' She laughed, the teasing tone returning in her last remark.

'Josie, *doudou*, as long as I living here, you and your mother going to continue to live in that yard. You hear what I telling you. And you know I have to paint all you portrait.'

Josie turned on him. 'Portrait! Portrait! Who thinking about portrait? I mean, Jeansie, put your mind to this business. This is life and death. You know what go happen if Mammy and me have to leave this yard? As long as you here, you say? But how long you go be here before you gone back to your wife and children? I know you have children with that Frenchwoman.'

'Josie, don't speak so, nuh.'

'And she French, and she's a woman?'

'Josie, I'll see to it that it get write down. I'll talk to Joseph and my sisters. I have to live somewhere and where I live you and Ernestine coming with me. You hear that?'

'Well, when I see it write, not that I could read, I go believe what you telling me.'

'Josie, close the door. It early still. No one coming upstairs yet. Come.' She sat on the bed as he folded her in his arms and kissed her cheek. 'Come, Josie, don't be vex.'

'Jeansie, is eight years. I accustom now. But is not easy. It not easy to undo something that hold we for so long. I not vex, but is true what I telling you.'

'Is true what I telling you, too. And you is my sister? How I go leave you?'

The cock crowed in the yard and Josie jumped off the bed. 'Is like that story the *abbé* telling we in the church, that gospel story. Before the cock crow twice you will deny me thrice.'

'You know the meaning of that, Josie? Never, Josie. Never. Not me.'

Betrayal, his pleasure in having a secret life, was that what it had become? If that was what it had always been, then it had now become a cruel force which made him hurt those that he loved the most.

Michel Jean reached for Louise's letter on the table beside his bed. '*Mon chéri*, I miss you. We all miss you.' He imagined the sound of her voice, and felt healed, but at the same time intoxicated by his desire for Josie.

In the weeks after his mother was buried in Lapeyrouse Cemetery, Michel Jean began to attend to those financial affairs she had cautioned him about. He met his uncle St Luce, a lawyer, who advised him that he would have to let Joseph, as executor of his mother's will, do his business. If he then thought there were irregularities he would take those up for him. He understood that, with his wife and small children in Paris without him, he needed money now. And that he needed money soon to send to Louise.

'You must bring your wife and family out soon. Don't be anxious about your white wife. I have coped, so can you.'

Michel Jean was thankful for his uncle's encouragement.

His solace now – from his grief at losing his mother, at the loss of how things used to be with Josie, and his missing of Louise and the children – was to begin painting again, to begin his once-imagined journeys, his imagined life, his pilgrimages into the interior of the island, into the bush where the light would be falling on the bamboos.

But before he had ventured too far from Port of Spain, he decided upon a visit to one of the haunts of his youth, Belmont Hill, when he had come to live in the town with his mother, when they had first left their house on the Café in San Fernando in 1837.

Before leaving the house he wrote to Louise in time to catch the fortnightly packet:

My darling Louise, I hope that the six hundred francs from my mother have now reached you. She said that it was especially for the children. But, of course, you must use it as you think best. She so wanted to meet you. I'm sending more money soon. I'm painting again. I'm hoping to sell. Watercolours. This morning on Belmont Hill, which looks out over the savannah to the sea, the islands and the continental mainland. I can't wait to show you the island. It is a view of hills, and in the foreground, an immortelle tree with its orangey-red flowers. Colour so different in this light. My palette must change.

He described how the funeral had gone. He did not tell her about his worries over the will, painting instead an optimistic picture of the family.

I think of you and the children all the time. I'm working to return as soon as I can, then to bring you here. Kisses for you. Kisses for Rosie from her *papa*. Keep telling Louis Michel about me and show him the pictures I painted when we were together. I don't want him to forget me. Is he walking as yet? That little left leg. How is it now?

Your loving husband, MJ.

As he handed the letter to Josie to catch the packet on time, he could feel the old struggle. It was not going to be easy.

'Is you wife, you write? That is good, Jeansie.'

'*Oui.*' As he touched her fingers in handing her the letter, he felt wretched, and at the same time utterly at home, as he looked into her eyes. 'I go see you. Watch me, nuh. I is a painter, you know.'

'You good for yourself, you know, Jeansie.'

'Till later.'

They smiled.

BOOK TWO

1849

I

Michel Jean paused on his walk across the Queen's Savannah to capture a fleeting moment, the scene of an African tulip tree that had lost both its leaves and its cups of vermilion flowers. He saw in the scene the dead tree in a Van Ruisdael. Cattle grazed beneath its branches with shadowed hills in the blue distance. Lilac clouds moved like slow caravans out towards the gulf.

He could not get Josie out of his mind this morning. He'd thought that eight years would have sealed their pact. And it was almost a year since his mother's death. He'd thought that marriage and children would have allowed his childhood obsession and youthful passion to fade. His return to the island had brought back the power of his and Josie's cruel past.

He set up his easel and laid out his paints. While the prospect that emerged promised a future, the past resurfaced. His departure for England, to go to school in 1826, had marked his first separation from Josie. They were both thirteen. She was Josie, Ernestine's daughter, the pretty girl in the house, who had played with him since they were babies and then, as they grew, between her tasks. Their hearts were one. They vowed to love each other for the rest of their lives, not understanding the world and its ways. They cut their fingers and mixed their blood. No one had told them. They must have thought there was no need. The children would grow out of it.

When he returned from England as a seventeen-year-old youth, he was shy when he met her. She was not a girl. She was a young woman. Those childhood intimacies, which started to end once her breasts began to grow, had seemed as natural as the breeze in the sugarcane fields. Yes, it had been exciting when they touched and kissed as children, playing at being grown-ups with all the thrill of doing something they felt they should not do. He felt her smell still on him; the scent that had long time lingered from their swim in the Cipero River, from their play in the bamboo patch. But then at seventeen she was cautious with her eyes, with her hands. It was as if she had been warned about something.

At that time, she appeared to be more under Ernestine's supervision than when she was a child. She was not in the house as much when he was there. He wanted to meet her, but it did not seem easy like when they were children. Still, no one had said anything to him. He remembered his mother arranging for him to meet Chantal, one of the Philippe girls on the neighbouring estate at Palmiste. That was a formal arrangement, which felt like the overture to a marriage. 'We'll soon make a man of you,' was how Joseph had put it when he was trying to introduce him to estate life. His brother had recently married Jeanne Genevieve. His sisters were both married and having their babies. Michel Jean saw that his future was being laid out before him.

It was too painful to go over it now. It was Joseph who had warned him. He wished it had not been Joseph. 'That girl is your sister, you know.' He had not wanted to believe him. His stomach churned. His head spun. He had tried to put it from his mind. He always felt, from that day, that Joseph had one over on him.

Looking up from his furious sketching, he saw a man approaching in his direction, a vague figure hanging in the heat haze, like a mirage, on the other side of the savannah. He turned his attention back to his painting. The light was changing fast. His brushstrokes were frenzied as he speckled the foreground. He lost himself in his work.

This was the way to separate himself from Josie, to banish his dilemmas. He also needed to let go of his responsibility for Louise and the children for the moment. He was on his own, painting. He must go with that elation. But it was difficult not to hear Louise's voice. The mention of the children in her letters continued to upset him. Also, she still talked of Theo and the other painters at Le Morceau contributing to her upkeep. That was good of them, but he felt that he needed to provide for his family. He was a little jealous of their chivalry, while at the same time knowing himself to be hypocritical. How would he explain Josie to Louise, even though they had ceased to be lovers?

When he looked up to judge the changing light, the figure in the distance had emerged from the haze. The mirage was closer. He looked like a white man, most probably English, unless it was Devenish, the local Irishman, the land surveyor, whom he often met on his sojourns. This one looked like a visitor. Michel Jean had encountered these travellers before, out to the colonies for adventure. They were often collectors of flora and fauna. He had even come across some of them in far-flung areas of the mountains, or along the coasts, with their notebooks and sketchpads. One he remembered sketching for some book; *An Account of Landscape and Negro Character* he had told him. What was his name? Bridgens? He never liked his illustrations of either landscape or his Negro characters, as he called them. They seemed too much like the happy pumpkin-eaters of Thomas Carlyle's discourse, living a life of laughing, drumming and dancing. The people were always so ugly. He would paint them differently. He might not quite do justice to the people's imperial qualities, but they would not have that ugliness which came from a warped sensibility. There was a prevalent view, taken from Thomas Carlyle's recently published *Occasional Discourse on the Nigger Question*, that black people should be compelled to work under punishment.

He could see now that the figure on the landscape was carrying a satchel with equipment that, from a distance, looked distinctly like the accoutrements of a painter. He was stopping and surveying the landscape as if with an eye for a subject, a suitable prospect to take back with him to England no doubt. That was their wont. The English had become so established since he was last at home. 'Blasted English, white people,' had been his mother's view when she allowed herself to rant against the administration, and when she wanted to rage against Joseph and his father, who were trying to work with the English. Michel Jean intended to stay out of the politics.

He returned to his own subject, the hills to the east, a little to the south of his favourite spot, Belmont Hill with its ruins of the old Government House. He must get going if he was to climb the hill for another visit. He thought of the letter that had recently arrived from Louise. She thanked him for some more money from his mother that he had enclosed with his last letter. She was going to use some of the money to get each of the children something special from their grandmother. She wanted him to write again about his painting. 'Darling, I love your words about painting. Tell me more of where you are visiting. I want to see the places with your eyes as I did on the Normandy coast. Remember? My father says that the old folk still ask for you, the painter.' He did remember. But he was now torn between her and all that had happened on the island. The past could still seduce him.

'Good morning!'

Michel Jean looked up. The man who had appeared out of the distance was waving and calling. He was almost upon him. He was blond, English looking.

'*Bonjour.*'

The man's eyes were a bluey-grey. Perspiration glistened on his upper lip. His fair skin was sunburned but had begun to go brown; no longer pink, but tanned. So he must have been on the island for a while, Michel Jean thought. Though his colouring was different, there was something about his boyishness as he hopped over the ti-marie's thorns across the short distance between them, which reminded him of Fitzwilliam from St Edmund's. It was the ready smile, the immediate friendliness.

'What weather!' he exclaimed, sounding very English. 'So, you're painting too? That's jolly good, I say. Who would've thought . . .'

The young man's interest in Michel Jean's work was instantaneous, peering over his shoulder. Michel Jean rose, washing his brushes and wiping his hands at the same time. His watercolour was drying fast in the morning sun. He laughed teasingly, asking, 'Who would've thought what?'

'A painter, an artist, here . . .'

'Here in this wilderness, this small island, on the periphery of the world, this lost boot in the silt of the Orinoco.' Michel Jean laughed at his own taunting exaggerations, his tone adopting that of a carnival character's ironic, satirical speech. He could win on his homeground, he thought. Or, could he? Did he even want to win?

'What? Yes . . . Exactly, to find a like spirit . . . I say.' Then, peering more closely at the painting on the easel, the Englishman drew back, correcting himself. 'A like spirit, maybe, but a far better painter. You must've trained at some studio in London or Paris, under a tutor of reputation?'

'*London Bridge is falling down, falling down* . . . Yes, I can see you come out to paint.' Michel Jean laughed off what sounded like praise, avoiding the invitation to rehearse his curriculum vitae. Unsure to whom he was speaking, he did not want, on the one hand, to appear too boastful, and on the other, he did not want to undersell himself and his accomplishments. If this was a gentleman who knew about art, despite his modesty about his own skills, he did not want to prejudice himself. Conversations on art were not commonplace in this town, nor were positions and commissions.

The white man then introduced himself. 'James Wildman, an apprentice in our common craft. Just call me Wildman.' He offered his hand to Michel Jean.

'Pleased to meet you, sir; Wildman.' Michel Jean shook the white man's hand and then glanced down at his own painting again, after looking into the distance, still measuring his scale by holding up his brush and squinting, peering like a surveyor through his theodolite. Then he introduced himself. 'Michel Jean Cazabon, *artiste extraordinaire*!' He laughed. 'Landscape painter and art teacher,' he concluded his introduction.

'I see a French influence. Is it? And finding you *en plein air*.' He sounded very pleased with himself, this Wildman. 'This is a revolutionary business as you must surely know, not something the academy would approve of.'

Michel Jean bent towards the painting on the easel and continued to peer into it and add to the foreground, choosing his brushes carefully.

The Englishman looked on with unbroken concentration. 'You know what I mean. Those French chaps out at Barbizon with the gypsies. But of course it was Corot, first of all, who cut himself off from the classical school and achieved his freedom from those romantic preconceptions. He goes for close observation and records what he sees. What do they say?'

Michel Jean looked up, but was still preoccupied with his work as the Englishman continued in his effusive way to drop names and references, which Michel Jean put down to shyness and a too-youthful cleverness. He remembered himself in Paris once he had found his feet; the sureness of youth.

'You must know Corot.' Wildman was insistent.

'Reducing a complex scene to a simple pattern of harmonious tones,' Michel Jean replied, as he continued working on his foreground. He remembered those conversations himself out at Barbizon, at Ganne's Inn, and with Rousseau in the forests of Fontainebleau, but refrained from informing the Englishman of this fact.

'Quite so. You don't mind me observing you, do you?'

Michel Jean kept on without answering. Wildman stared into the distance and then to the sketch on the easel. Michel Jean felt awkward at first, being observed, and then relaxed in the young man's presence. From time to time he stopped to wipe his brushes and allowed Wildman to comment and to ask questions. He noticed that the young man had set up his own easel and was preparing to paint. They worked together in silence in the heat on the open savannah, the Englishman reminding him afresh of Fitzwilliam. He remembered being with his friend at St Edmund's. It was one of his art-master Barnaby's painting lessons on the edge of the cricket field. It felt easy like that now. He glanced across at Wildman painting. He then remembered what had spoiled it. That summer Fitzwilliam had got sunburned on the cricket field, and he was teased. He himself, already brown, was even darker. 'Look, Cazabon, I'm a nigger like you.' That was the voice of the Rodney boy, baring his chest and bragging in a bullying way. He then remembered Fitzwilliam coming up behind him as they left the field after the game and putting a comforting arm around his shoulder. He did not say anything. His words were all in his gesture of camaraderie. He himself wanted to say something, to retaliate, but he choked and could not speak.

'Can I ask you about perspective?' Wildman put down his brush.

'How can I help?'

'Well . . .'

'You want to include the boys playing cricket in the distance? Yes, the chimney of the St Clair *usine*? At the moment you've not got enough foreground. And . . .'

'Yes . . .'

As Michel Jean intervened to alter Wildman's painting with the cricketers in the distance, the present was eclipsed by the applause in the past for William Hunt, considered the best bat in Hertfordshire. Then there was more applause for the crack bowler, Matthew Ryan, when the boys in the pavilion threw their caps into the air, and the surrounding fields, even more vast than the Queen's Savannah, were filled with voices shouting, *Hurrah, hurrah, hurrah!* He and Fitzwilliam had followed the

wicket keeper, Joseph Alberry, into the changing rooms. *Nigger.*
Tawny. Those darts still hurt.

'There, you've caught it. Much better, the smaller figures in
the distance.' How will it be here and now, he thought, with
this young Englishman? Will he be a Fitzwilliam, or turn out
to be a Rodney?

'I've interrupted your morning and I see by my watch that
time has flown. The sun is almost at its zenith. Would you
accompany me to my residence so that I can repay your time
with some refreshment?' Wildman had already packed up his
easel and paints.

Michel Jean was curious. The invitation was certainly unusual.
'Thank you.' Did this young man understand the etiquette of
the place and time? He would probably soon get into trouble
if he continued like this, inviting any coloured man off the
savannah to his residence for refreshments. He decided not
to continue to Belmont Hill that morning. He collapsed his
easel and packed away his paints and painting, which had by
this time dried. Wildman helped him pack up his things. They
began to stroll in the direction of the Botanic Gardens on the
old Paradise Estate.

'I remember eight years ago David Lockhart, who had been
sent out from Kew Gardens. Did you know of him? He brought
the first seeds in his pockets to plant the samaan trees you see
in our pastures.'

'Is that so? Yes, seen his name in dispatches, importing plants
from the Botanic Garden in St Vincent. There's a Mr Purdie in
charge now.'

'Lockhart said to me once, "Gardening, my man, is like
painting. We're both landscaping."'

'That's good. That's clever.'

They had crossed the savannah.

'Government House? You living in Government House? You
is not the Governor?' Michel Jean found joking a way to deal
with this odd stranger.

'No, I'm not the Governor. But I am his secretary.'

Michel Jean was a little taken aback by the discovery of his new acquaintance's connections. His curiosity grew. 'I see . . .'

'I needed a position after I came down from Oxford, and cousin George obliged with this wonderful opportunity, a job as secretary, with a living in a little cottage in the Arcadian grounds of the governor's residence in this tropical paradise. And it's actually called Paradise. Am I not lucky?'

'Cousins?' Michel Jean looked puzzled.

'Yes.'

'You and the Governor is cousins?'

'Yes, Cazabon, we is cousins.' Wildman imitated his verbs.

They both laughed out loud, their hilarity releasing the tension. It was the gushing spirit that reminded him of Fitzwilliam, he realized, though Wildman seemed a bit more hoity-toity, in that English upper-class way of the other boys at St Edmund's. Fitzwilliam was from Ireland. There was a music in his speech. He did not have a plum in his mouth.

After several glasses of iced lime juice, brought by a servant in the livery of Government House onto the veranda of the Cottage, Wildman suddenly said, 'You must stay to luncheon. And, what about a shot of rum with that lime?'

Over their pumpkin soup, red fish, christophine and mashed potato, the Governor's cousin was running on with an enthusiasm that Michel Jean started to feel uneasy about. 'It's all just so marvellous, this abundance,' he enthused, spreading his arms wide over the luncheon table. 'Quite peppery. Must be that wonderful cook we've discovered in the Santa Cruz valley. Señor Gomez recommended her.' This Wildman had got around the place very quickly, thought Michel Jean. He smiled, trying to assess the situation.

Joseph and his father would want him to use this opportunity, to petition the Governor through his secretary for their advancement. Maybe this would be a trump card to play against Joseph over his execution of his mother's will. '*Oui*, hot for so,' he laughed, in appreciation of the peppery food.

'I can hear the French now. You must be a Creole.' Wildman

said this as if he now remembered that it was something he should be noting. He did not seem dissuaded from venturing forth. 'Will you be my tutor? Will you come here? Paint with me and possibly allow me from time to time to accompany you around the island to paint? We might paint *en plein air* together,' he suggested, pausing over his mango and pommecythere fruit salad. 'Is it not all so delicious! What will you charge me?'

On the one hand, Michel Jean could not believe his luck, that he could be the tutor to the Governor's secretary. He knew he would have to be paid more than the five dollars per month he had planned to charge students with means. A governor's secretary must be able to pay more. But then he thought, on the other hand, he might have more to offer than fees for lessons. He was not blind to an opportunity. He did not want to overplay his hand.

'Ten dollars per month? Does that seem reasonable?'

'Absolutely!'

With Joseph delaying probate on his mother's will, and complicating matters with his desire to manage his brother's financial affairs, he would feel so much more comfortable if he had some employment in the interim. Wildman and Michel Jean agreed to meet the following week. He would come to the Cottage in the early morning and they would climb into the Maraval hills from the valley near to Port of Spain.

Back at George Street, Michel Jean reflected on his good fortune. He regaled Josie with his unusual tale of lunch with the Governor's secretary. They sat on the veranda and Michel Jean poured them each a nip of rum.

'Jeansie. You have to watch them English people, you know. You just come. You don't really know what going on. I expect you accustom mixing with white people in Fwance. But here, them white people is something else, you know. Them is English.'

'Josie, I don't forget so easy. But the fella nice. He go pay me. Ten dollars per month for lessons. He appreciate painting and thing.'

'Well, I tell you, watch yourself. Between them English and the white Creole we don't know where we is, you know. We does have to take care of we self. Things not as bad as when we was children, but for Mama and me things still bad . . .'

'Josie, don't bother your head. This rum nice, you know. You go stay tonight?'

'Jeansie!' She smiled. 'You not meaning what you say.'

'For old time sake, nuh. You know we good together.' The rum had turned his head.

'Let me go down and see Mama fix up for the night and I go come back and take another drink. You know we done with this thing, Jeansie. You is a married man now. I is your sister. Is like a sister I go love you.'

'You right, you know. Is the rum and a feeling for the old times.'

'Yes, but them old times was sad too.'

A mood of elation followed Josie's wisdom. He relaxed with the rum she had brought to the table. How young they had been when they had first started with their secrets. How natural it all was, too natural, or too much *commesse*, as Ernestine called it, once she had suspected her daughter's error. Why had she not stopped it? Had she known the full story? To himself and Josie it was not something that was a part of anything else. Their pleasure in each other was not part of their usual world. But it became a shameful secret after Joseph's warning, and still they did not stop. Did Ernestine think there was something to be gained for herself and her daughter? She had had so little from his father. It was his mother, in the end, who had given her a home.

When Josie came back upstairs it did not take long before they began to talk of how things had been. 'Let we leave those things, Jeansie. What good in it now? What kind of future we going to make?'

'Josie, you not angry?'

'I could be angry, *oui*. But if I let that eat me up what I go get? You go have to treat me good now, Jeansie. I have to look out for Mama. I want your assistance for that.'

'I tell you, Josie, I will take care of all yuh.' They sipped their rum like old friends, the brother and sister that they were.

The night closed in and Michel Jean was left wondering, once Josie had gone downstairs, whether his will was as strong as hers. She had not given herself to another man. At least, she had not told him whether she had. He did not know how he would feel about that. He could remember their bond as a joy and a pleasure, but, as Josie had said, there was also a sadness, a sadness in their forbidden love. He was a married man now. He had two children. The thought was a stark reminder of where his responsibility and loyalty lay. He must return to Louise soon, and then she must join him here with the children. Then he would be whole again. He felt that Josie's wisdom would help him, help Louise and the children to settle. All in good time, he thought. He wanted to do the right thing by both of them.

On the morning of the first official lesson, Michel Jean approached Wildman's residence across the stone bridge beneath the swaying, feathery clumps of bamboos, entering the Botanic Gardens and walking across to the Cottage.

They chose a view of a pasture with cows in front of the tapia cottage tucked away in the cultivated bush beneath Mount Hololo. Two young *blanchisseuses* were coming along the road, crossing the stone bridge ahead of them, returning with their pressed laundry, carrying it on trays upon their heads. '*Doudou*,' they called, and giggled between themselves. They waved.

'Let us include the figures of the women.'

'That's a challenge.'

'Yes. But try . . .'

'There, you've got a suggestion, build on it. It's not a portrait from this distance. It's the figure in relation to the landscape, part of the landscape.'

'Is that important?'

'Yes. The landscape is essentially theirs.'

'What? Even the washerwomen?'

'Think of where the washing is done, on the rocks of the river. You must've seen them in your travels. They've grown out of the landscape with their labour. Think of who the washing is for.'

Wildman learned quickly and enthusiastically. After completing his watercolour he was now anxious to talk. 'How did you come to paint? I would not have thought it was here, though I can see how the sunsets and sunrises which Ping loves so much must inspire you.'

'Ping?' Michel Jean inquired.

'You know, his nibs, the Governor. We call him Ping, a family name, what they and close friends have always called him, since Eton, I believe, and always up at Merton. His friends always addressed him as Ping in their letters. I've heard it since I was a child at Chilham Castle, and when we went to play out at Norton Court or Belmont House. Everyone cried out "Ping" on the cricket field. No idea of its origin. Probably some nickname given at Eton, or a mother's playful diminutive which never lost its hold.'

'You two very close?'

'Yes. Does that make a difference?'

'To what?'

'To us. To my painting lessons?'

'No, man.' Michel Jean found that he was being very informal with Wildman, just when maybe he should be more correct, given the closeness to his cousin, the Governor. He felt a sincerity about Wildman, and trusted that this feeling was right.

'Good.' Wildman continued with his expansive speech about what he thought must have first inspired Michel Jean to paint. 'All of this!' He stretched his arms to encompass the little cottage, the columns of *palmistes*. 'Doric columns of Greece,' he exclaimed, throwing his arms into the air to describe the height of the palms' lofty statures. His fancy went another way. 'They're the pillars in Durham Cathedral! And bamboo groves are your Gothic cathedrals. And there, above us,' he pointed to Mount Hololo, 'Parnassus!' His arms appeared to spread even further, as if he was accustomed to encompassing the universe.

Then he broke off. 'There, I know what got you painting, the hills. The hills go on and on.'

'Leave my hills alone, Englishman. This is my world.' Michel Jean smiled as he mixed his paints. How was he going to cope with this enthusiastic boy?

Wildman began to get his paints prepared for another painting. He had application. He looked up and smiled.

'*Bien, très bien. Bon.*'

'Good?'

'Good for now.'

He watched the young man's concentrated application.

Michel Jean was enjoying the lesson and the conversation, the kind he missed, now already finding his island too small, Josie's backyard too imprisoning. Wildman was a Fitzwilliam not a Rodney. He wanted back what he and Fitzwilliam had had roaming around London in the last year of school, allowed to saunter off on their own while Mr Barnaby went off to visit an aunt in Pentonville, arranging to meet them later at the Royal Academy. He used to set them their tasks to view the Turners and the Constables. 'Go and gaze into eye of the sun, or lose yourself in the Stour Valley,' Mr Barnaby had said, leaving them a few pennies for purchases. Years later they had regained their friendship when they were on tour in Scotland in '41, and he had done his Brown Studies. He was still protecting him then. What would Wildman have to protect him from? Fitzwilliam had had to guard him from taunts thrown in the street as they made their way to Piccadilly as boys. Once it was a couple of toffs with silk hats whom Fitzwilliam himself took on. They had smirked as they passed by with, 'There, see, a coaly!' One pulled the other around by the shoulder to stare. It was Fitzwilliam's theory, learned at St Edmund's, that bullies needed to be challenged immediately.

'Yes, you've got something there with those clouds.'

Wildman's basic knowledge contributed to the success of the first lesson, and another attempt at the prospect of the bridge and the cottage with the two washerwomen was a respectable beginning.

'I could never have done that so well on my own, Cazabon. It's jolly good, if I say so myself. Don't you think? And this one?'

'There's something there.'

'Something?' Wildman peered into his second painting.

'Yes.' Michel Jean was pleased. This might lead somewhere, he thought.

On arriving back home Michel Jean saw that Josie had left a letter that had arrived by the packet that day. It was from Louise. He read her messages of love – 'I keep hearing your voice in the house' – and then was alerted to the medical report in her letter:

Doctor Didon at Place Saint Georges says that the left leg will grow slower than the other and may never be quite right. He's a crooked little thing and so often locked away in his own thoughts. Rosie is very good with him.

Would his son not be normal? he wondered. How were they going to manage as he got older? Where were they going to find the right medical attention? And Louise? What was this going to do to her, having to cope on her own? He was plagued by these questions and worries, besieged by the sand flies swarming on the veranda.

Eventually, he fell asleep in the hammock. His dreams were of Louise. They were young lovers again. When he woke it was as if he could smell her scent in the room. He dozed off again. His dream changed. Josie was holding Louis Michel in her arms. He woke suddenly wondering where he was, almost falling out of the hammock. It had grown dark. He was still not accustomed to these early evenings. The heat made him want the long summer nights he had enjoyed with Louise. He reached for Louise's letter and read of the political situation in Paris. 'There are still fires in the city. The revolution is alive in Paris but less so in the countryside. The agitators are determined to press their demands.' What had he done, leaving his family at a time like this?

The night felt damp. It had rained. The jumbie bird made its hooting noise over and over. When he got up to relieve himself, he noticed there was a dim light burning in Josie's room downstairs. He thought to go and join her, slip into her bed, forget everything and spend the night with her. Yes, ironically, their passion had once been a way to try and forget, while getting deeper still into what was forbidden. That was how it had been when he was here eight years ago. He now found himself some bread and cheese and sat with his own thoughts of his wife and his children in a troubled world. He was taken back to the voyages, back and forth across the ocean.

As if she knew his thoughts, Josie came upstairs and joined him. 'Jeansie, what happen, you can't sleep? I myself can't seem to sleep.'

'Coming back, nuh, my mind full of memories. I remembering the first time I went away to England. My mother had written down my itinerary in a little notebook that she had given me as she kissed me farewell on the deck. "When you leave Trinidad you go reach Barbados, Grenada, Martinique, Guadeloupe, Antigua until you reach Atlantic Ocean, then no land till you reach Falmouth." I can still hear her voice. I remember learning to spell archipelago.'

'Archipela who? You learn to spell? Lucky you. I myself can't see to fall to sleep. Yes, I remember when you leave that time. I cry for so.'

'You does ever go back?'

'Go back when?'

'You know, back to Ernestine's stories.'

'Like what so?'

'You don't remember how Ernestine used to tell we stories between songs when she put us to sleep. I remember the one about a little boy. She used to begin it so. "There was a little boy who was lost. He did not know where he was. He did not know where his mama gone."'

'That was when you mother gone and live in San Fernando. Mama keep telling me that story. How you mother love you. She come back for you, you know? Take you by she.'

The woman he knew as Josie's mother was their Ernestine. *'Come let me give you a lift up.'* From inside his mother's bed, he hears her voice as she bends down, having pulled up the mosquito net. What does a small child understand when he finds another woman in his mother's bed, in his father's bed? What could a small child make of such abandonment and loss, but that his mother had disappeared never to return? For him, it was as if she had died.

Sleep did not come. Dawn began to etch the contours of the Laventille hills. A cock crowed in the neighbour's yard. They both, brother and sister, sat dozing and talking. 'Jeansie, boy, we still here. Let me bring some coffee.'

They sipped their coffee in silence.

'You remember the quarrelling voices out on the veranda? Who will win the battle for Corynth tonight? That was Joseph in the room next door, full of a false bravado.'

'And then your sister start up. This was her estate. Magdeleine Alexandrine always took her mother's part. She brought it into the marriage. It was her dowry. You don't remember how she used to say that?'

'And we all used to ask what a dowry was. You remember Rose Clotilde. She used to cry.'

'Magdeleine Alexandrine loved to tell that story and I used to listen at the foot of the bed.'

'Yes, your eye big like a jumbie bird,' Josie said, opening her eyes wide.

'You remember that?'

'Rose Clotilde was her father's favourite. Magdeleine Alexandrine had to be careful, otherwise there would be tears with Rose Clotilde, rushing out to the veranda to tell tales, crying, *'Papa, Papa.'*

'Joseph used to say, "You won't have a dowry."'

'Everybody used to cry about the piano.'

Michel Jean saw the piano teetering precariously, strapped to the back of the carriage and followed by two of his mother's slaves, Billy and George Williams, running barefoot behind the carriage, ready to prevent it from falling off. *Maman, Maman!* He sees himself holding on to the back of the carriage, dragged through the gravel. Ernestine and Josie assuaged his wounds.

'Let me go and rest my head, *oui*.' Josie went downstairs to her room.

'A fella all dress up like is carnival, bring the letter,' Josie said as she entered his room with coffee later that morning. 'When I look out in the street I see the carriage stop by the front gate, so I go to look. Well, I tell you, if the bearer of the letter look so important, the letter self must be more than important, *oui*! And he cheeky too. These fellas think they could get anything they like. Hmm! Not from me!'

'Not from you, Josie, sweetheart. I sure. And is only one fella that does get that?' He had his hand round her waist, pulling her into him, still wanting to nuzzle at her breasts where they were brim full under her tight broderie anglaise bodice.

'Jeansie. You still sleeping, dreaming or something? You need to get out of bed, *oui*. Too much spoiling. Here, read this letter.'

The Governor's crest was clearly stamped upon the letter. It was a personal letter written in the Governor's hand commissioning a view, a prospect, it said, of his residence, and inviting Michel Jean when it was finished to meet him at Government House. The writing sprawled, spidery. He wrote that he had heard about him from his cousin and secretary, Mr Wildman, who had showed him an example of his work, which had reminded him of a conversation with the planter Mr Hardin Burnley of Orange Grove, who had recounted only the other day that his wife, who was at the time living in Paris, had seen a number of paintings, three to be exact, at the Salon du Louvre by a one Michel Jean Cazabon from Trinidad. One was a view, a seascape, of the beach at Calvados in Normandy. One was a landscape near Poissy and another entitled *Little Fort on the Mediterranean*. They were all delightful, according to Mrs Hardin Burnley. The Governor had full confidence in his ability based on these recommendations and would pay his commission on completion of the painting. The letter was signed simply, 'Harris.'

Michel Jean turned the letter over in his hand. A commission from the Governor, he thought, just like that, something must be wrong. No, Wildman's doing. He saw again the view at Poissy. It was an oil. He had been trying for that green of Rousseau's, that tunnel of foliage and light taking you downstream into a distant point of haze and shadow congealed and clogged with water-lilies; one of those typical Fontainebleau forest views at Barbizon. The boy, for he did think of him as a boy still, had come up trumps. A Fitzwilliam indeed, with all that youthful enthusiasm.

'Who write you, Jeansie?'

'The Governor.'

'The Governor!' Josie took the letter from his hand, hoping to read some of its contents. As Josie puzzled over what must have been like deciphering hieroglyphs, he recalled his own retreat near Poissy; the second morning when this young girl had walked in off the country lane into the small yard, a country girl, like one of his own *blanchisseuses* here on the island. Her name was Isabelle. She had stayed long enough to be the figure on the landscape and to be his lover for the afternoon when she eventually said she had to get back to the chateau where she was a scullery maid. He had not looked at the painting for years. Soon after that he had met Louise. Then he remembered how he had erased Isabelle and painted in Monsieur and Madame de Noirmont from the village.

'I can't read this, Jeansie. You go have to tell me.'

'He talking about paintings I did in France long time ago. This big planter at Orange Grove, he wife see them in Paris.'

'Funny how things does come together.'

'I getting lucky.'

'Let me go see after Mama.'

He remembered how he had found a way for his double perspective, below and above the horizontal of the bridge. In the view, Madame and Monsieur de Noirmont are walking across the bridge. Madame is carrying her white parasol. There are white sheets and a red dress hanging over the railing of the bridge. The light is turning one of the sheets into the ochre of the brick. He remembers the day well. He had been disappointed in the cows making for the stream to drink. He found animals difficult. But the stream and rocks pleased him and the sky rose up tinted with dun and cobalt. Monsieur de Noirmont had bought the painting, giving him permission to exhibit it at the salon. He remembered that then he had been lonely, as he could be now. He would do anything to be with his wife. *Plage du Calvados* was a later painting, one of those which he had done on a trip to Normandy with Louise when Rose Alexandrine still stumbled and fell as she walked on the sands at Luc-sur-Mer and Louis Michel needed to be lifted into his mother's arms or carried on his favourite perch upon his father's shoulder. *Papa, Papa!* He heard his daughter's excited cries, demanding a ride on a donkey across the sands.

With the bedroom window open, he could hear Josie and Ernestine in the yard below.

'You is not a child no more, girl, come, time to have your own children.' He heard the disappointment of the mother for her daughter not getting married and giving her some grandchildren, now that she could with dignity and solemnity. 'And you must stop this nonsense with Jeansie. He gone, child, and good thing too. Let things take their natural course, is what I say. None of that *commesse* all you get yourself into. So long I tell all you, is against nature, child.'

'Mama, what you talking about? Is so long now Jeansie and I fix up we business. What you know?'

'So what you doing upstairs there? You think I don't know what going on.'

'Mama, nothing going on. Anyway . . .'

'So why you don't fix yourself up with one of them fellas that calling for you?'

Michel Jean thought how she had saved herself for him, seemingly unable to commit herself to any of her many admirers.

'Mama, you have time to meddle, *oui*. You want to see me leave you?'

Michel Jean listened to the sad conversation. His return to the island had made it all so real again, the tastes and smells of where he had learned to put his fingers to pleasure her. The very illicitness of their union had become even more the reason for continuing against all the warnings, against Joseph's nasty insults: 'You still with your nigger sister.' The beginning had been so innocent, the eventual knowledge so sweet with pain.

He reached, as if to pull her towards him now again, as she entered the room. 'Josie, sweetheart, *doudou*.'

'Jeansie, you need to get up, you know. You have to answer the letter. Is the Governor you say write you? Boy, you is a real big man now.'

'I doing that this morning.'

'I leaving some clothes hanging here that I iron.'

'Josie, you too good, *oui*.'

'You too bad.' She laughed as she left the room.

He read through the Governor's letter again. The small water-colour, *Le petit fort dans la Méditerranée*, had been done on a tour of the South of France with Fitzwilliam. That painting was charged with quite different memories of the two friends together with their own kind of companionship, their own love forged in the cruel halls of a public school, where to survive you had to have your secrets, negotiate your paths in a dangerous place. They were boys without girls, caught in the first flush of their desires. Then there were the priests trying to recruit you for God. The long hot summer, which he and Fitzwilliam had spent on the Mediterranean at Le Lavandou and in the hillside villages above the coast, was loud in his ears with the *cigales* reminding him of home, the locusts calling for rain. The scent of eucalyptus and the vivid red and orange of the bougainvillaea cascading over stone walls had reminded him of the gardens of his island. The Midi sea was an aquamarine which made him ache for home. Their longings found their consolation in comradeship, in a friendship that broke its bounds. Fitzwilliam used to say, 'Cazabon, is this what we really want?' In the music of that inimitable Irish accent. Their doubts faded and their embraces led to their own hot conclusions. But he did not remember that they ever spoke much about what they did. They followed desire. If they did give it thought, it seemed to be part of their sense of art and beauty, which they searched for in the galleries of paintings and sculptures, like when they stood, stunned, lost in admiration of the form of Michelangelo's *David* in the Piazza della Signoria, which they had eventually discovered off the maze of streets in Florence. In the delineations of that male form, beauty was the impetus that fired their desire and their common empathy for each other. Later, at night, after carousing in a tavern that led to a stolen moment with a young girl that came to nothing, they stumbled back to their *penzione* and fell into bed together as mates. A long, hot night quenched with spring water from the stone pitcher. In the morning, inspired by the memory of Michelangelo's *David*, he sketched Fitzwilliam's naked body with charcoal and a stylus.

Michel Jean wrote his reply to the Governor's letter while Josie moved around, dusting the relics of his mother's presence in the room.

'The Governor giving me work, that is something.'

'That's good, Jeansie. Your mother would've be proud. I does miss she, you know. With she gone, the times changing.'

'Times changing, for truth. I never hear of no governor before give we anything.'

Later, after Josie's breakfast of hot bake and more coffee, Michel Jean crossed the savannah to deliver the acceptance of his commission to a liveried footman, who took his letter away on a silver salver to be presented to the Governor.

He then continued over the stone bridge to Wildman's cottage. He was apprehensive. He felt conspicuous, viewed as he was from the neighbouring garden of Mr Warner, the Attorney General, one of Wildman's neighbours. He could see the white English children playing in the distance along the perspectives of Mr Lockhart's nutmeg plantation. He heard the call of a nurse for one of her charges. 'Bella!' They were singing nursery rhymes and ditties, English children with English voices echoing across the green. He could have been somewhere in Hertfordshire as he sat on the trunk of a fallen tree and sketched the scene.

'You've been talking about me?' Michel Jean said to his new friend, once they had settled down out on the veranda with glasses of iced lime juice.

'What about a dash of rum in that?' The young Englishman smiled. 'I could not help myself. Ping is so fond of views. Quite the collector, you know.'

'I see.' Michel Jean was still amused at the Governor's family diminutive.

'Yes, Ping, so cultured in that field, I felt sure he would want to meet you to see what you painted, so I showed him our efforts from our first lesson and what I had copied. I thought he would want to meet the one artist of Trinidad.' Wildman smiled, looking to see how Michel Jean would take this compliment. 'I thought you should be brought to court.'

'To court?'

'You know what I mean. You need to move in the right circles, man.'

'Who it is preventing people moving in the right circles, but you English, not to talk of the *grands blancs*? You royalists. There's been a revolution, you know.'

'Not in England there hasn't. Not the done thing, you know, to complain about your lot. Best to excel at what you do, which is what you do. So there!'

'No. Well, actually you cut off your king's head a long time before the French.'

'Come, Cazabon, I wouldn't pursue that line. You must know the talk about you southern, republican families, the Congnets, Saturnins and Philippes! And, I dare say, Cazabons! I'm not uninformed, you know. I'm the Governor's secretary. Anyway, you can't complain about the commission, and there'll be more, I can assure you. Has he named his price? It'll be a handsome one, I'm sure. He's very fair, is Ping.'

Wildman was so jovial, so keen.

'You know, I didn't ask the man that. I so excited to get the commission.' Michel Jean thought about this afterwards, that a price had not been agreed, that he was embarking on the work with no idea of what he was going to be paid. He did not like himself for this. He thought it was a sign of weakness. But he also felt that he would not be disappointed. Anyway, how could he barter with the Governor? He needed this commission.

'He'll pay you handsomely. Doesn't think much of my efforts. Dabbles a bit himself, you know. Probably will keep it a secret, though, when you eventually meet him.'

The following morning, Michel Jean began in earnest on the Governor's commission. He arrived early in the gardens to get the benefit of the fast-changing light coming over Belmont Hill. He set up his easel. He had decided to do at least two paintings that morning. He worked fast, trying slightly different angles, working from different parts of the gardens and catching different sorts of people: a *marchande* with her tray of sweets; a maid from the house walking into the gardens near the fountain.

A gardener entered along one of the pathways through the avenue of palms, disappearing into the nutmeg grove beyond the tall cedars and mahoganies. Another worker came through the clumps of Indian bamboo dwarfed by the royal palms that had been introduced by David Lockhart. Michel Jean wanted to include these figures on the landscape.

At the end of the day he had completed his different versions of the house and gardens. 'All gardening is landscape painting,' he said to himself as he picked his way through the nutmeg seedlings and along the avenue of cocorite palms as slender as pencils.

Back at George Street, Michel Jean kept to himself. He was exhausted. He rested.

Before retiring for the night he got all his equipment ready for the next day. He checked his easel, his box of paints, his charcoal and graphite. He cleaned his brushes. He was working in Trinidad!

Elated, he wrote a letter to Louise in the glow of the candle light.

Ma chérie, I'm working for the English Governor. He's going to pay me well . . .

Outside, fireflies lit the yard intermittently. He exaggerated the future to Louise, conveying Wildman's support. He had this good news to offset the disappointment about his mother's will.

Joseph has still not dealt with the will. I'm in the dark about procedures here. He still wants to manage my affairs. My sisters and Joseph are now disputing details of the will that I don't understand. They are demanding separate legacies for their children. There has been no mention of legacies for our children. Uncle St Luce is finally going to challenge Joseph to bring the whole thing to a speedy end. I'm going to let him advise me.

He sent his love to her, to his dear Rosie and to little Louis. He fell asleep, imagining his letter on the packet, crossing the ocean to his darling Louise. He missed her. In bed, he reached out for the warmth of her back where she used to curl into him, for her slender shoulders against his chest and his kiss on the nape of her neck.

*

He was up with the light of the foreday morning.

'I go wait for you tonight,' Josie said, as she unlatched the gate. A dog barked at the bottom of George Street.

'Josie, sometimes I need to be on my own, you know. You see with this work I doing for the Governor, I go need some time on my own.'

'But you need to eat.'

'Well, tonight then.'

'Tonight.'

He had his letter to post to Louise. 'Josie, deliver this for the packet.'

'You writing your wife?'

'*Oui.*'

'That's good. She must want you to reach back, Jeansie.'

'Now I have this work. But yes . . .'

Dawn was breaking over the savannah. His easel was strapped on his back. He carried his box of paints on his shoulder. With his folding stool and parasol, he set off. Dew was still on the grass. Sharp light picked out Belmont Hill. Parrots screamed, lifting off from the palms and the bamboos. They were vivid reds, yellows and greens. Their light and their screams faded over the Maraval hills. He headed for the governor's residence at Paradise Estate. He felt that he would have to show some of his work fairly soon, otherwise there might be some doubt in his ability. He could not allow this opportunity to fail.

He studied the house from a different angle this morning. He set up his easel. His mood changed as he considered the fact that this painting he was embarked upon had an immediate and particular audience. He did not know his audience, but he knew his position. 'Ping.' He did not want to think of his audience as 'Ping'. So instead he thought of him as 'Excellency'. Should he banish that thought at this stage? He thought he should. This should not primarily be a painting for an audience, no matter how important. It should be his painting until the time that he delivered it. But he was painting to please his nibs, as Wildman would say.

He was agitated. Joseph and his father, as he had thought, wanted him to influence the Governor's decision concerning representation on the council for the free-coloureds. 'Use the access you have to help us, man, put a word in for us,' they had insisted, that Thursday morning when he had gone to visit his father at Schoener's Import & Export on the wharf. He would have preferred it if Joseph had not been there. He would never learn to speak to his father with Joseph there at the same time. He could see that his father knew what he was feeling. When he said his farewell he said, 'I'll be here on my own next Thursday.' Michel Jean was going to keep out of the politics, if possible.

There was the architecture, the light, and then the landscape itself. As he worked, his attempts at the Roman Church came back to him, particularly his very first attempt when he had just come back as a boy of seventeen from St Edmund's, with great expectations, but inexperienced. He remembered his first lesson in drawing, which his mother had organized with the architect of the church, Philip Reinagle: 'Drawing, my boy, keep drawing.'

The old architect had been keen for him to return to England, but his mother had become set on Paris. Michel Jean's mind was a rage of reminiscence: Girtin's and Bonington's views, Corot. The English and the French, his twin influences. Their craft combined to give him hope in his own place this morning.

This far up into the valley of St Ann's, the morning mist had not yet lifted. Every shrub was a glittery wet colour with the details of crotons and hibiscus being gradually picked out by the light, which penetrated through the ground mist. There was an urgent sense of light, an effulgence, massing behind the scrim of mist. Crazy thoughts of Mr Turner ran through his mind. His own abilities at his craft were not up to those extraordinary furnaces that had begun as blotches of paint, puddles of colour, then worked into sunrises and sunsets, catching the waves of the river Thames on fire.

'Boy, if only Barnaby and Fitzwilliam could see me now, painting for the English Governor!' He spoke to himself, bending forward to wash his brush. Concentrating on his painting and lost in his thoughts, he had not heard Wildman come up behind him.

'Morning.'

'*Mon Dieu!* You frighten me.'

'Sorry. I thought you might be here.'

'As you see . . .'

'Yes. You're quite advanced, I must not interrupt.'

Michel Jean smiled.

'I wanted to leave you this. I worked on it on my own. It's for you. I'll leave it here. It's a copy of your prospect from Belmont Hill.' Wildman rested it on the grass.

Warmed by the young man's gesture, Michel Jean glanced at the watercolour. 'I'll examine it later.'

'Yes, sorry to interrupt.'

He knew that he would not get any work done if he allowed Wildman to continue. He would see him later. He watched him disappear behind the bamboos as he went back to the Cottage.

There was a sudden shower of rain. He gathered up his things and sheltered in the pavilion. He took the opportunity to look at Wildman's painting. He had made a quick advance in composition, but required more practice in drawing. Michel Jean thought of him bringing the painting to him. There was something impulsive in that. Maybe he too was finding it difficult to fit in to the island society. They both needed company and assurance.

The rain continued. He abandoned his session.

Josie was delighted at his early return. In the evening they had their nip of rum together.

'You need to go down south and see some of your old friends. Will Williams still there. I sure you ent see him since you gone

England. What about Engelle? He's a Cazabon, you know. He's your cousin. I ent know how Monsieur let him take the name.'
Them is free now, Jeansie.'

Why was Josie bringing up these boyhood friends now? he wondered.

'You gone and miss the thing when you went away. When you went was apprenticeship. You ent see us come out and dance we freedom. Where you was? Paris! Rome, Naples? Where you was when we get we freedom?'

He remembered again the disappointment in the Corynth yard at Emancipation that was no emancipation. He had stood on the veranda and watched his father talking to those who had formerly been his slaves, their children his playmates. He remembered particularly the Williams family, Patty and Success, Iain and Cato, standing there remonstrating with his father, Cato threatening to burn the house down in the night. 'Watch out, Cazabon, when the fire burning like the cane piece. But is no cane fire, you know!' He remembered the relief the planters had felt at the introduction of apprenticeship. The conversations at the dinner table had ended in rows about white people, their own constantly threatened rights, and the black people in the barracks. Michel Jean was torn apart as he listened to the grown-ups. He would leave the table to go into the yard to play with Iain and Success.

'Josie, why you bringing this up now?' he asked.

'Well, I thinking how you have these new friends. This Wildman, a young fella come to look for you.'

'When?'

'This morning.'

'Well, I'm teaching him to paint.'

'Hmm . . . It feel like more than painting when he talking to me. That young Englishman come here early after you left. He leave a painting for you.'

'Another one? I saw him in the gardens.' Michel Jean was intrigued.

'He sound surprised when I tell him that you painting in the

Botanic Garden. Here.' Josie handed him the painting. It was a copy of King's Wharf.

Wildman had not left a message. Josie had offered him some guava juice that he had accepted and he had stayed half an hour, chatting to herself and Ernestine, assuring them of what a good artist the Governor thought Monsieur Cazabon was.

Wildman had come to his house and then to the gardens all on the same day with two different paintings? Michel Jean was touched and encouraged by the report. But he was also curious about these surprise visits.

'Anyway, don't abandon your own people for what you think you go get from these white people.'

'I'll go and see them fellas down Corynth,' he assured her.

The next day, as Michel Jean painted, the Governor's house emerged out of Lockhart's cultivated wilderness. To capture its mixture of styles, he called on his architectural motifs from Italy, those he had drawn with Fitzwilliam at his side, searching for the perfect compositional angles while looking through windows and arcades into the Farnese Gardens and the Coliseum. Cedar and cassia trees framed this composition. The perspective drew the viewer into the garden through the foreground, then into the disappearing hinterland where the yellow light, building behind the mist, was flooding through into patches of deeper yellow on the green of the lawns. He went with the gravitational pull of the perspective. The fountain outlined in graphite opposite the house suggested architectural ornamentation to complement the larger presence of the house with its columns and wide steps to the veranda. The roofs and turrets faded into the dun mist and white cloud. Paul Sandby came into his mind as he put his finishing touches. It was his treatment of the trees, the translucence achieved by the body-colour. Michel Jean worked with quick strokes, the light changing quickly. The mist was lifting to allow a flood of light. He thought he had got what he wanted. He would try another the following day in the full light of noon. He would use oils next time and take in a full view of the front of the house with the hills climbing behind.

That was what he hoped for. But the weather might change. All his arrangements might be dashed.

He was despondent as he prepared to make his return journey back across the savannah. He heard, too, Josie's voice from the past accusing him: 'Where you was when we get we freedom?' – and felt less positive about his achievement. He put the painting away and packed up his equipment. He knew these feelings. They were old enemies that he had learned to entertain as friends to tame the effects of their persecution. It occurred to him that Wildman had not appeared in the gardens as he thought he might. Caught up in Excellency's business, he thought.

His solace now was to make for Belmont Hill on his own. Should he drop in to visit Wildman at the Cottage for lunch? He missed the young Englishman, who was fast becoming his *pardner*, not just his student or entrepreneur. He was touched by his visits the day before.

He took the sandy track along the river, passing under the arches of dark bamboos into the heights, leaving the lone fisherman on the bank he had stopped to sketch, making a note to return to that composition on another occasion. The solitude that he needed to tame his demons came with the increasing wildness as he climbed the hill. Looking out over the gulf he reflected on his present despondency. Somewhere was the nagging tug-of-war in himself between his longing for Louise and his desire for what he had had with Josie. Keep with the painting, he said to himself. Keep the demons at bay.

In the past, submitting his work to be viewed by Delaroche or Corot before he could dream of submitting it to the Salon du Louvre at the Palais Royal could mean that he did not paint again for weeks, or if he did he went through the motions, without belief that he was creating anything worth keeping. His craft was not up to his ideals. And, he was an outsider. He was still looking over his shoulder like on the corridors of St Edmund's when he was a boy, and then in the streets of Saint-Germain-des-Prés, or down the alleyways of the Mouffetard.

Out at Barbizon, he could get a rough ride at the Ganne, where his rented atelier was open for anyone who was staying at the inn to enter, comment and heap criticism. The lessons were hard. The forests at Fontainebleau were his escape from the turpitude of the city. They were a solace for his turmoil; dark tunnels of green in the high summer, kindling fires in the autumn, deserts of barren dried leaves and rocks in the winter. He submitted himself to nature's instructions in reality and mystery. He remembered Barnaby repeating Mr Constable: 'Still Nature is the fountain's head, the source from which all originality must spring.'

Michel Jean had longed for his island, despite how it had been complicated by the trade, remembering his vow as a boy to return and paint what he saw there in his own valleys and on his own hills, echoing with the cries which were shouted on the barricades in Paris for liberty, equality and brotherhood. He had to instruct his fellow artists at the Ganne on the politics of his island. 'All yuh talk about liberty, equality and fraternity while running the slave trade. Napoleon running the slave trade.' They sat around drinking, scoffing at his passion, laughing at his patois. 'All you don't like to remember Saint Dominique, or Toussaint l'Ouverture.'

Today, the brief dusk caught him unawares. He descended the hill. As he turned towards home, the savannah enveloped him in its increasing darkness, lit now by the furnace of a red and orange sunset he had not the power to paint that evening. Would a prayer to Mr Turner help him progress on another day?

As he crossed the yard at 58 George Street, he saw that Josie's lantern was still burning in the window. He knocked on the door quietly, so as not to disturb Ernestine and went in, remembering Josie's invitation earlier that morning to cook him his supper.

'Jeansie, you see how we good like this. Take a little more fish broth.'

He smiled at his sister.

*

Michel Jean had invited Wildman to accompany him south to visit Corynth Estate, which he had not done since his arrival, as Josie had recently reminded him. She wanted him to reunite with friends, while he wanted to revisit the landscape. A pilgrimage to Corynth and to San Fernando was a must. He loved his Port d'Espagne, but he did not feel that he had arrived home until he had crossed the Caroni River and headed south along the new Southern Road through the sugarcane estates.

Because of the rains they had had to change their minds at the last moment and instead board the steamer, *Paria*, and travel down the gulf's coast to the wharf in San Fernando. They were then equipped with horses from Joseph's estate at Mon Chagrin for their ride out to Corynth. This was their first *en plein air* class out at Corynth, of which he intended there to be others.

Michel Jean was getting the style of this young man, still a boy really he seemed to his own thirty-six years. He must be almost twice his age. 'Your last paintings have shown a marked improvement, James.'

'Thanks. You know I wanted to ask you about something now that we are here in the south. Ping talks of the free-coloured cause. He's sympathetic to some of it. They say the treasury is almost empty, though on the other hand, things, I hear, are getting better.'

Michel Jean had heard that Excellency was concerned with education, but the Governor not allowing local representation was what his brother and father talked about the most. 'I watch these matters from a distance.'

'But your brother and father are making representation, I understand. I've heard their names mentioned.'

'You want to be a painter or a politician?'

'Well, of course, it's why I've been brought out. It's my job to be concerned with these matters as I serve the Governor. It's why I'm here.'

'Well, you here to paint this morning.'

'Wouldn't miss it for the world.' Wildman looked a little sheepish.

'Don't be too heavy with the paint. Watercolour's not oil.' He watched his student's application. He had some of the rudiments. 'Watch your perspective. But above all, remember it's all in the moment with watercolour.' He returned to his own work. 'This is my politics.'

Wildman looked over from his easel and smiled. 'The power of art.'

The cane fields rustled around them. A chicken hawk hovered. 'Watch gabilan! See that hawk fly!' Michel Jean pointed upwards. They looked up to the wide expanse of wing as the bird soared. 'Notice the fast-changing light. See how it's opened up the landscape, erasing the shadows upon the cane fields.' The clouds fled towards the gulf with the Atlantic blast from the east. Then, almost as suddenly, the cumuli massed once more to obliterate the sun and create an *ombrage* over Corynth. Wisps of cirrus clouds, yellowing scarves, fading into lilac were strung out towards the gulf. 'See how much colour there is, when you might think you didn't have a lot to play with.' The quickly changing light, from brightness into shadow, reflected his own changeable moods, which returning to Corynth could sometimes provoke. They steadied their easels in the wind and worked away at their prospects.

The old pain of being caught between worlds, between the black and the white, between the white French Creoles and the free-coloured and their distance from those formerly enslaved returned to plague him. These feelings arose with the visit to Corynth. His mother had recognized these sensitivities that she thought should be put at the service of people. 'Be a priest or a doctor,' she would urge him, and if neither of those professions attracted him, he should be a man of law to take his people through the thicket of rights and freedoms. It took her some time to see where else he might use his gifts. 'Portraits? Yes, sweetheart, and these landscapes as you call them.' Michel Jean watched the Englishman at work and wondered at the choices available to himself now as an artist and teacher. He wondered at the choices available to this young Englishman. 'We're an odd pair,' he suddenly said.

Wildman looked up and smiled. 'I expect we are.'

'As a boy, I was a wanderer.' They were talking in their caves, each obsessed with his own painting. 'See the summits of Morne Jaillet.' Michel Jean told him how he had played there with Josie, losing themselves in the bush to catch semps and picoplats with the sticky laglee. She had loved the songbirds and kept them in cages. Something in him resisted this desire to have them in captivity. He hated to hear the chickichong calling for its mate from behind the intricacies of his cage.

'Yes, I met Miss Josie. Can we climb there later today?' Wildman was curious to learn more about the south.

'Maybe. Let's see how we get on here.'

'I, too, wandered away from home into the countryside of Kent, running wild among the apple orchards.' Wildman was keen to tell Michel Jean about his world. 'You must've seen the trees in blossom. In Kent, though, they are very special. All around Norton Court the orchards are a riot of pink and white in the spring.'

They half listened to each other as they painted.

'My mother painted,' Wildman was saying.

'I can see you've had some tutoring.'

'Yes, in the grounds at Chilham.' Wildman continued with his recollections of his home. 'Quite splendid views from the castle walls.'

'You make it sound like another world.'

'Well, I suppose it is from here. More natural when at home, but still quite splendid. I miss it sometimes, alone at the Cottage. It's been a real boon to have met you.'

Michel Jean smiled, cherishing this new companionship. He was understanding the young man's need for him.

Their view of Corynth was from the neighbouring estate of Petit Morne, looking towards the old family house with the San Fernando hill in the background. It was the dry season and the fields immediately in the foreground of their composition had been harvested; burned to the ground with the still faintest sign of stubble and the suggestion of the following year's ratoons. The high razor grass on the verges whistled in the wind.

'This is where I belong. Born and grew here.' Michel Jean applied ochre to his foreground.

Wildman kept with his own work, studying his mentor. 'The light changes so quickly.'

'What did you say? Why, that's very good.' He unpinned Wildman's painting from the easel, glancing at the young man's anxious anticipation for his opinion, and brought it towards him for closer inspection. 'This is very good.'

'Yes?'

'Maybe work faster. For the outdoor étude, speed is essential because of this fast-changing light. That is the way you will get the truth of this scene. And if you want to work this up later in your studio it is really important to have captured as much as possible that will help you when you are no longer out of doors, when you are no longer in this light and wind.'

'Yes, I see. I'm too careful at the moment, too nervous that a wrong dab might spoil it all.'

'No, but I see a little of . . . who is it? Girtin? I remember Barnaby at St Edmund's taking us to see Girtin in London. He had hopes for Fitzwilliam and myself. You remind me of him a bit. I remember something about the spaciousness, something about the browns and ochres being warm, optimistic. Sky and earth corresponding. That's what Constable liked about Girtin.'

'Do you know *The White House at Chelsea*?' Wildman asked. And the two men discussed the treatment of the sky and the expanse of the river reflecting the blues, greys and duns with the scratched-out white of the house reflected vertically in the water, a focal point of intense light drawing one right into the centre of the painting.

'The windmill and church steeples are suggestions for frames and the sloops are sunk into the watery foreground the same colour as the sky. It was pencil and watercolour, as I remember.

Think of your use of the *usine* over there in the gully and the royal palms on the hill.'

'You remember the painting so well. Your English influences? You speak differently when you speak of those things.'

'Do I? Well. They were the first, well not the very first influences . . .'

'And you bring them back here. That's admirable. But who's going to know what you do here?'

Michel Jean looked at the young man and considered his question; who would know what he did here? 'Good question. Indeed . . .' He laughed, leaving the question unanswered. 'Well, I must go back to Paris as soon as I've completed Excellency's commission. I've a wife and two small children there. I miss them.'

'You didn't tell me that you were married. You're established. I feel so much as if I'm at the beginning of my life.'

'You're . . . the world will favour you. It's more difficult for me. In Paris, or here. I must try.'

'And here I am painting your world. I should be back in Kent painting that light which breaks upon the North Downs, its yellow stone, the plain in the distance, Canterbury Cathedral, that place of pilgrimage.'

'Yes, I must paint in my light with the help of Girtin, Bonington and Corot.'

'That's what must compel you to stay. Everything here still fresh, undiscovered, to be done for the first time.'

'When I'm in Paris I am tugged back here. When here, like now, I'm excited to rediscover the place, to come here, to travel the coasts and the hills. But then I have responsibilities and loves there. But also I have the opportunity to see paintings, to talk with painters.'

'Who will win?'

'We've got to see. No sooner had I decided to leave to reach my mother before her death than the barricades went up. Louis Philippe gone. Paris erupted. I worried for the safety of my children and my wife.'

'Have you heard from her?'

'Letters take an age. But, yes, of course. Things are more settled now.'

'Look, the light has changed completely. We can start again on a view of ochres and blues.'

'Let's leave that for later, maybe. Come, let us go down to the estate itself. So you'll know what you've painted, so you will know where it started, what we talk about.'

After packing up, they retrieved and mounted their grazing horses and descended into the estate yard at Corynth. After all these years, it had remained much the same. It was hot and seemed deserted at first. There was a sudden clang of iron in the blacksmith's forge. The pens were open. Two young boys were cleaning out the mule pen and two grooms swept the stables. Flies buzzed. The shovelling in the pens echoed with a thud. There was the stench of the raked up mule dung mixed with the fragrance of freshly cut grass, and the pervasive smell of newly burned cane on the neighbouring fields from where the cane trash blew up in the sharp wind; swirling ash and trash floating in the air. Small children, boys as well as girls, barely more than six years of age, were picking up the trash with crooks.

They tethered their horses and walked about the yard. Michel Jean described how the estate had been in his childhood. 'There was always that grating and knocking of the treadmill in the *usine*.' As he spoke, he saw again their sweating, bent backs, their straining legs, the muscles on their calves. 'I used to peep through the slats between the whitewashed boards of the threshing room. Right here.' He winces now from the flash of the whip, the lash on the back. He still hears the drivers cussing the women and bullying the men. Wildman looked astonished, listening to his dark memories.

'Here would be where the manacles, chains, masks, bits for the mouth, the irons of torture and bondage were kept.'

'My God!'

'Just over a decade ago. Can you imagine?'

'No.'

Michel Jean pointed out the enclosures of the *usine* with the coppers and scum removers. Here again he sees the sweating bodies in that hot house, ladling the boiling syrups and molasses. He is taken beyond himself and Wildman into the sound of the lamentations arising out of the barrack rooms, Ernestine's story of the long slow swell, that wail like the Atlantic Ocean, breaking on the shore. 'You could hear their cries. That is the long groan from Guinea, my nurse used to say.'

'You talk about it as if it was yesterday.'

'I lived just there.' He pointed to the house on the hill. 'It was happening here where we are standing now. But look about you. See the beauty in the sky and the fields, in the contours of the land and the far hills.'

Wildman obeyed his tutor.

'I never wanted to record the dark visions.'

'Visions?'

'Only this light, the fields and the skies and something else I saw in the people, something I hoped for them, a kind of peace and harmony with the fields and the light.'

'I've lost you, Cazabon.'

Michel Jean smiled. Would anyone understand what he was doing? Did he himself fully understand? Did his thoughts, what he consciously wanted, get into the paintings? Maybe something else was there, which he did not see and others might discover in time. 'I expect you see it differently, without my disturbing memories.'

'So, this is where you lived as a child?'

'I left as a small child from that house on the hill which we have just painted. I went to live with my mother in San Fernando. But I used to come back to see my father, my brother and sisters. I would play down here with the children of the estate.'

'Gosh! I can't connect you, your talk, your painting, with this.' Wildman pointed at the estate yard. 'It's a kind of wonder that you became an artist.'

'It's why I'm an artist. There's no wonder about that. What else could I be?'

'A planter, yourself?'

'You're joking.'

'Am I?'

'Well, could you see me as a planter?'

'Maybe not.'

'Maybe not? Definitely not!'

The wind took their words and scattered them over the fields with the trash the small children were collecting. They returned to their horses. 'Let's ride up to the house.' Michel Jean turned his horse away and cantered off. The undulations and contours within the paintings they had done unfolded beneath them, sped beneath the horses' hooves, as they climbed the hill to the house where he had been born. On reaching the yard, they looked back across the fields to where they had sat with their easels.

'Set up your easel here. Look, why not try for that view of the palms in the distance and the *usine* in the middle ground. Maybe even those teaks on the round hill at Golconda. While you do that I want to walk about the yard and maybe go into the house if I can get access. I need some time there on my own. You can join me later.'

He never remembers how old he is at the time. But he knows he is younger than twelve. Maybe he's nine, seven even, maybe it is in the year he makes his First Communion, goes to Confession for the first time, the year that he had arrived at the age of reason, as Father Vessiny tells him, and he should know right from wrong. He always tries to remember it as young as is reasonable, so that he can be absolved from any responsibility for it.

The boy's name is Ignace. His mother scrubs floors up at the house. The boy comes with his mother and stays in the yard while she works inside the house. He sits in the gravel and plays with the stones. That is when they meet.

He plays on his own when Josie is working for her mother. She totes buckets of water, empties commodes, sweeps, makes beds for Ernestine. She is seven. When she plays with him she likes to play with his sisters' old dolls and to make a doll of him, or to play at making baby at the back of the house when she tries to put his totee inside of her. He can hardly breathe then. So, when he meets Ignace, he has his own new friend.

They play away from the house, roaming all over the estate, swimming in the Cipero, slipping down on the mud banks, catching guabeen and the tiny silver thousands fish that they keep in jars, the way they keep tadpoles, hoping to see them turn into frogs. Or, when more adventurous, they swim in the warm reservoir of the *usine*. The air is sweet with the steamy smells of the factory coming off the cooling towers.

Michel Jean knows that Ignace is not supposed to be roaming the estate, playing. He should be in the fields or in the yard with the other working children. He should be minding the mules in the pasture. He is a pasture boy. He graduated from his weeding job when he was six. Now he rides the mules. 'Come, Jeansie, come and ride mule, ride mule plenty.'

The voice he still hears so distinctly unnerves him.

'Oh, there you are. I wondered what you thought of this.' Wildman was suddenly there, a pupil with his sketch in his hand.

Michel Jean passed his eye over his student's latest sketch. 'Yes, well, there's still the foreground.'

'I thought I'd show you how far I had got.'

'I'll be with you shortly.'

He watched Wildman return to his easel on the other side of the yard.

He stood alone and looked about him.

It happens in the open yard that now lies below him. The stocks are in the middle of the yard. He remembers Ignace's cries as he is beaten for his crime and as an example to the other children. The guardian of the slaves, whom his father had brought from Martinique, is shouting as he beats him: 'Not because you playing with *béké* you must think that you could take *béké* toys away as if is your own, you is no *béké*.' With each word, a lash. And with each word Michel Jean remembers that he has told his father that he thinks Ignace stole his wooden carriage that had been brought from Paris by his mother. He stands at the edge of the yard and witnesses the beating and never tells anyone that he later finds the carriage under the back stairs of the house where he and Ignace had been playing. After he is beaten, Ignace is put in the stocks for the rest of the day.

Ignace never comes to play again. Michel Jean sees him in the fields riding the mules. Ernestine tells him, 'You know, Ignace riding mule now, riding plenty! Go down in the pasture. You go see him and he go give you a ride on the mule them.'

But he never goes. He sits at his favourite perch in the tamarind tree and watches Ignace from a distance. He does not confess.

'Cazabon!' Wildman shouted.

Michel Jean decided not to go on with the visit to the house. His memories of Ignace had unnerved him. He rejoined Wildman. 'Let me see your work. Yes, much better. You're coming on.'

'They're saying in England it's a new kind of slavery, this indentureship.'

'What?'

'The coolies from Calcutta.'

'That's ludicrous. I know their wretched lives, but it's not the same. After Emancipation some people deserted the estates, others stayed, living in the estate huts but planting their own gardens. The whole place would collapse without new labour. Anyway, I don't understand. I leave these things to my brother, Joseph, and my father.'

'How do they feel about that?'

'Well, they think I take the money but don't take responsibility. I never wanted anything to do with it. I left when I was thirteen. Did not come back till I was seventeen. Those were the last years. I left three years after the Emancipation that didn't happen, and then came back two years after the apprenticeships were over. That had kept the whole thing going. Then they had to stop it, but, you know? What was there for people? What was liberty?'

'Last years?'

'Before Emancipation.'

'And?'

'Terrible; the strife, the waiting, the anticipation and disappointment, and of course elation too. Then it came and it was not freedom. People had to wait. They shouted, "*Point de six ans.*"'

'But you had to have a position?'

Michel Jean told Wildman the history of the free-coloureds and their fight for their rights. He told him of his mother's republicanism.

'So, now?'

'I wait to see what she's left me and I must earn my living.'

'Well, I'm your first student. There'll be more.'

'We must get the horses back to Mon Chagrin and catch the *Paria* for Port of Spain before dark.'

There was a squall that afternoon on the gulf as they circled the rock island, Farallon, in the harbour. The choppy waves made it impossible to stay on deck. They sat at a porthole and looked out, catching the disappearing hills of Morne Jaillet. They made their painting equipment safe and shared a flask of rum.

'So, you had never painted at school, knew nothing of painting till St Edmund's?' Wildman was being the true pupil, learning of his master's progress, fascinated by a life so different.

'Well, that's not strictly true. Look! You can just catch a glimpse of a house in the foothills beneath Morne Jaillet. My aunt, my mother's sister, lived there. She was an artist. She was modest about her work. I think that seeing her paint was the first time I saw anyone paint with watercolours.'

'I too had an aunt who painted in the apple orchard at Norton.'

'The women of our households found ways to escape the harshness of the world that their husbands ruled. Mostly they escaped into the Church. But, if lucky, their education introduced them to the arts, to reading, embroidery, painting and drawing. Mostly through the nuns. Not remarkably different from what happens in Europe.'

'As I was saying . . . we had many paintings in the drawing room. But, that, you would now remember it as an influence?'

'Well, you absorb what you're offered. She came in a buggy to Corynth.' Michel Jean felt that he was stopping Wildman from telling him about his own experience. But he nevertheless continued, conscious of how obsessed he could become. 'As children we loved to have rides in the buggy.'

He could see that Wildman was indulging him. He carried on.

'Just where we were painting today, I remember her setting up her easel and paints. It was the way her fingers held the brush, the way her hands moved and the repeated motion from the palette or box of paints to the paper. I sat at her side and watched. Did not really try to do it myself then, not seriously. Maybe dabbled. But it left its mark.'

'I can see. I remember once . . .'

'Then the way she looked into the distance and then at her painting. What I loved was the almost imperceptible emergence of the whole scene, very gradually swimming up in the watercolours. I think my love for painting started there, beneath the light that falls on the bamboos. She was kind and let me stay with her at her house. She talked about colours and painting. I listened without understanding. It's gone now. What were you saying?'

'Oh, it doesn't matter. Another time, perhaps.'

He should have given the young man his space.

The rain drenched the deck, the wind causing the waves to lash against the sides of the steamer, making visibility impossible through the porthole.

'Have another nip.'

'It's good rum.'

'Yes, the Fabiens at La Resource have always had a good rum.'

'Excellent.'

'You know, when I was young and travelled on the ferry, we could not sit with white people. White people sat over there and we sat here and the slaves were below deck or right on top if there was no more room. The English . . .'

'What?'

'My mother once inadvertently sat on the wrong side of the cabin. She had sat on the side of the cabin reserved for the *grands blancs*, where those who were *gens de couleur* were not allowed to sit. She had been very rudely reminded, not by a steward who was a black man, and whom she noticed enjoying the contretemps, but by a young white Scottish planter who had rushed onto the ferry, which was very full that day, and not being able to find a seat, had demanded my mother's.

'My mother replied: "Young man, when you are a lady of my age and colour you sit where you like. You'll see, it will be quite soon that you won't be able to demand this and you'll have to stand out on deck in the hot sun to burn your red face even redder. Come, Jeansie, we don't want to sit here any more."

'There was great applause both from the side of the ferry to which we went and from the side of the ferry from which we had departed. The white people looked very embarrassed by the brash, young Scotsman's behaviour, all recognizing that these laws were foolish and would soon change. The ladies of the company were admiring my mother's wonderful gown in rich Martiniquan colours, her headdress tied so expertly that it made the English ladies whisper to each other with some consternation as to the time it would take while dressing to get things so well done. "Much easier to just put on a hat," one of them had whispered to her companion.'

Wildman listened, looking out at the rain. He felt awkward. He saw other people listening and smiling at Michel Jean's story. 'Pity about the visibility. I was looking forward to the view.'

'Well, this is part of it too. Cloud and rain, light and shadow. Sudden changes! Have you been up at dawn? We must go out into the Bocas, the channels between the western archipelago, between the island and Venezuela, and paint the people whaling. One of my tutors in Paris was Gudin, a wonderful marine painter. The trick is to capture the light in this darkness.'

'Turner,' suggested Wildman.

'Exactly.'

The clouds lifted and Port of Spain was lit up; a long town of white from this distance and the hills moving like whales among the lifting clouds.

As they came alongside the wharf, Michel Jean said his farewells to Wildman. He walked off towards the old Lapeyrouse Estate. As he approached the *marchande* at the corner to buy some lilies for his mother's grave, where his aunt Marie Lucille was also buried, he remembered that he had an appointment the next day with Uncle St Luce to hopefully finalize the details of his mother's will after the delay which Joseph was still using to impose his authority. He could feel that old anger against his brother rising in himself.

Before cock crow, Michel Jean was refreshed and energized by Josie's black Tortuga coffee.

'This Governor have you in his grip, man, Jeansie. I see the house you paint. It nice. It pretty. I only see it by the flambeau. Imagine when the sun catch it, boy. Like how you really paint it, eh.'

Michel Jean let the coffee warm him in the damp of the morning. He and Josie sat now on the back veranda and watched black fade into grey with the faintest dash of yellow and blue forming like a stain, spreading to the edges of a cloth. And then, suddenly, they looked up on the question of the first keskidee. *Qu'est-ce qu'il dit?* A sudden stroke of pink transformed the day's sky from foreday into dawn.

'I still have to paint you, you know, Josie. After all these years. You remember how I paint you long time.'

'To look like an empress, you tell me then.'

'No, but you know what I mean. I have to paint you.' He ran his fingers down her smooth arm.

'You could catch me any time. I right here. I ent going nowhere.'

He looked at her and smiled. Josie looked at him. They might still achieve a kind of peace. He decided to risk himself. 'You know, I want to bring my wife and children to live here.'

'That's good.'

'You sure?'

'Yes, man. That's good.' He saw the effort and the sadness in her face.

'I knew you would be your wise self.'

'I have to be that, Jeansie. I have to be that.'

'Thank you.' There was so much she had given up for him.

'We is family. Not so?'

'We is family.'

He knew what that meant to her.

The morning creaked with slowness, with Joseph's lawyers going through the codicils of his mother's will. The old Deed of Separation his parents had made was gone over again. He signed what he was asked to sign. Uncle St Luce made sure there were no more procrastinations by Joseph. He sat there with him and the lawyers at Philippe & de Montbrun's till every *i* was dotted and every *t* was crossed. 'Your brother needs this thing done, Joseph. You owe it to your mother to get it straight. Family must put aside rancour at this time. As far as I can see it is equitable and Madame Debonne Cazabon's wishes have been fulfilled. With the house in Edward Street added, everything should be fine now, yes, Michel Jean?' He agreed, relieved to be freed from his brother's bullying. His sisters smiled patronizingly. They had got what they wanted for themselves and their children.

Michel Jean took his courage in his hands and said, 'Of course, there is still the matter of Ernestine and Josie. But I will be bringing that up separately with my father. Though I notice that there is a codicil for a certain modest amount to be paid from my mother's legacy, which pleases me.'

'Well, yes, there was some challenge about that. But as you see I have managed to secure that as well.' Uncle St Luce looked at him reassuringly.

Rose Clotilde and Magdeleine Alexandrine departed the room at that point, gathering up their skirts and raising their eyebrows as they passed.

'As you see, there's still some strong feeling about the matter, but it has been settled and will be executed.' Uncle St Luce patted Michel Jean on the shoulder. 'All's well that ends well, as the great bard says.'

What Michel Jean wanted was for the whole business to be resolved so that he could get out of that office, take his money and return to Paris, to Louise and the children. He felt like booking his passage immediately. He knew that he would have to delay his departure because of his work for the Governor. But at last there was money to send regularly to Louise.

On his return home, there was a letter which had arrived that morning from her. She had gone with the children to Vire. Louis Michel had got worse, throwing himself recklessly to the floor in a tantrum. 'I'm so afraid that he will harm himself.' She needed her mother's support. She did not know how long she would stay in Normandy. 'I love it here when we go to the coast and I can remember how we were at Luc-sur-Mer. A mother now of two children, I can hardly believe it. My darling . . .'

He broke off, unable to contain himself. He replied at once to catch the returning packet. He informed her that the will had been settled. He told of his student, Wildman. He missed her. It was so important to get her letters, to hear her voice. Yes, he too missed the woman he had married, the woman before the children came. So wrapped up in his work, she seemed at times to fade away. He was alarmed by what she said about Louis Michel. Should he abandon his project with the Governor? He did not think that was wise. He had to keep the work for their future. He was able now to send another thousand francs.

'Master Michel, a word, please.' Ernestine came out of her room into the yard. Even with her age and even after the freedom, she kept with her 'Master'.

She stopped him as he was preparing to leave for the governor's residence.

'Ernestine, what can I do for you?'

'Son,' she said, holding onto his arm, 'is not long I have here now, before I go and meet your mother, I feel.' Then, she faltered.

'Come, Ernestine, you have years still. But come, you can tell me anything. You know I told Josie as long as I'm here you and Josie have a home in this yard where you belong. No matter who else say what.'

'I know that, son. I know that. Is not that I ever doubt. And you is my baby, my child since birth when I lift you from inside your mother and wash you and give you back to she. I leave my own bearing to help she with hers. Is I take the cord and bury it in the garden under the pepper tree. I could take you Corynth now and show you the very said spot. Is not my place in your heart or your house that I ever doubt. No matter how things turn out. They turn out for the best. Is what the good Lord plan for we. But is what I coming to. The good Lord ask we to do we best. I want to do my best.'

'You done your best, Ernestine.'

'Is Josie I talking 'bout, you know.'

'Josie, Ernestine? Well, she's your best.'

'My girl, my daughter.'

Josie? What did Ernestine want to tell him today, to make clear in a way that had never been made clear?

'Yes, Josie. My Josephine, my little empress. The day she born I say I calling she Josephine. People in the yard think I too grand. But I tell them is so she calling. Josephine.'

'Well, is what I telling you. She's your best.'

'But, Master Michel, you well know you not here all the time. You have your wife in Fwance. You have children. Where Josie in all of that? I not asking . . .'

'Ernestine, you right to talk. She's your daughter. You right to ask.'

'Yes, she's my daughter. But she's your . . . And François Cazabon, your father, he need to look out for her. He must not shirk that. He is she godfather, you know. It register right there in San Fernando. He send Cato Williams to register the birth. Cato can't write but he put his mark. He ent give the name but it register that he is the godfather. Some get name you know, but he never give she the name. But godfather, that is something.

People who know, know what that mean. I long in this family, as you know. My mother from Martinique. I practically born, too, in this family.'

'Ernestine, I know the history.'

'You know the history?' Ernestine's voice was stern now. 'All you is not children now, Master Michel. That is what I want to tell you, all you is not children now. That is my final word.'

Ernestine walked slowly back across the yard into her room. She turned again to face him, pointing and wagging her finger as when he was a little boy and she was correcting him. 'All you is not children now, playing in the yard, running in the rain, hardly any clothes on, climbing the hills of Morne Jaillet. All you . . . I ent know how I ent put a stop to this thing for so long. I not blind. Nobody blind. We at fault thinking it will stop for itself. All of us at fault . . .' Her voice faded. She turned to go back into her room.

'Ernestine, Josie and I fix up we business. You mustn't worry. As you say. We not children no more. I'll speak to *Papa*. He need to fix up *his* business. And you know this morning self *Maman*'s affairs get sort out. So something coming to you and Josie.'

'Praise God! With all that happen, that woman still good. She and I reach an understanding. She understand. Like a woman does understand. But François . . .' Her voice trailed off as she turned her back and walked away.

Michel Jean stood alone in the middle of the yard. He stood hearing Ernestine's voice over and over: 'All you is not children now!' Her saying so made him feel like a small child. He hoped for Ernestine's words to dissolve when he took up his painting. He saw Ernestine again now, as he had as a child, leaving his father's bedroom in the early morning. She had not spoken about that, or had she? 'Run along now, old man.' Those had been his father's words. In checking his father's responsibility, he was having to confront his own.

But him, this half-brother with his half-sister! This was not the same as his father's behaviour, surely. He knew they were not the only ones in the world to grow this way, but that did not alter their predicament. How would he make Louise understand this, even though it was all over now? There would be enough new things for her to accept. But as he said it, he felt how weak he was. The sadness of their history overwhelmed him. He wanted to get back to Paris, to his wife and his children. He wanted to look after them.

He had the full sun he wanted for his last attempt at the governor's residence. It had rained in the night and there were still puddles and swampy patches on the savannah that had not dried out. Sky and moving clouds made dun by the light on the muddy water rippled across the glittering reflection as he leaped over with the aid of the *bois* he had cut in readiness for his hikes. He marvelled how that small dirty mirror held the movement of the firmament. It was windy and the colour of the water changed all the time. Clouds were building up over the hills and moving out to the gulf.

The house was fully lit by the noon sun. When he set up he knew that the challenge was to work with the vertical light which flattens everything. He remembered Rousseau at Barbizon working with this challenge. He had met him in the forest the day he had begun *Une avenue, forêt*. Then he had seen it just before he had left. 'I must come back to see how you finish this, Theo,' he had said. Louise had written that they were missing him at Barbizon. 'You know how they love you, Michel, *ma jen piti neg*.' He could hear her voice humouring him, imitating his patois. 'This is what you have given me, sweetheart, your work, your painting and our wonderful children. Louis Michel is settling down. Such good news that you have received your mother's legacy.'

Two women and a child had walked into the fully lit foreground from the house. A yellow flamboyante behind the walkers lit the grass around the tree and the ground where the women and the child strolled. He would work further on this oil in his studio, but he was brisk to catch the moment. He worked with a confidence he had gained from Louise's words. The fountain fizzed like champagne. White pigment caught the streaming light from high above. The right side of the composition was balanced out in the shade given by the *bois canots* and the palms behind them. The main house, the quarters and then the turrets were caught full face on. The comparative height of the house was measured by a single *palmiste* palm. A Doric column of ancient Greece, Wildman would have called it. The accurate proportions of the whole were made authentic by the height of the hills bathed in light, catching the blur of the yellow poui trees. There was still space for enough sky: cobalt, lilac and dun.

He would have to work on the vertical light, work on depth and perspective to catch the outbuildings under the trees and the full depth of the valley behind. Then some *marchandes* entered the garden. '*Touloum! Pistaches!*' Light voices on the air selling their sweets and nuts to children. They offered their produce to the strolling party and then settled themselves on the lawns near the fountain, their skirts billowing around them.

He heeded Mr Constable's admonition, heard in his art-master Barnaby's voice, that a sermon had no place in art. Nevertheless, he balanced out his figures, allowing them to indicate the hierarchy of the world in harmony. Excellency might well want to show off after he returned home from his successful governorship of the colony. See how they live in harmony, he would say proudly of his good Negroes.

The two *marchandes* were taking the shade under the samaan tree. Let them roam where they will, take their liberty in the land of their freedom. Michel Jean chuckled to himself. Theirs was an audacity selling *touloum* and *pistaches* in front of the governor's house. 'Take your shade, girl,' he said to himself. Would anyone else discover his ironies? Would they be able to read the history which lay beneath? He was pleased with himself. He thought he was ready to submit to the Governor, His Excellency George Francis Robert, the third Lord Harris. He would have to get Wildman to introduce him to Ping. Ping! He played with the onomatopoeic ring of the name. What did it mean?

*

The introduction to the Governor came the following week when Michel Jean arrived at the house with the painting he had chosen to submit.

'What do you think, James?' Excellency asked his cousin, Wildman.

Michel Jean looked out into the garden where he had spent so much time. The three men were standing in the gallery of the house, the painting of which stood on an easel in front of them.

'I think it's excellent. I could not possibly have done anything like this.'

'My dear James, that's not the point.'

'I know. I don't know how I could even think of comparing my efforts.'

'Your efforts are wonderful, my boy. But we're appraising a work of art by Monsieur Cazabon.'

'Cazabon, what do you think?' Wildman was blushing.

Michel Jean could see that Wildman had been made to feel embarrassed. He wanted to defend his student. He had missed his opportunity. It would be too pointed if he said anything now. It would be patronizing. But he managed to smile reassuringly at Wildman, as if to say, just like old Ping. Except that he could never actually say it. Excellency did have at times an old-mannish way about him.

'It's not for me to say. Let Excellency judge. You judge, sir.' Michel Jean put down the challenge formally.

Excellency peered into the painting. Wildman and Michel Jean looked on. Wildman went up to the painting and then stood back from the easel, trying to be less compulsive and effusive in his responses.

Michel Jean stood with his back to them, looking out into David Lockhart's forest of palms and beyond them to his avenue of nutmegs. Did he ever make it up the Orinoco? he wondered: the Englishman from Northumberland laying out this garden; so keen to collect, draw and paint his orchids, hacking down his branches of calabash trees, sending them back to Kew with blooms still attached. Michel Jean thought of his own paintings being taken away to be hung elsewhere.

'Who are these?' Excellency exclaimed. 'Is this Mrs Warner and what's that young girl at the St James Barracks called, James?'

'You mean Elizabeth Prowder?' Wildman peered more closely into the painting to examine the two ladies strolling across the front lawn. 'Yes, that's her. Quite a plucky young thing. Do you know these people, Cazabon?'

'No, sir. There may have been the people that you mention, sir, strolling in the gardens while I painted. But to me they are figures on the landscape put there for effect, for the colours that I want, the shapes that I desire. They people the painting in a way that is necessary to the composition, to the meaning. They aren't portraits, sir.'

'Oh, I know that. But . . . And these, under the trees? Are these people you know, or, are they there for the effect?'

'No, sir. Yes, sir. They are some others of Her Majesty's subjects come to take the shade in their governor's gardens, sir.'

'Excellent! I like that touch. Makes things a lot more cheerful. Adds such variety.'

'Touch, variety?' Wildman echoed questioningly.

'Precisely, James. It is what makes your efforts admirable, but Monsieur Cazabon's art.'

Michel Jean and Wildman almost sniggered aloud behind Excellency's back as he bowed closer to the painting to look at the figures under the samaan tree.

'I see.' Wildman composed himself.

'Cazabon, let us stroll. I find it very well done. I look forward to more. James, tell them we'll be back for punches.'

'Excellent.'

The painting of the governor's house stood on its easel while the light moved away from the front of the house, leaving David Lockhart's garden in shadow.

'Do you notice, James, how it has the feel of Belmont about it? The proportions, I mean. Not the style, of course. It seems like a home.'

*

It was an easy climb beyond the Botanic Gardens into the gentle rise up Cotton Hill from where they had a view of the town of Port of Spain growing west towards the St Clair Estate and the sugarcane fields of Mucurapo with Mr Devenish's estate at Peru. The bush had been brushed low, and despite the sudden rain that fell before they embarked upon their stroll, there was still scorched stubble left over from the dry season with intermittent patches of green, which the rains had revived. They rested for a moment after the climb, looking out beyond the candelabra of the frangipani trees, the palms and bamboo clumps in the gully. The gulf lay stunned into a lilac haze. The brown smoke of clouds rested over the Venezuelan mountains on the horizon, rising at the end of the northern cordillera. It was a serrated undulation of ochres, olive greens and grey smoke beneath glimpses of cobalt sky and the ripening yellow light of afternoon.

They walked in silence, punctuated with observations made by Excellency on the flora, which were still startling and new to him and being exhibited in the new Botanic Gardens. 'I've arranged for plants to be sent from Belmont.'

'Oh, excellent. You have extensive gardens there?'

'It's a large acreage, including a paddock and shrubbery. There's a walled garden, stable yard and an extensive walnut tree walk. Modest but splendid, if you see what I mean. Wilson, the gardener at Belmont, has sent out the very first packages of seeds and some actual seedlings which they think may catch. Not sure exactly what they are. I must stroll down to the nurseries some time. You've been painting in the gardens?'

'Yes, sir. I've spent a great deal of time . . .'

'I can see that.'

'There're many more, but that's the one I thought would please you.'

'Well, I'm very happy and I hope you'll be doing many others.'

'Thrilled to be doing so, sir.'

'Will you paint me this cultivated wilderness?' He smiled at his own phrase as if he had heard it somewhere. He stretched out his arm and waved it in front of him, demonstrating the extent of the panorama that lay now beneath them and which he desired Michel Jean to paint. 'I want you to start on a series of views to do with my work. I want you to accompany me and record my work. This is a commission. I'll pay you well. Maybe you can tell James what your fee should be. We can arrange for that to be paid in instalments or all together at the end.'

'Thank you.'

Excellency had a hurried way of talking at times, hurried and emphatic, getting it all said, and all said decisively, sensitively. Michel Jean found him an unusual man to be a governor. He remembered Wildman talking of his delicate health. He wondered at the coincidence that Wildman should remind him of Fitzwilliam and Excellency of Mr Barnaby. Maybe it was because he had not had much experience of Englishmen, who on the whole he found to be cold and reclusive. The two men had remained for him gentlemen of refinement. From his mother, he had inherited the idea of an English governor as a Woodford, a Grant, a Hill or a Macleod, from whom the coloured Creoles had to wrest their power. Excellency did not seem like those previous governors.

Conversation with Excellency meandered through exchanges of biography. 'So, it was your mother who chose Paris rather than see you return to London. You may have developed quite differently as an artist if it had been the other way.'

'Yes, it was *Maman*. She had everything to do with how I am.'

'Everything? I've met your father with the delegation from the southern families.'

'I've nothing to do with them as a group. I'm an artist, not a revolutionary.'

'They sometimes go together. You must be their *bête noir*.'

'We're all *bêtes noirs*, sir.' He wondered if he had overstepped the mark.

Excellency blushed. 'I mean . . .'

'I know exactly what you mean.'

'Do you?'

'I respect my father and the others. But I was sent away in the midst of the real struggle before Emancipation. I know we've not achieved all that we want to achieve. But I made up my mind that I would keep my eye on different things in a different way. Or, on the same things but in a different way.'

'I'm glad you have. And it's how your eye views this that I am interested to see, the subject of my commission,' and he again described the panorama with his outstretched arm.

The light had changed. A sunset was beginning to form. 'I come here on my own after those long council meetings with Warner going on and on against de Verteuil. I tire of the antagonism between the English and the French, the Protestants and the Roman Catholics. Excuse my indiscretion. Then I look at this, the gulf, the mountains, and I'm revived to believe that the world is all of this and not just the injustice we've created. I wonder and I'm in awe.'

Darkness was closing in, as Michel Jean described his schooling at St Edmund's and his training with Mr Barnaby.

'I envy you that experience. My career has been quite different.' The Governor talked about his military ancestry, his great-grandfather's command at the capture of Saint Lucia in 1778, his going out to Madras, how he had been called the Tiger of Mysore. He told of his success at Seringapatam. 'He rose from nothing. It was with my great-grandmother's wealth that he bought Belmont House in Kent. My father followed along the same path. He was an athlete and swimmer.' Then, quickly, he added, 'I rather prefer pictures. You must take my commission.'

The burden of office seemed to be taken up again as they neared the house. Excellency had had his daily respite. 'And portraits? Do you paint portraits as well?' Excellency said, suddenly changing direction. He seemed distracted and was intent on taking another path, both through the gardens and in their conversation.

'Often they are part of the landscape I paint. The people have made this landscape. It's their cultivation, but I mostly paint out the hardship and keep the dignity. As I say, it's their landscape. I don't paint them as subservient to it. Not that I am blind to what has happened here. I grew up as a child here; I sucked the milk from her breasts.' Michel Jean lost himself in his enthusiasm.

'Whom are you talking about?' Excellency was astonished by what he was hearing.

'She is the land, but yes, she's my mother's woman who suckled me as a baby. Her name is Ernestine, once my father's slave, a gift to my mother at their marriage. She came from Martinique. He gave her a jewel made of jet, a cut of ebony, is how he once expressed it.'

'I see.'

He wondered whether the Governor did understand his colony.

They were now back at the house where Michel Jean accepted refreshment before leaving. He was learning that his governor was something of a philosopher and an aesthete. It was a risk that the ruling classes of England took with their sons, exposing them to a liberal education while expecting them to rule empires and fight battles. He wondered if the paintings commissioned by Excellency would one day hang as trophies of empire in that house at Belmont along with the portraits of their ancestors.

Excellency had guests for dinner.

'Before you go,' he said, 'I must introduce you to some gentlemen who will be useful for you. Mr Hardin Burnley and Mr James Lamont.'

'Mr Burnley?'

'Mr William Hardin Burnley, the richest man in Trinidad.'

'I see.' Michel Jean had heard these names from his father. James Lamont was known because of his uncle St Luce.

'They will want to commission you as well, I'm sure.'

'Really?'

'You'll soon have lots of work.'

Michel Jean took his leave after a glass of planter's punch, over which he was introduced to the two rich planters. They were polite, but too caught up in their business of the colony to take much notice of him, or the mention of his work as an artist.

He gathered up his easel and paints, brought in by the liveried footman, and walked across the savannah in the direction of town and George Street, expectation now in his heart.

He entered town among the flickering flambeaux on the roast-corn stalls and the trays of the oyster *marchandes*. He lost his way in the small alleyways, drawn by the scents of fried fish on sizzling coal-pots.

Young girls appeared from out of doorways as narrow as coffins. It was too late to turn back to choose the empty house and his studio. The figures in the darkness led him further into the maze of streets. '*Monsieur*, you look for something? *Une fillette.*' Then the voice changed into that of a boy. '*Monsieur*, you look for something? *Un garçon?*' They used their wiles, these children, for the pennies and occasional sovereigns they could filch in the moments of a gentleman's passion, to ascend themselves to the light of the stalls to buy some food.

He was pulled by the Yoruba drumming and the *bel air* dancing that had started at nightfall in the back streets of the town where the chattel houses were battened down, like the slave barracoons, housing those who had fled the cane fields and the cocoa estates in search of new work on the edge of town.

Filched, Michel Jean wandered home lost, asking the way from the rum-soaked guides along the old rue de Trois Chandelles. Having succumbed to temptation, there was no danger in him desiring Josie tonight. But as always he was then confronted with the reality of his life, his wife and children. Josie had left another letter, which had arrived from Louise. She mentioned again how grateful she was for the money, and now wanted to know if he had fixed a date for his departure. 'I don't know how much longer I can go on like this.'

He was kept awake worrying about how best to explain that he might get new commissions from Lamont and Hardin Burnley, and that these might further delay his return to Paris. He wrote before going to bed to catch the packet in the morning. He explained that his work for the Governor and the rich planters would establish him more firmly as a prospect painter. He understood her desire for his return. This was also what he wanted. But he might need a little more time.

Sipping Josie's strong coffee the next morning, he remembered what he had heard of Mr William Hardin Burnley of Orange Grove and Mr James Lamont of Palmiste. He knew Palmiste Estate, which bordered Corynth.

'I have work to do,' he said aloud to himself. 'I am employed.'

'What you say, Jeansie? You call.' Josie entered the room.

'Josie, you going in town? Make sure this letter reach the packet on time.'

2

There was a new regime at no. 9 Edward Street now that the house, one of Rose Debonne Cazabon's legacies, had been occupied. Michel Jean was not sure what he had sacrificed for this in Joseph's calculations, but he trusted the supervision of Uncle St Luce. This was to be the house for Louise and the children. She had written recently. It was better at her mother's in Vire. Louis Michel was less agitated there. He replied to her letter and told her of the new house, the home that he was preparing for them all. He had begun to plan that they might join him from Paris without him having to return. It would have to be seen whether Louise could make the voyage on her own, particularly with the delicate Louis Michel.

The house at the moment, though, seemed like Josie's and Jeansie's. They wondered what people said who had known, or suspected, their past. Ernestine and Josie were installed downstairs in more commodious accommodation; Ernestine saying, 'Is right here I go lay me down to rest.'

Josie had decided to sit for Michel Jean in his new studio. She was dressed for the part. He liked what she had chosen to wear. She sat in a blue *jupe*, the full skirt almost purple with the sheen changing as the light altered on the veranda with the moving clouds and the swaying fern baskets. The skirt was gathered. It was caught up and fastened below her breasts with a brooch he had brought for her from Paris in 1840. She wore it under her heart. He had not thought that Josie would have the patience to sit. They had their banter and fun as they prepared to begin.

'I just want you to sit, Josie.'

'You ent want the whole of me?'

'Josie, I know best. When we doing this kind of thing, I know best.'

'Okay, master, I go sit.'

'And quiet, too. Hold the position I give you. Just so.' She held her head at an oblique angle, crowned with a Madras headtie of yellows, blues and browns; mingled plaids and checks. A low-cut, embroidered muslin chemise hung off her shoulder, showing her brown skin for which he had used madder brown, raw sienna, cobalt and black. Naples yellow gave him that brownish *jaune* he needed. The line was broken with a rich purple foulard covering her shoulders and tucked at her waist. The scarf was a complement to her skirt and suggested her allure, but maintained her modesty. Her shining black crinkled hair was pulled back off her face and tied on the nape of her neck. She wore no necklace, no bracelets. There was the ring he had given her that he had brought back with him from England in 1830. Josie had picked from the garden some daisies called bachelor-buttons, fluffy white and purple buds, their stalks wrapped in their green leaves. She clutched them in her left hand. The portrait had its cryptic details: a story to tell.

She was no *mulâtresse*, but her fairness shone. She was a *chabine* like him. She had a touch of rouge on her cheeks and her eyebrows were dark arches over her full black eyes with their glossy eyelashes. All of Josie's personality played behind her stare, no smile, no disturbance of the smooth contours of her flared nose and perfectly formed lips betrayed her knowingness and her vulnerability.

'Josephine. I done for now.' They broke from the sitting.

'*Oui.*' Her lips parted as she moistened them with her tongue.

'You like the portrait so far?'

She came and stood next to him to view his work. 'Well, it ent finish, but it better than them young girls you bring up here from Corbeaux Town to your studio.'

'Josie, why you thinking about them? You go need to sit again.'
He put his arm around her shoulders.

'You know why I thinking about them.' She broke from him.
'And you have a wife. Madame Cazabon on the Champs-Elysées.'

'Champs-Elysées! The things that you does imagine, girl. I
wish. If only . . .'

'If only? Don't laugh, Jeansie. What? I does hear what go
on, you know, champagne and Veuve Clicquot cocktails. Is so
they does call it? On the terraces under the plane trees of the
boulevard. Is so they write about all you in *The Courant*, you
know. You think I don't read. I does well read when I want to
read. I has ways to find out.'

'People gossip. Don't believe everything you hear.'

'Anyway, your wife not going to like them young girls. Just
like I don't like them. That go have to finish before she come.
And you tell me that you want to bring she and the children
here?'

'Josie, you going to chaperone my life? Yes, you right. Look
at the portrait, nuh.'

'Is not portrait I want, you know.'

'You don't want posterity?'

'You go give me posterity?' She realized what she had said.
He saw her holding back her tears. The fact of what she had
given up for him made itself felt. They fell silent.

'Josie, I know.' He wanted to give her something back,
something lasting.

'I responsible for that as much as you.' She pointed to the
portrait. She smiled and changed her mood. 'The things we get
up to, the things we do. But you was up to all kind of thing from
small. Is your mother two eye you have. You confuse people
with those eyes, you know, and that charm.'

'Josie, what you talking about?'

'The boys, you confuse them too. You done with that I sure.
I could never make out how your desire went here and there
same time. Don't interfere with people, footman, and milkmaid,
you know.'

'Josie, what on your mind this morning, girl? Footman, milkmaid? Come, let me go, *oui*. Girl, you have an imagination!'

'You is the one with the imagination. Let me go do some work, yes. I can't afford sitting down whole day for you unless you go pay me.' Josie went downstairs.

Michel Jean's bohemianism had been reported to the family over the years. His youthful capers were frowned on by his sisters with their arched eyebrows. '*Mon Dieu!* That girl again, Josie should know better than . . .' And Joseph's sneer: 'Artist, my arse! Travelling companion! He should come home and do some proper work. Make a living instead of wasting the family money.' They had heard of his long tours to Italy and throughout France with his companion, Fitzwilliam. They had heard that he had been to Gibraltar and even North Africa. But it was what went on here that bothered them the most. 'Look at you, with the servants now, in true style. Or, you not see the colour of the girl skin. You think you is Toussaint. Is a revolution or something? We done with revolution, *oui*. No more Saint Dominique. Is we chance to rule now in this place.' Joseph had always loved to taunt him. His brother's outbursts were so irrational, his politics mixed up, when really it was only his wealth he was concerned about. He and his father had long departed from Jean Baptiste Philippe's or Jean Jaillet's republican politics, with their wanting to get close to the English party. How to get on in an English colony was their main endeavour. His mother would be turning in her grave at Lapeyrouse.

'Josephine, Josephine, somebody at the door!' It struck Michel Jean as he was shouting Josie's full name, hanging over the veranda the following morning, calling down into the backyard below, that he heard his mother chuckling at her own joke that every woman wanted to be called Josephine since Napoleon had chosen the Beauharnais girl from Martinique for his bride and empress, just like Ernestine had done. 'That Creole from La Pagerie,' his mother used to mock. 'Must be the one white girl Napoleon could find for himself in the whole island. If she white?

You know them *béké* and how they is in the yard. Hmm! And not *béké* only, you know.' He missed his mother's cutting irony.

'I coming,' Josie shouted from the yard. 'Who it is, so early, disturbing your sleep?'

'Don't trouble yourself with speculation, girl, attend to the man, make him comfortable with some coffee, sweeten it with muscovado, seduce him with your charm. He is a gentleman's man. Is not carnival, nuh, but he well dress up like is J'ouvert Morning, Dry River. Myself have to find a costume to meet the richest man in Trinidad. I forget and I late.'

'Forget what?'

'Work, girl. I think I must get the commission.'

'You good for yourself, *oui*, Jeansie. Seduce him with my charm! Is muscovado I have in the kitchen, you know; sweet and brown like your own skin. Let you mother hear you where she lying in Lapeyrouse. The richest man in Trinidad! Pappy Yo!'

Where his mother lying in Lapeyrouse! Josie could joke, *oui*; she could threaten him with the admonition of his mother because she knew what his mother had meant to him. She knew the whole story from the beginning.

A knock at the veranda door was followed by a quiet voice informing the household that Mr William Hardin Burnley's carriage was waiting to take Monsieur Michel Jean Cazabon to Orange Grove Estate. 'Monsieur Cazabon!'

This fella had respect, even if the age or his master had not risen there as yet. They continued with their contempt, those English, *petits blancs* and *grands blancs*. The introduction given to him by his new patron, Excellency, to the richest man in Trinidad, had worked. He was about to get his second commission, he hoped. He had not thought that the invitation would come so quickly. Lady Luck had blessed him. Fortune! Did Wildman know? He must know.

'You keeping the richest man in Trinidad waiting, Jeansie.' Josie fussed and busied herself with ironing his shirt and getting a small breakfast of coffee and fresh bread she had just taken from the oven on the wood-fire in the yard, where she was hotting up the flat irons. She scooped out some guava jelly from a jar into a small bowl to go with the warm bread. She always remembered Jeansie's desire as a child for her mother's fresh hot hops-bread baked in banana leaves.

Josie's nimble fingers fixed his collar. 'You looking good for the big man, Jeansie. First the Governor, and now Burnley of Orange Grove. Watch these people, *oui*.'

The carriage made its way out of Port of Spain along the old rue de Trois Chandelles and then on to the Royal Road past the inn, La Ventilla, where the groom stopped for more refreshment. He had been unable to persuade Josie to entertain him for longer.

'She not give you any food?' Michel Jean asked.

He turned and smiled with an open mouth, laughing out loud. 'She good for sheself, you know, sir.' The groom turned again, keeping his horses at a canter. 'But she give me a little something.'

Michel Jean noticed his cheek, despite the 'sir', and smiled. He imagined Hardin Burnley's man with Josie on her bed in the room downstairs, with the window looking onto the backyard where he had passed the other night and seen her in the oily light of her lantern undressing, like a flower opening and closing its petals, like a *bel air* dancer opening and closing her skirts, her brown feet dancing the stone floor. These fellas would take a chance if they got one. He imagined them now in his mind, the young groom with his Josie, the young man's fine torso, his back now naked, arched over his Josie, not dressed in Mr William Hardin Burnley's livery. The shadows of the room in the flickering light and their bodies moving in the dark on the bed were transformed with his present gaze. Their moving shadows changed with the contours of the land under the broad samaan trees on the wide savannahs. Why did he have to have Josie seduced by another man? Always, he thought, the clandestine and the forbidden had fascinated him; had entrapped him in that seductive pattern since so young with Josie, even when he found out she was his sister, particularly when he had discovered that frightening, alluring truth. They had made their pact, but when would the power of that enticement end?

They galloped along the Royal Road for some time. The air was mixed with the scent of coconut oil from a factory that imported coconuts from the Cocal at Beau Séjour on the east coast mixed with the putrid coagulations of the mangrove swamp. 'Mr Schoener factory, sir,' the groom pointed out, giving his information. 'New work.' Emancipation had meant that the blacks had abandoned the estates. But they had not taken to the bush in droves as had been feared. There were some Maroons in the hills. Mostly, they were squatting in the Laventille hills and along the verges of the Royal Road. 'People working for themselves.' As they galloped on, the groom pointed out new developments. 'This is the new Crown Lands, sir.' Michel Jean saw figures bent on the landscape. He painted in his head as the groom described and they swept by. The figures in the fields were bowed to the land with an endeavour different to the one that had harnessed them; apprenticed them to estates ten years before.

'Set at liberty!' he said to himself.

'You say something, sir?' Hardin Burnley's man turned, skilfully, keeping his horses at a steady trot.

'Yes, such beauty!' He pointed to the mountains.

'Beauty? Who? The girl?'

'*Non, non.* The land.'

'The land? Is the land, you say?'

'Yes. The landscape.'

'Is plenty land Hardin Burnley have, you know.'

'Yes, I know.'

'Is land you want to buy? You is a planter?'

'No, no, not buy, paint. I'm a painter.'

'Not a planter, but a painter. I ent hear you right, you know?'

'You must look where you're going.'

'Is true. I never see that, painting? What you say? Landshape?'

'Landscape.'

'What for? You must show me.'

'Certainly. I'm going to paint Mr Hardin Burnley's land.'

There was always this elation as the countryside grew around him, the landscape expanding outwards to the northern range on his left, the mangrove swamp on the plain of Caroni out to his right with the brown swollen river on its course out of the hills. Now they were cantering through the smaller estates in the foothills at Barataria and El Socorro. 'Them estate have blight.' The groom gave his commentary. Michel Jean was absorbed by the light playing on the land. They arrived at the wide savannahs of Aranguez, where the great house there, echoing the summer residence of the Spanish king outside Madrid, emerged out of the cane fields.

'Like in Spain.'

'What you say? Sir.'

'Where the palace is situated at the meeting of the Jarama and Tagus rivers.'

'Is a black man own that estate, you know,' the groom said proudly.

'Eh heh. Who is that?'

'Severe Laforest. Imagine! He do it.'

'You can imagine that?'

'I could imagine more than that. Give we the chance, we go own everything.'

'I can see.' Michel Jean saw the new barracks for the indentured workers. They continued on past the sugarcane fields that the groom explained had recently put this great estate, owned by a black man, into the news with its record productions of six hundred hogsheads of sugar and eighteen thousand gallons of rum.

'We have to imagine it, before we can do it. He uses Indian people now from Calcutta. You see them?'

'*Oui*. They come to save us, I hear them say.'

They passed Valsayn with Mr Guiseppi's house. 'That is where the Spanish Governor Chacon sign over the island to them English.' They crossed the San Juan River flowing out of the valley of Santa Cruz below the mountain of El Tucuche.

As they rattled along, Michel Jean kept thinking about his appointment with Mr William Hardin Burnley, a man of adventure, from the stories that he had heard. His father had had to flee America for England after the American War of Independence. He had been brought up in England. He was a man who had a formidable reputation for not suffering fools gladly and who apparently considered that there were not many people on the island of Trinidad, maybe three, with whom it was possible to have a conversation. It was reported that he had said he could only talk with Mr Warner and Mr Knox, the Attorney General and the Chief Justice.

However, Michel Jean was exhilarated. He had told his father at their Thursday meeting of the possibility of working for Hardin Burnley. He was taken aback by his cynical view. He did not want him to gossip with Joseph, about his brother going to paint pictures for Burnley, the champion of the planters, the clarion caller for the importation of coolie labour from Calcutta! Even Excellency had intimated his anxiety over Burnley's intransigence over these things. This was something the talkative Wildman had let drop. 'You painting for Burnley?' He could hear his father: 'You go paint what he tell you to paint, that's for sure. Sell painting is one thing. You go have to sell yourself. The one thing about Burnley is that he does own things. He does own almost everything in this blasted island.' How would he, Michel Jean thought, fare with such a man? What had Excellency let him in for? He preferred now to get back to his commission for the Governor.

They were now near the old capital St Joseph, San José de Oruña of Spanish days, with its ancient church and the Capuchin friary where the Maracas River joined the St Joseph to flow into the Caroni.

'Plenty land, eh?' The groom turned to speak to him. 'You have plenty land to paint. You ent want to own land?'

'I'd rather paint it.' He felt like a hypocrite knowing the land that his family had owned and still owned, and from which he was benefiting.

'I need some land now to grow garden.'

A pasture with a pond reflecting the sky suggested Daubigny as they splashed through puddles. Where had he heard, 'Take care of the light, and the shadows will take care of themselves'?

'One hundred and one windows.'

'Excuse. What you say, sir?'

'The windows. Is so many windows for truth that Mr Hardin Burnley have?'

'In the house, you mean? Yes . . .' He laughed.

'One hundred and one . . .'

'I never count. People say is more window than land, and plenty land he have.'

The groom's livery was a yellow as bright as an oriole's feathers and his breeches as black as a black black *cici-zeb*. Indeed, he was like a Johnny Jump-up on the grassy savannahs, the bumpy road lifting him off his seat. Like that little bird, he was jumping up and down. The popping-up movement of his bottom looked quite comical from behind where Michel Jean sat enveloped in the light of landscape and memory under the canopy of the carriage.

Looking beyond, the groom pointed into the far distance to Laurel Hill. 'That's the Scottish lady, Mrs Carmichael place. You see them whitewashed cottages by the almond trees.' He had heard his mother, when he was a boy, talk of Mrs Carmichael the missionary and her 'good Negroes' as she referred to her slaves.

'What happen to the people at Laurel Hill?'

'That's a long story, sir. We go need a next journey to go there.'

'I see. Maybe on the way back to Port of Spain. I went there as a child.'

'We had a fella from there, you know, sir.' Mr Hardin Burnley's man pointed, indicating Laurel Hill.

'And . . .?'

'He say, them Carmichaels and them gone long time. They find we people demanding too much. You know, it was in the bad days. They say the people too truculent and surly.'

'Truculent and surly?' He wondered where the groom had heard such language. 'What's your name?'

'Lazarus. Is Lazarus they call me.' The groom's first owner had been saved from drowning by the valiant young man. 'I bring him back to life, sir.'

'They should've called you Jesus.' They laughed together. 'Your master was Lazarus.'

'Is true.'

The dust was now building in the wind from the east.

'You don't have far to go now, sir.'

They had begun to see the outlying pastures of the largest estate in Trinidad.

Michel Jean turned his attention properly to Orange Grove, which was growing spaciously around him as Lazarus reined the horses into the gravel drive with its avenue of royal palms leading up to the main house and the factory with its chimneys beyond. He was excited by what he saw as he looked about him: the prospects he was to paint. Lazarus had the horses at a trot. He readied himself for his audience.

Lazarus reined in the horses. Then he fixed the footrest for him to descend from the carriage to be announced to the owner of Orange Grove. Michel Jean then saw close up for the first time the impressive residence he might be expected to paint. What the hell had Excellency let him in for?

Before he had time to think any more about what might happen, the man himself was suddenly there, descending from the long veranda. A large man of advanced years, nimble on his feet, agile and alert, came down the stairs quickly, stretching out his arm to shake his hand and beginning to fall into conversation.

Monsieur Cazabon! This is delightful! Welcome to Fontainebleau!' He laughed at his own identification of Orange Grove with the forests outside Paris. 'Welcome to Barbizon.'

Michel Jean rose to the occasion. '*Enchantez, monsieur*, to be your guest on such a beautifully landscaped estate. It's good of you to invite me and have me conducted so comfortably by Lazarus.'

'As you can see, what I have are the woods, the pastures, the mountains and the waterways. But I must ask pardon for the industry which I have tried to integrate in as appropriate a way as possible. You understand. Labour is a problem, of course.' As he said this, he pointed in the direction of the *usine* and the barrack rooms. 'The engine of the whole thing, but something we wish to accommodate in as comely a way as possible, if you see my meaning. Industry to civilize. That's the whole point of this estate, civilization through the profit from well-organized cheap labour. There must be profit at all costs otherwise everything will fall out of the bottom.' The big man smiled. 'And, of course, I have my gypsies, our own bohemians, some only recently from Calcutta and Uttar Pradesh, others from Madras.' He laughed jovially. 'An excellent addition to the island and our endeavours here.'

Michel Jean looked about him, taking in the acreage and the architecture held within the sweep of Hardin Burnley's arms and extending as far as the eye could see.

'My wife says I should have an artist. She's quite jealous that she's not here to welcome you. She is, of course, a frequent visitor to the salons in Paris and tells me that she remembers your views at the Salon du Louvre in the Musée Royal, or some such place, only last year. It meant, I must say, that when Harris mentioned your name, I knew that you must be a man of quality.'

'I'm most honoured, sir, that you should think so. That you should say so.' Michel Jean wondered if his acceptance was because he could be another example of the civilizing industry that Mr Hardin Burnley espoused so passionately. Michel Jean was not ordinarily short of words, but he was at this moment too caught up in the enthusiasm of Mr William Hardin Burnley to reply. It was not what he had expected. He smiled a lot and made attempts to speak that were quickly snatched away from him. He noticed that Lazarus was still there. The groom was rooted to the ground, holding the reins of the two horses together, a character from a seventeenth-century painting by Cuyp, or Wootton in the following century:

a groom and his horse. He had not been dismissed. His master was completely distracted from etiquette by his own enthusiastic greeting.

'I want you to think of this as your Barbizon, Monsieur Cazabon,' he said, repeating himself. Michel Jean began to think that he was becoming an idea in the mind of this millionaire, part of his project that was Orange Grove. There were many projects on the island that Mr Hardin Burnley controlled. It might be said that the entire colony was a Hardin Burnley project. He thought again of his father's advice at Schoener's Import & Export: 'You better watch these fellas. On the other hand, the favours of someone like Burnley might carry you places, so don't cut your nose to spite your face out of any prejudices. He's a rich rich man. So, you have to respect him for that, because here as everywhere else in the world, this wealth is power.'

Lazarus was still being kept standing next to the horses. Quite apart from the discomfort of Lazarus, the horses needed watering after their sweaty ride from Port of Spain. Hardin Burnley eventually noticed that the groom was standing there. 'Off you go now, Lazarus,' he said, with a flourish of his arm, and then he checked himself, changing his tone. 'That will be all, Lazarus, better get the horses watered and ready for the return journey to Port of Spain. You will stay to lunch, Mr Cazabon?'

'Delighted to accept.'

Lazarus turned and left, saying, 'Yes, Massa.'

'Shall we walk?' Planter and painter set off in the direction of the pond in the pasture. They left the paddocked lawns near to the house where the horses grazed, walking through the white picket gate. Once in the pasture, Michel Jean saw that there was a small boat on the pond, moored to a stake at the muddy edge. His eyes swept over the fields and the hills in the distance as Mr Hardin Burnley kept on with his commentary on the history of Orange Grove and its origins. 'I'm sure that Harris has told you of my desire to have a complete record of the estate. But you must see for yourself the best vantage points. Indeed, you must come again and stay and roam the estate.'

Michel Jean could not help chuckling to himself at the earlier idea that Orange Grove Estate was like Barbizon or the forests of Fontainebleau. The history could not be more different. It was well known that, when the end of the slave trade was announced, Hardin Burnley's response was to work the slaves on his estate even harder. Michel Jean had heard this from his father. Burnley moved slaves from less productive estates onto Orange Grove, so that it should then continue to thrive above all the others. And, at Emancipation, his compensation had been one of the largest.

'If it's too hot on the day that you wish to roam more freely, or if it's pouring with rain, Lazarus can conduct you around in the trap, or there will be a horse ready for you if you so wish. Do you ride?'

'I walk everywhere.' At last he was able to say something directly and break his repertoire of smiles and shakings of the head in agreement with his host.

'Excellent. Nothing could be easier, then.'

Michel Jean had not wanted to remember the history this morning as he began his tour of the estate with Mr Hardin Burnley, awaiting the precise figure of his commission. Hardin Burnley had deported himself with a certain charm, but Michel Jean could see what his father had alerted him to with his remark: 'You go have to sell yourself, boy.' He intended the planter to pay.

Quite soon Lazarus came with the trap to convey his master back to the house, as if knowing the limits of his stamina. He was already out of breath with the walk and the heat. Lazarus stood next to the horse, holding the reins tightly. 'Whoa,' he said as the large man mounted to his seat. Two hounds bounded up next to him for his embrace and then went wild with barking. Hardin Burnley leaned over to Michel Jean and said not too softly, 'Must be the *bouquet d'Afrique*, as they say.' Michel Jean knew well the inferred connection that the planter was making between the odour of Lazarus and the dogs going wild. An image of hounds chasing an escaped slave raced through his mind. Had he once seen a painting depicting that horror?

He stood and watched the planter being assisted into the trap. 'You'll be painting for posterity, my man. And then, there's your lunch.' He chuckled to himself. There still had been no mention of what his fee would be, what his prospects would fetch.

Lazarus took his trap off under the encouragement of his groom's cane. 'Heigh, heigh!' They disappeared into the kicked up dust. Michel Jean noticed two ladies in the distance through the scrim, their crinolined skirts in the breeze, welcome the trap at the front entrance. The figures shimmered in the haze. The scene unfolded in the distance across the green of the pasture. Who were the ladies of the house? he wondered.

Michel Jean set up his easel and settled down to work at his first view of the house. The mountains sloped steadily in the distance. The house began to take shape on his white paper. His charcoal scratched with the sound of the razor grass at the edges of the pasture. Above, in the blue air, was the screech of a chicken hawk. After a while, the ground was littered with his graphite, pen and ink drawings; sweat from his brow had dripped onto the paper and smudged the drawings. The house with a hundred and one windows established itself, the watercolour shimmering into view. Behind the *usine*, the barrack rooms gleamed with a whitewash which hid the sparseness and horror he knew existed in such places on the estates of his childhood: sharp delineations with his graphite fixed a subtle contrast. The underside of the belly of the great house was the barrack room. One hundred and one windows for Mr Hardin Burnley; one window for an indentured cane-cutter's family from Uttar Pradesh, not much better than a slave's barracoon.

As Michel Jean worked out in the pasture, a woman walked into his view, carrying her hoe on her shoulder. The facts of the story came as clearly into his mind as if he were still that attentive schoolboy at his father's dinner table. He had a name for the woman. He imagined her. She was Judy Brush. She was the common-law wife of Domingo Iriarte, a free man, who had cohabited with her for eight years and had come to Orange

Grove to buy her freedom. The court eventually granted her that freedom, but the just purchase under the law was ridiculed in the press. The truth had come in Judy Brush's own words. 'I have reason to dread Massa Burnley's lash more than that of all men.' Michel Jean was surprised how much he now remembered about his new patron.

Where would he find other patrons among the whites and the coloureds in these islands who had not made their money from the trade? His own complicity was a deep guilt which would take generations to unravel. Wealth was property. The essential property was labour.

He made his way back to the house.

Lunch was announced after a punch on the veranda, which he noticed the big man had refused, but drank instead the pure lime juice, brown with his stirred-in muscovado.

'I've never thought it of much use to the mind, though some of the best rum comes from Orange Grove.' Hardin Burnley tasted his lime juice and added, 'They all lose their heads and go silly; even Knox and Warner like the stuff. I notice Harris never finishes his. He keeps his head, but that young cousin of his downs at least three before a meal. He'll be a goner before he can say, *Salaam, bass*.' He laughed aloud at one of his new jokes. 'The limes, too, come from my orchards on the estate. Excellent for cleansing the system.'

Michel Jean was grateful for the punch. He knew that he needed to keep his head. There was his commission to discuss. He could just imagine Wildman getting tipsy. He was glad he was not here this morning.

Luncheon was laid, with the two men placed at opposite ends of the long mahogany table, which stood beneath a chandelier and was lined with three chairs along each side of the oval. They faced each other across the polished surface that held the moving shadows of a butler and a maid who hovered and served, trying to be as invisible as possible. How to be seen but never heard, that was one thing. How to serve but never be seen was quite another. The serving maid dropped a spoon, which brought forth a grunt from the big man. She hurried away to replace it with a clean one. The butler poured water.

After the pumpkin soup, they finished the entrée of fish and were then served their main course, which turned out to be a fricassée of chicken with christophine and creamed potatoes. Hardin Burnley helped himself to a morsel. 'Quite interesting to see what's happening to the cuisine, don't you think? I try to instruct them to keep things plain, but in no time there is a pinch of this and a pinch of that, and a "Oh gawd, Mr Burnley, is just a little pepper. It go taste good."'

Michel Jean feigned amusement at the Englishman's pretence, as he sliced into his christophine and let his tongue mimic the patois of his servants.

'All vegetables grown on the estate . . . Can you hear me down there? They insist on this arrangement. Ever since Harris came to lunch one day, and the idea of putting the Governor nearer to me was anathema to their sense of protocol. They banished him to the isolated splendour which you are now enjoying.'

'I'm doing fine down here, thank you.' Michel Jean wondered when he might mention the matter of his fee. In the silence of chewing and Hardin Burnley's instructions to his servants, he was calculating. In 1839, his *Assumption of the Virgin*, purchased by the Government of France to be placed in the chapel at l'hospice de Montignac in the Dordogne went for six hundred francs. He had been pleased with that after two years at the Ecole des Beaux-Arts, and then he had sold his *Colonial Landscape* six years ago in 1842 for one thousand two hundred francs. Everyone said that he had done well at the time. There would be the question of the passing of time. How much could he risk and not be laughed at by a man who could pay anything he wanted, who could have anything that he wanted. Excellency had not yet mentioned *his* fee, but he felt secure in a fair price. He was himself to tell Wildman and he was to decide whether to be paid in instalments or payment at the end of the project. It was a quite different affair with Excellency.

Michel Jean accepted a salad of fruit from the orchards of Orange Grove. The conversation turned to the recent immigration of East Indians arriving from Calcutta. 'I want one thousand Hindoos a year. That will begin to solve the problems left us by Emancipation,' Hardin Burnley said in a collusive tone. 'Your people down south will appreciate the need for new labour on your struggling estates.'

Southern, free-coloured republicanism was not where Michel Jean wanted to go with Mr Hardin Burnley. This was a conversation for his brother or his father. Except that they would want to convince the white planter now of their adoption of the new ways, agreeing with him about the state of labour on the island. He smiled politely, grateful for his father's counsel fresh in his mind; his warning ever more clearly etched in his memory: 'You go have to sell yourself, boy.'

'I understand very little of these affairs of economics and labour.' He spun that ball right down the centre of the table. If this conversation was like a cricket match, then sometimes he was bowling and then very suddenly he was batting again.

Hardin Burnley pretended not to hear and continued. His ball was allowed to flounder down at long stump. 'This is what I've told Harris,' Hardin Burnley said, opening another over. 'Don't stop the coolies coming.'

Michel Jean tried to imagine Excellency coping with the barrage of Hardin Burnley's balls. He was a bully, an affable bully, if that were possible.

'The idea that we can just switch to paid labour and that have no effect whatsoever on the profits is absurd. I can afford to shift things around, lose a bit here and gain it back there. But not the small estate-holders. They'll have disappeared before Harris can give another fine speech, before those fellows in London send out some more of their high-sounding moral platitudes about the new slavery. They should listen to Carlyle. He got it absolutely correct about the niggers.' That last ball was meant to bowl him out. Michel Jean pretended to cough in order to clear a bit of pawpaw stuck in his throat.

Holding his napkin to his mouth, his return ball came smothered by the blanket of linen. 'Must be difficult to balance things in a time of such change.' He then coughed profusely. 'Excuse me, something's got stuck.' This interruption allowed him to stretch for a strategic drink of water from a tall crystal glass. The butler was at hand to replenish it immediately. He felt pathetic. But he was here to gain employment. He began to feel that he might leave the table no better off than an indentured labourer. Hardin Burnley could not have cared less whether he was choking to death or not.

He kept on relentlessly. 'Civilization is not a matter of balance. It's how to keep your head when you know that you're right. Some people have civilization and others will have to be dragooned into it, through labour and punishment. Once we gave up the lash we forfeited our best chance of fashioning these islands into working economies.'

Michel Jean continued attending to the aftermath of his choking fit, wiping it up with his linen napkin. The butler removed the offending fruit salad.

'The half-breeds, of course, think that they are going to be the ones to lead us into the new world, and eventually into the new century. Of which there will be one. I won't be here to see it, but I will darn well make my mark before I leave.'

Michel Jean felt now that he was being openly provoked. In Hardin Burnley's terms, he should keep his head. He felt that all the big man needed was a trigger to propel him off onto another subject. He needed to choose one that might lead back to his painting. He thought of Excellency's letter and his mention of Mrs Hardin Burnley's presence in Paris. It was a surprise ball, bowled as nonchalantly as possible. 'So, you were saying that your wife happened to see some of my work in Paris?'

Hardin Burnley looked momentarily surprised by the switch in conversation. 'What's that you say?'

'Mrs Hardin Burnley . . . in Paris . . .' Michel Jean feigned shouting, as if he was at the other end of Hardin Burnley's vast acres.

'Oh, yes . . .' He looked a little disappointed to be distracted from his rant. He must be slightly deaf, Michel Jean surmised.

'Spends all my money. Won't stay in the London house. Yes, as I said, she mentioned your work. Good to know that you have done some other work and this isn't the first time you're embarking upon this sort of thing.'

The arrogance of the man was palpable. He was so openly playing now that Michel Jean felt confident to respond on his own ground with a bit more force than he had used before. He had not allowed himself to be provoked by the reference to 'half-breeds'.

'The *Colonial Landscape* I submitted in '42 fetched quite a nice sum. One thousand two hundred francs, if I'm not mistaken. Something in that region . . .' He kept on now, pulling Hardin Burnley to attention. 'Prices have escalated, of course, with this fashion for colonial landscapes, views to show what it was like when *they* return home.' While he might be one of the half-breeds, he could almost hear the word 'mule' in the mouth of the owner of Orange Grove. Hardin Burnley was isolated, an ageing white planter with no real hope of lasting into the next century, as he himself had admitted.

He suddenly saw the connection that he was seeking all the time he had contemplated painting for this planter with his father's reservations in his mind. He heard one of Hardin Burnley's first remarks again: 'You'll be painting for posterity.' That was why he was doing it. But he had to be paid for posterity. At least now, no matter what the future held.

'So, what's it to be? You're not going to ruin me, are you?'

Michel Jean nearly got bowled out with the speed of that delivery. He was not going to sell himself short.

'Well, if prices in Paris doubled in ten years. Then in six years they've not quite doubled, but probably are near to seven thousand two hundred francs for the collection. We need to sort that out in pounds or dollars, but then it's an album, not just a single painting, so there is that calculation to make.'

'What, even with the revolutions?'

'Maybe because of them.'

Michel Jean was feeling quite proud of himself by the end of lunch. He was playing confidently.

Michel Jean began to get the whole picture, when over coffee and Havanas he glimpsed for the most fleeting of moments a head peeping around the doorway, which led off into the corridor where the bedrooms were, as he imagined the inner structure of the great house that he had been painting from the distance of the pond beyond the pasture. A brown face with a colourful Madras had retreated as quickly as it had made its appearance. Then he heard giggles echoing down the corridor. Was this one of the ladies he had seen from a distance when he first arrived?

Hardin Burnley guessed the presence before he heard the retreating giggle. 'Beware a house of women, my man,' he declaimed, trying to silence the girlish laugh. 'I thought I was rid of them when my wife went off to London, but it seems not.'

Michel Jean smiled at the butler, who was witness to this statement of his master's, as he cleared the china and swept up crumbs.

'Anyway, enough of food and women. You need to get back to work or have you finished for the day with the hot sun?'

Both men rose and sauntered off into the glare of the veranda. 'You better let me see this work of yours if I'm going to be ruined.'

Michel Jean was not going to bargain. He got out his portfolio and lifted the first watercolour into the light. The house of one hundred and one windows was there in the small painting. It lay propped up in Michel Jean's arms as hardly anything, not something which might be worth the money he had mentioned. Confused, he kept looking at the painting in his hands and then at the face of Hardin Burnley. The big man bent to peer into it as if he could not see anything at all. A picture without a frame weighed nothing. As something fragile and delicate, just a bit of paper, it might fly out of his arms with the strong breeze off the mountains across the pastures.

It seemed an eternity before Hardin Burnley said anything at all. 'Well, it's much smaller than I thought it would be. But I expect when it's mounted and framed it will seem quite substantial,' he reflected.

'Of course, the mounting, yes . . . the frame . . .'

'It will be framed and mounted?'

'Well, in the first instance it will be mounted in an album. Remember, it will appear with other views of your estate. You've seen the albums I talk of . . .'

'Of course. My wife tells me . . .' Hardin Burnley took the painting from Michel Jean and held it at arm's length, looking at it intently. 'Yes, I can see the volume, which will sit in an embossed box. *Views of Orange Grove,* 1849. It'll sit on the table by the window. It'll be picked up and opened and viewed. It'll be circulated.'

Michel Jean kept agreeing with a nod of his head. He suddenly wanted to snatch the painting from Hardin Burnley, run out into the yard and hide with his watercolour. He was being made to feel like a child who was not getting the praise that he wanted, the praise that he deserved.

The truth was that Hardin Burnley did not know what to say about the watercolour. Eventually, he found a phrase. 'Very fine. Very fine. I look forward to other views. I can see how together they'll be effective.'

Michel Jean took the last comment as a criticism, that his views needed a cumulative effect to impress.

Then, at last, as if all these long moments had been a lesson in art, the big man held the painting away from him again and said, 'The colour is quite remarkable. You sat out there in that heat and drew and painted and here it is? That's quite something.' Michel Jean saw a change in the eye of the planter as he looked from the painting into the distance and the acres of his estate. He had moved him.

He himself wanted to cry. The confusion of feelings made him at once very angry, but then extremely vulnerable. He felt utterly exposed. He felt that he had opened up himself to the great planter, with all his power, to be inspected, to be probed and interrogated about the most sensitive part of himself. He did not think that he was as yet understood, but it was better than hearing Hardin Burnley going on about mountings and frames. Then he realized that he had done something quite remarkable, something he was just beginning to understand about his work, as he noticed the fragility and delicacy of his painting while he stood on the veranda of the enormous house that dominated the landscape for miles around.

'Thank you, thank you,' he said at last. He did not want now to talk too much about the painting, as much as he had thought he would. Surprisingly, or not, the planter needed an education in this craft. Maybe that was what had driven his wife and children to London and Paris.

Hardin Burnley had probably expected that his house would have expressed his power. The subtle, delicate medium of the watercolour had embraced the architecture of the house, made it part of the landscape in which it stood. But, in a subtle way, it had reduced its power.

The big man, having had enough of conversation, then retired to his siesta, leaving Michel Jean to stand alone on the veranda, as the acres of savannahs, cane fields and pastures descended into the heat haze with the throb of the *cigales*' piercing call.

As Lazarus conveyed him away from the estate and Hardin Burnley, back to Port of Spain, he could hear Louise's voice in a recent letter. 'It's a living, darling. Take the money and then you can paint what you want to paint.'

After the probate of his mother's will he had learned the reality of sugar in the island after Emancipation. He remembered now, because his mind was on it, that Burnley had received £50,000 in compensation after Emancipation. Being here on the estate brought home to him in the starkest terms the source not only of Burnley's wealth but the base of the island's economy. The trade had ended. Abolition, emancipation and apprenticeship, that joke, had taken place in its untidy fashion.

At least it was all over, legally. Now, it was indentured labour: Burnley's coolies.

There was a letter from Louise to greet him back at the house in Edward Street. She would consider the voyage with the children. It depended on Louis Michel. He was glad of this because he now had to tell her that, with this new commission from the planter, in addition to the one for the Governor, he would most certainly have to delay his departure.

On the following day, Michel Jean had set up his easel at the edge of the cane field from where he had a view of the full extent of the house and its foreground as viewed from its western boundary. The great house was framed by samaans and casuarinas. Royal palms rose on their slender pillars crowned with their wind-tossed plumes. They enabled a neat contrast by which to convey the height and breadth of the house itself and the grandeur it proclaimed, rising out of the savannah etched against the northern cordillera, itself rolling away into the further distance towards the heights of El Cerro del Aripo.

He worked away on the foreground with the grand water-lily pond. Here the shimmer of pink, white and yellow suited the light strokes of his fine brush, rendering the buzzing of flies, the hovering of butterflies and the zing of the *batti-mamzelle*, the dragonflies. The white and black piebald cows within the wrought iron railings of the pasture, under the broad samaans, bordered by the white picket posts of the inner pasture were drawn in; security for Hardin Burnley's herd. His graphite gave the big man his lofty portico and the dormer windows of which he was particularly proud, adapted from how his family home in Virginia was once described to him. And, of course, as many as was possible of the one hundred and one windows was etched in with precision. There was something about the whole enterprise he was embarked upon which disturbed Michel Jean's conscience and artistic sensibility, as he portrayed the harmony, pleasure and profit of Orange Grove.

*

He sensed the presence of someone else near by. It was not that he had been aware of an approach or anything so marked as a footfall. It was a change in the scent on the air. It was a lady's perfume. When he did turn around he was quite astonished at the young woman who stood beneath a blue parasol in her finery, as if she were off to a wedding or to church on a bright Sunday morning. He immediately rose, wiping his brush and laying it down on his palette. '*Mademoiselle*. Excuse me. I was just . . .'

'No.' She giggled into her frilly lace handkerchief. 'Is me to ask excuse. I disturbing you at Master's work.'

'No, *non*! No, *non, non, non*!' He took the young lady's hand to kiss it, taking in immediately her phrase 'Master's work', astonished at her first description of what she thought she saw him doing. She did not say a master's work, which would have been flattering. But he felt sure that she would appreciate the real matter of what he was actually doing, because he could see that she was intrigued to see the painting in progress on the easel with the paints and the palette all laid out, and the sketch in the early stages of composition. It was as if the realization of what it meant to produce a painting had prompted from her the phrase, 'Master's work'. Everything which took place at Orange Grove was indeed Master's work, at least work done for Master.

'I saw the other one.'

'The other one?'

'The first one.' She corrected herself.

'The first one?'

She pointed to the painting. 'I peeped.'

'Ah! The first view. What did you think of it? Not very good?' Michel Jean could not help himself. He could not tear his attention from her eyes, her slender waist, her petite feet in their pointed black shoes, her white stockings, which he noticed had got smudged as she crossed the savannah after the recent fall of rain. His eyes travelled over her bare shoulders and arms, shown off to absolute effect by her off-the-shoulder broderie anglaise bodice which cradled her small bosoms, and allowed the sheen of her brown skin to shine magnificently. She was a mulatto. She may have been the giggling girl at lunch, who then emerged later to view the painting left with Hardin Burnley. So absorbed, he barely noticed her protestations.

'No, no. Very good. Pretty. Very pretty, *jolie, très jolie*,' she insisted, then smiled sweetly at him. 'Master like it.'

'Ah, very pretty? Well . . . and Master likes it? *Bien!*'

'Master is so pleased with it. Mama, though, does not, I think, appreciate art.'

'Oh.' He noticed that she was making an effort with her diction and grammar. Art? He wondered what she understood of that herself.

'Master's wife sees many paintings in Paris and London. I would love to go there.'

'Oh.'

'Would you teach me to paint?'

'I'm not sure what I could teach you.' She was so beautiful, he thought. Hardin Burnley could buy whatever he wanted.

'You could teach me to paint,' she said again decisively.

He saw that she too, perhaps, could get what she wanted, lowering her eyes for a moment and then opening them so widely that it embarrassed him. 'Is this a sudden desire or an ambition you've had for some time?'

'I beg your pardon?' She struggled with the elaboration of his question.

'When you first want to paint?'

'When I saw how much it pleased Master,' she answered immediately and urgently.

'When was that?' Michel Jean was curious.

'When I looked at your painting,' she added quickly.

He could not help his surprise. He smiled at her wonderful innocence combined with what he suspected was her early tutelage in intrigue. So young, he thought, and already she could flatter so successfully. She must somehow know the sure way to an artist's heart.

She had moved closer to the easel and picked up one of his brushes and played with the bristles between her fingers.

'Master seemed more delighted with this,' she said, pointing nonchalantly at the painting on the easel. 'More interested in this magic, which you have performed here on his precious estate than with my performance in the wonderful frock which he brought me from New York earlier this year, when he was away longer than my heart could cope with. He used to like to see me dressed up in his gifts.' Her little speech had taken her beyond her usual syntactical distance. She had twirled away from the easel, allowing the white petticoats beneath her pink skirt with the blue pinafore to gush. He had forgotten what precise message the particular knot of her Madras headtie was meant to convey to possible suitors. She must be trained in the complicated science of love and marriage in which his Creole women were well schooled. They wished to marry well, but also keep their options for amorous liaisons open; the two were usually managed in combination.

This girl was not yet married and Michel Jean wondered whether she had as yet fallen in love; whether indeed it was her heart that had missed her master on his recent trip to New York, or her need for reassurance that she would continue to be in his mind when he was away from her, so that she would again be the recipient of another of his expensive gifts. Her fear would be that she might fall out of favour and be replaced. She must know he could have what he wanted. Michel Jean wondered what gifts Hardin Burnley bought for the mother of this girl. They might need still greater thought if he was to manage his household arrangements without rancour.

He remembered what else he had learned from his father: that Hardin Burnley had a woman from Tacarigua to keep him company and give, even a man as powerful and wealthy as William Hardin Burnley, those things a man cannot give himself. 'She is a Mandingo woman, they say, who will, if he allows, give him another breed of children to populate that big big house. He strikes a hard bargain, so watch out. Everything to do with Mr Burnley has a price.' What were the precise arrangements, what was the currency, at Orange Grove, he asked himself, with Mrs Hardin Burnley in Paris? He doubted that his 'magic' would count for much.

'Magic!' he at last exclaimed, recovering from her coquetry, as she opened and closed her eyes, smiled, looked stern, cross and disappointed, like an indulged child who does not immediately get what she wants. All the while she allowed her skirts to play with the sunlight, practically performing a ballet as she skipped and hopped over the rough grass and ploughed earth at the edge of the cane piece in intermittent attempts to prevent herself from stumbling and falling in shoes which were not meant for walking in the fields.

'Yes, magic.' She had found a mound of soft grass upon which to sit and watch him paint, arranging her skirts and petticoats around her like the petals of a flower in full bloom. She obviously intended to stay a while.

'I don't perform magic, you know. I paint.' It sounded silly to him to put it so simply when the girl felt that she wanted to be initiated into some esoteric ritual out of which the painting would materialize. 'Sit and watch me carefully.' He returned to his easel and picked up the brush he had been using before she had interrupted him. He then proceeded to do what he had seen his tutors as early as Mr Barnaby do, instructing on the kind of brush and the choice of pigment and mix of paints, as he moved about the painting, drawing and then dabbing at the foreground. 'Now, you must paint what you see, not what you think you see.' He fell silent for long periods, lost in what he was doing, rather than in the lesson he was teaching. All the while, she sat and watched.

She had not introduced herself formally and nor had he, though he guessed she had learned his name and his purpose up at the house. 'And, what shall I call you, miss?' he asked as he continued with his painting.

He heard her behind him, almost inaudibly: 'Augusta.'

'That's a pretty name. Do you know how you came by that name?'

'I born in August. But is also because the first house my mother, Mrs Farquhar, work in, the mistress daughter, who come from England, was called Augusta. My mother looked after that little girl as if she was her own till she have me. So when I come to christen, she say she want that name for me.'

'It's a very pretty name,' he said. She had told him a story he could well imagine; seeing her mother strolling out with the bonneted, and bonnie, English Augusta in her perambulator. He could see her charm and beauty. Distance allowed him to entertain this fancy. Drying his brushes, he turned to face his new pupil and said, 'I would like to paint you.'

'Paint me?'

'Yes, paint your portrait.'

'I not sure, you know.'

'Yes, a painting in which you are the subject. Not like this one we've been doing, which is a landscape painting.' Her beauty as a mulatto struck him.

She was now hanging on his every word, realizing that this magic, as she called it, had more to it than immediately met the eye. She was still concentrating on what must have seemed to her a phenomenon, how the scene before her came to be represented on the paper clipped to the easel. His act of painting excited her. It enticed her more than wanting to possess this magic herself to please Master, he thought.

'Perhaps Master would like to have my portrait,' she said, emerging from her pensive, frowning mood and allowing her brow to be smooth once more.

Of course, she must have seen paintings of people in the house, but perhaps had not really taken much notice of them, or given much thought as to why or how it was all done. Her ancestry had not been painted and hung. Could she imagine that her portrait might hang there among the portraits of Hardin Burnley's family from Virginia, London and Paris? Was she already choosing in her mind the dress she might wear, the jewels with which she might adorn her neck, and what other gems she might hang from her ears and wrap around her wrists? This was *her* magic: prettiness. 'A penny for your thoughts.' He turned from packing his brushes and folding up his easel.

'I just wonder what go happen.'

He knew that it was Hardin Burnley who would have to agree to Augusta being painted. She was not the Mandingo woman his father had spoken of, but her daughter. She, too, must belong to him. She would also have to get his permission to have lessons. That use of his time was not within the contract for the painting of a dozen views of Orange Grove. Maybe when she asked her master he would agree to humour her, to get from her some delight he had not as yet tasted; use it as a bargaining chip in the buying and selling of affection which Michel Jean suspected was going on at Orange Grove.

Michel Jean watched Augusta's diminishing figure disappear as she left the pasture, then the yard, and eventually re-entered the house.

Back at Edward Street he replied to Louise's last letter, encouraging her to think of planning to make the voyage with the children. He suggested that there might be an opportunity to find her a travelling companion. He expanded on his previous account of getting Hardin Burnley's commission and his first prospects at Orange Grove. He kept his thoughts on the darker side of life there to himself.

The following morning, he left the house in Edward Street without seeing Josie. He left his letter, hoping she would make sure that it reached the packet that morning.

He travelled on horseback, a loan from the Orange Grove stables. He was soon out of the town and on the Royal Road.

When he arrived at the great house Lazarus took his horse. Then he went straight out onto the savannah to continue his work. He would leave it to Augusta to find him, or for Hardin Burnley to request his presence to instruct him to tutor Augusta and paint her portrait.

The situation reminded him of the young girl, Angelique, who had come to the house when he had just moved into the studio at 24 rue de la Rochefoucauld. She had been Martiniquan. That morning, in his Paris studio, he had wanted to paint her skin, which had meant that he needed to find the paints to render the young mulatto girl's skin. She spoke her French with a patois accent he recognized from his mother's speech. It had occurred to him that when she was not modelling for him, she was modelling for someone else. She was not, after all, his private property. What an entirely scandalous idea! But it was the same proposition as with Augusta, who was also bargaining with herself. How would she use the portrait? How would he use the painting of the portrait? And what, indeed, if he agreed, would the portrait be to Hardin Burnley? These questions perplexed him.

The view from the western boundary that was emerging on the easel led the viewer's eye along the road into the estate up to the house with the factory in the further distance. The heat haze on the savannah altered the horizon. Michel Jean wiped his brow. He erected a large parasol to give himself more shade than that afforded by his wide-brimmed straw *chapeau*. He had a drink of water from his flask. Augusta had not appeared. He wondered if she had been prevented from seeing him. There had been figures on the landscape; some had walked towards him from the house, but none of them ever arrived. They appeared in his landscape but got lost in their own.

Seated on his small stool, he was finding the increasing heat difficult. He raised the brim of his hat and there she stood. She had stepped out of nowhere, it seemed. He turned towards her voice. 'Mr Cazabon.' As the young girl stood there against the haze he saw her as a figure arising from one of the many Baker & Dawson slaves who had been sold to the owner of Orange Grove in the early part of the century. Michel Jean thought he could see, rising and falling behind her, a gang of cane-field cutters raising their cutlasses and swiping at the base of the sugarcane, lifting the cut cane and laying it down to be collected. Then all that rose and fell in his landscape was the shimmer of the light; the shadows of the broad branches of the samaans moving in the breeze, along with Augusta's skirts. She had walked into his watercolour landscape.

'Miss Augusta!'

'Monsieur Cazabon,' she called across the short distance that separated them.

You belong right here, he said to himself. He reached for his brush. His fingers tightened and his brushstrokes quickened as he returned to his painting. This would be his first portrait of her, seeing her now, picking her way delicately over the thorns of the ti-marie on the savannah. A light touch of his brush brought up the pink of the ground mimosa. Her face was in the shadow of her parasol. She lifted her skirts and petticoats. She was a shimmer of light, like the butterflies and the *batti-mamzelles* on the water-lily pond. She would not even know. No one would know, except him. Hardin Burnley would not know. It would be his secret; a cryptic portrait. She was almost completely formed by the time she arrived at his side, peering over his shoulder at the painting. It was her form, but not her face. The figure fitted into the composition impressionistically, creating that sense of leisurely strolling in the park; one of Burnley's ladies. This was the kind of grace that Hardin Burnley would want conveyed. This was the sense of civilization that Wildman talked about when he spoke of the prospects around Chilham Castle and Norton Court. But the subtle indication was the suggestion that she did not belong to the fields beyond the savannah. The viewer would ask the question as to how she came to belong to the house. He heard again his mother's words on her deathbed: *And you have work to do, darling, painting to paint, an island to give to the world . . . don't forget the ideas of freedom which have carried us this far; the republic we seek in this corner of the world.*

'Art does not preach a sermon.' He heard another voice from his past, a correcting voice.

'You've finished another one.' Augusta interrupted from behind. He let the perfume that she wore overwhelm him, as it had done the first time she had ventured out to the savannah.

'It's almost there.' He sighed, sitting back, taking the whole of her into his view now.

'And you've put in what you've imagined rather than what's there,' she said, pointing at the figure strolling across the savannah.

'Oh.' He tried to sound surprised. They both looked towards the empty savannah from where she had come. 'Yes, there's no one there now. But, there might've been, as there used to be,' he said, still thinking of the Baker & Dawson slaves.

She was a young girl dressed in satins, silks and tulle. Her parasol's fringe was gathered into scallops. It was how he wanted to paint her with her own face, not a figure to represent a world. He employed the colours for her skin that he had learned in painting Angelique.

'So, have you come for a lesson *en plein air*?' he asked as he washed his brushes.

'What you mean?'

'Not in my studio, but here, under the sky, in the pasture with the natural light, in the open air.'

'Where's your studio?'

'In Port of Spain.'

'That would be a long way to come for a lesson.'

'Yes. Better I come to you.'

'I tell Mama I want to paint, you know. She laugh.'

'She laugh?'

'Master say, Mama don't understand art.'

'Yes, you said.' He remembered their conversation from the day before. 'So you've talked to Master? You've asked him about the lessons?'

She was looking into the painting and then into the distance that had yielded it, as if puzzled. 'You paint the girl with my dress? It could be me?'

He did not reply; he was embarrassed, caught out. Then he said, 'You suggested her to me.'

'You really go teach me to do this?'

'It's possible.' He didn't want to promise too much. He didn't know whether she had an aptitude.

Then she said, thinking aloud, 'Master coming and going, no time to ask him.'

'Coming and going?' he enquired.

'He have plenty estates to visit. Sometimes we don't know where he is.'

'Oh! He doesn't tell you where he's going?'

'Mama say she sure he have other women on the other estates.' Then, abruptly, she stopped talking. 'Anyway, I mustn't talk their business.'

'No,' he said, but desiring her to go on.

Michel Jean could not help reflecting on the goings-on at Orange Grove. Hardin Burnley had not chosen the mother, closer to his own age, he surmised. It clearly was not the companionship of the absent Mrs Hardin Burnley that he missed. Augusta's seductive beauty was much more what the planter must desire.

As Michel Jean looked about him and at this beauty sitting on the grass before him, he realized that Hardin Burnley needed to own things. Owning was his satisfaction. This millionaire planter was not interested in his painting but in owning his paintings; paintings of Orange Grove, his prize possession with all that was in it, including Augusta and her mother. He might then be interested in her portrait. That would be another way that he might own her.

Michel Jean began to paint her as she sat under her parasol. She was alert to his every brushstroke. The insects ticked in the scorched, dry-season grass. She slapped her arm nonchalantly. 'Them mosquitoes.' He heard her sigh. He would rather paint her without all Hardin Burnley's finery; the frocks from New York. Maybe she should be persuaded to travel to Port of Spain. He mused on this, while Augusta stared from beneath her parasol.

Augusta interrupted his painting and his thoughts. The heat had become intense, making her irritable. She needed to return to the house. He definitely wanted her to sit for him. He devised an excuse to accompany her to the house. He wished to leave a message for Mr Hardin Burnley about his progress with the album.

'Mama, is Monsieur Cazabon.' Augusta brought him into the drawing room where he was met by Mrs Farquhar. Augusta then left them to talk.

She must be the Mandingo woman his father had talked about, Michel Jean recalled. He saw at once where Augusta had got her poise and beauty. He wondered about the journey of this woman to this drawing room. He did not believe that she had always been here since she had first come to the household. He wondered at what stage Hardin Burnley had given her her freedom. What had it cost, that freedom?

He heard Augusta call from the adjoining room: 'Mama? Where them red ribbons Master bring me?' The mother ignored her daughter's plea.

'We've been viewing your landscape, Monsieur Cazabon.' He noticed the easel with his painting still prominently on display. She strode across to a corner of the drawing room to where the easel stood supporting the first view of the house for the album. Michel Jean thought it looked surprisingly fine. She stood next to the easel, pointing to the painting as if she were about to deliver a lecture. 'We're very pleased with your efforts.' He wondered when she had acquired this tone and from whom. How different it would have been if Hardin Burnley had been at home. He remembered Augusta's remark that her mother did not understand art. She was clearly being an ambassador for her master dressed in what were clearly *her* latest New York fashions. Hardin Burnley knew how to keep both women happy.

'And have you an opinion, my lady?'

'Mrs Farquhar.' She put him straight.

'Mrs Farquhar, I would be grateful for your appreciation, how you see my efforts.' As he spoke, he could hear Augusta in the next room. She was still fretting over her lost ribbons.

'Mama, I can't find them.' There were the thuds of sharp, stamping feet. Again the mother ignored her daughter, raising her eyebrows, as if to say, What a little terror. Michel Jean could well believe that. He allowed himself the faintest flicker of a smile. There was some kind of collusion going on between him and the mother that he did not quite understand at the moment.

'We find your painting a capital achievement.'

'Thank you, Mrs Farquhar.' That sounded quite solid, he thought. Clearly, she thought she had done her duty to art, because she briskly moved away from the easel to the tall window of the drawing room to look out onto the entrance to the house, as if surveying her estate. She obviously liked playing lady of the manor while Hardin Burnley was not in residence. He did not think she would be quite so haughty if the planter was present. This might well be part of the bargain, might be what the lady got in return for the girl in the adjoining room.

'You've come to see the master.' He was intrigued by the way both women continued with the title: Master.

'Yes, I wanted to inform Mr Hardin Burnley of my progress.'

'He's away visiting his other estates. Of course, he's not long from Orange Grove. This is his home.'

Michel Jean noticed her insistence on the preference Master gave to Orange Grove, at least in the view of the mistress. How much of a mistress was she now? How perverse was the ménage? Augusta bounded into the room at that moment, more like a twelve year old, rather than the young lady she had presented herself as on their previous meetings, still demanding the presence of her red ribbons. He wondered how knowingly he was being brought into the family drama.

'My daughter wants to learn how to paint,' Mrs Farquhar said in a manner that did not reveal her view of that proposition.

'Does she now? That's splendid.' He thought he might mask his embarrassment in being an accomplice in Augusta's deception by seeming enthusiastic, and as if he had just heard the suggestion for the first time. Augusta had recovered her poise. She had found her red ribbons under a cushion on the couch. She was busy untangling them and pressing out their creases on her knee.

'Is there an advantage for a young lady in learning to paint, Monsieur Cazabon?' Mrs Farquhar persisted with her French title.

'An advantage, Mrs Farquhar?'

'Materially, I mean. Will it better her position?'

'Well, I don't imagine there is much to better in Augusta's position, my lady.' A look of disapproval greeted his remark. He realized he had implied that he knew her daughter was spoken for and provided for by the richest man in Trinidad, so what better advantage could she possibly achieve, least of all by learning to paint. He doubted very much whether Augusta had the patience for painting. But that reality was neither here nor there in this game. He continued. 'I would be very happy teaching Miss Augusta to paint.' He looked directly at the mother, thinking that he might not be able to keep a straight face if he met Augusta's eyes at this moment. Augusta was now ignoring her ribbons; her eyes were flashing between Michel Jean and her mother, as she enjoyed the fact that her mother was unaware of the previous conversation between her daughter and her proposed tutor. Michel Jean realized that Augusta was trying to catch his eye.

'Well, of course it is for the master to decide,' Mrs Farquhar said decisively.

'Of course.'

'Well, Mama. I must decide too.'

'You'll do as the master says, young lady.' The mother smiled at Michel Jean, trying to smooth over what was clearly another intermittent row with her strong-headed daughter.

Mrs Farquhar wanted to offer him tea in the new style that had taken hold of the island since the English set had gained the ascendancy. But Michel Jean escaped, claiming that the journey back to Port of Spain prevented him from being detained any longer.

He gave Augusta a knowing look that he knew would leave her feeling comforted that he had indeed collaborated with her silently. He ventured to say quietly as he passed her, 'Maybe we'll meet again while you're strolling in the savannah.'

Just as he was departing the drawing room, Mrs Farquhar followed behind saying, 'You should really stay at the house, Monsieur Cazabon, while you are engaged in this artistic project.'

'I thank you for the offer, Mrs Farquhar, but business in Port of Spain dictates my return.' While he had found a form of words to satisfy the moment, he wondered at the mother's intent and whether it was courtesy, hospitality, or some other scheme to benefit herself and her daughter.

When Michel Jean awoke he was still stained with the dream of the night before. He had been seasick on a merchant seaman's vessel. The night had been an ordeal. Lying on his bunk in the lower berth, he watched his luggage and all the necessities of his life swim away as his stomach lurched and then foundered. His mouth tasted of rancid butter, bad biscuits and tainted water. Rust, and some metallic poison. All night there had been the buckling of sails and the straining of ropes. Then his bed was up on deck beneath an interminable sky, floating on an immeasurable sea. He was surrounded by coops of chickens with scraggy heads and pens with consumptive pigs. The dark blue surface of the sea flooded the deck. Then, like a blacksmith's bellows, the billow of the sea drowned out the cheering crew who had come to see him vomiting out his guts. This confusion changed imperceptibly into a silent peace.

The light had changed into a phosphorescent fire that boiled on the surface of the water where shoals of fish glided past him, while pods of dolphins leaped and flying fish landed on the deck. This was mixed with a story that his mother had told him when he was a boy of her voyage to Barbados. The clouds were delicate tints of lilac, orange and the flame of the flamboyante flower. Then the sea was running as high as a mountain range. Leaping as high as their peaks, the dolphins were as transparent as crystal, streaked with the green, orange and purple hues of the sea.

On waking, there had been the immediate feeling that this was a dream of a voyage that embodied his worst fears and anticipations of what might happen when he had left Louise and the children; the fear that his ship would be wrecked and he would be lost at sea. He now felt a growing fear of Louise and the children making the voyage without him. Even the solution of them travelling with Uncle St Luce alarmed him.

His fever had run for four days. Each day Dr Marryat came to attend with poultices and Josie attended with clear chicken soup. 'Only consommé,' he heard Dr Marryat saying, as he descended the back stairs. 'Only consommé, or you'll lose him.' He heard Josie crying and Ernestine in the yard below begin to wail, a soft rising wave coming up to his window where a palm scratched at the jalousies. 'Take control, woman,' he heard Dr Marryat say, as he left the yard.

Oh for a cool breeze off the sea, he thought.

'Jeansie.' It was Josie's voice. She was leaning over him and then quickly going to the windows and opening the jalousies to let the sharp yellow sunlight fall in ribbons upon the floor. 'What happen to you? You still sick? But you was better yesterday. How you sleep so long? I say you gone long time. I not looking to find you here. Long time now he out in the road, I say, on his way to Orange Grove to paint them pictures for the big man. Remember is days you not gone.'

She went on with her questions and speculations as he continued to lie, drained, with his eyes closed, emerging from his dream. The fever had subsided. He speculated himself that he had sat for too long in the sun, out in the savannah with his watercolours and then sketching Augusta. Obsessed with his painting of the girl, he had forgotten the time. But then, of course, Dr Marryat's fear had been malaria or the yellow fever.

'You know, last night you fall off to sleep just so.'

He had a vague recollection of Josie cradling his head between her breasts. That would have been part of his dream.

'I leave the house before cock crow to reach market early so I could get the best ground provision before they tell me all finish. I say you gone by the time I get back. I hope the big man don't vex with you for this. So many days now you ent gone to work.'

Josie continued with her domestic preoccupations, but also, as he now heard, her solicitous concern for his welfare. He had not realized before that Josie would be taking care of this in her mind. He did not think that she had thoughts of this nature. He knew that he was the world to her and she would have feared that he would succumb to the fever. But he had not thought that she would, while on her own, be concerned with the detail of what he did at Orange Grove. It moved him that, quietly, alone, she had pondered the success or failure of his project.

'I suppose it too late now to be looking to go to Orange Grove? Let me see whether I can't hire a messenger boy to take a letter that you must write, because you know I can't fit them letters together to make any sense at all. You have to tell the big man you not well these days. Is more and more people I hear getting this influenza they talking about, you know. If only writing was like talking . . .'

'Josie, sweetheart, is coffee I smelling down in the kitchen?'

'Well, I make coffee, yes.'

'Bring me some, nuh, girl. That will get me out of this bed.'

'And I bringing pen and paper too. And let me run out in the street and see whether I see one of them messenger boy. That young fella from Dry River does pass up this way with errands, you know. He have a nice horse with a buggy. He go go Orange Grove if you pay him a little something.'

Michel Jean fell back into the mood of his dream as he heard Josie busy in the kitchen outside and then opening the gate onto Edward Street. He wondered how aware Josie was of the importance of Hardin Burnley's commission. She was aware that he had to establish himself on the island in order to bring

Louise and the children to Port of Spain. What were her real thoughts on that matter? He did not want to hurt her. He felt that fantasies still lingered, fantasies with their origin in their past relationship. No matter how resolute they had been, there was still heartache for both of them. The coffee she brought him revived his spirits and he took up the pen she had laid on the side table.

'*Garçon*; come, boy! Wait eh. Monsieur Cazabon have errand for you.' Michel Jean could hear Josie's voice from the street below. She was not going to be defeated in her efforts to put his life straight.

He wrote a letter of apology for Mrs Farquhar's attention, surmising that Hardin Burnley himself would not yet have returned from his progress through his estates, progress through his women. It gave him the opportunity to mention his hope that Augusta would soon be beginning her lessons. He mentioned that maybe a portrait of the young lady, and indeed of Mrs Farquhar herself, might be something Mr Hardin Burnley would like to consider.

'You write the letter? The fella waiting. And I need to give him something.' Michel Jean looked up as Josie re-entered the room.

He handed her the letter for her to fold. Josie's idea of a letter was now completed and signed with a flourish. But it was not the letter to the big man that she had advised. 'I ent see the big man name here,' Josie said, searching the letter, trying to fit together the letters and syllables, forming them slowly with her lips.

'I've written it to his housekeeper. Mr William Hardin Burnley is not in residence at the moment.'

Josie looked up. 'I hope she'll tell him that you write. It important, you know.' She folded the letter some more, still forming words in her mouth. 'Mrs Farquhar. Is so she call?'

'Yes, Josie. Take the letter now for the fella and give him what you think with the change from market.'

'Is so? That is for other purchases.'

'Josie, you know where the money is in the drawer of the sideboard. I leave it to you.'

'Yes. You leave it to me. I hope that Madame in Paris know what work it is I doing here for she and she children.' With that, Josie left the room.

Michel Jean lay back, wondering how he had ever under-estimated Josie, above all people, to understand the predicaments of his life. Only, he now saw, that his predicament was also Josie's. She was taking care of all of them. She had thought out her position since her anticipation of his mother's death and his arrival.

Belmont Hill was not the balm he'd hoped it would be when he went there to paint. He was anxious that he might have lost the chance of his commission at Orange Grove. He wanted to get back there. But, immediately, he needed to go home. Would there be a letter from Louise, telling him what she thought of the idea that Uncle St Luce might be a companion on her voyage?

Michel Jean descended the slopes to the upper reaches of the St Ann's River. He looked for a place to cross into the savannah; a place he knew where the river ran shallow over a shoal of rocks and pebbles. As he crossed, some washerwomen were returning from their long day's work. So often they had walked into his paintings with the cadence of their song: *Doudou, ou abandonné mwe, mwe pan ni peson pou soigné mwe.*

'So, you leaving me, darling. I have no one to care for me, you know,' one of the bolder and older women now called out.

'She tiefing young boys now,' one of the younger girls called out.

He waved, keeping his eyes on the rocks as he crossed the river a little downstream from the women. As he reached the other bank and made his way through the bamboo arches to the savannah, he was interrupted by a familiar voice: 'Good gracious, Cazabon! You're quite lost.' He was trudging along, deep in thought. 'Where've you been old chap? It seems as if I've not seen you for weeks. I simply did not know where to look. Have you been staying out at Orange Grove?'

Michel Jean set down his easel, stool and parasol and leaned up against the bridge, which would take them to Wildman's cottage. 'No, no, no. I . . . Anyway, you exaggerate!'

'Is there new work here, old man?' His friend pointed to the artist's portfolio. 'Something I've not seen? Something you've done today? Can I see it? Let me see!' Wildman was his usual cheerful self. If he would take him to his cottage for a good rum punch that might be just the balm needed to erase his anxiety.

By the time evening fell away into the burning cauldron of a sunset over the gulf, lighting up the poui and immortelle trees on the savannah, the raucous hysteria of the parrots had subsided in the bamboos on the hill above. The two men had finished the punches a butler had offered them on a tray and were now drinking neat nips of rum from the bottle left on the veranda ledge.

Night closed in, loud with the tick and creak of insects and the singing of frogs. The lamps were turned down to prevent the frenzied flapping of moths around the flame. Wildman had his captive audience for the talk he enjoyed the most: art and artists. 'I've got another painting to give you, another copy I've made.' Michel Jean was content to grow slowly slewed by the rum and listen to the young Englishman, who had kicked off his boots and opened his shirt. But he did not give the painting the attention that Wildman craved. With the drowsiness caused by the rum and his melancholic mood, he dozed away.

'Cazabon. It's night. Have you looked at this?'

Michel Jean woke to the heat, the loud stillness. 'Sorry.' He noticed the painting he had not examined. 'I'll look at it later.'

'There's a pool within the grounds. That'll waken you. I'll get a lantern.' Wildman led the way.

Under the broad samaans, a pool fed by a stream from the St Ann's River had been artificially created and paved with blue stone. 'It's for Ping and his guests, but they won't be here tonight.' Wildman threw off his shirt and stepped out of his trousers. Michel Jean was reluctant to follow.

'Come on, Cazabon. It's not that cold.' Wildman caught him in a clench around the neck, and pulled him under the water as schoolboys might do, their bodies tied in a playful wrestle.

'Where've you been? I've missed my tutor.'

'I had the fever. Couldn't even go out to Orange Grove.'

Despite his reluctance, Michel Jean was invigorated by the river water and felt young again, enjoying this camaraderie with Wildman. Images of his childhood with boys in the Cipero River near Corynth mingled with images of Fitzwilliam in the river Lea, boys finding their pleasures with each other.

After their dip in the pool, Michel Jean returned with his friend through the shadows and the bamboos, thinking that they formed a macabre bathing party in the grounds of the governor's residence as they skipped over the sharp stones on the path to the Cottage. There they towelled and had a tot of rum.

'Let me look at that painting. Not the best light. I'll examine it in the morning.'

Michel Jean slept the night in one of the hammocks slung between the pillars of the veranda.

It took him a while to register where he was as he awoke into the tones of subdued, morning voices. It was Excellency and Wildman chatting in that familiar way of cousins.

Excellency had strolled over from the great house to the Cottage, to walk and exercise his dogs. Michel Jean, hidden in the cocoon of the hammock, contemplated his second failure to rise early for his appointment at Orange Grove. He felt that he had now so blotted his copybook that he would not be able to redeem himself.

Hardin Burnley, the hard employer, would certainly not approve of this slovenly progress. He could imagine that on his return from his estates in the southern Naparimas he would want to be greeted by several prospects of his estate. He would want to be boasting about them to Mrs Farquhar and Augusta and showing them off to his friends, Warner and Knox. He could just hear him saying how he couldn't depend upon these coloureds: 'Just like niggers.'

Bleary-eyed and dishevelled, Michel Jean emerged from the hammock to join the men, expecting a chilly reception from Excellency.

'Well, my man. You two have had quite a night.'

'Excuse me, sir. I must apologize.'

'Not at all. I can see that our James has found an equally adventurous type for his japes.'

'Sir, this is most unusual.' Michel Jean was still retrieving items of his clothing that he had hung over the banisters of the veranda.

'I don't believe a word. It's the kind of thing I imagine you artists get up to quite frequently.'

'Sir, I can assure you that this kind of thing won't happen again.'

'Well, it's not the kind of thing to have been found doing when Woodford was governor. Not a risk to be taken, I'm sure.'

Wildman was immediately in peals of laughter. Michel Jean eventually thought it fine to join in. Excellency was shaking his head censoriously in mock-seriousness. 'They say the entire barracks had to be careful on parade days. There was no knowing where it would lead when summoned by Governor Woodford. Came to an early death, you know.'

Michel Jean remembered the gossip about Woodford, the least favourite governor of his youth. He was rumoured to have had a penchant for young officers and would contrive ways to obtain their favours. A view of himself and Wildman naked in the moonlit pool flashed through his mind. His own genuine affection for Fitzwilliam and their youthful passion for beauty tempered his disapproval even of Governor Woodford.

He could see that Excellency and Wildman were exchanging knowing looks, teasing him with their eyes. But you could never tell with these English, he thought. He needed the work. He worried now that he had run the risk of losing both his commissions.

He was heartened when Excellency, in continuing good spirits, was immediately involving him in a project which he was conjuring with his young cousin and would not hear of Michel Jean not joining. 'You must come with us. I need my artist to chart my expeditions.'

Michel Jean protested. He was still commissioned by Hardin Burnley. He had to get back to his work at Orange Grove. 'I'll get a reputation for being unreliable.'

'Nonsense. I'll speak to Burnley. You've had the fever, James tells me. That should clinch it with Burnley. I know he's a stickler, but . . . I'll sort it.' He laughed.

Excellency was enjoying himself and was looking forward, as he then described his plans to Michel Jean, to take time away from the business of governing in exchange for a couple of days of exploration and hunting. 'After all, you have completely neglected my commission and have gone off to Orange Grove without the least excuse,' he said with a twinkle in his eye.

Michel Jean did not always understand English irony, though he could also tease with his Creole *picong*, which left Wildman puzzled, a lingering, quizzical look on his face. Getting the mood of things this morning, Michel Jean replied, looking at Wildman and not at Excellency, which might have seemed impertinent, 'You'll have to have me whipped then.'

Excellency and his cousin were not sure that they should laugh. 'It's okay, gentlemen; there won't be a massacre here this morning, no riot and affray.' The Englishmen were seeing another side of their Creole friend.

'I like the copy,' Michel Jean said, holding up Wildman's recent work. 'Do another. We'll soon get back to our regular sessions.'

When Michel Jean learned that the destination for Excellency's expedition was Mount Tamana, he realized that the Governor had extensive plans. They would be away for more than a morning and an afternoon.

Josie was in the backyard washing clothes at the tub and beating them on the bleaching stones. She was singing a mournful-sounding hymn. 'Josie, how you going?'

At first, she did not turn. Had she not heard him at the gate? 'Jeansie, I've a bone to pick with you, *oui*.' She said this without turning to face him. She continued speaking, in the mood of her hymn – 'Rock of ages . . .' – singing snatches of verses in between what she had to say to him. 'So where you been? You leave here since yesterday morning to go Belmont Hill or some place. Is not as if is Fwance you gone. What cross is this? What Mama and me do you, Jeansie, that you want to worry we so?'

'Josie, what trouble you?'

'I make the effort to fix up things at Orange Grove for you. Because, you know, that housekeeper, Mrs Farquhar, send back a message with the same messenger boy. Like she at least have manners. And a next letter get include, which I didn't know not to open. I thought that was from Mrs Farquhar too. Is lucky. I lucky, *oui*. For when I run out in the street to see if the messenger boy disappear, I find him by the corner drinking a mauby.'

'Josie, what you talking about?'

'Listen to what I say. Is the messenger boy explain to me, how when he leaving with the madam letter. Is so he calling Mrs Farquhar, madam, a young girl call him back. Young girl, is the messenger boy description. She find sheself out in the yard to give him a message sheself to bring to the artist – that is a next word she use, artist . . .'

'Josie, I feel there's a misunderstanding. Let me explain.'

'Monsieur Cazabon, is so the messenger boy refer to you. Is not me that making up the story. Only, the messenger boy add that she good for sheself you know, that red girl. Is so he call she. So when I try to read the message again to get it straight I begin to see what happen. I now know who it is send these messages to you, Monsieur Cazabon, the artist, in Port of Spain.' Josie stopped singing verses from her hymn. It was at this point that she threw down her clothes on the bleaching stones, water soaking all over the front of her dress. She turned to face him. Her voice was mounting to a scream. 'That you could be chasing young girls. That you could have a young girl . . .'

'Josie, let me explain.'

'When I thought you was working hard at Orange Grove to get the work to bring your wife and children to their rightful home.' Josie continued with no intention of halting her attack.

'Josie . . .'

'How old she is, this girl? You not shame? Is not only that you not telling me and I sure you not telling the Madame in Paris you carrying on with Hardin Burnley little piece of black pudding. Or, how I is to really describe the little red-nigger, blood pudding, that have you so mix up in your head?'

'Josie . . .'

'Don't Josie me. I truly wonder what that young girl go feel when she find out the true story of how things stand with Monsieur Cazabon the artist who so want to paint her portrait and give she lesson in the bargain. You must've make she think she is the only one in the world when you tell she you want to paint she portrait. You pinch she bottom yet? You painting she for posterity?' Josie laughed a cruel laugh.

Michel Jean stood and listened. He bowed his head to gather his composure. He had known Josie's temper since she was small. He was not going to interrupt her now.

Mrs Farquhar's letter absolving him from the sin of absence lay open upon the sideboard, while Augusta's lay strewn upon the floor. Josie's outrage had torn it into shreds. It was impossible to fit the jigsaw together. He guessed at some of what Augusta's sentiments and words might have been. But what was it that could have enraged Josie this much? Looking at the shreds of the letter, he could see only conjunctions and prepositions that created tension and anticipation without revelation. A vivid memory evoked Augusta's voice on the savannah: 'I born in August.' He could see her brown-sugar hair and the glint of her green eyes, her smooth ochre skin where her hands fell to her side and her fingers, clutching at her skirts, raised them above her petticoats. This was the portrait he wanted to paint.

Mrs Farquhar had expressed her master's assurance to see him resume his commission as soon as he was in good health. There was no mention of lessons to be taught, and similarly there was no mention of a portrait to be painted. He wondered again what had been in Augusta's letter.

He could still see Josie from the back veranda, scrubbing clothes and putting them out to bleach. He knew that some part of Josie's anger would have been her frustration at not being able to read clearly what was written in Augusta's letter. Which were the words that could have jumped out of that jumble of hieroglyphs? That was when she would have begun to tear the letter to pieces.

As he watched her bent over the tub in the backyard her hymn changed and he heard her soft chant. '*A re! A re! Yemanja! Olomowewe!*' He heard now the words she had learned by heart and had never written down, or seen written down, words learned at the lips of her Yoruba elders, passed down as the prayer to the mother of multitudes, the goddess of the water and the ocean who lived in the rivers. She sang; her arms submerged in the tub of water. He listened again to the words she had brought back with her on those nights when she went with her mother out of the yard at Corynth into the gully to the *palais* in a barrack room to pray to the Orishas. He felt sorry that he had not ever gone there with her, that he had been excluded from the ancient rites of Africa.

He could hear his father's voice even now: 'Come from that window, boy, go and sleep, that is them black people *commesse*.' He remembered looking down at his own skin, so black he could almost not see himself in the night.

'Josie, I need you to understand, girl. Is a mistake,' Michel Jean said, descending into the yard.

She looked up from her scrubbing. 'Tell me.'

'Josie, I am arranging to paint and to teach painting to Mrs Farquhar's daughter. That is all. It not arrange yet. The daughter want it, but the mother and Mr Hardin Burnley not given permission. Nothing going on with this girl. I don't know what she say in the letter.' He held out the scraps of paper. 'But I tell you, nothing going on, Josie. You have to believe me. I need you, Josie. I need . . .'

She looked up to where he was standing on the back veranda looking down at her. She rinsed her arms slowly in a bucket of water and wiped her hands on her apron. 'I coming.' Her words were hardly audible.

'I going away with the Governor. I need . . .'

'I know what you need.'

Her brow and cheeks were wet with her sweat when she came close and held his arms and leaned to kiss him on the cheek. 'I know what you need.'

He smelled the labour in her sweat. He remembered when in the midst of her chores they used to steal away and lose themselves in each other.

'Josie.'

She stopped him from talking. 'You can't afford to get involve with no young girl.'

'Josie, you have to believe me.'

'I working here with Mama for you to get this house ready for your wife and children. I not working here for you to be interfering with no young girl, who think she go get she portrait paint for posterity.'

'That is not what going on.'

'You must think about she too.'

'I do . . .'

'You need to grow up, yes, Jeansie. You have children now. You have a wife and children.' All the time she talked, she was folding clothes and getting what he needed ready for his expedition to Tamana.

'Josie, you don't believe me?'

'I want to believe you. I believe you.' She looked at him strong. 'I believe you, but I warning you.'

The Governor was keen on riding and rearing horses. He had opened a stud farm out on Bande-de-l'Est at Beau Séjour, where he visited from time to time to stay at a cottage he had had built. From there the horses were brought by boat along the coast to Port of Spain, the eastern forests still impassable.

Michel Jean rode alongside Excellency with Wildman bringing up the rear, supervising the porters and the men on the donkeys carrying their hunting equipment and supplies in panniers. Michel Jean had got one of the fellas to strap on his easel and folding stool with his parasol together with the satchel, which Josie had packed with a fresh change of clothes and the particulars of his toilette.

'We'll breakfast at Orange Grove,' Excellency said before breaking into a slow trot. Michel Jean fell forward in his saddle, his heart in his mouth. He then regained his balance. He turned in the saddle to see Excellency smiling. 'You'll have an opportunity to offer your apologies in person to the big man.'

'Yes. But I thought . . .'

'All taken care of, old chap. Irony,' he said, chuckling.

'Oh.'

'Hardin Burnley is back in residence and insisted, when he heard we were coming east, that we should break our journey.'

'Excellent.' Michel Jean tried to sound positive for his own sense of equilibrium. He did not know quite what to expect at Orange Grove after the letters he had received. He would have to play it by ear.

He glanced behind him to see where Wildman was. On the second occasion, his friend waved cheerily from behind with the donkeys. Michel Jean would have preferred to have been riding alongside him.

By the time they had arrived at the front of the house and the Orange Grove grooms were coming forward to take their horses away to be watered, he had fully convinced himself that all would be well. They were met at the front by Mrs Farquhar. She was dressed in her best morning gown to greet the Governor. 'Excellency. Gentlemen. Monsieur Cazabon. Mr Wildman.' She was outdoing her position and her sense of importance in the tone of her greeting. She was the front behind which, he was sure, Hardin Burnley conducted his liaison with Augusta.

Michel Jean felt at that moment that the relationship with Mrs Farquhar and all its details must be entirely known to

Excellency. So that, when everyone was at last gathered in the breakfast room, everything went off without embarrassment. He apologized to the planter for the delay in his commission, owing to his recent illness. The only moment that created some slight nervousness was when Augusta appeared and began to contradict Hardin Burnley on a matter of New York fashion and Mrs Farquhar raised her eyebrows fiercely and shot her daughter a silencing look of disapproval. Michel Jean continued to wonder what had been in the letter. Augusta looked a little glum. At an appropriate moment, he smiled in her direction. She returned his smile, but he felt the questions in her look.

In the end Hardin Burnley was invited to join the hunting party, as half suggested by the gentleman himself. Mrs Farquhar arranged that on their return journey the following day, they would dine and spend the night at Orange Grove.

Wildman, as they cantered down the drive, now riding alongside the Governor and Michel Jean, leaned over and said, 'That young girl is thoroughly agreeable, don't you think?'

In that fleeting moment Michel Jean was irritated by the Englishman's remark. He was again consumed by the present, mounted upon a horse, riding next to the English Governor. With his privilege and white skin, he would not be able to tolerate Wildman making advances. The combination angered him. He would hate to see Augusta fawning over him.

Before the Governor's hunting party realized it, they were out of the heat and into the cool of the forests, an entrance broken into by the beaters, cutlassing down the sharp razor grass. Here they dismounted from their horses and walked them carefully along the narrow track. At first, the climb was slight, but then began to grow steadily steeper. Through a break in the tall silk-cotton trees there was a shaft of light and they glimpsed their destination, the table mountain, Tamana, rising sharply above them. They were now out of the cocoa estates and into the Mora forests with the tall silk-cottons, *bois canots* and the majestic balata, their crimson leaves fallen to the ground.

The Governor was ahead with Hardin Burnley, who was regaling Excellency with the foiled Maroon revolts for which Tamana had already entered the history books. 'Captain Taylor was the man in charge, I think. Three Negroes shot. Twenty-five or twenty-seven captured. That was back in 1819. Quite a business in those days, dealing with these chaps.' Hardin Burnley nodded in the direction of the porters. 'It's taken some time to get it all under control as you can imagine. Civilization is no easy thing.'

'Yes, indeed.' Excellency listened without comment, knowing full well that Hardin Burnley was talking of a time when he was the owner of two hundred slaves at Orange Grove and had fought against the abolitionists and then struggled even further for the maximum compensation at the time of Emancipation. 'A very trying time for us all, that abolition business,' Hardin Burnley continued. 'Nothing to compete with it, except of course the free-coloureds up in arms. Though some of them took it and benefited in the end like all of us.'

The remark did not escape the attention of Michel Jean.

Wildman walked his horse alongside him with one ear cocked to the conversation ahead, always solicitous about Excellency, but more interested to be talking about art and the natural flora and fauna. From time to time he stopped to tether his horse and collect specimens of ferns and leaves, then press them into a notebook as subjects for his drawing exercises, the flora becoming a collection in themselves. 'I'll take these away with me, back home to Norton.'

'Don't hold us up, James,' the Governor called from the front of the party.

'I remember those days so well.' Hardin Burnley was still at it. 'There was the incident at Terre Bouillante. I remember the names of the men. Ralph Short was one of them. Always amused me, these English names that they carried. And there was one called Carlo. Spanish breeding, no doubt.'

Hardin Burnley was away on his own with his reminiscences of a time which Excellency and his administration were trying to distance themselves from, with their own reform programme for the betterment of society; something Michel Jean knew that Hardin Burnley and his friends, Knox and Warner, were not at all in favour of, preferring to keep children illiterate and working the fields from the age of six.

'But we must look ahead. What a paradise! And with this African labour you can imagine the dollars rolling in if we take the opportunity sensibly. We must go with this freedom movement. Captain Stewart had been saying this as far back as '39, just after Emancipation. I'm a liberal man really.'

Smiling at his young cousin just behind, Excellency teased him: 'Not what you thought you were coming to, is it, James? Not quite Norton!' Excellency was trying his best to get the subject off Hardin Burnley's politics.

'Extraordinary!' Wildman shouted from the rear; the noise disturbed the toucans and they flew up into the canopy, transforming the upper branches with their yellow and blue plumage.

'You'll have to be painting this soon, Cazabon,' Excellency called back.

Michel Jean listened. He was one of the party, but he was also detached. He watched the English ahead and the beaters and porters behind.

Hardin Burnley was insistent. 'Had to bring in the treadmill in '23. There were civil servants sent out to chair committees and write voluminous accounts of their finds on the Negro character under slavery and freedom. What an idea! We've seen it all.' Then he was back in the present. 'But now, this indentureship problem. We've got to get it straight. Otherwise we're dashed, I say. The colony is dashed!' It became evident that Hardin Burnley's decision to join the Governor and his party was so he could air his own concerns and bend the Governor's ear on the current problems of the colony.

As they again mounted their horses and as the bush tracks

became wider and clearer, Excellency dropped behind to accompany Michel Jean, leaving Hardin Burnley in the hands of his young secretary. Wildman's enthusiasm for the flora and fauna of the forest soon quelled the flow of Hardin Burnley's historical reminiscences and complaints about labour.

Hardin Burnley was silenced as they sat on the rocks overhanging one of the fast-running streams coming off the heights. Wildman was enjoying the opportunity to show his finds from his botany box and from between the leaves of his notebook. He looked up from his collection at Michel Jean and said, 'That young mulatto, I can't wait to see her again.'

Michel Jean, surprised by the sudden remark, did not reply. Wildman turned back to his collection.

'This is what I want you to capture for me,' Excellency said to Michel Jean, finally escaping Hardin Burnley. 'This mystery in the landscape.'

Michel Jean wondered whether any mystery would be left. The hunting party had crowded the forest. And they had not yet begun the hunting.

'This is what Bates and Gosse write about,' Excellency declared.

Michel Jean nodded uncomprehendingly, not knowing well the writings of the British naturalists and travellers of the Amazon to whom Excellency referred. His smile encouraged the Governor to continue. He wondered whether the Governor was for a moment seeing himself as one of those discoverers of the new world; or, at least, of the beetles which crawled through it. Did he want Michel Jean there to record for posterity this visit to Tamana? 'Watch out for that beetle, Excellency!' he joked.

'Is that a coleoptera?' The Governor stopped to inspect.

'Coleoptera! What's that? I ent know, boss, but watch out for them *bête rouge*, they does sting no arse.' Michel Jean's levity had got away with him and he immediately apologized to Excellency for his language. He put it down to the light-headedness caused by the increasing altitude.

'Glad to see you so relaxed, Cazabon, being yourself. You must realize that we're just ordinary human beings, governors and all the rest of us. When it comes down to it, man, we're as insignificant as that ant you were mentioning just now. Look at all this splendour! What are we?' He stood, awestruck.

'You better watch that ant for true, yes, sir. When he bite you, you go itch and itch and scratch and scratch all night. Watch them *bête rouge*.'

Hardin Burnley was lecturing Wildman. 'Take advantage of your position. Acquire an estate and make your fortune in sugar before the bottom completely falls out of it. What's a young man like yourself doing with all this frippery?' he said, pointing at Wildman's botany box and notebooks. 'This is lady's stuff.'

'How can we stop him?' Excellency suddenly blurted out. Hardin Burnley was so absorbed in his own discourse that he didn't hear the outburst.

Michel Jean observed the English. If Louise were here she would save him from these thoughts about white people and their ways. 'Just be charming, sweetheart.' When his mother first heard about Louise in one of his letters, she wrote back to say, 'Thank God for Louise!' Ironically, his mother thought that a white Frenchwoman would be good for her son and his advancement. Had she fully understood the changes coming in an English colony?

Wildman finally managed to escape the tyranny of Hardin Burnley by stripping down to his underclothes and plunging into a river-pool they had come upon. 'Irrepressible,' the Governor said, laughing, coming up behind Michel Jean, who was staring at Wildman's white body. A shaft of sunlight, piercing the canopy above, lit his blond hair, sleek and seemingly painted onto his pate as he came up to breathe, and then tousled as he shook his head, freeing his locks of water.

'Come on in,' Wildman shouted.

The carriers also wanted to cool off in the pool and, before anyone could object, they too were slaking their thirst and diving beneath the cascade which fell about ten foot from the rocks above.

'Look at these wretches,' Hardin Burnley grumbled. 'And that silly young man cavorting with them.'

After a change of shirts and refreshed by the plunge into the cool water, they were on the move again. As they began to climb more steadily, they caught a glimpse through a break in the trees of the plain, the Aripo savannah and the mountains of the northern cordillera with the heights of El Cerro del Aripo, before the horses moved on steadily.

'I can see, lad, that you have attractions at Orange Grove other than matters of perspective,' said Excellency, a twinkle in his eye. Now he was Ping, not Excellency.

Michel Jean noted Excellency's intuition into Wildman's interest in Augusta. He thought back to Wildman's repeated mention of the girl since leaving Orange Grove.

They were nearing the summit of the table mountain. The path had flattened out and they were travelling along a narrow ridge. They walked the horses in single file, the guides having gone ahead to clear the path. The hunting lodge was near to one of the missions the Capuchin monks had built in the interior of the central cordillera. It was not as if they were journeying into a real wilderness. It had already been conquered and converted. They were walking in the footsteps of conquerors and conquered. Cross and sword had both had their way with the original Amerindians. And now, an English governor had brought an artist to record his progress through the colony.

Tamana was estimated to be approximately one thousand feet above sea level. Whether it was the heat or in some part the increased altitude, Wildman was elated. He could not stop talking, and the rest of the party recognized a trance-like quality in the descriptions the young man gave of his first journey into the tropical forests. As they sat, exhausted by the last climb from the ridge to the summit, they slaked their thirst from their goatskin bottles. 'You're drunk with beauty, James?' the Governor asked, concerned for his cousin.

'Absolutely. Have you seen the tree ferns, like the ones in the conservatory at Norton? And the creepers! Some of the flowers are almost ornithological. I nearly took one for a bird with its bright plumage.'

'My dear James. It's the sun. They say the moon makes one mad. But in your case . . . here, have a drink of water.'

They had at last arrived at the hunting lodge. The porters assisted in the provision of a meal, cooked on coal-pots and served in the lodge.

After resting in the hammocks slung to the rafters and swinging between the tree pillars of the rustic lodge, preparations for the hunt began with the gathering of the dogs and the cleaning of the guns.

Michel Jean let the men get on with their hunt while he laid out his paints and stayed within the shade of the lodge to capture its interior with the board tables, benches, the carat screen and the rafters of saplings. There was a roof of more carat palm leaves, laid in the traditional way to create the modest *ajoupa* of country people. This was something to present at Belmont, something Excellency would want to show to his family and guests when he went back home.

The alarm of intermittent gunshot echoing through the forest and dogs barking told him that the hunt was on.

The afternoon had moved on; the sun was now lighting the entrance to the lodge. The yelping dogs heralded the returning party. Everyone was excited by the wild pig. Quenk and wild ducks were laid out on the earthen floor. The local fellas were impressed by the English hunters. The fire was being laid and lit for the roasting of the wild pig. Michel Jean sketched furiously to capture the atmosphere.

Strenuous physical activity had silenced Hardin Burnley's discourses on history and Negro character. He had stopped reacting to Wildman's visionary account of the flora and fauna. The soft patter of rain on the roof soothed everyone's nerves, as the sun continued to shine brightly through the clouds, expressing a local myth that the contest between sun and rain was God and the devil doing battle.

The Capuchin Prior suggested a late afternoon walk to Cedar Point. Excellency strode forward to the head of the party, to the very edge of the plateau, clearly recognizing some aspect of the topography that he began to explain to Hardin Burnley. 'There, what's it called? El Cerro del Aripo?'

'Indeed, indeed.' The old man was puffed after the walk, not having rested sufficiently from the trek and the hunt. The old bull, Michel Jean thought, watching him clambering to the very edge. A childish thought had him falling over. Maybe someone might just push him. That might be the end of his commission. He sketched without stopping, his mind on fire with frustrations as he contemplated his role here and his true acceptance in this company, with whom he had lost patience.

Wildman stood behind his cousin, his enthusiasm for the view overwhelming him as the savannah of Aripo and the Caroni plain were lit by the setting sun. 'We're lucky to catch it. The sunsets are so brief. In fifteen minutes the sun itself will dip away beneath the horizon. Look . . .' He was looking back over his shoulder, hoping to catch Michel Jean's eye, seeking confirmation that his perceptions were accurate. 'See, where there was light, there is now shadow. See the shadows move and fill the plain.'

'I've never seen anything like this,' Excellency explained. 'Not tropical. Extraordinary to feel that we're practically on the equator. Seen the Massif Central, seen the Alps coming out of winter into spring. Extraordinary thing at this moment to think of chasms of snow and ice, glaciers on the move.'

'See the Caroni. That's it, isn't it, Cazabon?' Wildman asked, without turning this time. The question lost itself in the forest. Michel Jean did not look up, but kept sketching. He ignored Wildman. What these sketches would become in his studio he did not know. One of the porters had been urged to sit next to the Governor, so that he could ask him questions. The man did his best, pointing out places of interest.

As they stood and sat and watched, and as Michel Jean observed and sketched, the sunset continued to light the landscape as the river curled its muddy way to the delta and swamp, which were lost in haze and the bright line of white light that stretched across the horizon.

In front of Michel Jean, the porters ignored what the gentlemen were gazing at and instead relaxed, now that they were no longer being asked to run and fetch. They were instinctually part of it all; the gentlemen were visitors. The English brought memories of what they had read and what others had seen and described to bear on what they saw.

It was inevitably Wildman, speaking from memory and from the literature of an earlier time, read in the library at Norton and learned for his tutor in the schoolroom, who exclaimed, 'Wasn't it Raleigh, Ping? He said . . . I remember memorizing it once. Let me see. Something about birds and their colours. I remember words, but not sentences. Carnation, crimson, orange. Yes, tawny, purple, green . . . I forget . . . yes . . . and something else about rowing, the deer coming down to feed by the river. That might've been the Caroni or the Orinoco. They thought they were on their way to El Dorado.'

Michel Jean listened to the conversation without commenting. He felt that he would rather be talking to the carriers and porters sitting in front of him, who were cleaning their guns, oblivious of the talk. He caught the foliage in the foreground and drew in the tall *bois canot* that was cantilevered over the cliff. Vision was growing dimmer as they watched the sudden green flash, as the sun dipped beneath the horizon leaving only the dying embers of its furnace.

Night closed in as they picked their way back to the lodge. The porters had kept the fire going as the wild pig was roasted. The bush started up its orchestra: insects, frogs, bats, falling fruit, the crash of a branch and, in the far distance, the tinkling sound of water over rocks and gravel as of many quiet bells chiming. They ate in silence. From the valleys beneath them, Yoruba drumming told them that they were not alone in this world. There was a place to return to the following day.

As the fires burned down and the darkness was complete, the planets hung low and bright. Mars, Jupiter, Venus and Mercury were picked out clearly from the summit of the mountain. Inside the lodge, the Governor, Wildman and Hardin Burnley slept in their hammocks, the porters and beaters on the ground.

Michel Jean lay in his own hammock, which he had slung near the entrance. While he watched the swoop of bats and caught a glimpse of the great stars in the night sky, he reflected on what the expedition had taught him about where he stood in relation to his patron and about his own role as recorder of events. It was not only the wonder of the landscape that was uppermost in his mind while he painted, but the figures who traversed that landscape, making and leaving their mark. He had sketched in a portrait of himself sitting beneath the silk-cotton tree, the artist at his work, in the last painting of the Governor. He was master of all he surveyed, looking out over the savannahs towards the mountains and the gulf. But there, at the edge, was himself, the artist, the recorder, without whom this moment would not be known or remembered, preserving the young porter leaning in and pointing, instructing the Governor on what he was looking at.

He wanted to share this moment with Louise.

The following morning the party set out on the return journey to Orange Grove.

Augusta wore red taffeta that evening; a bustle to accentuate her already pronounced posterior. She was well corseted. Her frock was deeply cut, so that her bosoms were held to brim full. It was a miracle of New York couture that they did not spring out of their constriction and surprise Wildman, whom Michel Jean could see was unable to take his eyes off her. Could he stand aside and let Wildman have his way?

Burnley and the Governor sat in the drawing room while a liveried footman brought Cazabon and Wildman their punches on the veranda. Augusta had not kept them waiting. She had made sure she was present at the strategic moment to be able to lift the glasses off the tray and hand them to each gentleman at the same time, so showing no favours to one rather than to the other. 'There you are, gentlemen; to your good health.' She gaily sipped a little punch from each glass before handing it to them.

Michel Jean wondered if she would indicate that she remembered and still valued their secret, previous acquaintance; she made such an effort not to distinguish between himself and Wildman. What was in her letter that he could not imagine? Of course, not distinguishing between them was a great compliment. Was she trying not to favour a white man over a free-coloured? But she might very well have been trained to respect the white Englishman the most. She dallied and flitted and flirted with each of them in turn. The rum was working its own magic with the heat of the night.

Wildman was clearly enjoying Augusta's attentions and perhaps even enjoying that she was being playful with each of them. Michel Jean knew this might suit his sense of camaraderie; the liberality of mind which he had noticed was characteristic of himself and Excellency. But he wondered if tonight it was a strategy to foil him.

Wildman would be enthusiastic about wenching, he thought. Augusta's language of the eyes and the touch of her fingers, as she twirled her fan, spoke to Wildman. She let herself almost touch Wildman's arm while turning, spinning and hardly standing still for a moment, creating a continual rustle of her taffeta in her restlessness. Perhaps her favours were more bestowed upon the Englishman than upon himself, Michel Jean now thought.

'Mr Wildman . . .!' Augusta never seemed to get beyond his name in a continual ecstatic series of exclamations. 'Mr Wildman! Mr Wildman!' She was carried away by the 'wild' in Wildman, as if she wanted him to *be* that wild man at this moment.

Michel Jean rescued her from her pitch of over-excitement. Wildman seemed too overcome with her visual charm and her vivaciousness to help her out with her conversation.

'Mr Wildman and myself have been hunting!'

'Hunting!' Augusta almost screamed with laughter.

Hardin Burnley, at the other end of the room, talking to the Governor, shot Mrs Farquhar a look, as much as to say: Get that daughter of yours under control or take her away from those young gentlemen.

Mrs Farquhar's look did little to silence the girl. Michel Jean, observing the drama of eyes between planter and housekeeper, was sure that Augusta had noticed her mother's cautionary look but decided to ignore it, continuing with, 'Hunting! I thought it was painting you was doing in the mountains. You not painting?' The last piece of rhetoric had an accusatory tone and, to Michel Jean, it sounded like a declaration of intimacy.

Wildman and himself looked at each other and smiled. But he could see that Wildman was asking himself, What has Cazabon been up to with this girl? He had not mentioned to his friend that they had had a previous acquaintance. Michel Jean tried to placate Augusta's accusation and Wildman's interrogation by exclaiming, 'Look at the fireflies!' They all stared at the off and on flicker of the fireflies out on the lawn, where at that moment Michel Jean wished to be alone with Augusta.

'Yes, they pretty, *oui*.'

'Indeed,' Wildman underlined.

'Are they new to you, Mr Wildman?' Augusta positioned herself so that she could put her arm through Wildman's to gain some assistance in her descent from the veranda to the bougainvillaea arbour.

'Yes. You could say so, though I have in fact observed this flickering candlelight from the window of my cottage in the grounds at St Ann's. It was on my first night in the colony. I was very tired after the voyage. I wondered at the arrival of this large group of people at my window with lighted torches – a kind of illusion, a *trompe l'oeil*.'

Michel Jean could see that Wildman had lost Augusta with his description. The punch must have gone to his head because he continued to lose her further with another story.

'Then it came back to me that I had read of this phenomenon in one of the early sixteenth-century travellers to the island. It was in a volume in my grandfather's library in the house at Norton in Kent. Yes, I think it was indeed Robert Dudley or his notary, a Mr Wyatt, who wrote of the young nobleman, the illegitimate son of the Earl of Leicester . . .' Wildman trailed off as he realized that Augusta's attention had indeed strayed.

'Is that where you come from, Kent?' she said, trying to respond.

'Absolutely.'

Michel Jean could see that, despite the long stories, Wildman had caught Augusta's imagination. He was showing off his English heritage. But, at the same time, he could see the annoyance of Hardin Burnley, who at that moment was looking out onto the veranda, irritated, no doubt, by Wildman's indulgence in rum. He did seem to be getting drunk. That would not help his conquest of Augusta, Michel Jean thought.

'But I must continue with my story . . .'

Augusta supped on every word like a colibri sucks the nectar from a flower. She hovered in her taffeta like that hummingbird, sharing the iridescence of the fluttering jewel. In his excitement, Wildman had forgotten the tale of the fireflies that had surprised the early travellers in search of El Dorado.

He then began on another story. This did not seem to matter to Augusta, who seemed more entranced by his voice than by what he actually said. 'He, that is, Sir Robert Dudley, was the first man to teach a dog to sit in order to catch a partridge,' Wildman concluded nervously, laughing at his own memory of an absurd tale.

What was Wildman talking about, dogs and partridges? 'James!' Michel Jean, lighting himself a cigarette, which itself burned like a firefly in the darkness, leaned over and whispered in his ear a word of caution concerning rum punches. Augusta looked lost. Wildman was drunk.

'No, I must tell you.' He was not to be deterred from continuing. 'This is not about dogs and partridges, which I dare say is a little off the point, though relevant to Robert Dudley. This one is about fireflies, cicindela, or the great firefly *Fulgora phosphorea*. This last one lights up into azure. It has a crimson ruby upon its abdomen. A wonderful contrast. It's able to turn these lights off and on as we can see. Probably, what we are seeing are the cicindela, candle-flies, which offer, as we see, "transitory scintillations", as the historian Mr Joseph tells us is their habit.'

'The historian Mr Joseph, indeed! You really have been a secret student, James, when I thought you were indolent, except in respect of your painting, of course. What else goes on at your cottage?' Michel Jean said, smiling at Augusta, including her with the embrace of his eyes.

'Don't laugh. What I tell is true.'

'You know so much about things I never even think about,' Augusta responded. 'I catch them when I was a little girl and put them in a glass jar. Like a lamp.' She had moved closer to Wildman to say this.

'Well, there you go. I read by a large number of them I collected once. Yes, in a jar, just the thing. The footman had not lit the lamps in the cottage that evening.'

'James, you're full of the most extraordinary stories, that I wonder Miss Augusta has not fallen entirely for your ardour.' Michel Jean packed another cigarette.

'For his ardour? He tells nice stories nicely.'

'Indeed, he does.' Michel Jean pretended to agree.

'Do you have any stories, Monsieur Cazabon?' Augusta asked teasingly, so that Michel Jean could see that more was going on in that head of hers than she had first revealed.

'I paint pictures.' He looked at her in her flame dress brightened by the flambeaux that burned as torches held in bamboo stakes.

There was a lull in the conversation and they could hear drumming coming from the barrack rooms down in the estate yard. Michel Jean would have liked to escort Augusta into the darkness. He shuffled his feet to the tempo of the drums.

Wildman had replenished his drink once more. He was now more than ever inspired to continue with his stories of fireflies, which he had read about in Mr Joseph's, the Scotsman's, recent history.

'Apparently a Spanish lady in Port of Spain, at carnival time, had bedecked herself in puckered . . . I think that's the right word – finest gauze. Between these puckers she had inserted the great fireflies. As you can imagine, the phosphoric scintillations were remarkable. Azure, red. The lady wore this dress as a masquerade at one of the great houses. Everyone else was so amazed that they took off their masks and gaped in awe at the creation. What Mr Joseph says, is that all the gems of Golconda could not compare with such an appearance. Golconda! What a thought!'

'What a story! I could listen to you . . . for ever!'

Michel Jean coughed, interrupting Augusta's exclamation, then added, 'James, you have surpassed yourself.' For ever, he thought, dismayed. Had Wildman won her?

'But what about the fireflies? What happened to them after the carnival?' Augusta was enthralled.

'Excellent question. Just what I was coming to in conclusion. Another lady informed me that when the dress was taken apart and the insects given their liberty, none of the fireflies had died. They simply flew off, lighting up the darkness.'

'Their liberty . . .' Augusta echoed Wildman. 'Liberty. I love that word. I learn that word from my father. Liberty!'

'From your father? Who is your father?' Wildman asked.

'He is Mr Farquhar from Tacarigua. He owns a shop.'

'Indeed, a shop?' Wildman arched his brows. Michel Jean had by now understood these signs, insinuations of understatement, in the tones of the English. He could guess what was going through Wildman's mind at the thought of Augusta and her father, the owner of a shop. Leave her alone, Wildman, he thought. Don't begin what you don't intend to honour.

'Yes.' Augusta looked vulnerable to Michel Jean, as if she needed his help. He was not sure what her face said, but he knew that he understood her predicament more than Wildman could imagine. Though, he did wonder if Norton Hall in Kent might not be too different from Orange Grove in the attitudes of the manor to the village.

In the difficult hiatus, Wildman, alluding to the drumming in the distance, suggested, 'Should we go, later, to see the Negro dancers?'

At that moment, the Governor called for Wildman upon some business, thus giving Michel Jean the opportunity he had been longing for. Alone with Augusta at last, Michel Jean hoped to return to the mood of the acquaintance they had begun in the pasture when he had painted her before he was ill.

No sooner had Wildman disappeared with Excellency and the big man of Orange Grove into the recesses of the drawing room for their conference than Augusta detained a passing footman, inviting Michel Jean to replenish his glass, and herself to be poured some more planter's punch. He noticed that she had a way of managing this complicated task while keeping her poise and urging him into the darker shadows of the veranda. Her hands moved as she talked; her eyes sparkled. Her fingers touched his fingers where they clasped his glass in the wet condensation of the iced drink.

'Master has ice delivered to the house each day. Mr D. P. Cotton's man brings it out from Port of Spain. The cargoes of ice come from Boston.'

'Indeed.' He wondered that she knew so much about the trade.

'Isn't it just wonderful to have ice,' she exclaimed, licking the wetness on her fingers while drinking her punch and looking up at him with her large green eyes; checking her elocution and grammar when there was less reason to do so, now that it was just the two of them and there was greater freedom for the patois. 'Ice, ice, ice, I just love the idea of it!'

'Ice?' He was taken aback by this ecstatic observation. He did not want to talk about the wonders of ice.

'Master get a refrigerator, you know. Mama beg him for one since Mr Cotton import refrigerators to keep the ice from melting and also to store desserts,' she concluded with delight.

Michel Jean had been told of the excitement in Port of Spain. It had become quite a story, what with the expectation which had built up before the arrival of Captain McCurdy on his brig, *New England*, from Boston. But all of this factual information about ice was delaying the conversation he wanted to have.

'And tonight we going to have ice cream. I tell Mama we have to have it. And Master say I must have it if that is what I want.'

'I see.'

'Because we can keep that in the refrigerator now.'

'I see.'

'You like ice cream?'

'Pardon?' He had lost her. They were not going to have their intimate conversation about her lessons and her portrait.

As Augusta flowed on, her fingers extracted some stray bit of nutmeg sprinkled upon the surface of the punch that had got stuck to her lip. This extraction she made into a gesture of sophistication, licking her lips with the tip of her tongue while flicking the erring splinter of nutmeg away from her into the darkness. Michel Jean fell for her gesture, for the fragrance of her perfume, for the texture of her taffeta. There was that scent which was her particular odour. Each little glancing touch of her fingers and twinkle of her eyes was lit by the light of the fireflies and the torches along the arbour. All the while he felt that she wanted to say something more, but words did not come, only her excitable breathing, the gentle undulation of her breasts as she manoeuvred him even further away from the earshot of footmen and the servants, who were now putting the finishing touches to the dining room and lighting the candelabra at the centre of the table.

At last, the moment arrived for words. 'So hot! I can hardly breathe,' she exhaled, the sweet rum and nutmeg on her breath;

the nectar of Demerara, which he sucked in with his own breath. They were that close, without any single part of her touching him, but certainly poised to do so. Never, he thought, was denial so sweet. She was seducing him with delay and anticipation. Not only did her chest undulate, but her lungs, held in, corseted and laced in by those fine criss-crossings of ribbon down her back, gasped again and again in almost imperceptible inhalations for their own breath of liberty, as the pulsing fireflies in Wildman's story of the Spanish lady did in their efforts to escape their trap of gauze.

'Yes.' His glass sweated in his hand, the moisture trickling over his fingers. 'Yes.' He slaked his thirst. 'Yes, you must have some air.' He now manoeuvred her to the balustrade where she could lean backwards.

'Such a long and tiring day,' she sighed.

At first he did not understand, imagining that she would have had the whole day at her leisure to choose and choose again which frock she was to wear that night, and then to rest in the afternoon and spend the time with her toilette: baths, towellings, lotions and creams; intimacies which made his mind spin with desire to know them. He had not thought that all those preparations could be exhausting for her. How did she imagine what she was preparing herself for? Did she ever feel that she was quite ready to present herself? Yes, he supposed, the waiting for the performance would make the day long, and the pent-up emotion would make it tiring.

His day, too, had been long and exhausting. There had been the trek back from Tamana, his emotions used up with the business for Excellency. Judging his palette, that had sapped him; trying to fully understand the light as he painted his sense of the sublime. Their tasks for their respective masters were so different; their tasks for themselves such a contrast.

They had both gone beyond their endurance and found that in the seclusion of the darkness they revealed more than in the light. This time her fingertips did rest upon his neck and on his cheek and were not the fleeting glances that they had been. This time he allowed himself to suck her breath into his by placing his lips upon hers.

She had chosen him rather than the Englishman.

A footman's footsteps drew them apart for an instant. With the following silence, they were linked even more passionately than before with their embraces. 'I've not stopped thinking of you,' he said, between longer and longer kisses. She did not answer, unable to catch her breath. A nightjar's trill startled them into consciousness. At that moment dinner was announced and they had to leave the darkness to the fireflies, and enter the light and the presence of the full company of men and her mother.

'Miss Augusta, my dear, you will sit next to your mother. Harris, you can give us the honour of taking the head at the other end. Mrs Farquhar at your right will look after you. The two gentlemen can resume each other's company on this side. Monsieur Cazabon, we have not spoken for a while about my commission, so you can sit next to me. Wildman, you can tell the ladies about your pressed flowers.'

The company laughed and Wildman blushed. Michel Jean gave him a reassuring smile, hoping that the effect of the rum punches had worn off somewhat.

Michel Jean gave an account of his progress to Hardin Burnley. He apologized again for the time lost due to his illness.

'We'll hang them along the walls of the drawing room. Right here in the other room. You'll come and hang them yourself. And, of course, I will require them as prints in an actual album. I understand you are doing this work now.'

'Yes, sir. Lithographs?'

'Excellent. So you can do it for me. These lithographs. My wife tells me that they are quite the fashion in Paris and London.'

'Very well, sir.' Michel Jean thought of his father's descriptions as he spoke to the big man. He seemed to take his own power so casually. Perhaps that was how it was with power.

'Of course, you'll be well paid.' He lowered his voice and leaned in towards Michel Jean, as if he was hatching a conspiracy. Then he spoke across the length of the table to the Governor. 'You heard of these, er . . . what's it, lithographs, Harris?'

'I beg your pardon, William, I'm so taken up here with the account the ladies are giving me of the decoration of your wonderful house.'

'They'll spend all my money if I let them.'

'Master. You know that not true.' Augusta spoke to him more like a daughter talking to a father, than a mistress talking to her lover. Mrs Farquhar restrained her from talking further, otherwise there was no knowing what revelations Augusta might make.

'Harris, lithographs? Is that what Monsieur Cazabon is doing for you? I won't have him doing things for you and not for me.'

'Well, he's completely deserted me since your commission. Yes, they're a wonderful idea, those albums. I want watercolours and oils. I'll give him a free hand. Something to take back to Belmont to hang in the old house, so that I can remember my time here.'

'Nonsense. You're not off already, are you? I know this indentureship trouble is a spot of bother. You'll get it right.'

Excellency was not keen to get into the politics of the colony again and looked glad to be rescued by Mrs Farquhar.

'Maybe, sir, yourself or Monsieur Cazabon,' Mrs Farquhar said, speaking to Lord Harris, 'might explain lithography?' This was Mrs Farquhar's longest speech to the table. Hardin Burnley continued with his hors d'oeuvre of *petits pâtés à la pâtissière*; this speciality being served in the Governor's honour. Hardin Burnley was not usually given to entertain with rich, lavish meals at Orange Grove.

'Maybe the artist himself should do the honours. Cazabon?' Excellency smiled warmly at Michel Jean, bringing in his protégé.

Michel Jean agreed. He caught Augusta's eye. She was radiant at the prospect of hearing him speak to the company. 'Well, I'm not sure, madam, how much you're acquainted with the art of lithography, so excuse me if I prolong the explanation. You must stop me when you will, if you tire of my description.'

'You go straight ahead, young man. You can be sure they know nothing,' Hardin Burnley boomed.

'I'm sure . . .'

'No, you go straight ahead.'

'Well.' Michel Jean faltered. 'It's a wonderful process, madam.' He smiled charmingly at Mrs Farquhar, both because this was the way to her daughter's heart, but also feeling aggrieved for her because of Hardin Burnley's bullying manner. 'As I was saying . . .'

The rest of the company got on with the entrée of *pieds d'agneau farcis*. Wildman was too drunk to eat. He had folded his knife and fork and looked forlorn.

'The word itself is instructive. *Lithos*, which means stone in Greek, and *graphos* of course means one who draws.' He smiled nervously at Augusta and Wildman. 'Thus, a lithographer is one who draws on stone.'

'Draws on stone!' Augusta echoed him.

'Yes. The lithographer will draw with greasy chalks and inks. The best stone is limestone from Bavaria. When the stone is damp, printing ink can be rolled onto the drawing. But the ink does not take where the stone has not been drawn on. This way you can get the texture of the pen-line or grain of the stone on your paper. But I'm not the lithographer. I prepare drawings, paintings for him to copy onto stone with pens, needles and even brushes.'

'I see.' Mrs Farquhar and Augusta nodded at the same time. Michel Jean wondered if they did see.

'It's a way of getting several copies of the same painting.'

'Who will be your lithographer, Cazabon?' Excellency asked.

'I hope to get the best. I know of Levilly and Ciceri. Lemercier or Geny-Gros will do the printing. But of course we're a long way away. I have to finish the work here and then return to Paris.'

'You see, Harris. These young free-coloureds have all the freedoms which they ever wanted.'

An awkward silence fell upon the table for a moment.

But, as Michel Jean was talking of having to go to Paris, Augusta listened attentively, and the look on her face became less vivacious. Michel Jean glimpsed for the first time what a sad little creature she was in this house of Hardin Burnley's, offered up as the mistress of the gentleman by her mother. This was his conclusion. He could hear her saying the word 'Liberty'; the word she had been taught by her father. Was he intent upon entrapping her for himself, while she was pursuing her freedom in trying to form an attachment to him?

Later that evening, alone in his room, he continued to see her face and its bemused, sad expression as he talked of his plans to go to Paris.

The night ticked with the creak of insects and the call of the jumbie bird. A cool breeze came off the hills and the valleys to the north, bringing in the music of the frogs. Michel Jean lay awake, alert to every sound, until he heard nimble footsteps in the corridor and a gentle tap at his door. '*Monsieur*.' It was Augusta's inimitable voice, whispering '*Monsieur*', as she entered his room and slipped into his bed.

The Governor's party prepared to return to Port of Spain early the following morning. Breakfast had been laid out in the dining room from six o'clock. Wildman was reluctant to leave. Michel Jean was staying on to continue his work for Hardin Burnley.

'I expect there is more than one fortune for you to win here,' Wildman said in a disappointed tone.

Michel Jean guessed that his friend felt that he had not been the one to win Augusta's favours. He kept her visit to his room a secret, leaving Wildman to continue guessing at the truth of his own remark. He himself felt rotten and ashamed that he had not acted more responsibly.

'I must keep to my painting,' Michel Jean answered, implying that his fortune was what he hoped to be paid for his paintings. Augusta was not for sale. What, poor girl, was she expecting for her favours? He was concerned about how he would face her in the light of day. She had escaped from his bed in the darkness before the first glimmers of dawn; the screech owl with its alarm beneath the window.

He could still smell her. He did not want to wonder about where she had gone to when she left his room. He had listened to her retreating footsteps down the corridor, inhaling again her scent, which seemed to permeate the room. It was as if she had left some part of herself there in the bed with him. He had wondered if she had left him some garment, some small token of her sex tucked beneath the pillows. He had pressed his face into the sheets and conjured her. Emancipation. Was this her liberty? His mind turned sour with the thought. He was alarmed at what they had done, not just in the house of the planter, but that he had in the end allowed his obsession to become a liaison. What could their promises mean? What had he promised?

Not only did his guilt conjure Louise and his children, but also the thought that he would have to face Josie's inquisition when he returned to Port of Spain. She would be looking out for any changes in him after his stay at Orange Grove, well aware of his weaknesses. Maybe he should have left the way open to Wildman, not allowed the rum and the threat he perceived to his manhood get the better of him. Wildman would not offer her anything. Augusta was the one who was seeking her fortune. How could he blame her for where she sought it?

From the distance of his position in the far pasture he had a view of the entire estate. While he painted he forgot his guilt and let his mind work with his composition and the selection for his palette. Whenever he began a new painting, his mind returned to times when he was first learning to paint. That morning he was starting at the Ecole des Beaux-Arts, laying out a palette for a different kind of light. He was reminded of when he had ventured out into what had felt like a funereal city as he discovered Père Lachaise and Montparnasse. But then he had realized that the city was a delicious monster. Though he had been still racked by the Atlantic passage, his desire drew him forth, a *flâneur* from the Antilles. '*Le petit marmoset*,' was how the concierge saw him. Working again he remembers Paris, its allure, but also his isolation and the remark by the concierge.

The new prospect of Hardin Burnley's estate was almost finished: the chimney of the *usine*, the sheds of the estate yard, the whitewashed barrack rooms for his newly imported labourers from Calcutta. Michel Jean drew what he was asked to draw. He painted what he had been commissioned to paint. His intention was his patron's, a place where the planter and his labourers were at harmony. His composition softened the divisions, allowing the pastures and cane fields to merge with the savannahs and wild foothills of the steep mountains, giving a sense of expanse and freedom.

But he secreted his own secret into the hazy portrait of a girl who sat beneath a parasol beneath a samaan tree, her skirts gathered around her like the petals of a full hibiscus. She belonged in the commissioned painting. She had been commissioned to perform her duty and for that she had left him in the darkness to enter the bed of her master. Would anyone understand his irony? It was intended as a secret; not even Wildman would find it hidden in the rules of the genre. Hardin Burnley would be glad that he could boast to people like Harris and those liberal British, who came out to the colony travelling after Emancipation, that his estate represented stability. He would point out the benign figures. He would not credit them with looking beneath the surface for the harshness of his estate, which had been softened by the suggestion of a young girl placed so delicately in a world the planter had described as Barbizon, a tropical Fontainebleau. Unbeknown to him, Augusta was the gypsy of his tropical estate.

More and more Michel Jean adopted the sarcasm of his father about these white planters. He could hear him still on the veranda at Corynth. 'Watch that man. He will have anything he wants. He has the power.' He would take their money and they could hang his art on their walls, fold it in their albums. But he liked to imagine that sometime, somewhere, someone would look at the gypsy girl and wonder about her. He could hear Barnaby quoting Mr Constable: 'We see nothing until we truly understand it.' Let them see their nothing, their houses and their barrack rooms, their railings and their one hundred and one windows.

He painted furiously now, using his pen to incise the blasted railings in even more detail. He remembered Hardin Burnley's boast as he walked him about his estate, more concerned then with the importance of the imported iron railings from Glasgow than his imported labour from Calcutta. He had almost had one of his fabled tantrums; he was notorious for his temper. 'If the niggers won't work we can transport the coolies to take their place. Let them walk off my estate. I can do without them.'

Michel Jean had tried not to listen, so he would not have to engage or pretend to show agreement. Instead, he had bent to the ground to inspect the pink, fluffy flowers of the ti-marie; the ground mimosa under their feet; her leaves closing to the crush of a foot or the touch of a finger. The flowers and leaves knew how to protect themselves. It was more than this whole land could do to save itself. The breezy air contradicted the harshness of the history. The gentle, waving palms denied the violence. The visual surprise, the daily epiphany of radiance, assuaged the brutality with which people had dealt with each other. The cruel contrasts filled him with a rage that resulted in him beginning another painting, almost as soon as he had finished the view he was working on. He put it aside on the grass, still wet with the fresh paint. The red of the girl's skirt bled a little into the colour of the foreground, as wet as the perspiration which ran down his arms and back and trickled along the furrows of his brow. He had taken off his shirt and now painted bareback. Then he saw her walking across the fields into her master's prospect.

'So, you taking a stroll in this hot sun?' He pulled his shirt back on, leaving it to hang loosely.

Augusta looked at him in a sulking way. Then he noticed the tears in her eyes. He stopped painting and wiped the tears from her cheeks with his rag that smelled of turpentine. His fingers were engrained with paint. The colours of his palette smudged her cheeks. 'I really painting you now,' he said, laughing a little.

He tried to wipe off the paint, but it only made it worse as it mixed with her tears. 'We go have to go by the ravine so you can wash your face.'

'You too full of sweet-talk, you know.'

'Augusta, what happen?'

'You asking me what happen? Like you don't know what does take place in the darkness? Is only light you know? I does hear you talking to yourself about the light all the time. Like some mad man talking to himself. You think I stupid?'

'Augusta, I'm sorry. I should've . . . Who you talking 'bout, your mother?' He had never heard her talk this way before.

'You think it easy in that house?'

He saw the pain in her face.

'You should paint darkness, then maybe you go understand darkness.' As she spoke to him, she pointed with her finger, as if instructing a child.

He looked at her, astonished at the profundity of her statement. He had not credited the light-headed, frolicking, flirtatious Augusta with her love of New York frocks and bright ribbons with such an insight. 'No, I don't think it easy.' He saw what he did not like to imagine, the old ram-goat Burnley with his sweet girl. 'No, I don't think it easy,' he said again. He wanted to hug her up right there. He wanted to protect her.

'I hear you, you know,' she said.

He put some spit on his finger to rub off the paint on her face. 'Come, let we go by the ravine.'

'Take me in some gully and rape me.'

'Augusta! What happen? Someone do you something?' Then he noticed that her dress had been torn.

'Nobody ever touch me before. Nobody ever so bold as to touch me on this estate before. One slap they go get. But like since Master artist come to paint pictures everybody think they have permission to touch me.'

'Augusta? Who touch you?' He went to draw her close to him.

'Don't you even touch me, yourself. You not go want to touch me when I tell you . . .'

She walked with him to the ravine between the pasture and the lawns of the house, Hardin Burnley's attempt at a ha-ha. A small canal ran there with water. As they sat in the shade of the ravine, Augusta eventually told him how she had been forced to the ground by one of the footmen, who had followed her out into the pasture; one of the footmen who had served them with rum punches before dinner. 'He say, what is for some is for all. What is for red-nigger is for black. What is for white man is for he.'

Michel Jean felt helpless. There was no way for him to protect her. He could not challenge the man because then what had happened between them would become public knowledge.

'This footman is the one who always in Master's bedroom, fetching water for the closet. He always about the place, even at night. I does see him. He must've see me come to your room. You see this place we living in. I fight him. I give him one lash with my parasol it break. When I begin to scream, he run. Because he know is lash he go get if Master find out, right there tie up in the yard. Master is no respecter of what take place here called liberty. You hear him talk?'

'Augusta, I'm sorry . . .'

'He still with the lash, you know. Just provoke him. But if the man have to take lash, he go talk when he bawling, and then is my name in that, and I go lose everything. Your name in that, and you go lose everything.'

'You don't think . . .?' Michel Jean looked helpless. It would truly be absurd if it happened the way Augusta described that it might turn out.

'You must stop staying the night.'

'Stop? Yes.'

'Yes. You not hear what I saying?'

'Very well.' Then, he said, 'Let's get Master to agree to your portrait being painted. You can come to my studio in town. You must find a way to persuade him, to persuade your mother.' The suggestion seemed to cheer Augusta up, but he could see the struggle on her face.

'Let me see how it turn out.' She had not completely adopted his suggestion. He did not think that they could continue with their liaison. She would not risk giving up everything she and her mother had gained at Orange Grove, and nor could he risk more.

In the weeks that followed, he completed his commission for Hardin Burley without going up to the house. And he was glad when he no longer had to visit Orange Grove and could engage himself with the Lamont commission at Palmiste near Corynth.

Michel Jean waited in his studio in Edward Street. He was all prepared for Augusta's arrival from Orange Grove. He had had a message from some market cart-man coming in from the estate to Port of Spain, whom Augusta had clearly paid to bring the letter and keep her confidence. He had delivered it to the house, giving it to Josie at the gate. Josie had brought it to the breakfast table, suspicious of the fact that it had come from Orange Grove.

'This ent smell like it come from the big man,' Josie said, as she hovered behind Michel Jean as he tore open the letter.

'Josie, give me a chance.' He was irritated by her prying.

As Josie had observed, it did not smell like a letter from Hardin Burnley. It had been scented with tonka beans. The writer had taken great pains with her sentences, and it stated briefly that she, Augusta, was coming into Port of Spain with Mrs Farquhar in one of Master's carriages, and while her mother was visiting an ailing aunt in the Belmont area of town, she had persuaded her mother that it might be an opportunity for her to sit for Monsieur Cazabon for the portrait that they had both decided might be a suitable gift for Master.

While Michel Jean was delighted at the prospect of Augusta coming to his studio, he doubted whether what was stated in the letter was indeed the case. This did not sound like the commission they had planned.

He did not say anything to Josie. He did not know exactly when Augusta would arrive.

After breakfast, he could not keep still. When he was this nervous he would start tidying his studio.

'What the matter with you this morning? Mr Big Man say something you don't like? Or, is some other kind of news from somebody else?' Josie called from sweeping in the corridor outside the studio. Michel Jean did not want Josie starting on her suspicions about Mrs Farquhar or her daughter.

He did not reply, but kept on with stacking his canvasses and cleaning up his tubes of paint. Josie understood these signs. There was nothing for her to do but sweep between the spaces and then leave him to himself.

Talk of his mother's will used to bring on these states. A visit from his brother, Joseph, could mean days of tidying. The last letter from Louise had meant that she did not see him for over a week. He had had to explain that Louis Michel had been taken to the hospital, for Josie to sympathize with his obsessiveness.

There was not just the tidying. Sometimes he would lock the door and not come out. The best that Josie could do then was leave the tray by the door and hope that he would at least open the door enough to drag the tray in. At least then she could feel that he was not starving himself to death. He knew that she did not like these times. The best thing was for her to go out and leave him. She would prepare some buljol and bake, thinking the saltfish would not go off in the heat. Her voice offered him some comfort: 'Jeansie, darling, some buljol there, eh.'

That morning he had felt the tension of how to receive Augusta with Josie hovering around and Ernestine sitting out in the yard. Josie would not tolerate the visit. She would not rest from letting him know what she thought of his philandering at Orange Grove with a girl half his age.

Silence descended on the house with Josie's departure into town. Ernestine went with her to help bring provisions from the market. Michel Jean stood in the middle of his studio, a prepared canvas on his easel. There was a stool for Augusta to sit on and a chaise-longue on which to recline if she wished. His imagining of this studio session came abruptly to an end with the reality of Augusta's voice calling from the front gate. Maybe because she was outside where she thought she would be heard, she called out formally: 'Monsieur Cazabon.'

He knew her voice at once and raced out of the studio to the veranda above the front gate. Leaning over the balustrade, he called, 'Augusta, come, come.' He looked about him to see if there were any gossiping neighbours to carry news to Josie.

This was not *en plein air*; this was not like catching her in the pasture strolling or posing under her parasol or seated under the shade of the samaan trees. This was to have her in his studio with the natural light, which came from the street, a light from an ever-changing sky above the encircling hills which transformed themselves again and again with the shadows of clouds slipping imperceptibly away as they drifted across the sky, following, as if instinctively, a shower of rain over the gulf.

The hills could be jade. They could be lilac. They could hang in a haze of the Sahara's harmattan. This ever-shifting light slipped through the wide windows he had had specially made for the studio. There was a light breeze, but it was not the capricious wind that could blow up her skirts to show her frothing petticoats.

She stood at the door of the studio, seemingly nervous of entering.

'Come in, nuh. You shy?'

She played with her half-closed parasol. 'So is here you does live?'

'Well, this is my studio, as you can see.'

'I didn't think you was so tidy. I imagine you need somebody to keep house for you. I ent see nobody in the yard. The yard empty. It quiet here.'

'Yes, it quiet here, except for the neighbour cock crowing in the morning.'

'It does wake you?' She smiled.

'I wake with the first light. Cock does crow even before that.' He laughed.

'Like you ready to go one time.' He realized that he was standing with his brushes in his hand and at his easel. He put down the brushes. 'Just getting ready for you. I get the message. You mother in Belmont?'

'Master bring we, you know. He say he have to come and see the Governor so he go drop we one time. He think I with Mama. But I make the man come back after he drop Master, and bring me here.'

Michel Jean did not want to wonder how she had made the man bring her. He knew well enough the currency of Orange Grove that he himself was exchanging. But he did not want to know the details of that exchange between others. He knew from the story of the footman that Augusta could well look after herself. Maybe the driver of the carriage had been made happy with hard currency, her allowance to spend on ribbons. Or, was this extravagant subterfuge of Augusta's, while Master was meeting the Governor, still to be paid for on return to Orange Grove; a promise to be extracted from her later?

'So you come. I tell you it easy.'

'Who say it easy?'

'I mean . . .'

'What you know? You don't want to know.' She had put down her parasol and moved away from the door of the studio. She played with his brushes. He held her hands where they held the brushes.

'Don't let us rush it then. We go take it easy. You must be thirsty.' He took the brushes from her and put them back on the table with his palette. He poured her some guava juice from a cool pitcher. He watched her drink eagerly. Then he leaned over and licked the juice from her lips. 'Is paint I want to paint you, you know. This go be better later. Sit here, nuh.'

'The dress nice? All night I only changing and changing me mind about how I go dress to come in town to meet you. Master say, "You looking particularly pretty today, Augusta." He don't usually say that kind of thing in front of Mama. Because you know before it was me, it was Mama. He don't want Mama to get jealous. He tell me that one day. But I know Mama only too please to rest she self. She tell me, "Girl, I ent able with that now. He go make things good for you."'

'Why you telling me all of this?'

'So you go know.'

'Know what? Sit, nuh. You looking real pretty. Forget Master.'

He worked the paints on his palette. Everything needed to be a little darker, but it was the same madder brown he had used for Angelique and Josie, the same raw sienna with cobalt and black. He would pencil her features. He would use a largish brush for tint composed of madder brown, raw sienna and Naples yellow with madder, carmine and white. To be able to have the colours right here for her skin enthralled him. She had not seen him work his magic with oils before and in the studio. 'Don't keep looking at me. Keep looking out of the window. Think of something nice. You know what I mean?' He smiled.

'Monsieur Cazabon, is my portrait you painting, you know.'

He continued as they both, sitter and painter, worked for the composition. It was not long before Michel Jean felt he had got something from his sitter. Augusta wore a white dress, which had belonged to her mother when she was younger, a gift from Master; damask with embroidery. The challenge was the extent of the white he had to use. But the effect was for the white against her brown skin. Then he suggested something that he knew he would not show in Trinidad.

'I need to see you now. Take your time. I want you to lie on the chaise-longue. I go get you some more guava juice.' The fragrance of the fruit juice was close. Josie had made a lot of juice because there were plenty ripe guavas in the yard.

Augusta did not resist his request for her nakedness. In fact, he thought that this was what she most expected. He had already painted her out at Orange Grove in her fine clothes with her parasol and her petticoats caught in the capricious breeze. He felt that he was doing something bold by putting her on the couch and not at the edge of a painting as an attendant. She and her naked body were at the centre.

She was not looking inwards. She was not a black shadow at the edge, an erased face whose appearance out of the darkness was lit, by say, a bouquet of flowers presented to her madam. *She* was the madam. This was how he would rescue her. These thoughts swirled in Michel Jean's mind as he brought intention to bear upon instinct, as he drew and painted the body of the woman he had held in the darkness of the bedroom at Orange Grove. She was not then as brightly lit as this. In the night, the treatment was more chiaroscuro; intensities brought by candlelight and the turned-down oil lamp in case their presence together should be detected. Through the half-open window the moon and the stars had shone through.

Here, the fully lit studio showed her in all her blacks and browns against the white sheet he had thrown over the chaise-longue. She was his Venus, his black Venus, his *capresse des colonies*. He wanted to protect her, own her, and paint her. Ferns and crotons at the window he picked out with a fine brush as colour to contrast with the darks and whites of the central painting. She took to the pose naturally. She kept still and showed herself without embarrassment, looking straight out beyond him. She had placed her hand upon her sex, but allowed the line of her other arm to flow naturally with the cushions and the folds of the sheet.

He was proud of her. In the currency of Orange Grove she would have to owe him for this gift of herself. He felt his own cruelty and brashness. He was torn between freeing her and entrapping her for his pleasure. She would be flattered when she saw it.

This would be his payment. He was no better than the massas. Why was he doing this? He paused with the portrait, deciding to continue and finish off later. He poured some guava juice for himself. He replenished her cup, then stooped to kiss her on the lips and to join her on the couch; slipping off his clothes, as if this drama was one with the act of painting. She was eager to see herself, but he prevented her from rising, and would not let her see the painting till he had worked at it some more. She was tantalized by her anticipation of the painting, but let herself be seduced by the painter.

When she did look at herself, taking a peep before leaving, as Hardin Burnley's carriage arrived and the groom came to the door to request 'Miss Augusta', there was a delay as she took in what she saw. Michel Jean could see a mixture of pleasure and doubt on her face, realizing that she had given all of herself to him.

The groom was kept waiting at the door while she continued to stare, and then she collected her things that had become scattered about the studio.

Michel Jean came to the veranda to assure the man that Miss Augusta would not be long. 'She coming. She say, wait for she.'

The man, as Augusta had called him, was a young fella, and Michel Jean could not avoid picturing him with Augusta. He placed them in one of the outhouses in the yard at Orange Grove, where she would be able to keep her rendezvous to pay for the drop, and also for his silence. In an attempt to prevent what he was imagining, he reached into his pocket for the coins which jangled there, and leaning over the balustrade, he threw them to the young fella, calling out, 'Catch.'

The groom looked up and smiled. Holding out his hand, he caught the coins expertly and counted them, laughing, and asking as he did so, 'That is how much she is? She much more, you know.'

Michel Jean would have poured purses of money over the balustrade in his confusion but, cut by the fella's insolence, he turned his back and called into the house, 'Augusta, the fella waiting for you.' He could feel his anger against the young man being displaced and expressed against Augusta. Then, in his own guilt, he blamed himself as he slammed the door of the veranda.

'Tell him wait, nuh.' She smiled at him while biting her lower lip.

As the afternoon light declined over the gulf, he watched her departure from behind the half-shut jalousies. She frolicked and flirted, as was her way, as she let the young man open the carriage door. She turned and waved in the direction of the house. The masquerade was not lost upon any of them. They knew the kind of carnival they were each playing for their own limited advantages. Once the carriage had disappeared around the corner of the street, Michel Jean turned to the unlit portrait, going close up to it and peering into its darkness. He felt that the well-being he had experienced at Tamana when he had hung in his hammock beneath the planets in the darkness of that night and understood his work as a painter, desiring his wife to be there to make the wholeness complete, was now entirely lost.

Later, in the night, he heard Josie returning to her room. She did not come looking for him. He expected that she had guessed at what had taken place that day in the studio, and would eventually go looking for evidence in order to reprimand him.

At last, the long-awaited letter from Louise arrived. Josie brought it up from the wharf the following morning. The packet had been delayed and had had to go via Georgetown in Demerara. Michel Jean sat out on the veranda and read the full story of Louis Michel's hospitalization and his prolonged stay in the care of the nuns at St Lazare. He had been taken into the hospital coughing up blood.

I thought we had lost him. I left Rosie with the concierge downstairs and sat with him. Sister Philomena was very generous in allowing me to spend the night next to his cot despite the dangers to myself. She brought me warm milk in the night. The consumption that has been diagnosed has subsided. It means that he is even more withdrawn and intense than ever. He moves between elation and depression. The doctor says, that because of his overall condition, he will be prone to illnesses. He says we will have to be very careful when we travel to the tropics. I wish you were here. I am full of trepidation to make the voyage with or without a companion.

He folded the letter, pressing it down on the table of his studio, anchoring it with tubes of paint lest the wind blow the pages away. The image of Louise at Louis Michel's side, feeding him warm milk, erased the memory of himself throwing coins into the yard for Augusta's man to catch. It was not the sound of the carriage wheels departing with Augusta that filled his head now, but the persistent coughing of his young son in his cot at night.

What did he think he had been doing, risking everything?

He resolved there and then to go to Paris on the earliest steamer that he could book a passage on. He sat down and wrote to Louise. 'My darling, I'll be with you within the month. I need to be with you. We need to be together with our children.'

He wrote the required letters to Excellency, Wildman and Mr Hardin Burnley. He explained his responsibilities to his family, but to Hardin Burnley he argued that he would be able to supervise the printing of the lithographs for his album. He did the latter in person, visiting Orange Grove and leaving the shortest of notes with Augusta, seeing her fleetingly, sensing her disappointment but informing her that his work had suddenly taken him to Paris. He felt sure of what he was doing, and hoped that time would solve his dilemma.

By the end of the week, his passage was booked. 'Josie, I coming back.' He reached out his hand as if to touch her.

'I know. I waiting for you.' Josie waved him farewell at King's Wharf.

Michel Jean had been lucky with the availability of a steamer and the favourable weather.

BOOK THREE

1850–1851

I

The invitation to the governor's residence for dinner was delivered on the morning of Michel Jean's arrival back in Port of Spain on the *Olympian*. That evening he was thrown into a spin. 'Josie, you have that shirt for me? Josie, I can't put on this collar stud.' Josie was running hither and thither through the house. At last, he was dressed and ready to go.

He said *au revoir* to her, as she stood and watched him leave in the last of the evening light.

'Jeansie, you ent even have time to tell me how your visit to Paris gone?'

He was conscious that Josie herself was not going anywhere. Ernestine was now bedridden. He noticed the deterioration in her health over the last six months. Josie was not going anywhere at all. Nothing had changed in that regard. She had kept watch over her mother and the house. 'I still here, don't frighten.' Those had been her words of greeting that morning on his return from France.

Six months had flown. The journey to Le Havre had seemed like an eternity through rough seas and storms. Luckily, he had been able to travel to Paris by the new railway. Now he was already back in Port of Spain, satisfied that Louise would follow either with Uncle St Luce and his wife, or on her own with the children, once Louis Michel was able. His visit remained vivid in his mind on his return trip, while sailing on a moderately calm sea. His memory was refreshed with the cries and smiles of his children. He could feel his son's warmth lying against his chest. The boy's heartbeat was one with his father's before he put him down to sleep. He had recovered from the consumption but was still delicate. They laughed and played together. '*Papa, regarde!*' Louis Michel was always crying out for attention. Then he was pulled away by Rosie, who was constantly at his side looking at everything he did, curious, asking questions all the time about everything. Once the children were asleep, he and Louise had their time alone, often in his old studio looking at work he had left there, deciding on what they could sell to help with her finances. It was there that they rediscovered their intimacy; finding again in themselves those times when they were younger and had learned that instinctive language of touch. Why did he ever need to leave her when this was where he belonged and where they both lost and found themselves in their passion, a passion that erased time? They listened out for the children; the creak of a footstep on the stairs, a quiet pushing against the studio door of a child unable to sleep. They stifled their laughter, returning to their kisses in each other's arms. On his last morning he had caught her hanging out the laundry in the courtyard; her petticoats and underclothes hanging on the line, catching the breeze. The bright morning light gave him the opportunity there and then to paint her, golden hair in the wind, looking back over her shoulder with her blue eyes. 'Louise.' He heard himself whisper her name.

Louis Michel had still been too delicate to travel, so they had decided that Michel Jean should return without the family to hand in his album of lithographs to Hardin Burnley at Orange Grove, and to continue his work for Excellency.

Michel Jean's thoughts moved to the company he was going to meet at the Governor's as he strolled across the savannah illuminated by fireflies. Of course, there would be Excellency and Wildman. He was sure that Hardin Burnley would be there. He did not think he would bring either Mrs Farquhar or Augusta to Government House, though one could never underestimate the boldness of the big man. Michel Jean had to eventually deliver the album of prospects to Orange Grove. Wildman would want to be taking up all of his time with talk of Paris and painting. He must have had a hand in this unusual invitation to dinner at the Governor's. He wondered if, in his absence, his young friend had tried to see Augusta. He could not imagine anything would have come of that. Instead, he wondered how she would view him on his return. He hoped that his absence had brought their liaison to an end, for it could not have continued satisfactorily for either himself or for her. She was clearly looking for a way out from under the old ram's haunches, but did not seem willing to sacrifice the material advantages she received in exchange. He must not now offer her any expectations. Reflecting on how many coloureds or blacks would be present, he wondered whether Uncle St Luce, a respected free-coloured man, would be at the dinner with his white wife. Or had they left for Paris? Already he felt thrown into the tensions of Port of Spain society.

These thoughts were left on the savannah as he crossed into Paradise Estate where the governor's residence twinkled in the darkness, set among the plantations of the Botanic Gardens at the end of the avenue of Mr Lockhart's nutmegs. The flambeaux lit for the occasion made the path clear.

'Cazabon, there you are, old man. You must tell me everything. Your family? Paris? What's going on in the metropolis? I've so many sketches to show you.'

'James.' They embraced. 'Yes, we must talk.'

Excellency greeted him warmly. 'Good to have you back. We heard that you were arriving. Hope all's well with the family?'

'Thanks for enquiring, sir. All is as well as it can be. My little boy is too weak to travel, but I am preparing for the whole family to join me as soon as is practical.'

'Excellent.'

He noticed at once Hardin Burnley with Mr Knox and Mr Warner; the English set were here in full force. Wildman whispered in his ear that the old planter was not well.

'Is he here on his own?'

'What you mean is, has he brought Miss Augusta?'

'Yes, or Mrs Farquhar?'

'Did you get your payment in the end?'

'Half on completion; the other half on delivery of the album.'

'So.'

'I'll arrange a visit to the estate tonight I hope.'

'Capital. Look forward to seeing the work and his response.'

'What do you mean?'

'Probably got wind of your amorous desires.'

'What are you talking about?' he said, deliberately side-stepping Wildman's suspicions. 'Anyway, Lamont at Palmiste paid up handsomely before I went away and I have his album completed by Lemercier as well. He was a different kind of character altogether. I loved it down there, close to Corynth. We must make another trip once I settle back.'

Dinner was served. They were called into the dining room. At that point Michel Jean tried to put all worrying thoughts aside. He found this a strain, but had felt that he had to turn up to show good will and secure his work. He was now in a bauble of glitter and chat in the chandelier-hung room with the long mahogany dining table laid with damask linen, glittering with crystal, silver cutlery and china. The centre of the table was decorated with blooms of cattleya orchids, thanks to the specimens of Mr Lockhart. Footmen attended to the oil lamps and helped the ladies into their chairs.

Outside, the insects and frogs played the music of the night, as the bats swooped in the darkness beyond the perimeter of light that fell from the lamps the footmen were replenishing out on the veranda. He sat back and took it all in. A Miss Birmingham had been hired to sing light arias. He noticed that she was a coloured woman and wondered at the liberalism of the Harris house. At least he was not the only nigger here, he thought, laughing ironically to himself. Of course, the invisible butlers and servants were other dark shadows at the edge, beyond the spill of light; a hand which placed a plate, refilled a glass.

'I'm Mrs Elizabeth Prowder. How good to meet you.' She was a young English lady, next to whom he had been seated.

'Michel Jean Cazabon.' He noticed a number of stares from around the table as he introduced himself. How was he going to cope with the evening? He found that he did not have to make polite conversation as there was no end to Elizabeth Prowder's talk, which was made up of her observations on every subject as they naturally suggested themselves to her, from the overheard conversations of the other guests to the events in the country and the world which came to her regularly on the packet from her *dearest mama*. 'I see,' he found himself repeating several times.

'I spend one week awaiting Mama's letters and the following week writing to her.'

Michel Jean smiled at the young woman's youthful exaggerations. She must only be in her twenties, he thought. Maybe she was as nervous as he was and this was her way of expressing it. He tried to be polite with his smile and his attention, accepting the wine that was poured and the courses that were served.

They spooned through the turtle soup in silence. Then came the *rissolettes de volant*. At this stage of the menu he exchanged with the young lady observations on the qualities of the cuisine. But by the time a choice of Baron of Beef *d'Angleterre*, *casserole au riz à la Polonaise* and curry of fowl *à l'Inde* were offered, he was exhausted by the descriptions of the dishes and overwhelmed by the choice. They confided in each other the difficulty they were having in getting through the courses, how they were both accustomed to a much more frugal diet. But they also admitted that they were enjoying the novelty of the event.

'This is an indulgence,' she leaned over and whispered to him, as she tried the *riz à la Polonaise*.

Across the table, Michel Jean then noticed the watchful eyes of a gentleman Wildman was trying to engage in conversation, but who was obviously distracted by the young lady's talk and was trying to gain her attention. She was speaking quite loudly and he could see others at the table looking in her direction. Or was it him? Was it that others at the table were curious as to what she was saying to him? She was unaware of the efforts of the gentleman opposite or was deliberately ignoring them and continuing to remark on the courses. 'What is *ramières*? What is it?'

'The local wild meat.'

'Good gracious. Like wild boar, I expect. It's too rich for me, and too much. I'll explode.'

'I couldn't agree more.'

He noticed the same gentleman staring and arching his eyebrows, as if he might lean across the table at any moment to engage Elizabeth Prowder in conversation. 'My husband is trying to catch my attention.' She leaned forward to speak to him. 'Charles, what is it? Am I doing something I shouldn't?' she whispered.

Michel Jean felt embarrassed. While Elizabeth Prowder made conversation across the table with her husband, he was allowed to exchange pleasantries with Wildman, who smiled at him knowingly, showing that he understood the awkwardness he was feeling.

But now Elizabeth Prowder was again ignoring her husband. He was a military sort, who seemed to be trying to correct her exuberant behaviour. She was now telling of her home on the Isle of Wight, of her sister, Lottie, and more again about her dearest mama. He listened attentively, but was beginning to wonder how much of this kind of chat he could take. He told her in turn of his recent visit to Paris.

'Paris. I've never been there. I've never been anywhere but here really and the Isle of Wight. No, I do go to London. But, why Paris?'

He told her of his family and the albums of lithographs. This led from one thing to another. She was enthralled to find out that he had been educated in England. 'I had not thought . . .' she said, trying to continue before he interrupted her.

'Thought what?' he asked.

'That a Negro would've had that sort of education . . . and that you would be painting and . . .' Then she quickly changed the subject. 'Your family?' Looking around her, she noticed the silence at their end of the table. She had obviously not yet acquainted herself with the subtleties of race, or with the inflammatory possibilities for conversations about the free-coloureds. To her, everyone was a Negro who was black. The look on the faces of her fellow diners began her instruction. Michel Jean imagined that she had made a mental note to question her husband on the subject later that evening. Sensing her faux pas, she called to him across the table, 'Oh, Charles . . .'

Michel Jean went to her rescue. 'Yes, my wife. She's French and we have a girl of six and a boy of five. My son is a worry with his poor health. I miss both him and my daughter.' He found, as he spoke of his children, there was a quaver in his voice.

'I'm sorry to hear of your son.' He could see that she understood his anxiety. 'We also have two small children. They are such a concern.' Her eyes indicated her husband as she spoke. She then felt happier to talk about her husband's work as an engineer and draughtsman for the Governor, where he was stationed at the St James Barracks, than to pursue her enquiries about his life any further, or to allow him to tell her any more. Her impulsiveness was youthful. She was being herself, even if that self was a little irritating and offensive. He excused her. It was her class and type. He wondered, at times, if she listened to what he said as she went ahead with her own observations in her original, excitable manner. So, he was surprised, when in quite a different tone of voice, almost conspiratorial, she said to him, 'So, you are an artist. You paint.'

It was as if she had just remembered what he had told her of his early time in Paris. He smiled and nodded, realizing that she had taken in his travels in Italy with Fitzwilliam.

'Yes . . . as I was saying.' Then she was again responding to the caution of her husband, who was leaning over to say something to her.

At that moment Michel Jean caught Wildman's eye. He was still trying to interest Charles Prowder, who was now more concerned, it seemed, with supervising his wife. His young friend was trying to say something to him with his eyes, which he could not understand as he had to give his full attention now to his exhausting dinner companion. He smiled back reassuringly.

Michel Jean was feeling more and more in this company as if he were in England. He thought that it had as much to do with the bowl of fruit at the centre of the table. He wondered how the russet apples and pears had survived the voyage of the Atlantic crossing, which had given them that sort of wrinkled look that reminded him of fruit arranged in one of Chardin's still lifes.

Then Elizabeth Prowder interrupted him. 'You've been away with the fairies. As I was going to say, I've been learning drawing at home. I had a master in London and a teacher on the Isle of Wight, but I would very much like to learn to paint. Can you advise me how I might receive such lessons in this town? I must have some views to take home with me.'

'I see.' He had not looked at her properly all this time. He turned to face her. A young bride with an older husband, he thought. Just arrived, she was already thinking of leaving. Her voice had taken on a very different tone. She was not chattering and leaping from one subject to the next. He was trying to listen to her more intently now, leaning in towards her to enable him to hear her more distinctly above the clatter of the crockery, the tinkle of the cutlery and the crystal.

Then he noticed the cornflower-blue of Elizabeth Prowder's eyes. They were bluer than Wildman's, which were bluey-grey. He thought her hair should be blond, but it was jet black. The combination unsettled him. She was not at all like a Frenchwoman, or like any of the French girls he had known in Paris. She was not like Louise in her looks. She did not have that confidence. But her nervous, distracted chatter was being replaced by a thoughtful frown. He suddenly saw a quite different character looking at him searchingly with an intelligence he had not recognized before.

'Yes, painting lessons . . .' He was lost for a moment both in her enquiry and in the sudden memory of a landscape he had not thought about for some time, an England of gardens with arbours of roses as large as cabbages, an England of orchards he did not often think of, an England of hot summers and dangling bare feet in the icy cold of a stream from a stone bridge on a walk in the country; an England where, as a youth, he had stood and thrown stones into a river, its surface marbled with trout. He was taken back to when he raced across the fields during haymaking to get back to prep on time. He imagined Excellency, Wildman and Mrs Prowder in that England. And then the thought that, yes, he had been painting that kind of landscape for Hardin Burnley. He had been painting the English landscape at Orange Grove. He had been painting English light in the tropics, drawing English perspectives of avenues up to the great house, giving to the millionaire planter his prospect as if he were an English country gentleman in his great house. His mind was on the album he had to deliver to the big man at the other end of the table next to Excellency. 'Yes, of course . . . painting lessons . . .'

Elizabeth Prowder was wiping her mouth with her linen napkin, as white as a cloud; not wiping but patting, blotting up, and then smiling with her full red mouth, her cheeks blushing either with rouge or the heightened mood of excitement with which she had been talking. His impressions were running away with him. 'You were asking . . .'

'About painting lessons. Are they available in this town?' She was being insistent.

'Well. They must be. There's the now-elderly Mr Reinagle, who was my first tutor here. He was the architect of our two famous churches.'

Wildman had encouraged Michel Jean to start giving lessons. Then he had got lost in the Orange Grove commission and not done anything about it. Here was a student. He had not been able to imagine who his students might be. Now, without any planning, here was this young lady from the English set presenting herself for lessons. He did not say anything about his own project. He told her that he would make some enquiries in the town and then he would endeavour to send her a message through Mr Wildman, indicating his friend with a glance across the table where he was engrossed in the business of building bridges in Arouca with Mr Prowder.

'I know Mr Wildman. He's been so helpful to us settling in.'

By this time they were onto the desserts. They were both amused by *la pyramide meringues d'arlequin* and wanted to see what the confectionery would look like. The occasion was the Governor's birthday and the chef had exceeded himself in the length and ambition of the menu. In the brief interlude between the last of the savouries and the desserts, Michel Jean took the opportunity to survey the table, while Elizabeth Prowder turned to the guest on her other side, whom she had largely ignored. He was a reverend recently out from Somerset, Michel Jean learned, overhearing their conversation. He thought he must describe all of this to Louise in his next letter. She would be amused and intrigued by the company he was keeping.

Dinner was concluded after a toast to Her Majesty, the Queen. Then there was another toast to Excellency on the occasion of his birthday. At first, the ladies were ushered away by the footmen into the gallery for coffee after being shown where they might attend to their toilette. The Governor did not have a wife, which meant that duties, which might have been performed by the lady of the house, were left to the footmen and other servants, in particular, the major-domo. Lord Harris did the best he could. But it was noticed that Miss Sarah Cummins, the Venerable Archdeacon's daughter, whose father was from Trinity Church in Port of Spain, assumed some of these duties informally and did indeed seem to have the eye of the Governor. This created a bit of a stir in the room as the women left for the gallery and the men stayed on in the dining room to be served with port and smoke Havanas.

Michel Jean took the opportunity to speak to Mr Hardin Burnley and make an appointment for the following week to deliver the album. 'Jolly good, my man. Glad it's all completed. I'll be looking forward to your visit.'

Michel Jean escaped the company of the planter and his friends, Warner and Knox, neither of them as friendly as Hardin Burnley. He joined Wildman, who wanted to know everything about Paris. 'You must tell me everything, old chap.' Wildman had been having his usual fill of wine and now port. 'So, you were subjected to the charm of Mrs Prowder?' he asked.

'You don't find her charming?'

'Elizabeth Prowder? You must've noticed her husband at my side, gesticulating to his wife. I have to say, I could hear her voice over on our side of the table. It seemed to bother him. He kept saying into my ear in guarded tones, "She does get quite excitable. She doesn't quite understand the etiquette."'

'Yes, at first she was quite excitable. I put it down to nervousness and shyness.'

'That's very generous and sensitive of you, Cazabon.'

'Well, what do you suggest?'

'It's our job to pick up the pieces.'

'Pick up the pieces? What pieces?'

'Well, there was some trouble when they first arrived . . .'

Michel Jean frowned.

Wildman lowered his voice and looked about him before continuing. 'You know how it can be in the early stages of a marriage with small children in a strange land. Of course, he's a bit older and was being a little patronizing to his young, strong-headed wife.'

Michel Jean was so surprised to hear Wildman speaking in this tone, a much more mature tone, that he wondered when he had developed it and where he had gained the experience to talk of being married and having children. 'What've you been up to while I've been away?'

'I know it's a way of talking, but I do help people.'

'I see . . .'

Wildman explained that Elizabeth Prowder had not been able to settle on first arriving in the colony, and he had had to try and find a suitable governess for her two small children: Kate, a precocious girl, and her younger brother, Eddie.

'Have they been married long?'

'Well, not too long. You can see how young she is.'

'I see.'

'What do you see? See. See. You sound like Iago. Think, think, my lord. You speak as if there's some monster in your brain.'

'What are you talking about?'

'Are you already smitten with the English lady? You've hardly met her. Have you forgotten your brown-skin girl in Orange Grove? You can leave her to me. Remember Cassio fancied Bianca, the gypsy girl, while Othello fell for the white lady of the state. You can be Othello. I shall play Cassio.'

'As I remember, he could not hold his drink.'

'Not you as well, Cazabon!'

'What nonsense are you talking?' He felt irritated with his young friend. 'What melodrama. Augusta, and now these ridiculous insinuations about Mrs Prowder.'

Michel Jean then thought that Wildman had not considered the conclusion of the play in ascribing him the role of the Moor. 'It was a tragedy, you know; he smothered her on their marriage sheets.' Flashing through his mind was a poster he had seen long ago of the American actor, Ira Aldridge, playing the lead part in *Othello* at one of the London theatres. He had stopped and stared at the black man, who was looking down on the people passing in the street as he held a white woman in his arms about to murder her. As a schoolboy, the image had fascinated and disturbed him. He thought now of Louise. He wondered how people were going to see the relationship between himself and his white wife. Where was he bringing her?

They had ventured onto the balcony overlooking the lawns at the front of the house.

'Where've you gone to now?' Despite his jealous outburst, Wildman was eager to find out all that Michel Jean had been up to since he had last seen him, following him to where he stood under an overhanging samaan.

'Do you hear that? Do you hear him?'

'What's that? Yes. Yes, I've heard it in the night, waking in the Cottage before dawn. I hear the call in the bamboos.'

'The jumbie bird, a pygmy owl. I see them when I go out early to paint up the valley, hoary and staring with those all-seeing eyes of the night. I saw its flight once in the valley which leads to Macqueripe.'

The moon was now up over Belmont Hill, flooding the savannah with its white light.

'What a sight!' Wildman seemed to be feeling all the better for the good Sauternes followed by the port and the Havana he was luxuriously inhaling. 'What an extraordinary space, encircled by the hills and the sea lying out before us, just there.'

'Indeed. What a traveller you are, Wildman! You have the eye of a traveller for exotic places.'

'Are you laughing at me, Cazabon?'

'No. I'm glad to be home, but missing my wife and children. I've arranged for them to follow. My little boy could not travel. I'm just teasing you. I get jealous of anyone else loving my island the way I do.'

'Why would that be? You should cherish that I love it too.'

'Yes, I should, if all things were equal. But they aren't, are they?'

'What do you mean?'

'Well, my good friend. You are my friend, you know?'

'Am I?'

'James!' He was touched by the young man's affection.

'I'm sorry. I've really missed you, you know? All that time you were off in Paris. And it's a bit tiresome here with Ping and the irksome affairs of this island. This coolie question just won't go away. The whole scheme is about to be suspended, you know, and that will be the ruin of the colony.'

'Count me out of the politics of labour. I was relieved to be away from it all for a while.'

For a moment they stood in the stillness of the night, gazing out over the moonlit savannah. 'It's good that you're back in town, Cazabon.'

'That's just it.' Michel Jean broke away to walk down to the terrace that overlooked the Botanic Gardens.

'What now?'

'The island. It's mine. But you own it.'

'Please, not now. Poor Ping, he's caught between Warner and de Verteuil. Did you see the French creole there tonight? Ping's been trying his best.'

Wildman described, like a secretary, the tensions between the Romans and the Protestants, the whites, the Creoles and the coloureds, and the great black population pressing from beneath. The indentureship problem had become the straw on the camel's back. 'Ping knows. He's a sympathetic soul. Caught up in Her Majesty's affairs. He's often hurt.'

Michel Jean wanted to move away from the politics. He was fed up with the same old stories, the politics of race and religion, royalists and republicans.

'Your way is to live differently. But you can't deny your privilege,' Wildman said.

'There's no place else for me.'

'London? Paris?'

'I might even fit into Boston if I could get into that country. No, I belong here. This kind of belonging has nothing to do with owning.' He changed the subject. 'You know that woman wants to learn painting.'

Wildman persisted. 'But of course it does have to do with owning.'

'Liberty is a new word on this island, but it's a rare experience. What is it to set people at liberty? How do we do that, set people at liberty? Truly. My mother wondered about that.'

'Sorry. What did you say?'

'My mother, she understood.'

'No, before that.' Wildman had now grown tired of the argument.

'Oh, Mrs Prowder, the Englishwoman . . .'

'What about her?'

Michel Jean related his dinner conversation with Elizabeth Prowder.

'Why didn't you offer there and then to give the young lady lessons for a good fee? Her husband can afford it. I know what he gets paid. There's nothing here to spend their money on. He might at least give his wife some pleasures.'

'Does he not pleasure his wife? Is that part of your job, too, to find out who does and who doesn't pleasure his wife?'

'There are things I could tell you, my friend.'

'I'm sure. I heard a bit of tittle-tattle about Excellency himself this evening. A couple of other English ladies down the table from me were all eyes and a number of words about a certain Sarah Cummins.'

'Not tittle-tattle, I'm sure. But I have my integrity to preserve. It will all be out sooner than you think. Then it won't be tittle-tattle any more. But until then . . .'

Wildman took the opportunity to talk about the painting he had been doing in Michel Jean's absence. They had strolled off into the grounds, but time had run away with them and they had to return.

'I must take my leave.'

'Do you have a carriage?'

'A carriage?' Michel Jean laughed. 'No. I'll have a sumptuous stroll across the savannah in this wonderful night.'

'There're rumours of highwaymen. Attacks along the road from the estates in St Ann's.'

'Nonsense. Do you smell the earth, the dry earthen floor beneath a dry season grove of bamboo? Do you smell the night juice of the orange blossom, the ylang-ylang? Then you know why I must be back here to walk out each morning into my island. I was given it with my birth. I was given its smells, its touch and its visual surprise at almost every turn. I must paint for myself and not just for patrons.'

'But you do . . .'

'What is it to paint for myself? I sometimes do at sunrise. When I'm there alone at Carenage or Corbeaux Town, or when I am the first to walk across the savannah before dawn, or the last to fade into the darkness after the sunset. There was freedom in Paris. I know what it is to paint for a patron. I know what he wants. It isn't that there's not any of myself in that, or any of my island and her beauty.'

'You do both excellently.'

'It's that the audience of a Hardin Burnley, a Lamont or Excellency makes me see it their way. I look at it for them. It's a kind of homage to them. But I must see it my way.'

'I had not realized that you resented it so much.'

'I did a sunrise at Carenage before I went to Paris. I must show it to you.'

'I would be delighted.'

They had kept on strolling some distance from the house into the Botanic Gardens. Michel Jean explained himself, saying how they, Excellency and Wildman, would not be staying on the island for ever. 'No doubt you'll leave when Excellency leaves. There's already talk of India.'

'Well, these islands and their sugarcane fields are almost over. England's sway is moving elsewhere.' They agreed that the lack of free labour would change the island. There was no knowing how much longer the ships would be arriving from Calcutta with their cargo.

'Where've you two been? Shunning good society?' They met the Governor and Mrs Prowder strolling along the path at the front of the house. 'Let me introduce Mrs Charles Prowder. James, you will know Mrs Prowder. But, Monsieur Cazabon?'

'I was delighted to make the lady's acquaintance at dinner. We were seated next to each other. I expect she's completely forgotten me by now among the hosts of such interesting and delightful guests here at your birthday, Excellency. Happy birthday.'

'Many thanks, Cazabon.' The Governor then turned to Mrs Prowder. 'So, my lady, you will already know about our resident artist. He will have told you about his work.'

'Well, I certainly haven't forgotten him. How can he think that? I think that the gentleman must be fishing for compliments. He's been quite reticent, actually. I've heard about his travels in Italy and France, but not a great deal about his work here. And, he's going to look into the possibility of a tutor in the town.'

'I'm sure he will. He himself may teach you. But he's in much demand from the great and the rich. So much so that he can hardly find time to paint a couple of views for the Governor of the island. Isn't that true, James?' Excellency and Wildman laughed teasingly.

Cazabon bowed his head in embarrassment and then laughed himself. Elizabeth Prowder looked on, unsure what to make of this banter between the men. While the Governor, Wildman and Mrs Prowder bargained over him and the lessons he could offer, he looked at the young Englishwoman from where he now stood at a short distance from the party. He saw her in quite a different light under the flicker of the flambeaux that lined the path. He saw her face in another shade. He was able to take in quite another impression she gave as she stood in her full-length, dove-coloured satinette, which hugged her upper torso tightly, buttoned to her neck with fine mother-of-pearl buttons, finished off with sleeves to her elbows, which were continued in full-length gloves, fastened at her wrists with the same mother-of-pearl. The satinette slipped around her like water. The skirt, slightly *bouffant*, was pulled back into a bustle, falling into the folds of a train that she so fetchingly held and dropped at intervals, as if she was a kind of Nereid of the water standing in the midst of some fountain. He was sure that Charles Prowder would approve of her being so buttoned up. Her breasts were held in. It was a pity that her neckline did not break into a cleavage, that her narrow shoulders were not bare.

He realized that he was assessing her for a portrait. She had an exquisite neck, shown to good advantage by the style of the collar. Her black hair was lifted to the top of her head into a crown of black curls, some of which refused to be constrained and fell in strands along the side of her neck and against her flushed cheek. These, she tried to control by lifting them lightly with her fingers to fit them back into the arrangement on top of her head. But they inevitably tumbled out again. It was a beautiful gesture. He might have thought it was an affectation. But with Elizabeth Prowder it was an innocent gesture, something left over from her girlhood. She was an odd mixture, he thought, this pretty girl with her lovely clothes and perfume and the upright, military husband whom she had accompanied to the tropics with two small children; all of that, and then this desire to learn how to paint watercolours. It excited him that he could teach this English girl to paint. That was his ambition.

'Cazabon, Cazabon!' The Governor had to call twice. 'Where are you, my man? Is it the rum or the good wine and whiskey from my cellars and vats? Why have you wandered off? We've got another job for you.'

'Excellency. What a wonderful night! Don't you think?'

'Yes, indeed. But James here and Mrs Prowder have hatched a plan, while you seem to have been bewitched.'

'Hope it does not involve me. There're so many plans afoot and I've not yet progressed with the Governor's views.' He smiled teasingly, more at ease now in Excellency's company.

'I may have to release you from that commitment for the moment. Because this is a very favourable plan both for yourself, I'm sure, and for this young aspiring artist here who is seeking a tutor, a master, I might say.'

Cazabon looked at James and at Elizabeth Prowder and then at the Governor. He had been trapped, but also had been relieved of the duty to pretend to look for some tutor for her in town while in the end offering his own services. But here was

Wildman and the Governor offering it to him with the lady's consent on a platter. It wasn't *his* head on the platter, was it? He suddenly doubted himself. How was he going to cope with the English set, so loathed by the Creoles?

'What does Mrs Prowder think?'

'Mrs Prowder is thrilled,' Elizabeth Prowder replied to his question.

What was he getting into? The questions, the arrangements he should be putting in place were tumbling through his mind.

'Very well. Very well, then . . .'

'You sound doubtful,' Elizabeth Prowder said directly to him.

'*Non*. No doubts. Where would the lady like to be tutored?' Michel Jean saw visions of Augusta arriving at the studio in Edward Street. He saw Josie caught between Augusta's departure and Elizabeth Prowder's arrival. He saw the young girls from Corbeaux Town wanting to earn a few shillings as models. It would be absurd for her to come to his studio.

'I'm going to leave you artists to make your arrangements. James, I need you for a moment.' Excellency and Wildman strolled off towards the house.

Michel Jean and Elizabeth Prowder were left standing alone under the stars and the white light of the full moon.

'We seem to have been thrown together.'

'I'll ask Mr Wildman about the arrangements,' Michel Jean said formally, 'and then we can take it from there.'

'You come to St James Barracks. It's a little grey cottage with a white picket fence. You'll be directed.'

'I think I should escort you back to the house and to your husband. I'm sure he must wonder where you've got to, especially as he'll have noticed the Governor return without you.' Michel Jean had already begun the return journey, striding off, so Mrs Prowder had to catch up.

'I'm sure my husband will feel entirely at ease with the knowledge of where I am at the moment. But you seem in a hurry . . .'

'Yes. I must leave as I have to cross the savannah on foot.'

'We could arrange to drop you in our carriage.'

'*Non, non, non.* I . . . I actually do prefer walking. I walk a lot . . . I must go, take my leave.'

'It has been delightful meeting you, Mr Cazabon.'

He took her hand. 'Mrs Prowder.' They separated at the entrance to the veranda, where Charles Prowder was waiting for his wife. Michel Jean acknowledged the gentleman and left Paradise Estate.

Michel Jean stood alone in the middle of the savannah bathed under a moonlight that lit the surrounding hills. He let the noisy silence of the night envelop him. The orchestra of frogs played in the canals and waterholes of the pasture. He stood still and listened. The wine, the heady atmosphere of the Governor's birthday dinner, and the attentions of an eager young Englishwoman seeking painting lessons, had played the necessary tricks to flatter him and provide enough excitement to anticipate his next meeting with her. What was it about her that intrigued him? What he knew was that he wanted to teach her to paint.

Once at home he settled down to write to Louise about this extraordinary evening. He had to talk to someone. Josie was asleep. Anyway, he did not think she would be impressed. She would be warning him about the dangers of white people. He gave Louise the details of the dinner party, the different characters and this new work, tutoring an English lady, part of the English set. This would amuse Louise.

'It is work, darling. I need to have more students, more commissions.'

A week later, Michel Jean woke to the hot sun forcing its way through the cracks in the jalousies and Josie's voice in the yard. 'He tell you to come at this hour of the morning?'

Who was Josie talking to so early and so imperiously?

He went out onto the veranda. There she was at the gate. 'Augusta! Come.' He went down into the yard. 'So long. I missed seeing you at Orange Grove last week.' He had not expected to see her so soon. He had had to leave a message for her with the groom, Jean Pierre, which did not please him, but the young man was compliant for a small fee. He had written that he would like to see her if she was ever in Port of Spain.

'I come too soon, too early. I get your message. I need to see you.'

'*Oui, oui*. You look weary.' He noticed right away her changed condition. She was as beautiful as ever. But now she looked like a woman with her full breasts and the child she was obviously bearing, rather than the young girl he had last seen before going to Paris.

'Jean Pierre bring me. It still dark when we leave.'

'Is that safe?' He was still taking in her appearance.

She explained that Hardin Burnley had left the estate on one of his visits south and that her mother was under the impression that she had come into town to see her aunt.

He had not counted on Augusta simply turning up without warning. He had hardly got himself organized after his voyage back, his six months away. He was also intent on arranging lessons for Mrs Elizabeth Prowder that same morning. He had resolved to bring to an end his liaison with Augusta. He could see too plainly now the results of that risk. On the other hand, he was not sure. Could the child really be his? He thought of that one night at Orange Grove and then once again in his studio. Surely . . . Augusta was the planter's goods, his property. He had acted foolishly, getting drunk, allowing a competition with Wildman to encourage jealousy, to threaten his manhood, and then thinking that he might rescue her from Hardin Burnley, the monster; thinking that he could offer her a life. What could he possibly offer her? He had a life with his wife and children. He hated these thoughts. But he did not want to be callous to her now.

'I have not heard from Mr Hardin Burnley about his commission for your portrait.'

'Is no commission I come about. You think I want you to paint me now?'

'No, I can see that. Augusta . . .' They were still standing in the yard. 'I can see that. Come inside. Come, take some refreshment before you leave.'

'I just reach. Jean Pierre coming back later.'

'I see. Come.' He was confused and embarrassed. He led her upstairs to the studio. He did not know what he was saying. Of course she must stay as long as she needed to stay. Leaving her there in his studio, he went back downstairs to the kitchen to get coffee and bread. Josie would not want to come to the studio. He wanted to avoid a quarrel with her. But he had to listen to what he did not want to hear.

'So, is children you bringing in your mother house now?'

'She's not a child, Josie. And, this is not my mother house.'

'I can see she is no child. But is child she bearing. And, she is child still, that's the worse thing. Who child is that? Anyway, house is money. Money is house. Is your mother house. That girl go want money. All them young girls making baby all over the place. What I sure of is that they can't make baby on themself. I know something going on at Orange Grove. And I tell you so?'

'Josie, give me a chance this morning, *oui*. You don't know she is pregnant with my child.'

'I sure it could be anyone with them kind of girls.'

'Josie . . .'

She turned her back on him and left the kitchen.

The light increased in the studio as the dawn faded. Michel Jean opened the jalousies and the shutters onto the veranda. The street was coming alive with the smell of fish and burning garbage from Corbeaux Town, borne on the early morning breeze.

Augusta chewed her bread slowly and sipped her coffee. She still did have a childlike look about her, though she was so much more a woman this morning, sitting there in the increasing light. She was not dressed in one of her usual pretty frocks from New York. There was no parasol to dally with. Images of her as he had painted her went through his mind. Those paintings were hidden here in the studio somewhere. She was now dressed like any *marchande* or *blanchisseuse* you might find on the road. She wore a white cotton blouse with simple embroidery, which she might have sewed herself during those long evenings at Orange Grove with the old man and her mother. The dress was too tight for her now. She had dressed to travel incognito, not as Augusta Farquhar from Tacarigua, the mistress of Mr Hardin Burnley. She wore a blue and red striped skirt. She had hitched it up so that it was rucked around her waist, and that on her seemed a fashion, even in her pregnancy, not the necessity it was. She seemed more black than brown this morning. Her headscarf was a Madras kerchief that was tied on the side, simple; no cryptic message for a paramour in the knots and twists. Michel Jean felt sorry for her. He felt sorry for himself, for the risks they had taken with their lives. Pity welled up in him. He looked at her plain innocence this morning. He had been attracted to her beauty and her coquettishness. She was one of his people; she was part of the confused allure of Orange Grove. She looked now like those women carrying babies in the cane fields right up to the birth, dropping their newborn infants right there in the furrows under the hot sun.

How was he to correct his error?

'So, you hide me away?' She was looking about the studio where she had sat for him, where they had lain together.

'I didn't think they was for Port of Spain.'

'For posterity, you tell me. But it was never for no posterity. Them was just pretty words, sweet-talk. It was for you, for you to get your hands on me like that fella in the pasture, who want to throw me down in the ravine, like this same Jean Pierre who I have to give . . .'

'Augusta, I don't want to know . . .'

'You don't want to know? What happen? It go offend your feelings? Monsieur Cazabon from Paris. *Artiste extraordinaire! Monsieur.* Look at me now. You don't want to know?'

'I don't mean that. But, Augusta, I was being true. True to your beauty.'

'So, what, I turn ugly now?'

'No. *Non. C'est impossible!*'

'This is another truth. I ask you before. You think it easy in that house?'

'I know it not easy. I get carried away with my own work. Your beauty, the house, the whole situation.'

'Don't spoil it, nuh. I thought it was liberty you was offering me.' Then she changed the tone of her voice. 'I go have to wait, because I tell Jean Pierre I go take some time. I ent dress to walk about town.'

She looked abandoned, lost. She had come on a mission to confront him with her pregnancy. He saw now how much she had to lose, how much she had risked. She was looking for the road to that liberty she pronounced so clearly, that sweet word she had learned as a girl from her father's lips.

'You must stay. You can stay,' he said. He did not know what he was saying, though, what he was thinking of doing.

He left her to sit and to look at the paintings in the studio. Each time he passed through the studio she looked more and more upset. While she sat and sometimes walked around, he busied himself with getting ready to go out to St James Barracks to arrange his painting lessons with Mrs Elizabeth Prowder.

'You going out? I can't believe I make all this effort.'

'I staying with you. I not going anywhere right now. Anyway, you could go and see your aunt in Belmont later.'

'My aunt? You think I come all this way in town travelling before dawn to town to see my aunt? Risk the wrath of Master to see my aunt? Give what I have to give Jean Pierre, even in my condition, he want it, the wutless little scamp, to see my aunt?' She turned her back on him and went behind the canvasses and hauled out her portrait on the couch. 'Look at me, like some naked whore. What it is you say? You can't show this in Port of Spain? I wonder why. Where you go show it? Anywhere to show it, to show Augusta, the whore? This was about you all the time. Who go buy me? Who go want me now? You think Master self want this pickney.' She cradled in her arms, as she bent down, the baby she had still to bear for some months to come.

Michel Jean hoped Josie was not hearing Augusta's outburst. He stood rebuked. He reached out to touch her.

'Don't touch me.'

'Augusta . . .'

He had dressed for St James Barracks. He went into his bedroom, changed into his work clothes and came back into the studio. He began to mix paints and prepare a palette of oils. Josie came into the room carrying a tray of laundry. When she saw Augusta there she put the tray down and walked out. 'I have work to do, *oui*.' With that, she slammed the door and each step she took down the backstairs echoed through the house.

'Augusta, while you waiting for Jean Pierre, will you sit for me?'

'Like this?' She did look like a child.

'Just your head and shoulders, a bust. Your pretty face.'

'You not going out again?'

'I waiting with you. While we wait . . . sit so. You mind? We go rest from time to time. You working. I go pay you.'

'I not looking to get pay, you know.'

'I know, sweetheart, I know. This is for me. This is for you. For us. I need to paint like this, you mind? Till Jean Pierre come.'

He had painted her skin before. He had smelled it. He had held it close to his own body in the night at Orange Grove, lost himself there in a bamboo patch, in a cane field, down in a ravine; under the spread of the samaan. He had tasted the very salt of her earth. Augusta, born in August, her mother's daughter; Mr Farquhar from Tacarigua sweet child, rescued from poverty, but at a price. Everything was property. Everything had a price. He too had his price. He had played with the girl. He had dallied with her feelings, seduced her with expectations that he knew he could not fulfil.

Michel Jean had primed his canvas. He was painting her in oils. This was no watercolour moment. These were the oils he had stored since he had first come back from Paris. Some he had found from a colour-man in a back street of Port of Spain on Chinnet Lane behind the bridge, still using pigs' bladders for his tubes. He wondered what he was doing there. He had said that he had mixed paints for an Englishman, who was travelling through with an explorer. They had gone up the Orinoco.

He drew as he painted and painted as he drew. His brushes worked furiously as he built her breasts and shoulders, her neck and her head. He had the basic form.

'Augusta, sweetheart, you tired?' He had spoken to her in the past as he spoke to the girls from Corbeaux Town who came to sit for him. This sweetheart-talk she had recognized was not his love, not the love he thought he had for her that night in the hot room at Orange Grove when he nearly stifled her because of how she cried out for him, pressing his chest against her face, his hand on her mouth when he cried out for her, burying his pain with his mouth on her neck. For it had been a kind of pain he felt as he took her, knowing in that moment that he would abandon her.

'Take a rest, girl. You doing good. I go get it.' He wiped his hands of the oil paint. 'In time,' he reflected. 'I get the main part and I go have to work on it later. This is not like watercolour. I go have to work on it alone. But you doing good. I thank you. I go pay you.'

'I tell you, I ent looking for no pay, you know.'

'You working, girl.'

They looked at the portrait together.

'You want some juice? I go get you some juice.' He went down to the kitchen and came back with some guava juice. It was guava last time she was here, the nectar that he had licked from her lips. But he didn't want to think of that time now.

'You have plenty guava.' She licked her own lips.

'Let me take a smoke and then we go try again. You have to pose same way, eh.'

Michel Jean leaned up against the banister of the veranda. The sea burned at the end of the street.

He was in Port of Spain, painting. He had a real sense of that. Is painting he wanted to paint, not to fall in love, not get up in some *mamzelle* skirt and call that love. Have a child! What was he thinking of?

'You ready to start?' Augusta called from inside the studio. She had taken up her pose. 'Is so I was before?'

'Just right, darling. You just look straight ahead of you. I want you natural.'

'It look like me? It pretty?' Augusta had come around the easel to peep at the painting.

'Girl, hush, nuh. You too vain!'

'You want something ugly?'

'Nothing ugly about you, darling.'

'So why you sending me away?'

'And I painting you.'

'But is not *the* portrait.'

'Who tell you is not a portrait?'

'I thought you say . . .'

'What I say . . .'

'You say . . .'

'Augusta, girl.' He put down his brush. 'Who child is this?' He reached out to rub her belly.

'Boy, how I go know? I tell you it not easy in that house.'

'Augusta, I want you to take this for now.' He went to the drawer of his desk and drew out some notes that were there. 'For the moment.'

'Is not money I come for. I come to see you. I come because I hope . . . but I know is wrong hope. You fix up. I hear you have wife and children. I always know that. I just didn't want to know for truth. I know I want the pickney to be yours. I just want that. But it could be Master's. It could be Jean Pierre is the father. Any of them will look after me one way or another. Mama not going to abandon me. Master go provide. So is not money I want.'

'But let me give it you. I ent bring you a present self from Paris.' She took the money.

'You ent bring a perfume? Now you talking.' She smiled, teasing him.

'I go come and see you. I go bring more.'

'I hear somebody in the yard.'

As she readied herself to leave, he saw the full portrait in his mind's eye that he had wanted to paint with the landscape building around her: the dry red stone where her black feet walked the earth with the rock stones, the plantains, the ridges of the mountains falling away in the distance, in the haze all dun and pink with ochres rendering the devastation of the sun, the Sahara dust. She was striding out of the painting in the heat of the dry season. 'Sweet Creole woman.'

'What you say?'

'Take it easy, girl. Whoever child it is, it go be pretty because is yours.'

'You will come, eh?'

'I will come. Augusta, we mustn't, you mustn't, take these risks again.' While he could speak for himself, he hoped, he wondered how she would survive Hardin Burnley, Jean Pierre or any of the other dangers of Orange Grove.

'I ent go have time for nothing but this baby. I gone. I go come again if I don't see you.' Her voice trailed in the breeze – 'Bye-bye' – as the buggy, driven by Jean Pierre, rattled down Edward Street.

The burden of the realization, that if this child turned out to be his he would have to take responsibility, weighed upon him. He could not abandon her and the child, and he would have to explain the truth to Louise and his own children eventually. The thought appalled him, as he imagined actually telling Louise to her face what he had done, seeing his children's eyes staring at him with disbelief. The clandestine did not seem so alluring now. The very fact of her there, large with child, the reality of Augusta with a child which might be his, clouded the expectation of a new beginning for his work; teaching Elizabeth Prowder.

*

There were stares from the guards at the entrance to the barracks, but Michel Jean was not detained when he stopped and announced his intention. He was not given any precise directions. 'Move along and ask again at the end of the yard.' He recognized a Scottish accent. He made his way along the avenue to the stone buildings; reddish brown in the light of the late morning.

He asked a washerwoman for the quarters where Mrs Elizabeth Prowder lived with her husband and children.

'Ask that old fella down there,' she said, pointing ahead.

Once he was inside the barracks itself, he noticed there was a lot of activity; comings and goings of soldiers making ready for a parade, for drills, he did not know what. He asked for the Prowders' quarters again and was directed by an old man who was sweeping drains.

'I does plant garden for she,' he said. 'Down by them palms and then take a right by the bamboo. You go see it.'

Right by the bamboo brought him to the little grey cottage with a white picket fence; someone's idea of creating a piece of England in the tropics. He guessed that it must be the Prowders' house. A white woman with auburn hair, about his own age, was standing in the patch of garden at the front. The old man's plants had hardly taken and were in need of rain. A hen with chicks had strayed from the back of the house and there was a cockerel strutting around proudly. A turkey had fanned out its feathers in a territorial manner.

The woman was supervising the play of a little girl and rocking a baby's stroller, a smart contraption that looked like it had just arrived from England on the packet. Elizabeth Prowder had said there were children and Wildman had spoken of a governess. The woman noticed Michel Jean at the garden gate and came striding over, leaving the stroller standing.

'Can I help you?'

'I'm here to see Mrs Elizabeth Prowder. Have I got the right house?'

'Indeed. Whether she's available is another question. I think at this moment she's buried in boiling forty pounds of marmalade.'

'I see. I can come back later.'

'No. You must introduce yourself.'

'Monsieur Cazabon, about painting lessons. We met at Government House.'

'Yes, of course. She has mentioned you. Sorry, it's Miss Lavington. Just Lavington. I'm the governess of these wonderful children, who use up all my energy. But it leaves Mrs Prowder free to pursue her artistic ambitions, besides making marmalade, of course.' She laughed aloud.

Michel Jean was amused at the absurdity of his arriving at this moment.

'Mr Wildman sent a message to say you would be coming.'

'Excellent.'

'She's eager to start. You know she spends a lot of her time drawing. She may spend as much as four hours a day. She is gifted. I must look after the children constantly during that period. But today it's marmalade. Let me see where she's got to with the boiling. Unhitch the gate, Kate . . .'

The little girl came running towards her nurse and then took charge of the stroller with the little boy sitting up in his sun-bonnet.

'Monsieur Cazabon, do come along. Do you mind waiting on the porch? I'll just see what the state of play is inside. Do you enjoy marmalade? Please just keep an eye on Eddie, see that he does not leap up!' She laughed that laugh again, a laugh which was a language all of its own, and which he was beginning to translate.

As the screen door banged, Michel Jean heard the voice that he recognized from the Governor's dinner table. 'Lavington, dear, is that you? What a day! Do you have Eddie? Is Kate with you?'

Michel Jean listened to the exchange between the governess and Elizabeth Prowder. He had chosen a bad time to come. He kept his eye on the children. Kate was getting impatient with the waiting, rocking the stroller too roughly. Eddie was beginning to sulk.

'Who? Who did you say? Monsieur . . . Mr Cazabon! Gracious, that coloured man, who is an artist. I must remember Charles's words of caution before he left. I'm not dressed to receive anyone, far less talk about painting lessons. I'm marmaladed.'

Michel Jean could just make out the conversation. He heard her description of him: 'That coloured man, who is an artist.'

'Should I tell him to return?'

'No, no, Lavington. You must bring the children in. I must leave this now. You can just keep it simmering. I'll change. What would I do without you? I've been up since dawn. Into town and back. Charles embarked at four this morning. He's gone to Chaguanas by row boat.'

He heard Elizabeth Prowder's voice again. 'The poor gentleman must be dying of thirst. Offer him some lime juice. I've squeezed gallons. There's ice. The man came an hour ago.'

Lavington re-emerged from the house, laughing and speaking at the same time. She obviously copes through laughter, Michel Jean thought. 'Mrs Prowder's very keen to see you. She apologizes for the delay.'

Having heard the original, Michel Jean was impressed by Lavington's diplomatic translation. What, indeed, would her mistress do without her? Elizabeth Prowder was another of her charges. Lavington was back in the yard relieving Kate of her duty and attending to Eddie. 'Isn't he just a wonderful boy?'

Michel Jean admired the child. Going to be like the father, he thought, while the girl had her mother's eyes and hair. He could not help thinking of his own children, how like her mother Rose Alexandrine was. Would Louis Michel grow up to be like him? The domestic scene made him envious for the one he had left in Paris.

The porch was a quiet place for him to rehearse his introductions and plans for the lessons. As he stood and surveyed the barracks yard beyond the picket fence of the grey cottage, he noticed that the earlier activity of the soldiers had increased. Preparations of a sort were in hand. Soldiers were running back and forth. They certainly seemed to be at the ready to cover any contingency.

'Mr Cazabon! What a pleasant surprise! You caught me in the middle of a million chores. Mr Wildman did say you would be arriving this morning. Time simply runs away with one. Do you find that?'

'I'm just a short distance. On the edge of town. If it's not convenient . . .'

'No, absolutely not. You're here. I've not drawn this morning. I must this afternoon. It's not with drawing that I need your help. It's with painting. Watercolour. Lime juice? I've squeezed a gallon. Lavington? What would my life be without Lavington? And I'm drowned in oranges. A Mr Metivier from an estate near Gran Couva, Los Naranjos, left us a cartload, repayment for some favour. Charles was supervising one of his projects in the central hills, a bridge I think. Metivier. He's rather like you.'

He smiled, guessing at which Metiviers they were, the coloured ones.

Silence was easiest with Elizabeth Prowder as she moved hither and thither between offering lime juice and talking about oranges in the same breath as her drawing and her need for tutoring in watercolours. He needed to fix a time for them to begin, so that he could be earning a little money. She seemed even more like a girl in her morning dress than the woman he had been sitting next to at the Governor's dinner table. But it was her keenness that excited the teacher in him.

They went to sit out on the veranda at the back of the house that was really the front. There were some samaan trees shading the back yard that was part of the St James savannah. The shade from the trees enveloped the house in copious shadow. The bright light at the perimeter was intense.

'It's the yellowest green I've ever seen,' she exclaimed, pointing at the scene. 'Do sit.'

He noticed her pencils and drawing paper. He looked intently at her sketches. They were fine work. She would be an able student. He imagined that they would look at them together more closely later. He could see that at the moment she was nervous.

'Charles left at four o'clock. Can you imagine rowing from Port of Spain to Chaguanas? He'll be rowed, of course. Though I expect he'll want to take his turn. You must get about quite a lot yourself.'

'Yes, I use the steamer, the ferry, or I might sail. I've been rowed in the past. Quite a chore for those doing the rowing and then if the weather is not good you can get soaked.'

'All for the love of art.'

'Well . . .'

'What are your plans?'

'I thought we might like to work *en plein air*, if I may suggest . . .'

'Yes, I want to learn that, to paint what you see rather than what is in the head. And, the light is so different.'

He could tell that she was serious about her passion for learning to paint.

'This open area is wonderful for the children. But I can send Lavington further afield with them. We can't have them under our feet. Kate is very demanding. And if Eddie cries, I won't be able to resist him.'

'I understand.'

'Yes, of course. Your wife and children are in Paris. You must miss them.'

'I do. And my small boy, as I told you, is not well.'

'The consumption. Poor mite.'

'Yes, I hope his improvement continues.'

She changed the subject once more to arranging her lessons. 'I want the best that I can get here for my painting.'

'Well, there isn't a lot to choose from, but I'm sure I can get you started.'

'You're modest. Charles, my husband, does take an interest in what I draw. I draw for him, for his projects. But I want to advance.'

'I understand.'

'So?'

'I suggest Tuesdays and Thursdays at five dollars per month.'

'That seems more than reasonable.'

Lavington raised the alarm just as they had settled his fee. Michel Jean was about to take his leave.

'What is it, Lavington?'

'I'm not quite sure, ma'am. One of the guards has mentioned that there is a spot of bother in town.'

'What kind of bother?'

'Apparently to do with that new ordinance.'

'Yes, quite extraordinary. Have you heard of this, Mr Cazabon?'

They discussed the recent ordinance concerning persons being committed to prison for not paying debts below the sum of fifty dollars. They were to be tried as criminals and have their heads shaved.

'It's outrageous, ma'am. These rules and regulations are obnoxious to the people. It's that Mr Warner again.'

'Lavington! I dare say. The people, did you say? We're not in France, you know, Lavington. This is a British colony.'

'And, also, ma'am, to have their heads shaved like common criminals.'

'It does seem extreme, even unjust. But, you know, matters here in the colony are not the same as at home. We must remember where we are and the kind of people we're dealing with.'

'Ma'am!'

Michel Jean noticed the formality of the household now that it felt itself under siege.

'Lavington, is Eddie asleep? While we debate questions of state, my little boy may be in danger.'

'He's fine, ma'am, quite peaceful. And Kate is actually drawing, like her mama.'

'What do you think, Mr Cazabon?'

'It does sound extreme.'

'And that's just it, ma'am; the people are taking extreme action in reaction. That's what this guard told me. This bother in town may be something more. It may be a riot.'

'A riot! What time is Charles back from Chaguanas? You know Charles mentioned something, but I was not paying enough attention. I had already begun preparations for my marmalade. Some disturbance was anticipated yesterday and the troops were in readiness, but then nothing occurred. The calm before the storm, I suppose.'

'Will you be safe here?'

'This has to be the safest place on the island, Mr Cazabon. You may want to get off immediately so that you are not caught on the road and I dare say cause any suspicion.'

'Suspicion, ma'am!' Lavington looked quite surprised at her mistress's insinuation.

'No offence to Mr Cazabon, Lavington. Are you aware that not very long ago there were severe restrictions on the movements of coloured people?'

'Ma'am, yes, ma'am.' Lavington looked uncomfortable, as if wondering how best she might restrain her young mistress.

Michel Jean smiled. 'I'll be fine. If there's a spot of bother, as you describe it, I may want to record it.'

'Record it?'

'Sketch it, yes. I do some work from time to time for *The Illustrated London News*.'

'I see.' Elizabeth Prowder was genuinely surprised and now seemed a little embarrassed at her insinuation that he could be seen as a rioter.

'I'll have to get down there and see what position I can take up to get the best advantage for a sketch.'

'Isn't that dangerous?'

'It can be. Probably won't be for me.'

'Yes, I understand. I hope you won't be taking Mr Wildman with you. It might not be quite the same for him.'

'He'll be safe. I'm sure.'

'He met with an accident the other day which might have proved very serious.'

The newspapers had described the accident. Lord Harris's horse had taken fright on the savannah and had run off.

The groom and Mr Wildman were thrown. They had got off with minor bruises. Lord Harris had been injured by a horse falling on his leg. Michel Jean had not yet seen Wildman to enquire after his well-being and that of Excellency. He had been remiss.

It was past lunchtime, and still they were trying to find out what was going on in town. As they stood on the porch, Elizabeth Prowder saying farewell to Michel Jean, Lavington attending to the children's late lunch in the kitchen, the temporary peace of the parade ground was disturbed by the furious entry of a rider and his horse.

'It's the Inspector of Police,' cried Elizabeth Prowder.

They were stunned as the Inspector turned his horse and left as suddenly as he had arrived, only to return at an even greater speed. The rider's second sudden entrance to the barracks was followed almost immediately by the 88th with all the officers on horseback headed by the colonel and the artillery with two guards on carriages and powder barrels wrapped in blankets.

'My God! It's what you read of in war,' Elizabeth Prowder remarked. Michel Jean stood close at her side and stared in astonishment.

'Lavington! Stay inside. I don't want the children to see this. It will alarm them. And Charles, where's Charles? Where's their father at this moment?'

'I'm sure he's safe.' Michel Jean tried to be reassuring.

'You know no such thing, my man. You don't know my husband. He'll have gone straight into the fray if it was necessary. You had better get off. If you're a reporter you need to be on the spot. You've been very kind staying all this time.'

'I don't think I should leave you alone with the children.'

'I thank you for thinking of us. But, as you can see, we're well protected. Though I expect they will be replenishing their ammunition and heading back into town if there's indeed a riot. You must take the back lanes. I travel that way myself in the mornings when I go to shop in town.'

As Michel Jean prepared again to take his leave, a young boy ran through the gate and up to the cottage. 'Message, madam, message from the boss.'

'What are you saying, boy? Come quickly.'

Lavington, overcome by her curiosity, came out onto the porch. She had a protective arm around Kate and was holding Eddie by the hand.

The boy unburdened himself of his message, the words spilling out with the rapidity of the horses that had just entered the yard. 'They break all the window in the Treasury, but when the soldiers come they run like hell!'

'I see. And you have a note for me?' The boy had been waving a piece of paper. 'Lavington, we must give him something.'

Lavington retreated into the house for the messenger's reward, fetching some coins kept in a bottle on a shelf for this purpose. Elizabeth Prowder read the note aloud, paraphrasing. 'Charles says that all is under control. I must not wait dinner for him. He has recently returned from Chaguanas. Luckily, he caught the steamer coming back, instead of the sloop. He has business with the Governor, who of course is in Council. He says things have quietened. Thank God. But, Mr Cazabon, you must hurry. What will you record?'

'I'll take my leave now as things do seem to have abated. I can see what has been left in the aftermath.'

'Remember what happened in St Lucia when twenty or thirty people were killed by the troops.'

'Let's hope that no one gets killed.' Then, as he was leaving the yard he turned back for a moment. 'I'll be here on Thursday morning at eight o'clock.'

'Of course. You know, I quite forgot what we were discussing, our morning so transformed. All my drawing time gone. *Au revoir*, as you say.'

'*Au revoir, madame.*'

Lavington put her head around the screen door. 'I'm very pleased to have made your acquaintance, Monsieur Cazabon. We hope to see you again soon.' He noticed how Lavington spoke for herself and her mistress. She was a different kind of woman. There was something commanding and capable about her and, at the same time, protective of her young mistress.

Michel Jean made directly for the town, hearing from people on the road that the matter was far from being resolved. Charles Prowder had been anticipating and placating his wife's fears.

No sooner was he halfway down the St Clair Estate road, taking short cuts through the traces between the cane fields, than the 88th, the colonel and the artillery passed him, headed by the Inspector of Police. He thought of Paris just before he had left in '48; the barricades and the assaults by the cavalry. He had not experienced this kind of thing in Trinidad before. Things had been more settled in Paris on his recent visit.

When he eventually got down to Marine Square, he found that the crowds were immense. He took up a position on one of the balconies opposite the Treasury. The roar of the crowd was deafening. He knew Mr Schoener, the German merchant, from his father's visits. They had met in the store beneath. 'Absolutely, Cazabon. You make yourself comfortable, my man. Yes, you must get it all. It's madness. This colony will be ruined if this kind of thing goes on any longer. This is disastrous for business.'

Michel Jean worked with his sketchpad on his knee. He begged for some water first of all, as he was dying of thirst after the walk from the barracks. Then he knocked back a shot of rum. 'Yes, this is Mon Chagrin rum. You've got good taste.'

The crowd were chanting. 'The law stink! No shave head. No tax!' Then there was a heave and the crowd surged towards the Treasury. As they pressed in on the Treasury, the artillery forced their way between the people and the entrance to the building. Men and women were digging up the stones in the road and pelting them over the heads of those in front towards the soldiers defending the main entrance. Michel Jean tried to capture the opposition of forces. Once his first sketch was done he sat back and had some more of Schoener's Mon Chagrin rum.

The German merchant fed him. 'You draw all you want. It's good to tell the world what's going on here. Where did you say you're sending these sketches?'

'*The Illustrated London News.*'

'You're an important man. How did a coloured fella like you get such a job? I thought things were bad for you lot here.'

'Well, I've a friend who respects my work. I went to school with him. Got me the contract.'

The crowd were going mad with their chanting.

'It's that Englishman, Warner, speaking. The crowd hate him,' Schoener said. 'They detest that man.'

Michel Jean spotted Charles Prowder on the steps of the Treasury next to Mr Warner.

'They won't let him talk,' Schoener said. 'They'll stone him.'

The stones began to fly. He saw Charles Prowder ducking out of the way, protecting Mr Warner. Would Wildman be in the Treasury? Would Excellency be there? Michel Jean left Mr Schoener's store to get closer to the action. He thought he spotted Wildman going into the Treasury. This was not the kind of event that either Wildman or Excellency would want to be mixed up with. He felt the outrage of the crowd, but was concerned for his English friends.

He found another shop-front balcony from which to work. A Portuguese shopkeeper, Mr Jardim, invited him in. 'What's that he's saying?' Jardim called down to someone in the street.

'He say he go change the law. It not go have the shave head. He take that out,' an old gentleman explained.

'How the crowd taking it?'

'They want the whole thing take out. They go stone he arse.'

Soon the crowd had started their chant again. 'The law stink. No shave head. No tax.'

'People stoning,' Jardim shouted.

Michel Jean thought he saw Charles Prowder being hit, but he could not be sure.

'Yes, the troops are firing. They better not fire into the crowd.'

There was intermittent gunshot all afternoon. Darkness closed in. People began to disperse in the half-light as the police cleared the square.

The following morning the news came that the rioters, as far as Tacarigua, had attacked the house at Orange Grove and thrown Mr Hardin Burnley from his carriage. They were rioters from the estate, but none had been caught or charged. Michel Jean was anxious about Augusta. He also wanted news of whether Charles Prowder had been hit. He was sure that he had seen a stone hurled in the direction of the gentleman standing on the steps of the Treasury. So far, he had not heard any adverse news about Excellency and Wildman. He felt the responsibility that he was reporting on events for the London papers.

He wondered if Louise might read the news in Paris. He wrote to tell her of the riots, that he was safe and sound, and that he had got some good sketches to send to the papers in London; another bit of work he was lucky to have.

Later that week, on Thursday morning at eight, no longer meeting his father at that time, Michel Jean and Elizabeth Prowder had their first watercolour lesson. Charles Prowder greeted him at the door on his arrival. He had by now recovered from his injury at the Treasury, and at that moment was leaving for a journey to Couva. 'She's excellent at drawing; it's simply in watercolour that she'll require your help.'

'Yes, I understand that.'

Michel Jean was amused and a little irritated at the insistence of this request, repeated both by Elizabeth Prowder, and now again by her husband.

The first lesson and those in the following weeks continued with the painter and his student working in the garden of the small grey cottage with the white picket fence at St James Barracks. Michel Jean hoped that soon they would venture further for their *en plein air* classes. Elizabeth Prowder was making great strides. It was obvious that she had a natural talent and an aptitude to learn quickly. He arrived at each lesson excited to be with her and to move on with her progress. At the end of each month he was paid his fee of five dollars.

The regular routine of lessons allowed Michel Jean to settle back into life in Trinidad. There were also mornings out in the country doing his own work; some of the paintings that formed part of Excellency's commission.

He was often distracted by thoughts of Augusta. He had seen her at Orange Grove after the riots and left her another gift of money. Her pregnancy had another three months or so to run. Hardin Burnley had suffered complications after his accident. Life on the estate was quiet.

He had made further advances on the Governor's commission. He had recently recorded the building of the new reservoir in Maraval, a project close to the Governor's heart. It was a surprise when he received a letter from Excellency, in the midst of all of his matters of state, repercussions after the riots earlier in the year, and the continuing indentureship problem. He was inviting him to join the honeymoon party that would be embarking for the Five Islands after the wedding. His marriage to Sarah Cummins had recently been announced. Michel Jean thought of it as an honour. Excellency explained that he wanted him to have a free hand to paint views that he thought were appropriate as a souvenir for himself and his new wife. He needed portraits done. He also expected him to record the wedding ceremony at the Trinity Church.

His letter had crossed with one from Louise reassuring him of Louis Michel's steady improvement. Rosie had written a few words to her *papa*. She missed him. He could not have borne bad news from them. He read Rosie's little message to Josie and Ernestine. 'We looking forward to the family coming, Jeansie,' Ernestine said. 'You tell them about we? You must tell them. We go pull together. Not so, Josie?'

Josie was looking out of the window with her own thoughts.

'Thanks, Ernestine,' Michel Jean replied.

*

While visiting his father and brother at La Resource, Joseph laughed at the idea when he told him about his commission. 'Boy, what kind of honeymoon that go be with you painting pictures, snooping around, when the Governor and his lady trying to find a little romance down Five Islands. How you get yourself in there, boy?'

'Watch yourself that you don't get taken for a ride,' his father added. 'You know what I mean. And I don't just mean the boat ride to Five Islands or wherever it is the Governor, that friend of yours, have his seaside residence.'

'You sneer. He's a friend, you know,' Michel Jean insisted.

'How he could be a real friend?' François Cazabon asked his son with concern in his voice. 'First, he's the Governor and second he's a white Englishman. Friends are equals.'

Michel Jean did not answer at once. He thought of himself and Fitzwilliam, their intimacies, first at school and then travelling across France and down into Italy as equals. He was not naive. He knew that people had stared. He knew the times when Fitzwilliam had taken his part to defend him against attack. But he knew what that friendship was and what it meant. Then he thought of Wildman. He knew what Wildman felt. He believed him. They were *pardners*. Were they not equals?

He could not think whom he had been close to as a child, not counting Josie. There was Ignace, but he had been a bonded slave at the time. In a social sense they had not been equals, but in an intimate way they had been. Then Michel Jean had betrayed him. His friendships had been bounded by taboos and by the terror of physical punishment if those taboos were broken.

He was not inclined to pull skeletons out of the cupboard for his father, or to tell him of his comrades in the Parisian studios and out at Barbizon among the artist community in the forests of Fontainebleau. He did not remind him of his white wife. It was on his tongue to compare himself to Uncle St Luce and his wife. He just said, 'You would not understand.' Then, he added, 'You've not had, or given yourself, the opportunity to experience the friendships which I've had. I know what Joseph is thinking about. I know the politics. But Excellency and I have found a common humanity in things as brief as a sunset. We've shared an enthusiasm for things as fleeting as the wind in the bamboo or the light on their leaves. We've marvelled at something as ordinary as water flowing in a river, the light changing on its surface . . .' he said, stumbling out his descriptions. Michel Jean stopped himself. He could see François Cazabon looking at him and smiling in disbelief. He did not want to patronize his father, nor did he want to make too certain a case for something which had been tarnished with the stain of the trade; the memory of that commerce which had so complicated their lives and which had become so embedded in the philosophies which rationalized that brutalization, so alien to the Enlightenment and its cry for liberty, fraternity and equality.

'I may not have had your experience,' François Cazabon acquiesced, 'but I know that we are caught up in something way beyond these intimacies, as you describe them, these common sensitivities. You may well have found community among your bohemian artists. And while individuals may achieve the kinds of allegiances you describe, the vast majority of people continue to remain at the edges of society as outcasts. You must think about what you can do about that. Your mother was always talking to you about our republic. And, I expect, you're well aware of your art and its purpose beyond the common appreciation of, as you've put it, sunsets, light on bamboos, ordinary water . . .'

'Don't talk of art. What do you know about it?'

'I know that it's an art which shows off the white man's property to good advantage and which will indeed grace their great houses back in England when they exhibit their West Indian estates to those back home, over coffee and tobacco. Views to take away, my boy. Views that conceal more than they reveal, as far as I can see. It's property and trade which run this world, not art! You may be part of that property.'

'I do more than you think with the craft that I've learned,' Michel Jean stated with a sense of hurt, well aware of the truth in his father's little speech, or, at least, its partial truth.

'I hope so,' François Cazabon said decisively.

'What about Uncle St Luce?' Michel Jean changed the subject from art to race. 'Uncle St Luce with his white wife.'

'You're talking there about the business between a man and a woman. St Luce is an exception.'

'Maybe.'

'It's a different matter, as you know. Yet you've not brought your own wife, Louise, back home to meet the family and to live here. Do you fear for her, a white woman married to a coloured man?'

'What do you mean? I am planning for her arrival with Uncle St Luce when he returns from Paris.'

'I don't blame you. But you can't have it both ways. I understand what you're doing. You're an artist, God protect you, and you must make a living. These English types, they like your work. They want what you can do. But what about the white French Creoles? They ever ask you for a painting? They ever ask for one of those views of light on bamboo, or a portrait of themselves or their wives? You ever ask yourself why you never get a commission from a d'Abadie or de Verteuil, from a de la Peyrouse or a Vessiny?'

'Maingot ask me.'

'Maingot ask you? I see. Good for Maingot.'

Michel Jean looked at his father. He did not want to have to live in a society hedged round with these irrational laws. He thought of how society had changed since his father's youth. He admired him now. He had been so distant when he was growing up, visiting him in Corynth, while he was so much his mother's son in her house in San Fernando. His father and his generation had had to struggle with those insults, those humiliations, which were, now at least, no longer law. That older generation had had to steer such a dangerous path before 1829, walk such a narrow line. Philippe's *Free Mulatto* was their rational cry, their enlightened argument. But there was such a long road still to travel to enlightenment.

But they knew that beneath them was a mass of black people

agitating and ready to burn the place down, making, as they saw them, uncouth speeches, behaving in vulgar and common ways, speaking a broken language, making music out of stirrups and blacksmith's irons, the thud of bamboo on the ground, the beating of skin drums. They were a people mangled by history. Their hope had taken longer to be fulfilled and then, when it came, it was so little; so little after all those struggles for manumissions and the extraordinary idea that you had to buy your freedom, or to have your emancipation postponed for an apprenticeship.

Yes, his views would hang in their great houses in England and here on their estates and there was a beauty that was the beauty he knew his patrons wanted represented. But he also knew that a discerning viewer would see more, see beneath the surface to a more honest truth of what was actually happening in this part of the world when they turned the pages of his albums.

He took the ferry from the wharf in San Fernando and was back in Port of Spain as the sun set over the Five Islands with the towering mountains of the Paria coastline on fire. Sitting on deck, he sketched the orange and red sunset in crayons, making a note of how soon the sky turned to lilac.

Before going home to Edward Street he made his way to Corbeaux Town to find his old friend, Pompey.

'Eh, Pompey, how you going, man?'

'Boy, work for so! You taking an evening stroll? You can't paint in this light. Must be something else you after. Them ent come out yet, you know. Them does wait for darkness. You should've come last night. Plenty people, stick fight, cock fight. Plenty *jamette*.'

'Pompey, you studying one thing. I don't want no *jamette*, them. Maybe later. Anything nice these days?' He could still be tempted by the women of the darkness.

'You know how it is. They ent giving Pompey nothing with all you rich fellas coming in the town. Take a nip, nuh.' Pompey passed Michel Jean a flask of rum.

'You all right, *oui*, boy. I might be here early in the morning.'

'Pappy, you trying to catch the first light.' Pompey liked to show that he understood Michel Jean's needs for his painting. He had been with him at Chacachacare on the Venezuelan coast for Michel Jean to paint the whalers from Point Baleine.

'I go reach five thirty, then I go see the change in the light.'

'What happen? You is a weathercock? I thought you was an artist?'

'Boy, you see how things is. You have to take everything into consideration.'

'Yeh, you tell me, is not just to paint anything in your mind. Is to paint what you see.'

'Eh, eh, Pompey, you taking lessons?'

'You see the one you paint with Miss Melville factory in the background with me and the madam? I like that one too bad. Corbeaux Town looking smart in that one. Another one you have Corbeaux Town looking rough, boy.'

'Is how Corbeaux Town is.'

'For truth.'

'*Demain.*'

'*Via con dios*, as them Venezuelan cattle fellas does say. *Adios.* Take another nip, nuh.'

'Fire! That is a real punchin'. Burn my throat.'

'Fire in your belly.'

Pompey's voice faded with the light as the fish *marchande* offered him the last of her catch.

There was a letter waiting for him on the dining-room table. Josie and Ernestine had retired. He sat on his own and read.

Mon chéri,

It has been a while since I've written. I don't know where time has gone. Louis Michel is back home. Those nuns were saints. Louis has recovered, but Mother Philomena says that the illness can recur. The tuberculosis can recur throughout his life. If he has a life. He's been scarred. She says we must take care, great care, otherwise we can lose our son without knowing. He might just slip away without us noticing. Rosie is now showing in her behaviour that I have neglected her. She misses you. When you were here she had you when I was taken up with Louis Michel. I must make it up to her. It's hard, sweetheart. It's hard being here alone again. I am pleased at all the good work that you're getting. Your students, the young Wildman and the English lady. *Mon Dieu!* Paintings for the Governor! But at the same time they keep you there away from us. When will you return? I expect it's too soon to know. Thanks for the francs from the paintings you sold here. I keep thinking what it would be like for us to come to you. But I don't think I want to make the voyage on my own with the two children, particularly with Louis in his condition. I'm decided against that. I say that today, but will think differently tomorrow. To travel with your uncle St Luce is a possibility but still I think it will depend on Louis Michel's fitness. I miss you so much.

Michel Jean let the letter drop onto the table. He was weighed down by the responsibility he now felt for his family. He planned for some of the Hardin Burnley money to be sent. At times it seemed unreal that he was here again, living this life with the English Governor and his cousin, at home with Josie and Ernestine. There was the distance and the time it took to travel. He felt unsure of his plans. He did not think that he could resettle in Paris. What would life there be like for his mixed children? Once he had completed Excellency's commission, he should be able to get back and then the family could return together with him. That was his plan. He would look into Uncle St Luce accompanying them, but then it was always so unpredictable about his travels. When would he be going to France again?

There were all these anxieties and, not least, the thought of having to tell Louise about Augusta and the child, if it was his, appalled him. How would that affect their plans for her and the family to join him in Port of Spain?

The lessons at St James Barracks had been going well. Michel Jean's student was progressing. They had had the house and garden to themselves at the last lesson and had then ventured beyond their usual bounds. Lavington had taken the children to the pasture at Paradise Estate through the St Clair Estate on a morning walk. Kate was not at school, but was convalescing after a mild bout of influenza. The walk was Lavington's prescription of fresh air and exercise to put her on her feet again. Eddie, of course, was under the tutelage of Lavington herself. The little boy seemed more active than it was possible for his mother to control. She felt she had to hand him over to the good Lavington for her own peace of mind.

Michel Jean and Elizabeth Prowder had gone along the Long Circular Road to where a stream flowed through an arch of bamboos. 'Ah, these confounded bamboos. I can't manage them.' She was agitated, not herself.

They retraced their steps to the cottage after barely an hour.

On the Thursday he was expecting to see some new advances in Elizabeth Prowder's progress. She had been planning to work all of Wednesday on her watercolours.

Lucia, the Portuguese maid, let him in after detaining him with some conversation in the pantry before she left for the market.

Lavington was taking the children over to the Warners for the day. Michel Jean witnessed their departure from the drawing room as he looked through the house to the veranda at the back and the garden beyond, catching the children leaving their mother in the accumulation of sunlight; the effulgence of light trapped where the coralita vines, mixed pink and white, covered the arbour. Kate was part of the light in her white muslin. Eddie was dressed in a sailor's suit, his collar piped with blue; his mother's little admiral. He chased a yellow butterfly into the garden with his net. Michel Jean envied the settled domesticity. How happy the children were, how healthy Eddie looked. Would Louis Michel ever grow into a strong boy?

The house was quiet. He waited a moment before he introduced himself. He stood in the shadows as the grandfather clock ticked, soon to chime the hour of their lesson. He stared as Elizabeth Prowder recomposed herself. She rose and erected her easel, pinning her paper and arranging her paints; her box of watercolours and a palette of oils she had recently taken to preparing. She arranged her stool and sat with her back to him. She had scraped her hair off the nape of her neck and tucked it into a roll that allowed wisps to stray from their informal but nonetheless purposeful arrangement made secure by a nest of hairpins.

As the clock chimed eight o'clock, Michel Jean stepped forwards like an actor hearing his cue to enter onto the stage to play his part. He caught a view of himself for a second in the mirror over the sideboard as he walked across the drawing room. He looked like an intruder. He coughed to clear his throat on arriving on the threshold of the veranda, but also to warn Elizabeth Prowder, lest he startle her. She turned towards him. He had half expected her to be alerted by the chime of the hour, but she had remained steadfastly staring into the garden at whatever it was she was thinking of working on this morning as her composition.

She turned her torso slightly, looking over her shoulder, and he would have liked to have said, freeze, and painted her in that posture of expectant surprise with the light and shadows playing behind her. He was reminded of a Vermeer; the yellow light and the interior of the room. There was something very knowing in her look as if, no matter how preoccupied she seemed with arranging her composition, she was in fact awaiting his arrival. There was a sadness, too, a glimmer of melancholia. He put it down to the farewell she had just made to her children.

His thoughts were again of his own children and Louise's last letter, describing the effects of Louis Michel's condition on Rosie.

'Mr Cazabon!'

'*Pardon*, I surprise you.'

'No. Not really. I was preparing for you, as you can see.'

'Yes, you're very prepared. And you have chosen a view as well.'

'I've had time today. Lucia is at market, the children with Lavington. Mr Prowder departed at dawn on one of his expeditions to La Brea.'

'La Brea! He's gone to the end of the world!'

'Oh, you Creoles! You do exaggerate!'

'Well, you do know where it is.' Michel Jean liked to have a bit of banter before starting work. He needed to exorcise his own nervousness. There was a restraint he found difficult. He preferred to joke and even to tease. 'You've not gone yourself? Surely! To see one of the wonders of the world? The bitumen with which your countryman, the poet buccaneer, and I dare say royal lover, caulked his ships before returning with fool's gold to his queen.'

'Mr Cazabon, what are you talking about? You're full of stories this morning.'

He realized that he had overstepped the mark. Was it the word 'lover', introduced so casually into their privacy? He did not know what she thought about anything like that. But she did seem to blush for a second. He was sure that he had seen that sudden rush of blood resulting in that tint upon her cheeks, that hint of rouge spontaneously appearing, and then fading in the instant.

He changed the subject at once. 'So, have you been invited to the wedding? I'm sure . . .'

'The wedding? What wedding? Whose wedding?'

'Is there another wedding in town worth talking about?'

'Are you talking about Lord Harris's marriage to his Creole lady?' She was pinning and unpinning her paper on her easel.

'Indeed. It's going to be quite an occasion.'

'Do you think so? The Governor's a very discreet man. A very low-key sort of person. I'm surprised it's going to be at the cathedral, though. I would've thought that one of the smaller chapels of ease, say the lovely All Saints at Tranquillity, built with that wonderful Laventille stone, might be more to his taste.

Such an elegant gable and the morning light coming across the savannah transfigures the double rose window. It's smaller, but with its buttresses and lancet windows it never fails to inspire. And, you know, they've transferred the old Seraphim organ from Trinity. So, there could be quite suitable accompaniment. I must say, I imagined the whole thing happening there the other Sunday while attending Eucharist. I'm quite disappointed.'

Michel Jean stood and listened as Elizabeth Prowder transported herself with her talk and fantasy. He wondered why it meant so much to her.

'Reinagle's neo-Gothic has never really impressed me. I think it must be the abbreviated steeple, which I've understood was thought noble by that Governor Woodford. One hears odd things about him for all his municipal developments. I don't know. It's beautiful enough in its surroundings with its enclosed lawn. I'm surprised to have read that that traveller Coleridge, only recently here, thought that it was one of the most elegant and splendid things in the Empire. I really don't think so myself.'

Michel Jean noticed that the watercolours were drying up and the few oils that Elizabeth Prowder was beginning to experiment with were oozing from their tubes onto her palette, their red and blue secretions glistening in the sun; blacks, yellows and greens reminding him of the caterpillars he had noticed feeding on the frangipani at the bottom of the garden.

He then realized that he had been standing all the while, without putting down his bag of paints and easel that were still strapped to his back. He lowered his equipment to the ground, thus indicating that it might be suitable to begin work. He was half expecting to hear the children returning with Lavington. That would mean that the lesson would have to be interrupted, and, if lucky, resumed after Lavington had settled them down to a new occupation after the telling of their savannah adventures. This had happened before. But Elizabeth Prowder was not to be deterred from her now frenzied talk about architecture, so that Michel Jean began to wonder if there was something wrong.

Had there been some recent event in her life of which he was uninformed? Of course, there could be many. What did he know of her intimate life?

He did not want to tell her then that he was about to paint Trinity Cathedral as one of the Governor's commissions. That might release even further lengthy criticisms of Philip Reinagle's design. He was not going to tell her that the gentleman had been one of his earliest teachers and mentors.

'At least that other traveller, Day, is it?' Elizabeth Prowder continued with her lecture on architecture. 'Thought it handsome, referred to its extinguisher steeple as pocket size, which he put down to a fear of earthquakes. Quite sensible I suppose. Did you feel that tremor the other morning? It gets so still and hot before the quake.'

Whether it was her own story which had begun to terrify her, Elizabeth Prowder suddenly changed tack. 'Really! What are we doing, whiling away the time when you should be tutoring me in art, Mr Cazabon? You do think I'm improving, don't you?' She asked this with a quite forlorn expression.

'Of course. You get better with each new effort. And look at all the work you've done since the last lesson.'

The wedding and the architecture of churches was banished from their thoughts and conversation as they prepared their paints while discussing their composition. The morning sun was high in the sky, and a drizzle, which had fallen when they were talking, allowed the light on the wet foliage to increase the lushness of the green and the brightness of the variegated leaves of the crotons which seemed to be still wet, to have been painted with vivid reds, ochres and yellows. Particularly startling was the wet, streaked olive and purple of the riau at the boundary of the garden.

Michel Jean concentrated on the improvement of Elizabeth Prowder's foreground as she built her composition, a partial view of one wing of the military barracks, which was taking on a terracotta glow, framed by a royal palm on one side, and a cluster of mahoganies on the other. He leaned over and intervened with the small detail of a soldier's scarlet jacket. 'There, that completes it. That splash of red.'

'Do you think so?' She looked up at him quizzically. Her white hand with its brush still lay alongside his brown one, where he had intervened in her composition.

Michel Jean did not know how to read Elizabeth Prowder's agitated distraction throughout the lesson. No sooner had they started than she was rising from her stool and offering him lime juice. As he awaited her return from the pantry, he inspected her prospect of the entrance to the barracks. He had painted this view on a number of occasions since their lessons had allowed him the opportunity to visit the barracks, and he had also lent her one of these views to copy from. First of all, he was judging her sense of perspective as the viewer is drawn into the painting along the road that leads to the barracks; the soldiers' quarters filling the space at the end. The frame was one in which angelin trees made an arch over the road, so that there was a sense of tunnelling through light to a horizon at the end.

He kept holding the painting away from him to better judge the depth of the perspective; the architecture of the barracks and the naturalness of the arch of trees. He was judging her use of greens and blues and the splash of red in the dresses of the women reclining on the grass beneath the almond trees. He was so absorbed that he didn't notice how long it was since she had gone off to the pantry for lime juice. A scream from inside the house startled him.

He hurried in the direction of what was now a call, not exactly for help, but of spontaneous anguish and pain. He found Elizabeth Prowder lying on the pantry floor, trying to raise herself. He noticed at once that her skirt of white muslin was growing a stain of blood all down the front. He thought, incongruously, of her jams, her guava jellies and marmalades. He thought at first she must have cut herself, but then realized the pain was not from a cut hand or foot but from her abdomen, against which her hands were pressed.

'No, no, don't come in here. Fetch a doctor. Fetch the doctor.'

Her face was as white as chalk, desperate. At first he did not want to leave her.

'You must hurry!' she urged.

'She's on the floor of the pantry,' he kept repeating. 'Mrs Prowder needs a doctor.'

The guard looked at him suspiciously.

'She's bleeding.'

'You stay here,' the guard ordered.

Michel Jean felt helpless. He kept seeing Elizabeth Prowder's face. She had been so insistent that he did not come near her. He then felt that it must be women's business, something relating to her menstruation.

The doctor arrived with the guard, who was still looking at Michel Jean suspiciously.

'What is it?' the doctor asked.

'It's Mrs Prowder. She went off to the pantry and then screamed out for help. I found her on the floor, bleeding. She insisted I call a doctor.'

'What were you doing in Mrs Prowder's house?'

'Doing? I'm here to give her painting lessons.'

'Painting lessons? My good man, you better stay here with the guard. Hold him here while I go and see what the matter is,' the doctor instructed the guard. They both looked at each other and then at Michel Jean.

Michel Jean protested.

'Sir. I must prevent you from leaving.'

'She's my student. I'm concerned about her.' He wanted to mention that he thought it was women's business, maybe nature's way. But he knew that to say any of this would sound too intrusive.

'The doctor will examine and assist her. If what you say is true . . . I'll get the resident officer to go and investigate further. You must stay here.'

'Why are you doubting me?' Michel Jean could see that the soldier had every intention of barring his departure.

'This is a military barracks, sir. We have intruders. We must investigate.'

'Ask the guard at the gate. They let me in this morning. I have an arrangement with the Prowders. The Governor and his secretary know about this arrangement. I insist.'

'Sir, you must do as I say, or I'll be forced to restrain you.'

'Restrain me? I'm an artist doing his job.'

'That's what you say.'

Michel Jean was frustrated by what he saw as the injustice of his confinement. He knew the suspicion must be because of his colour, and he resented it.

'The laws were changed in 1829, young man. I expect you've not been in the colony long.'

'Sir, I must caution you.'

'The Governor's secretary will investigate this.'

'Sir, I must caution you again.'

Michel Jean relented. There was no sign of the doctor returning.

Michel Jean was sent to Colonel Ward for the investigation.

'Were you alone in the house with Mrs Prowder?'

The consternation that this notion created among the young officers on duty standing near by was noticeable. Their hostility towards the idea of a coloured man being alone in the house with a white woman was palpable.

'What were you doing before Mrs Prowder went off to the pantry?'

'We were talking about architecture and then getting down to our painting lesson.'

'Architecture! Painting lesson? Oh, yes, that's your claim.'

'It's not a claim. It's what I'm employed by Mrs Prowder to do. Have you checked? It will be very easy to corroborate.'

'I don't need your advice, sir, as to how we carry out an investigation.'

'I don't see why you need an investigation at all. Just talk to Mrs Prowder.'

'We have . . .'

'And?'

'You were alone with Mrs Prowder, you say?'

Colonel Ward was not listening as Michel Jean explained again that he was an artist and was giving Mrs Prowder a lesson in the use of watercolours for landscape painting.

'Are we meant to believe this? Do you think we're stupid, my man? You're a fantasist, or a scoundrel.' Colonel Ward added, 'I think we can deduce that Mrs Prowder experienced some kind of shock.'

'What sort of shock? Speak to the lady,' Michel Jean insisted.

'Mrs Prowder is in no state to be interrogated. The doctor is attending to her.'

'I thought you said you had spoken to her.'

'Mr Cazabon! Is that your name?'

'You know it's my name.'

Michel Jean could tell that the colonel and the soldiers thought he was telling them a preposterous tale. They took his story not as an explanation for his legitimate presence, but as a pretence to hide his guilt. Michel Jean did not want to even imagine the offence they were suggesting by their suspicion. He hated the thought that Elizabeth Prowder herself might be interrogated as to its possibility, when the doctor and the accompanying officer in charge attempted to discover what had happened.

After being detained for the rest of the morning he was told that he could leave. He was allowed under supervision to return to the house to retrieve his painting equipment from the veranda. This evidence did not seem to impress the officers.

The doctor and the two officers were in the pantry as he passed through to the door. He felt sure that Elizabeth Prowder was in the house, probably in her bedroom.

'Is it possible for me to see Mrs Prowder?' Michel Jean asked the doctor.

'Are you mad, my man?'

There was an unusual quiet in the house that was normally full of talk and laughter and the voices of children.

He was asked to give his address and told that he would be required to submit himself later in the day to an interrogation, which an officer would conduct at his home. Or, he might be asked to return to the barracks. He was then ordered away from the house and escorted to the main gate.

Humiliated and angry, Michel Jean walked back towards the town. He felt harrowed by the fact that he had not been allowed to see Elizabeth Prowder again, and that she might think he had deserted her.

On passing through the pantry, as he had exited the house across the drawing room from the veranda, he had overheard the doctor sufficiently to confirm his impression that Elizabeth Prowder had suffered a sudden miscarriage. But what remained imprinted on his mind was the look on the officer's face as he looked up from the blood-soaked floor. He could see that both the doctor and the officer shared a suspicion that Michel Jean had been responsible for bringing on the miscarriage.

He had not realized that Elizabeth Prowder was pregnant. The information made him think differently about her relationship with her husband, in a way which he had not done before. His brief encounters with the gentleman at Lord Harris's dinner party, and then on arriving at the house for a lesson, were all that he had to go on. He was a man who was anxious about his wife. He remembered Wildman's view of their troubled time when they had first arrived on the island. Now, she had lost her baby.

He wondered about the aftermath: the return of the children with Lavington, her husband's return from La Brea, the continuing investigation and the increased suspicion about his behaviour.

How would he resume their lesson the next week? Would they ever resume lessons, given her health, but, more particularly, given the ridiculous way in which he was now viewed? His one solace was that, among her carers, Lavington was admirably capable. Maybe she would be the one from whom he might seek advice about the resumption of their art lessons. Had he heard the officer's remark correctly as he left the house? 'We'll get you for this, artist,' he had said under his breath. Was it artist or rapist? This word formed a dread mantra in his head.

Who could he talk to about all of this? He felt so isolated. He could not possibly write to Louise about the event, about his humiliation. It was she whom he wanted above all, though. It was too disturbing, too difficult to describe in a letter. He would have to complain about his treatment by the soldiers. He would have to choose a moment with Wildman. There was Uncle St Luce, maybe his father? He had doubts about each one.

The following day, Michel Jean was at Corbeaux Town. Pompey had not yet arrived at his boathouse. The light was poor. What with the looming rain, the first intimations of dawn, the foreday morning was not as bright as usual. He sketched the boathouse in the shadows.

With fast strokes followed by quick scratching-out, he had caught the instantaneous contrast between what little light there was and the gloom of the morning in black and white. His speckling gave the effect of a lively sea as the sun struggled to rise and bring some brightness to the metallic grey of the water.

He had been plagued by dreams which he could hardly remember, but which had possessed a mood of anxiety related to the uncertainty he now felt about returning to St James Barracks in a few days' time for his next painting lesson.

No officer had come to visit him. There had been no interrogation as threatened. What was he to surmise? He could only imagine that Elizabeth Prowder herself had made it quite clear that Mr Cazabon had indeed been giving her a painting lesson and she had gone to make lime juice when she was quite suddenly overcome with pain. Yes, she had called on him to run to get the doctor. They would have to believe her. Because, on the doctor's more thorough examination, there would be no question of what was being suggested about him.

He hoped that they had never actually made their suspicions and fears explicit to Elizabeth Prowder. Though he knew that she knew the truth, he felt that the suggestion might act like an infection, which would continue as an idea every time she thought of him, or met him again. He thought that she would think, How can I ever sit alone with him and paint; travel with him to some remote spot to find the bamboos or the waterfalls? The mere insinuation might cause her to be wary about his behaviour in the future. How could she trust herself in his presence, if her doctor and an officer of the Queen's Regiment could so quickly jump to conclusions about him?

All these imaginings and their consequent feelings troubled him more than if he had been interrogated. He had waited at Edward Street all afternoon in anticipation.

The weather became brighter. The small beach at Corbeaux Town was transformed from grey into ochre. The shift in the light transfigured the water near the shore so that it reflected the blue that had now appeared in the sky. The yellow and dun of the sand, and the reflections of a sloop that had entered the bay unnoticed, built the scene. Michel Jean tried to concentrate on his sketch, but was distracted by his anxieties over Elizabeth Prowder.

Pompey appeared. 'You ent waste time. You up with the cocks. And I see you get a sketch and half a painting. Continue while I brew up some coffee here for we on this coal-pot. I have some nice Gran Couva coffee.'

Bright sun caught the friends still talking about fishing, boat-building and painting.

The day of the Governor's marriage to the Archdeacon's daughter was nearing. Michel Jean was down at Trinity Cathedral to get a sense of the setting for what was to be the society wedding of all time in Port of Spain. He was unsure of what he would be able to do with a full congregation. He walked about the cathedral, getting a feel for its detail. He had a growing sense of the effect he wished to create through sepia watercolour heightened with white. There were treasures here, he remembered, that he would not be able to record for his patron.

As he sat in the transept and allowed the atmosphere to envelop him, his thoughts were inevitably of Elizabeth Prowder's remarks on Reinagle's neo-Gothic architecture during that fateful morning of their most recent lesson. His mind was racing ahead with his plans, while his emotions were troubled by not knowing what had happened to her. He could still hear her cry of agony coming from the pantry. The loss of Elizabeth Prowder's baby inevitably reminded him that he should have heard about the arrival of Augusta's baby. He would have to try and get some news from Orange Grove. He continued to sit in a pew that caught the sunlight through the transept door leading in from the enclosed lawn with the frangipani trees and palms, reflecting on these worries and responsibilities, while trying to imagine the paintings he had to do for Excellency.

There was a voice at the front of the church, but when he turned he did not see anyone. It must have been one of the ladies arranging flowers, whom he had seen on entering the church earlier.

A resounding thump of a seat, or some large prayer book being dropped onto the stone floor and echoing through the silent vault of the church, startled him. On turning around, he couldn't see anyone who might account for the disturbance. His reverie interrupted, he was leaving by the transept door into the hot yellow noise of outside, when he heard rushing footsteps behind him. Looking around, he was astonished to see the girl, Kate Prowder, running down the central aisle, followed by her little brother, Eddie, both pursued by an agitated Lavington. Her green skirts were billowing behind her, and her bonnet was struggling to stay on in its appropriate position because of the draught down the centre of the cathedral.

She was running and calling out to the children in loud whispers. 'Kate, Eddie, stop at once!' The children were not paying their governess any attention and Michel Jean stood looking on at what at first appeared quite comical, as the children had now turned into the transept aisle and were running towards him and calling out his name.

Kate was shouting, 'Monsieur Cazabon. Monsieur Cazabon!' Clearly, her governess had had more influence upon Kate on the use of titles.

But Eddie was calling him as he had heard his mother address him. 'Mr Cazabon, Mr Cazabon.'

Michel Jean could see Lavington scowl still further; now she was not just impatient with the children for tearing away from her supervision to destroy the tranquillity of this place of worship. She arrived just in time, flushed from the exertion of her running, to rescue him from the children's excitement. They were practically throwing themselves at him in a way he had not experienced before in the garden at St James Barracks.

'Monsieur Cazabon! Do excuse us! We have quite lost all sense of proper decorum. Kate, Eddie. You must quieten down. Monsieur Cazabon is here for meditation and prayer.'

Michel Jean smiled at her words of concern and reassured her that the children had not disturbed his meditation or prayer, but that his visit was an entirely secular one.

'Can I show you the church or have you already benefited from Mrs Prowder's knowledge of the building's architecture?'

He hoped his embarrassment at the sound of her name did not show. What did Lavington know of the events of that morning?

He was sure that the children would have been spared the details of both their mother's condition and the soldiers' suspicions and insinuations about him. Kate and Eddie's exuberant attention seemed to show that they were, if anything, enamoured at seeing him on this expedition to the town, this visit to the cathedral where the grand wedding was to take place. They were still very animated and he had to drop to his knees to be at their height to give them the close attention that they craved.

'What are you doing here, Monsieur Cazabon?' Kate enquired in her usual very articulate way, so like her mother, while Eddie kept holding onto his arm and dragging him away to view the handsome brass lectern that sported an eagle with outstretched wings and a daunting head and beak that had caught the boy's attention.

'Is this where Lord Harris is going to get married to Miss Sarah Cummins?' Kate asked with curiosity.

'It is indeed!' he replied in an exaggerated voice so as to match her own excitement. He looked into her wide, astonished eyes, those of a child but so like her mother's.

'I wonder what her dress will be like as she walks down that long aisle.'

'Well, we'll have to see. That's the surprise for everyone, especially the bridegroom. What will the bride be wearing and how will she look?' Michel Jean turned from the girl's rapture to the governess looking down on them, puzzled as to how to conduct the encounter any further.

'Come, children, we must not disturb Monsieur Cazabon any longer. I'm sure he has many more important things to do than be distracted by noisy children.'

'But, Lavington,' Kate pleaded. 'This is such a surprise to see Monsieur Cazabon here.'

'It is indeed. Eddie, come here!' Eddie was extending his curiosity about the lectern by climbing into the pulpit to reach the outspread wings of the apocalyptic eagle upon which the book of the Gospels was opened.

'I'll fetch him,' Michel Jean quickly volunteered, enjoying the children's company, while planning how he might enquire about their mother. Kate gave him his cue.

'Mama says you're going to represent the wedding in a painting.' Kate spoke to him very directly and maturely. He could see that Lavington was not entirely approving of this precocious statement.

'Kate . . .'

'Yes, I've been commissioned to paint views of the Governor's wedding.' Michel Jean was surprised that Elizabeth Prowder had spoken of him to her children. But he did wonder where she had got this information from. Was it from her husband who had got it from Lord Harris or Wildman? Or, was it from the dreaded Mr Warner? She had once dropped the name into her conversation, saying that she had been at the Warners' and had borrowed books from that gentleman's private library. The child, Bella, though older, had played with her children. Lavington often took them on walks past the Warner house. He remembered her stories.

Kate continued. 'Mama says we can't come to the actual wedding. She and Papa will be there. But Lavington can bring us to stand outside to watch.' She had such an open face. Michel Jean thought how he would love to paint her. Portraits of children were not his expertise, but this little girl's face would be worth the challenge.

'I see.' Michel Jean noted this information. So, he was at least to see his student, if not actually speak to her. But, did he have to wait that long? He took his chance at this juncture, looking directly at Kate, but really asking Lavington to answer, glancing up at the governess, who was now a little more composed and less eager to take the children away. 'How is your mother?' Then, more directly to Lavington, 'How is Mrs Prowder?'

Kate did not answer the question. She was pulled away by Eddie to explore some other object that had caught her brother's attention, leaving Michel Jean alone with Lavington.

'We've missed you at the house,' Miss Lavington answered. 'This is such a coincidence.'

Michel Jean was taken aback by the governess's reply. It was not an answer to his polite and formal enquiry, but altogether a much more intimate communication. He wondered for an instant whose statement it was, the governess's or her mistress's. He had not before appreciated Lavington as much as he did at this moment. She could appear a bit stiff, emphasized by her starched dresses and even crisper aprons. But she was clearly more warm-hearted and sensitive than he had imagined.

In the absence of the children she was now more forthright. 'As you know, Mrs Prowder has been indisposed and not up to her painting lessons. She expressed the other day the hope that you had received her message sent by the messenger boy from the barracks, as she wondered that she had not had a message in return.'

He thought that maybe he was again being sabotaged by a member of the St James Barracks, some lad with ambitions to be a soldier, or to join the Royal Engineers.

'No? Well, that explains . . .'

'No. I've never received a message from Mrs Prowder and have been wondering . . . but not thinking it appropriate to come to the house in case Mrs Prowder was still indisposed. So, I haven't acted on my concerns for her. Foolish of me really. You must apologize for me.'

He felt the blood racing to his cheeks as he spoke. He found he sounded so English, like Barnaby, whose accent he had at times imitated because it was easier to be understood rather than look into another's bewildered eyes as he spoke in his French-sounding English, his inflections so musically affected by the patois, by the modulations of his mother's Guadeloupian voice.

'Foolish of me really.' He tried it once again, and thought it genuine to his ears, but wondered what discordant jarring it made to Lavington's hearing, as he tried to interpret the almost imperceptible play of a smile on her half-opened lips.

'No, I'm certain that Mrs Prowder will feel that she should apologize to you, when she learns that her message never got to you. I expect it could be something as simple as the boy not being familiar with the street or the way the houses are numbered . . .'

'I'm sure. You must convey my best wishes to Mrs Prowder and thank her for trying to contact me. Tell her that whenever she feels she might like to resume her painting lessons, I would be more than happy to oblige. I wish her all the best for her health.'

Lavington listened to this little speech without interrupting. When Michel Jean had had his say, she reached out and touched his arm and said, 'I will convey your message and your wishes to Mrs Prowder. I'm sure a resumption of her painting lessons is just the balm that she needs at this time to aid her convalescence. I must tell you that she has been copying your view of South Quay more than once, and her efforts, despite her indisposition, have shown quite remarkable advances in the use of watercolours, because, as you know, she is already accomplished in drawing.'

Michel Jean smiled at this last comment; Lavington's defence of her mistress's accomplishments.

'*Oui*, yes, yes indeed. I'm so pleased.' He reached into his portfolio that he often carried around with him and drew out a recent painting of the Maraval dyke. 'Would you mind . . . if I fold this carefully . . . I would be most grateful if you would give this to Mrs Prowder in order to allow her some fresh experience while she is still unable to have lessons. Do ask her to send me another message.' He wanted to tell Lavington how angry he had been, how angry he could still get, how difficult returning to the barracks would be for him. He felt that she knew, that she understood his restraint.

'Certainly. Children, I think we should go now. We've detained Monsieur Cazabon long enough, and time has sped on, so we must return to the barracks.'

Kate and Eddie were ready to leave the Trinity Church, but disappointed that Monsieur Cazabon was not to join them in the square opposite for one of those iced confections still such an excitement in the town, especially among the children.

'*Au revoir*, Monsieur Cazabon,' Kate called, already racing away with Eddie in hot pursuit.

'Bye-bye, Mr Cazabon.' Eddie ran looking backwards, almost stumbling as a consequence.

'Eddie, it's Monsieur Cazabon. And, watch where you're going. Do forgive us.' But he could see now that Lavington was feigning her apology, there now being a better understanding between them. They both understood the exuberance of children; he at once catching a remembered glimpse of his own on an afternoon in the Bois de Boulogne: Rose Alexandrine stumbling into a puddle and almost falling under the wheels of Louis Michel's perambulator.

He watched them bustle their way out of the opposite transept into the light of Brunswick Square. He turned to make his own exit as they became part of the light, disappearing into the haze of the late morning brightness. He longed for his own children, for their play and laughter on the Saint-Germain-des-Prés.

He walked down Clarence Street to Marine Square, finding his way to Almond Walk. He kept on walking to Fort San Andres, towards the lighthouse on its mole. From there he looked back from the breakwater upon which the lighthouse stood and saw one of his recent views of the town. He saw how his fiction had subtly altered the reality of the place, though the commendations from Excellency were of how well he had represented South Quay and the King's Wharf, reflecting the growing economy of the colony with the hogsheads of sugar and barrels of rum, the *marchandes* sitting amid the produce from their country gardens.

'Some lady say she come to Monsieur Cazabon.' He knew that it was not one of the girls from Corbeaux Town, who liked to earn a small sum and inquisitively observe his business and on whom he liked to practise his figure drawing. Josie would not have introduced any of them with the title 'lady'. His sister's usual expression on those occasions was, 'Is a jamette come to maco the place!' Her fierce judgement on the gossips of the town would have him rescuing the poor girl from any more insults and from the nosy neighbours at the windows overlooking his yard.

When he looked down from the veranda he caught her framed in the gateway of allamanda and bougainvillaea in her green bonnet. Today she wore a skirt and bodice of browns shot through with yellow ribbon. 'Miss Lavington,' he called out. She looked up, startled, maintaining her dignity under the assault of Josie's rude introduction. She raised her arm and waved, but looked embarrassed doing so. 'I'll be right down,' he said.

He hoped that she had not caught him shoving his shirt into his trousers. He was unwashed, uncombed, caught as he worked in his studio in a vest and old trousers. He hoped, too, that she would interpret this as the appropriate attire of a Parisian artist, one of those bohemians. He could not see the children.

Had she come on her own? As he passed through the pantry, he met the censure of Josie.

'Who is this old woman now! I thought you tell me is some young English girl you giving lessons. Is old woman you chasing now?'

'Josie, give me a chance, nuh. The woman is the governess.'

'Governess? What is that? I never hear them big name for my mother and myself. Governess! Is servant and when is not slave is housekeeper. And we know what that mean. All you ent change, nuh.'

'Josie, what is all of this in aid of this morning? When the poor woman gone you could say what you want to say. She ent do you nothing. Give she a chance. Coffee? I smelling some nice coffee. And a nice piece of that cake. You never know, she may want to see my studio.'

'Well, so, excuse me, Monsieur Cazabon, *artiste extraordinaire*! Don't worry. I ent go bite she.'

'Josie, sister.' He leaned over to kiss her on the cheek.

'Watch yourself. You better go and bring she in from the gate and see what message she bring.'

'Message?'

'You must think I stupid in truth. You think I don't know that you waiting to hear from the young girl. I ent deaf, you know. And, I ent blind. I does hear and see what go on, you know. Jeansie, your face is an open book.'

'Josie, sweetheart, a favour, be nice to her. I go make it up to you.'

'I hearing that my whole life. That is what you say since I know you. You forget? You does forget, you know.'

'Cake, cake and coffee, Josie. I depend on you.'

All the time Miss Lavington had stood in the welcome shade of the allamanada arbour, interested in the yards in this part of the town and collecting stories to relay to her mistress, but with some censure, he was sure.

'Miss Lavington. You must excuse the delay . . .'

'I must beg to apologize. I barge in . . .'

'*Non, non, non . . .*'

'You must be in the midst of your work . . .'

'Very happy to see you . . .'

'I could not depend on that messenger boy to deliver responsibly. I realize now that you never got Mrs Prowder's message because the silly boy lost it on the way and was too scared to admit his error.'

'That's absurd. The fates conspire against us at times.'

'Do you believe that?'

Michel Jean was leading her along the paved way. 'Would you like to come in for some refreshment?'

'So kind. It's just a message from my mistress that I bring.'

'Excuse the entrance from the back. The front door is around the side of the house. It's the way the yards were first constructed and then altered. Did you find it easily?'

'Absolutely, and I found everyone so helpful on the way with confirmation of the directions. I had heard alarming stories about bandits and even cannibals, but I knew they were untrue.' She smiled, drawing a complicit smile from him at the nonsense that could be heard in the drawing rooms of those great houses.

They were now coming into the pantry. 'This is my sister, Josie. Josie, this is Miss Lavington, Mrs Prowder's children's governess.'

'Pleased to meet you, madam. You're from London, aren't you?' Josie actually curtsied, which Michel Jean knew they would have to talk about later.

'Pleased to meet you.' Miss Lavington extended her arm to shake Josie's hand. This threw Josie into a spin of trying to wipe her wet hands in her apron before reciprocating.

'I hope you enjoying your stay on the island and it not too small for you coming from the big world out there.'

'Well, actually, England is also an island. And an even smaller island than yours is the Isle of Wight where I come from.'

'Oh ho!'

'I know so little of your island that it seems very large with all the things I have still to discover and learn.'

'I see,' Josie said, making Michel Jean relieved that she had decided to perform appropriately, though he knew that later he would have to pay.

They proceeded into the drawing room where Josie had already arranged the table for their repast, and now followed with a tray beautifully laid with a lace cloth and the best china that had belonged to Madame Rose Debonne Cazabon, and was part of the division of the spoils after her death.

'This is very comfortable,' Miss Lavington remarked, looking around her at the furniture and ornaments.

'Yes, I must get it ready for my family.'

'Of course. Mrs Prowder has mentioned your wife and children in Paris. You must miss them.'

'Very much. But I'm forced to delay my departure till after I have completed some of my work for the Governor.'

Miss Lavington listened sympathetically. She then drew out of her unclasped purse a note on folded writing paper and handed it to Michel Jean. 'Mrs Prowder again apologizes for leaving you in the lurch in this way. I can assure you that when she found out she gave the messenger boy a sharp telling-off as only my mistress can do.'

The note was a short one. It was written in that inimitable handwriting, which he remembered seeing on her writing table in the living room, aware that when she was not painting or reading she was often seated at that table writing to her *dearest mama*. The note read: 'I do apologize for my messenger's negligence and wish forthwith to have you again as my tutor if that is at all possible. Yours gratefully, Elizabeth Prowder.'

Michel Jean folded the note and put it into the pocket of his smock, already wanting to reread it to see if he might discover between the lines, however brief they might be, any indication of embarrassment concerning the awful circumstances of their last meeting.

Miss Lavington finished her coffee and cake.

She was a funny-looking thing, he thought to himself. He had had no real experience with women of her kind. She was not like her mistress. She carried herself about the town in a way that showed she was at ease with her surroundings and, from the conversations with her mistress that he had listened to, he could tell she was more liberal and open-minded than the family she worked for. She seemed comfortable with the people of the island as they were, rather than viewing them as objects of curiosity or alarm, as Elizabeth Prowder so often seemed to when she pointed out people and their characteristics on their walks near St James Barracks.

'How are the children?'

'Oh, I thought my mistress should have a morning alone with her little terrors.' She smiled.

Josie had come to the door of the drawing room.

'Miss Josie, that was the most delicious cake I have eaten in a long while. You must give me the recipe, for I'm sure my mistress would be so interested to try it. She is a great maker of cakes, or, should I say, is becoming so. She's young and is still learning. I would imagine that this recipe would enhance her reputation. Her husband loves cakes.'

'Is what left over from the Christmas. We does call it black cake. Not too much rum for you?'

'Rum! Is that what it is? Gives it quite a kick I would say.'

They all smiled.

'I'm sure Mr Prowder would enjoy that. I overheard him only the other day commending Mr Warner on some rum or the other he had tasted out at Arouca.'

Josie kept smiling at the compliment and at the interest of the lady, and she kept on curtseying which was something Michel Jean had never seen her do before until today. But then he had not before experienced Josie in the presence of a white woman. Is this really what Josie thought was appropriate, or was she laughing at him and Miss Lavington? She did look genuinely pleased with the governess's compliments on her baking. But he must speak to her about the curtseying. He did not like to see Josie in that role.

'You must write it down.' Then, as Josie looked appealingly to Michel Jean for help with this, she added, 'Monsieur Cazabon

can bring it along the next time he visits St James Barracks.'
Miss Lavington corrected her faux pas with aplomb. Michel Jean
noticed her tact, her insight into Josie's illiteracy. 'Absolutely. It
can wait, the measures, the recipe . . .'

Josie did her last curtsey and left the drawing room to Miss
Lavington and Michel Jean.

Michel Jean took his cue from Elizabeth Prowder's note and
wrote a brief reply. 'I would be very happy to resume our lessons
at eight o'clock for an hour or more twice a week on Tuesdays
and Thursdays. I will be there next Tuesday.' Again, he wanted
to tell Lavington of his anger, but restrained himself.

On the way through the pantry, Josie offered Miss Lavington
a portion of her black cake parcelled up as prettily as she
could manage with some paper that had been tucked away,
which had once contained a present Michel Jean had brought
from Paris.

'I hope you and your mistress enjoy it. Maybe the mister go
like the kick it give him, as you say.'

They all laughed and Miss Lavington took her leave, shown
to the gate by Michel Jean.

'And what is all this curtseying?'

'I thought you tell me to behave myself.'

Michel Jean looked at Josie without replying and then closed
the door of the studio. He locked himself in for the rest of the
day, instructing Josie that he was not to be disturbed, that he
didn't want her barging into his room as she could at times
with suggestions of juice, mangoes or some confectionery off
the street.

He worked on an oil of a view of Port of Spain from Laventille
Hill for the rest of the afternoon, which included the figures of
Excellency and one of the notable Muslim personalities of the
day. This was to be a major contribution to the collection he
was completing for Excellency. He emerged from his studio at
dusk and sat out on the veranda.

He and Josie spent the evening with easy talk as the lamps glowed amber. The dusk fell and the darkness enveloped them and the house in shadows. Another Port of Spain came alive with the drumming from Besson Street. The smell of fried fish came from the coal-pot fires in the backyards; plantains and melangene grilled on the cooking fires of Corbeaux Town.

'People settling for a life, *oui*,' Josie remarked.

Michel Jean dozed off. Later that evening, he wrote to Louise about the eccentric Miss Lavington. He still could not bring himself to describe the awful scenes which had taken place the last time he had been at St James Barracks.

Michel Jean's entrance into the barracks was unimpeded. He was nervous at first about arriving. The soldier at the gate nodded him through, seeming to know who he was. He must have been told of his arrival. Lavington would have made sure of that, he thought. Anyway, there was not going to be another coloured man with an easel on his shoulders passing through these gates with an appointment with Mrs Prowder to conduct a lesson in watercolours. He would be that painter they would have all been told about. He imagined his notoriety in the officers' mess since Wildman had taken up an enquiry on behalf of Excellency. 'You're now known as the court painter,' Wildman had informed him. Both he and Excellency had apologized profusely about the way he had been treated. He was unsure, though, whether any of the offending soldiers had been reprimanded. He could not be sure of the Wards.

He strolled along the avenue in the shade of the low-lying flamboyante trees, cutting across the St James savannah. The trees made a wonderful parasol, a welcome shade from the hot morning sun. He prided himself that he was what he had begun to call an artist-plantsman, ever since his meeting with David Lockhart had developed his botanical understanding of the landscape.

He tried to keep his thoughts on the coming watercolour lesson, but the inferences within those questions of Colonel

Ward and the interrogating officer after the events of his last visit kept going through his mind. He felt slightly sick in the stomach at the thought of what they had suspected him of doing. He wanted to tell someone, the soldier on duty, just how wrong they had been, how unjust.

Michel Jean stood for a moment at the door of the little grey cottage, hesitating before knocking, rehearsing his introduction, preparing himself for seeing Elizabeth Prowder after such a long interval. He knocked twice in rapid succession.

'Just coming!' He could hear her shout from within. She must be out on the veranda, he thought. 'Just coming,' she repeated, signalling her almost arrival. And then, there she was, flinging open the door with an exaggerated enthusiasm. 'Mr Cazabon, what a pleasure after all this time.'

It was as if nothing had happened. It was as if he had not witnessed her in the extremity of her pain, in the exposure of her privacy. She was almost shrieking, which he thought must be a sign of her nervousness. He was nervous, too, fearful of what she might say and how he would reply. She did all the talking, sweeping him into the drawing room and out to the veranda. He hardly took in what she was saying, something about Lavington and the children having gone out half an hour before. 'We have the morning to ourselves, if we so choose to make up our lost time with an extended class.'

'Yes, of course,' he blurted out. He was surprised at this choice of an extension. He had imagined that she might want to keep to the original arrangements till they had become better reacquainted with each other.

'I thought we'd work here,' she proclaimed, standing next to her easel and paints.

He had thought of an *en plein air* lesson in the full view of those who came and went from the barracks, maybe even on the bank of the river under the bamboos, would be what she wanted, lest there be any suspicions. That was what he had thought she might desire. But then he thought that maybe she imagined that would be like giving in to the suspicions of the Wards and the interrogating officer.

'This is excellent here. We can find a lot to work with here,' he said. 'Light and shadow and the colours at the end of the garden.'

Walking through the house, he remembered again the morning that had forever altered that space. He could still hear her scream; see her lying on the pantry floor, clutching at her abdomen, curled in upon herself. He thought she looked pale today, but she appeared high-spirited. He had remembered that this was one of her moods. She noticed him staring at her.

'Can I ask Lucia, the girl, to bring us some juice? And we have ice today, you know.'

'That's wonderful.'

'The man brings it in the morning and Charles has had an icebox made at the back in a shed. We wrap it in crocus bags; crocus is what the man in the yard calls them. They bundle the cocoa beans on the estates into these kinds of bags, I understand from Mr Warner.'

Then she remembered that she should be asking Lucia to bring in the juice.

'It's soursop juice. Lucia picked the fruit and made the juice,' she said on returning from the pantry.

'Delicious,' he said with anticipation, turning from erecting his own easel next to hers. He noticed that she had already begun to lay out her palette. He would have to work with her choice. He did not want to contradict her, not this early on at any rate.

'Yes.' She had been observing him examining her palette. 'Yes, an entirely new taste for my palette. The soursop.'

They looked at each other and laughed, enjoying the pun.

Lucia, at that moment, came in with a tray on which there was a jug of iced soursop juice and two glasses.

'Thank you, Lucia. That's splendid.'

Michel Jean smiled at the young girl, who looked confused and shy, unsure what to do with herself. Then, she hurried from the room.

'Very difficult to train them,' Elizabeth Prowder remarked, 'but they are far quicker than the Negroes.' She looked up from pouring the juice and he realized that he was the sudden cause of her self-consciousness about her views on Negroes as compared to Portuguese.

They drank their juice in silence while sitting at their easels, looking out into the garden. She edged her chair a little away from his. 'Yes, this is a better angle from which to look at things.' She rearranged her muslin skirt to prevent it catching in the legs of the chair.

He was choosing a composition. 'Maybe, the bamboos as they lean towards the stream which feeds the river? See how the light filters in between the clumps.'

'Bamboos! Confounded bamboos. I still can't quite get them. Well, not like you can.'

He looked across at her. She had not lost any of that spirit he had first recognized. 'Well, it comes with practice. I can show you again.'

'I can draw, as you know. I've been drawing. I've been trying during my convalescence. Little by little,' she added.

Michel Jean stopped what he was doing at that moment, preparing his paper with a light wash. He looked across at her. It was the word, convalescence, which had startled him. Lavington had used the same word, but it was Elizabeth Prowder's first explicit reference to her miscarriage, the first conscious exchange about that day and its repercussions.

She was trying to secure her paper to the easel. She had paused and had looked up and allowed her stare to continue into the garden where the light caught the white stone birdbath, in which a number of palm tanagers were splashing in the water. He could see that she was fighting against the emotions her own words had evoked in her.

'Well, we must get on,' she said, breaking from her reverie.

She began and he intervened with his brush. 'It's a feathering technique. Corot was a master at that, as you well know.'

'Yes, oh yes, I see. My tutor in London once told me that.

Yes . . .' She continued while he got on with his own painting. They worked steadily, with him keeping an eye on her careful application.

The morning had run away with them and she had progressed with the bamboos. He intervened with a light touch at the base of the clump, then sensed her irritation at his intervention.

There was a sudden downpour of rain that released the fragrances of the hot earth and the scents from the grasses and flowers. The bush, just beyond the perimeter of the garden, steamed, and there was that continuing *drip drip* of rainwater from the branches of the wet trees. 'I thought there would be rain. It's been so hot.' He noticed the beads of sweat on her brow and a patch of damp in her white muslin as she raised her arm to reach for her paints and brushes. He could smell her clean sweat. The green of the lawn and the variegated leaves of the crotons glistened with the sudden burst of sunlight that followed upon the shower.

'Look at what has happened. Light on wet leaves,' she exclaimed.

'Yes, you might be able to catch some of it with your cobalt green. Look, like this.' He made rapid dabs with the end of his brush over the surface. After washing his brush, he observed, 'Yellows for lantana.'

'That's something else you do which I find quite difficult.'

'You can build the colour lightly that way. Not too much. See, it begins to shine. Like those red leaves of the riau on the boundary. The extremities of the Barbados pride. Very feathery.'

'That's just it. Give me a pencil. But a brush and my hand becomes so heavy.'

'You're too hard on yourself.'

'Well, that's the only way.'

'Yes, I know what you mean, but you must give yourself a chance to learn and then practise. What do they say?'

'Practice makes perfect?'

'Yes, there's something in these old maxims.'

'Let's finish. Some more of that juice?'

'*Oui, merci*. Thank you.'

'Lucia! Lucia!' She sang out the maid's name. 'She sometimes pretends not to hear me.' Lucia appeared almost at once. 'Lucia, Mr Cazabon will have some more juice and ice. I'll just have some iced water. Have you begun the lunch?'

'Yes, madam.' Lucia took the tray to the pantry while they washed their brushes, dismantled their easels and shut up their paint boxes.

The silence as they occupied themselves with their cleaning and packing away was like the silence of the house on that morning when he had been made to leave the yard with his tail between his legs. He felt twinges of resentment. He did not have to be here, teaching this young girl.

Lucia had now reappeared at his side with a tray carrying a glass of soursop juice.

'*Merci bien.*'

She smiled and almost curtsied. This he found disconcerting. He felt she wanted to show him a respect she sensed he did not always receive.

When she had left the room, Elizabeth Prowder remarked, 'I observe that you must be bilingual. Is this something you persist in, that you think will be altered by our, by the English presence here, if you don't?'

'It's just the way I've always spoken since I was a child. I went to England to school and later to Paris. So, I'm equally fluent . . .'

'I see. It's just that I've been told the coloureds have republican views and the retention of the French language is important to them.' Then she laughed, saying, 'You won't send us to the guillotine, will you? Or, have us slaughtered like they did in Haiti?'

'I paint, Mrs Prowder. I'm not a politician. But I do wonder where you've acquired such extreme views.'

'No. I won't continue now. Charles tells me that I should be careful with what I say and how I say it and to whom.'

'You are fully entitled to your views, madam.'

'Mr Cazabon, I sense I've touched a sore point.'

'It's only sore because some people insist on irritating it with their barbed comments.'

'Is that what you think I've done?'

'I didn't say that. You have entered our society at a very complicated time. It's easy to misunderstand.'

'Let's agree to continue with painting. On Tuesday next week?'

'Yes, definitely. I was thinking, though, you must be getting prepared for the wedding.'

'Mrs Ward and myself must get seats right in front of the altar,' she said. 'I expect you'll be at some distance to take in the whole.'

He winced at the mention of the name, Ward. He hoped she had not noticed.

'Yes, I think I'll position myself in the choir loft to get a full view of the proceedings. So you've heard that I have been commissioned to illustrate the ceremony for Lord Harris.'

'Oh yes, that young Wildman thinks a great deal of you. We were dining at Government House the other night and he proclaimed your virtues to the whole table and then Lord Harris himself told us all that he had commissioned you to record the wedding for *The Illustrated London News*. Is that correct?'

'Good old James. He's a true friend.' Michel Jean smiled to himself at her view of Wildman as young, given that she must be about the same age. 'I'm going to leave my effort this morning with you to help you complete your painting, if you think that will be helpful. As you know, it's one of the ways I particularly like to teach my students, let them copy my sketches.'

'Yes, thank you. I do appreciate your patience. And thank you for the painting you sent by Lavington during my convalescence. Sorry too, yet again, about the messenger. I just found it too frustrating getting back to things after the interval.' They looked at each other, but neither of them said a word.

Then she said, 'I do apologize for what you were put through on my account.' Without elaborating further, she broke off. 'I think I hear Lavington with my treasures.'

This was his signal to leave. Before the moment was lost, he said, 'I trust you are much better now, and I'm sorry for your loss.'

She looked at him and he could see her eyes fill with tears. 'The children are . . .'

'Yes . . .'

He left before the children entered as they and Lavington would certainly have detained him further. He needed to go. 'Till next week. I'll let myself out.'

As he collected the last of his things and she went into the garden, Michel Jean guessed that Elizabeth Prowder had many things still on her mind about their last meeting. As he left, he could not help seeing on the small desk, where she wrote her letters, the beginning of her latest to her *dearest mama*. She had found the accomplishments of letter writing and painting to be ways in which to assuage the loss of her baby and her mother's absence, he thought. These thoughts lessened his anger and increased his sympathy for her.

'Such a young girl, and Lord Harris so much older. Of course, that's very secure. I'll have to give Mama a full description of the matter and of the whole ceremony once it's over.'

When he had arrived for their lesson the next week, Elizabeth Prowder was talking to Lavington in the drawing room. Lavington was listening politely to her young mistress. She was patience personified. Michel Jean could not help but overhear the conversation from where he was on the veranda, and wonder at Elizabeth Prowder's preoccupation. He had been examining her homework. There was the scene of the stream leading into the river beneath the overarching bamboos. He could see that she had improved on the foreground that they had worked on last week. He moved on to the portfolio of her earlier work that she had left open for his inspection; to prove that she could draw, he thought. She could indeed draw. There was no doubt about that.

Time was hurrying on. It was her time. He waited.

'You know some people do wonder at his choice of a Creole. They wonder if it's at all political. Such a gentle soul, the lord, I cannot but think it must be the genuine choice of his heart.'

'Indeed. I'm sure, given all that you've told me of his person,' Lavington responded circumspectly. She was busy with getting the children equipped with the right shoes for their morning walk and, no doubt, hike into the St Ann's valley, or up Belmont Hill, if Lavington was allowed to have her way over the will of Kate and the peevishness of Eddie, once the heat of the day had increased.

'But you must wonder about what sort of stability these marriages can have.'

'Why so?' That was abrupt for Lavington. Michel Jean listened for the answer. He almost missed the mistress's reply with Kate bounding onto the veranda and demanding that she too have lessons from Monsieur Cazabon.

'Lavington. What can you be thinking? Across cultures, the husband not knowing the background of the wife.'

'She is the Archdeacon's daughter. She may have been born here, but she's from good English stock. Isn't she? And not a hint of colour, if that's what disturbs you, ma'am.'

Those should be words Elizabeth Prowder could admire: good English stock, he thought.

'Not a hint, did you say? I suppose. But it does worry me what goes on out here. You know, to use your word, with the stock. That's the point; breeding, interbreeding. It does go on, you know, half the town of Port of Spain is the result. What can happen outside one's home, family and friends. What desires are bred I can hardly bear to imagine!'

'To look at the Archdeacon and Mrs Cummins, I can't imagine that anything like you're suggesting has gone on.'

'Lavington! You do continue to surprise me. Do we know everything that has happened to the family out here?'

'Happened? What do you mean, ma'am, happened?'

'Well, just what we've been talking about. There's no knowing what people will do when they come out here.'

What must she think of him? Michel Jean thought, now thoroughly distracted by the conversation. He could feel himself getting irritated. How much more of this could he take?

Kate and Eddie were at last ready for their walk. They wanted to drag Michel Jean into the garden.

'I must just look at your mama's work a little longer. Why don't you both run into the garden and play hide-and-seek while Miss Lavington gets ready?'

'Mama won't let her go,' insisted Kate.

'No, she won't,' echoed Eddie. 'Mama!' he screamed.

Michel Jean did not want to miss any of this revealing conversation between Elizabeth Prowder and her children's governess. He had noticed Lavington's protectiveness, but now he noticed a strictness, an ability to be the one in authority. He noticed her looking in his direction from time to time, no doubt worried about the tone of her mistress's views with him, a coloured man, there. He had to admit to himself that he was hurt and angry.

Lavington's patience must have reached its limit because she said with finality, 'I must take the children for their walk and you have a lesson to commence, ma'am.'

'Yes, of course.'

How much more of this could he put up with? he asked himself.

'Mr Cazabon, I've kept you waiting.' Elizabeth Prowder joined Michel Jean out on the veranda.

He wondered at Lavington's command of the situation and at Elizabeth Prowder's ability to turn so amicably from that conversation to the tutelage of her coloured teacher. What was it, despite all her appalling prejudices and her very particular fears, which kept him so fascinated with this young woman?

She could draw, and soon, he thought, she would be painting quite well. To witness that progression under his guidance pleased his sense of irony; it was one of his pleasures. When he allowed his thoughts to become quite wild fantasies, lessons offered themselves as the perfect opportunity for a progressive seduction, the slower the better. He was falling into something he could never fulfil. Who was that conversation with Lavington for? She must have been aware that she had an audience. Was she sending out a very direct signal of *noli me tangere*? Could she have guessed any of his hardly visible desires, which had crept into his real sense of pleasure in her as a student?

When she had mentioned at the last lesson her intention to go down to the church for the wedding with Mrs Ward, he did not know whether she had noticed the irritation on his face at the mention of the name, Ward. She could still seem so unaware of the society in which she was now living. She was so sensitive about some things and quite shockingly insensitive about others.

She was still not ready to start the lesson. He had planned a walk along the Long Circular through the canes and into where the bamboos were in abundance near Dibé. There might even be a waterfall there. She seemed to be pleased with this idea, but was making it impossible to leave the house. While they waited for Lucia to pack a picnic she went on and on about the wedding preparations to the Portuguese girl, who looked as if she was not understanding half the information or opinions which her mistress was imparting, but was having to nod and smile and look interested.

She was now onto describing what the Creole girl, as she persisted in calling Sarah Cummins, might wear, and how she would conduct herself. Then she moved on to Lord Harris and his ability to deal with such private matters in public.

She was so different when she painted, he thought, when they were sitting side by side in some secluded spot, or in the quiet of her garden or veranda. He sometimes did not recognize her when she was holding forth in this way. Was it just her youth, or was she simply repeating the views of her husband and the English set?

In the end, after their *en plein air* lesson between the cane fields off the Long Circular, Elizabeth Prowder's mood changed to one of concentration and then elation. They returned to St James Barracks with a sense of accomplishment.

Once Lavington arrived back with the children she was unable to concentrate on anything else. 'My darlings.' She drew them both into her embrace.

Michel Jean took his leave, having regained the equilibrium which he had lost at the beginning of the lesson.

2

Once the carriage with the governor and his bride had left Trinity Church, Michel Jean said that he would accompany Miss Lavington and the children back to the barracks. He would not leave them to manage the crowds who had gathered for the wedding in the street. She protested. But he said it would be convenient as he would then proceed on to Cocorite, where he was to meet his friend, Pompey, who would be taking him to Craig Island, where he had been invited to record the honeymoon party. He had not been invited to the Archdeacon's house for the *déjeuner à la fourchette*. He was very happy to partake of a light lunch with her and the children. He was satisfied with the sketches he had made of the scenes both inside and outside the cathedral. He was pleased with his collection on the wedding, with the portraits he had done of Excellency and Lady Sarah earlier. He now had to make these ready for *The Illustrated London News*.

They left the square, which was now suddenly deserted, after all the pomp and circumstance, about which the children had been particularly excited, having seen their mother arrive and leave by carriage, their father on a horse as part of the guard which escorted Excellency and his new wife, Lady Sarah.

Miss Lavington served him cold meats and potatoes. He was struck by the English fare. It took him back to St Edmund's when he was a boy.

'I do apologize for the plainness of the meal.'

'It's substantial. I was famished after the long morning.'

With the children off out to the veranda, she served him coffee and continued with her talk.

'Miss Lavington . . .'

'Alas! In vain I would recall
The features hidden from my sight
Too truly is the funeral pall
For ever spread 'twixt him and light.

That was one of her verses at the time of the miscarriage.'

Lavington then changed the subject to events earlier that morning. She described her mistress's state of mind before leaving for the wedding. 'She was already dressed in the blue satinette her mama had sent in the box that month, which arrived by the packet from Barbados just in time. She made me call Dr Drumreck.' Lavington was unusually unsettled as she told this story. 'But then she didn't want to distress Lieutenant Prowder, who was about to leave to join his regiment, nor the children, who were already at a peak of excitement. Then, suddenly, she felt herself again.'

'Miss Lavington. You don't have to break confidences. There's no demand on you for that.' He wondered at how these feelings and memories were at the very surface of her emotions. Her distraction was forcing her to tell the story in fragments.

'It just came back to me. I thought you should know what has been happening here.'

Michel Jean had never broached the subject of Elizabeth Prowder's miscarriage, or the repercussions of that loss in any detail.

'You do realize, Monsieur Cazabon, the suspicion that you were under when you announced Mrs Prowder's condition to the officer in charge that morning?' Lavington asked, gazing steadily at him.

'Yes, of course. But, Miss Lavington, why are we going through this now?'

'Things are still changing. She may not always seem herself.'

'I understand.'

'There were the Wards and her husband, too. They took quite some persuading. It's extraordinary them thinking this, but it's the way of the world. It is beyond them really, that you, with your colour, that a man like you should be an artist and be teaching lessons without some ulterior motive. It's in the mind. That you should be civilized, is how they put it. They can't quite believe it. This worries them so. The idea that you are enlightened is quite beyond them.'

'I must admit I was losing my patience with many of Mrs Prowder's views. As regards the Wards, I . . . But what makes you different, Miss Lavington?'

Lavington looked a little taken aback at the directness of the question.

'What makes me different?'

'*Oui.*'

'It's my nature.'

'Nature? A difficult concept.'

'And, there's nurture.'

'Of course.'

'Some of us have always thought differently. It goes back to the trade. I was fortunate to have a father who was an early abolitionist. So the talk in our household was different to some of the talk I still hear in my employers' household. We're Quakers. You know, even now still, Thomas Carlyle's outrageous piece on the Negro question! But you must not mistake my frankness as betrayal of my loyalty to Mrs Prowder. I've said this to you before. She's just a girl, really. Thrown into a world of huge change. We live at a time of huge change. Yes, nature is a difficult concept. But, nurture, education, is so important. And I've always been a bit of an outsider.'

He wondered what she meant by 'outsider'. Was that why he had a growing sympathy for her? He was an outsider to this English set, and she was caught between servants and mistresses. He found, though, that he did not want to prolong his stay. 'Miss Lavington, I can't thank you enough for your hospitality.' He had been surprised by her openness and forthrightness.

With the children settled into reading and jigsaw puzzles before siesta, he left Miss Lavington after lunch with her own thoughts and imaginings. He would have to be so careful, he thought, on account of both the mistress and her governess and their vulnerable sensibilities.

Michel Jean thought of how, later, as darkness fell upon St James, Flora Lavington, the governess, would, in her solitude, construct her own version of events. She might fall asleep with an image of Sarah Cummins, an eighteen-year-old, a mere girl, a child almost, and her older, more mature husband. This image might be replaced by that of her mistress herself, a girl, too, really, and her husband. Secretly, he thought, she would be jealous, to have been left out as the others were whisked away for the celebrations. Were there other feelings, intimacies, that Miss Lavington might not describe to herself? With whom did she share her intimacies? There was only her mistress, possibly. Michel Jean reflected on how she might let these thoughts and feelings convey her into a slumber, once she was assured that the children were asleep.

He imagined her peeping in at them before retiring to her own bed, to tuck in the mosquito nets once more, the yellow fever being such a scourge. 'I fear the fever so,' she had said to him one day when Eddie had looked a little weak and flushed. 'I could not bear him to be snatched away from us.' He noted how she talked of the children almost as if they were her own.

He thought of his own children at that moment: Louise's last letter about Rosie's messages, and how easily they could have lost Louis Michel to the consumption that had reoccurred. The most recent letter told of good health, but that Louis Michel was again withdrawn. Thoughts of Louise's letter brought him back to his real responsibilities. The Governor's commission, Mrs Prowder's art lessons, these were proving to be too consuming. And, just beneath the surface of these thoughts, there was Augusta and her child about to be born or already born. He needed news.

Taken up with his lessons, his commission for Excellency and the preparations for the wedding, he still had not been to Orange Grove. He felt that he had been procrastinating, dreading the news. He had to act soon.

The weather was changing, but Pompey insisted that they could still make for the Five Islands, despite the choppy waters and occasional white horses, which endorsed the reputation of the gulf for sudden squalls and dangerous currents; the *remous* which might drag you to Venezuela and out through the Dragon's Mouth into the open sea.

Caledonia and Craig were a ghostly presence with an outline of Lennegan Island. Pompey was not to be deterred and pointed to the smallest window of indigo. 'Watch the light, nuh?'

The Five Islands began to take on a blue hue and a lilac tint. The cry of the parakeets filled the air. The regiment's flag on Nelson Island fluttered above the fort. *The Duchess of Argyll*, recently arrived from Calcutta, was moored just off the island. It was being used, since the vexed importation of the indentured workers, as a place of quarantine in order to delouse and register the indentured before their transportation to different sugar estates. 'They say that might be the last ship. They not bringing more. Is another kind of slavery them abolitionists in England saying.' Pompey rested on his oars.

'Yes, Hardin Burnley and Warner lose out,' Michel Jean said with some pleasure. Then he thought of how Hardin Burnley would pragmatically make the best of it, become the advocate of the new arrangement.

'For now. Them does always win.' Pompey sneered.

The white-walled house on Craig Island, where the wedding party was to stay, emerged as the contours of the islands refashioned themselves. Michel Jean chose the sites he wanted to sketch and paint. He excluded the ragged band of East Indians supervised by soldiers. He did not think that they would be an appropriate prospect for a wedding day. Then he thought of how he might record the scene later. He would keep the fort and the flag, symbols of order and dominion. They were quite close to the shore now, and the faces of the East Indian men, women and children on the jetty were just there in front of him. He could stretch out his arm and touch them with his hand. One of them called out, but he could not understand the greeting in Hindi. He waved feebly, embarrassed. Once Pompey had pulled away from earshot, he said, 'Is a real slave trade, *oui*.'

'Burnley go get that lot, *oui*. I was painting out at Orange Grove. He already build his new barrack rooms.'

'They say they sending some of them to Bande-de-l'Est, to Ganteaume at Beau Séjour Estate.'

'Yes, the Governor has an interest out there. He has a cottage and a stud farm.'

Michel Jean looked back from where they had pulled away. Pelicans swooped and fed in the wake. The squatting East Indians from Calcutta formed a line and processed up a small incline from the jetty to the quarters on the hill below the fluttering British flag above the garrison. Pompey dropped him off at the jetty. 'I go see you tomorrow.'

The staircase up to the house on Craig Island was decorated with flowers. He could see that lanterns had been hung in the trees for illumination once evening approached. He positioned himself discreetly on one of the terraces above the jetty to give him a vantage point from which to view the arrival of the barge bearing the Governor, his bride and the honeymoon party.

There was a bustle at the side of the jetty as Excellency and his young bride alighted among their wedding guests, who had arrived in two barges accompanying the Governor's. There was the landing of the luggage and the hazardous climb onto the jetty. The crews did their utmost to help everyone, particularly the ladies and the elderly gentlemen like Mr Hardin Burnley. There was Mr Warner, who was sprightly, but Mr Knox looked like he might need quite a shove to get him out of the barge onto the jetty. Two or three of the crew had to give a hand with great skill and courtesy.

He did not think that Elizabeth Prowder could see him. She was accompanied by her husband and the Wards. Both the colonel and his wife were chaperones. Unknown to them, he caught their conversation as they mounted the stairs beneath the terrace on which he was positioned. Mrs Ward, all eyes on arrival, had spied him in his hideaway. She expressed this fact as she mounted the stairs.

'Do you see that man again? I quite wonder at the Governor having that coloured man in his employ. I wonder that he can continue to trust him.'

He did not hear any reply from the others. The lady's remark was part of her offensive rhetoric, not requiring an answer.

But, as Elizabeth Prowder gained the top of the stairs, she turned to lift her dress that had got caught among the flowers strewn for the bridal procession up to the honeymoon house. As she did so, she directed her gaze at him and he was sure that he saw there the faintest flicker of a smile, a parting of her lips, a comment of reassurance. He was lucky at that point to have lifted his own gaze as he kept on working at his sketch. Then, almost before the moment was over, she had disappeared into the house amidst the chatter and the laughter, embraced by her own people and whisked away from him. Everyone seemed to have vanished to their own quarters. Even Wildman did not come out after the light repast served on the gallery overlooking the jetty. A long siesta was clearly needed for the entire party after the emotions of the day and the celebration at the Archdeacon's house.

Michel Jean had found out where he was to sleep. He was on the island of Caledonia across the causeway. With the tide still not completely in, he was able to make his way across. He found himself with the more senior staff, the very lowest housed in the outhouses right on the water's edge. He settled down to a short siesta. At least he had his own room.

No one in the main house across the causeway on Craig Island seemed to be rising from their siesta. The sunset would surely bring them outside, he thought. There would be a gathering on the jetty for rum punches. Would he be invited?

Looking up from one of his prospects, he saw her on the rocks of the causeway between the two islands, struggling with the slippery surfaces. She had changed into a white muslin dress. He was worried about the increasing tide trapping her.

Should he leave his easel, boxes of paints and brushes and go to her rescue? It was impossible now for him to continue painting. He did not want to draw attention to himself. He was there to be invisible, to paint some representative prospects of the event for Excellency, as a memento. He could not afford to get embroiled in actions, which if wrongly observed, would bring up again the whole affair at the barracks when Elizabeth Prowder had had her miscarriage. He did not want that humiliation repeated.

He could see her more clearly now. She wore a wide-brimmed straw hat. Her dark hair was caught up on the nape of her neck. She did not appear to have on very sensible shoes for this particular hike. She seemed small and fragile against the immensity of the sea and the sky. When would high tide begin to rush in? He would then have to act. He thought she looked up in his direction. He collapsed his easel and packed away his paints and brushes. He inserted into a portfolio his prospects of Carenage and the channel, tying the ribbon securely.

There was still no one out on the jetties or the walkways around the Governor's house on Craig Island. Its white monumental presence across from Caledonia seemed to become more menacing because of who might emerge to view what was happening. No one, no one at all, was visible, not even a servant shaking out a tablecloth.

He could not help himself. He waved. He was not even sure that she was looking in his direction. He waved again. He felt ridiculous, thinking that if anyone saw him he would look quite stupid, but not, of course, if it was Colonel or Mrs Ward. He would look dangerous to them.

Elizabeth Prowder had now stopped clambering over the rocks and was sitting down and bending to reach one of the rock pools. Paintings of oyster pickers along the Calvados coast came back to him.

For a moment, it was like a forgotten life suddenly returning, his wife and children, those trips up to the Normandy coast. He was keeping an eye on Elizabeth Prowder, but it felt like looking down into the bay at Luc-sur-Mer and seeing Louise that time in white muslin and a straw hat among the rock pools, collecting *huîtres* and *crevettes* with a large basket. He felt unnerved by the coincidence. He had made such a fool of himself on that occasion, looking so visible, a black man running across the sands shouting in patois, so heightened were his emotions, waving at Louise to come in from the encroaching tide. He could see her astonishment. They held on to each other, her body cleaving to his as he held her tightly and kissed her tenderly.

Elizabeth Prowder was looking around. She had nearly lost her straw hat to the wind. Then she was waving. He waved back.

He collected up his equipment and clambered down the side of the cliff along a natural path made by the way the wind had twisted the trees, and the sea had corroded the outcrop of rocks where the agave grew, exploding their tall yellow torches. He was throwing all his previous caution to the wind. They were going to meet in the open in front of everyone who happened to be looking out of windows, from the gallery or the jetty.

This might be Mrs Ward's opportunity to call to her husband to see just what that 'nigger' was doing now.

Elizabeth Prowder was calling out to him, but he could not understand what she was saying. He stopped to get a better grip upon his satchel and to hoist it onto his shoulder.

She was then stooping to prod with a stick the rock pool on the edge of which she was standing. She seemed unaware of him as he picked his way over the rocks towards her. Then she stood up as he was almost there. He had to rest his easel. She turned to look up at the house on Craig Island. He followed her long stare across the causeway. There was someone now looking out from the staircase. He did not recognize who it was. Elizabeth Prowder turned towards him as he reached the stable rock on which she was standing. He was out of breath.

'Are you all right?' she called.

'Yes,' he managed to say. 'And you? Are you all right? I was worried that you would get stranded.'

'Perfectly. It's been quite an adventure.'

She was exhilarated.

'Have you seen what's in this pool?'

He rested his things carefully next to them and stooped down to peer into the rock pool. He then noticed that the rocks were alive with crabs that scuttled away at the least disturbance into crevices and fissures. They lost themselves like small children, abandoning themselves on the seashore collecting seashells, with their parents wondering whether they have got lost.

'How has your painting been?'

'I've managed to complete a number of prospects.'

'Wasn't it splendid, all of it? From the moment the organ sounded,' she said, raising herself to sit on a higher rock, gathering her muslin skirts around her legs. She had scratched one of her ankles on the barnacles and there was a drop of blood on the bone, shining like a ruby.

'I've tried to catch the atmosphere and mood.'

'In sepia heightened with white, as you said you might?'

'Yes, both the arrival and the ceremony as seen from the choir loft.'

'I know. I thought of you there. I turned around and saw you, but then I thought it would be noticed so I turned away.'

'I knew exactly where you were.'

'I'm sorry.'

'Whatever for?'

'They won't leave me alone.'

'I can see.'

'At first it was Mrs Ward, insisting, and then the colonel. You know the colonel. It was like a military exercise. I'm not sure what they think you will do to me. I almost called off, claiming sickness.'

'Yes, Miss Lavington said . . .'

'Lavington. What has Lavington told you? When were you with Lavington?'

Michel Jean described the meeting with Lavington and the children in Brunswick Square outside the Trinity Church. He then mentioned that she had served him lunch at the barracks.

'Lavington! You know . . . She really.'

'She's very much . . .'

'Very much . . . indeed. Something is the matter with Lavington, which I've not got to the bottom of . . .'

'She seemed very well . . .'

'Very well? Yes, she's excellent. I don't know how I would cope without her. She's so good with Kate and Eddie and then, you know . . . I don't know how I would've survived without Lavington. But this morning . . .'

'She's been quite excited by the event herself.'

'Is that it? Weddings? Poor Lavington. It disturbs us all.'

'What? Weddings? Did you hear someone call?'

'Maybe a parakeet!'

She looked up, straining to see through the glare. She laughed at her own fancy, throwing back her head and nearly losing her straw hat once more.

Then they noticed the sun was beginning to set and the parakeets were flying in to roost for the night in the branches of the acacia trees. 'There's an old Spanish myth concerning these islands which gives them the name Los Cotorros.'

'Oh?'

'The parakeets.'

The time and the tide did not seem to matter as she curled her legs under her on the rocks and listened to him tell his tale.

'A mother, a witch, had cast a spell, in jealousy, upon the most beautiful of her daughters. The girl's sisters, less beautiful than her, encouraged by their own jealousy, goaded their mother to perform her magic. First, she had called upon the devil to help, but he with his own wickedness and intentions for the beautiful girl, instead bewitched the mother and the four sisters, turning them into parakeets. He shooed them away from their home. On their flight he turned them into rocks that fell into the sea. When he then looked for the beautiful daughter, he realized that in his haste he had changed her into a parakeet as well.'

'Oh, no, poor girl.'

'And, then, into a rock. So, actually, there are six islands. And, that is why from one of the islands they can still be heard, rocks that cry out like parakeets. The cry of the most beautiful daughter is still begging in her distress to be freed from her prison of stone.'

Elizabeth Prowder looked around her, counting the islands. 'Of course, there are indeed six. Poor thing. Is it really her calling from her prison of rock?'

They both stood and looked back at the house. It was now unmistakable. A small group were down on the jetty. One of them waved. He looked to see if she would return the greeting. She kept one hand anchored on her hat and with the other she was lifting her skirts to negotiate the jagged, slippery rocks. He followed with his equipment, unable to lend any assistance, but warning her of possible obstacles.

'I can still hear that poor girl's voice imprisoned in rock.' The last of the parakeets flashed green against the darkening blue.

'Take care where there's moss. It looks harmless, but you'll soon be sitting down in a pool of water.'

She laughed. 'I'll need your help, but your hands are full.' They crept over the rocks, her white dress getting muddy at the hem.

They paused to rest and to see how they might cross to the causeway. The tide was trickling in. 'I think we'll need to retrace our steps and go in that direction.' Michel Jean pointed to an alternative route to the causeway. When he looked up at the house it felt again as if they were being spied on from afar.

'Tell me what else you've been painting here.'

'Oh, some landscapes, views of the mainland. Carenage.' He pointed into the distance.

They picked their way carefully between the slippery rocks, making for firmer ground. When they reached the causeway they stopped to look back from where they had come. Elizabeth Prowder had collected round pebbles, smooth like gulls' eggs.

'Reminds me of being a girl on the Isle of Wight. I do know the sea.'

'Yes, you don't seem afraid.'

'I'm not. You seemed more alarmed.'

'I was worried about you.'

'Don't be.'

They were delaying their parting and her return to the house.

Even her white muslin had caught the pink and orange of the sunset for a moment. 'Look, it's all been transformed,' she declared. They stared at the continually changing colours that played over the islands and the mountains of Venezuela. This is when I should be putting my arms around her, he thought.

'I'll catch the scene tomorrow.'

'It'll be different.'

Elizabeth Prowder stooped to write on the beach with a small stick. He crouched down beside her. She drew squiggles, like hieroglyphs, not a language he could read. Was it a coded message for him? Or, was this simply the memory of a child, a young girl on an Isle of Wight beach, idly drawing. He kept seeing Louise collecting oysters into her basket.

'I can't get her out of my mind.' Elizabeth Prowder interrupted the silence.

'Who?'

'That Creole girl in her veil and orange blossom.'

'Excellency's bride?'

'So young! Her dress was so open, no scarf or mantilla covering her shoulders, just that long lace veil and the wreath of orange blossom.'

'Why does that bother you?'

'She did look lovely. But so young, just eighteen.'

'But you were . . .'

'Yes . . .'

'You were young yourself.'

'Just eighteen, a perfect child. There they are . . .'

They turned towards the house, looking along the strand that led to the steps of the jetty. Excellency and his bride were walking towards them.

'I must go.'

'I'll leave you here.'

'I'm sorry.'

'For what?'

'For how it is.'

She reached out to the portfolio under his arm. 'Let me see what you've done.'

'Yes, there's a moment.' She clutched his arm instead of the portfolio.

'Mrs Prowder.' He reached out to touch her arm.

'Not here.'

He opened the portfolio and she drew out the view of the ceremony from the choir loft, the wind snatching at the papers.

'Careful.'

'Yes, beautiful; sepia heightened with white.'

'Mrs Prowder?' He sought her permission.

'Not here . . .'

'When?'

'Depending on the tide, but I love walking out at dawn.'

As Michel Jean tied the ribbon on his portfolio and Elizabeth Prowder turned to leave, the married couple were almost upon them.

'Cazabon? Mrs Prowder?'

'Your Excellency, Lady Harris.' They spoke together.

'I was just showing Mrs Prowder my sketches of the ceremony.'

'They're wonderful,' Elizabeth Prowder exclaimed nervously.

'The portraits were finely done,' Lady Harris added, seeming unsure of herself.

'I'm glad your Ladyship is pleased.' Michel Jean bowed slightly. He did not know why, or whether that was the protocol.

'You must bring the wedding views up to the house.' Excellency moved the awkward conversation on. 'Come on up to the house later. They'll be a place for you at supper.'

'Excellency.'

'As it should be.' He smiled. 'Come on, dear, we must try and get to Caledonia and back in time for punches on the terrace.'

'I must go.' Elizabeth Prowder took her leave.

Michel Jean stood alone as she, the Governor and his wife departed. He could see that Elizabeth Prowder was again agitated. He guessed that it was in anticipation of the inevitable meeting at supper in the presence of Colonel Ward, his wife and her own husband. He looked back at her crossing the causeway, her white muslin cleaving to her body in the wind. He turned back to Caledonia and walked some distance behind Excellency and Lady Harris along the causeway. He turned to look back again once or twice to see that Elizabeth Prowder had crossed safely to the Craig jetty. The last time he turned she had disappeared. He stood and listened. He could swear he heard the cries of that beautiful girl imprisoned among the rocks of Los Cotorros.

That evening some of the wedding views were exhibited at the house. Michel Jean stood and watched as the honeymoon party came and went from the room, sipping punches. Wildman rescued him from isolation by stopping to chat, but then was soon taken away by Charlotte Bushe. Michel Jean had noticed the young lady, who was rumoured to have caught the eye of his friend. He had not spoken of her to him. She was from an English Creole family. Wildman was following in his uncle's footsteps. Michel Jean felt excluded. He had not been introduced to her. He tried to put this oversight down to the nervousness of his young lady, though he felt somehow that Wildman himself had been remiss as a friend.

The next morning Pompey arrived to row him back to Corbeaux Town. Elizabeth Prowder had not appeared at dawn. Michel Jean was disappointed both by what he felt as Wildman's snub the night before and Elizabeth Prowder's failure to meet him on her morning walk. He could get so close and no further with these people.

'You spending time with some real big people. Here, take a drink.' Pompey handed him a flask of rum.

Josie brought a letter in from the packet. 'Letter from Paris.' Michel Jean left it lying on the table for a while. 'Like you in another world, *oui*. You not anxious for news? How that little boy of yours?' Josie was right. The lessons at St James Barracks and the wedding had consumed him these last weeks. The letter was a relief because life for Louise and the children seemed more settled. This made him feel better, less guilty about his preoccupations. He replied with a gossipy letter full of details about the Governor's wedding, the honeymoon party and his commission.

Painting lessons were resumed at St James Barracks. Michel Jean and Elizabeth Prowder strolled a little way along the road to the Rookery beneath the bamboo arches. The Maraval valley opened up in front of them as they emerged along the river. The water was running swiftly after heavy rains that week. It was a deep brown colour, the effect of landslides further up the valley on the cocoa estates at Moka.

'A lesson in bamboos, *oui*?' Michel Jean tried to be himself.

'I still find it very difficult to master the line, to get both that sweep and the feathery effect, both the grandeur and the delicacy.' Elizabeth Prowder seemed overwhelmed by the beauty of her subject as she spoke.

'Well, I think you already possess the approach, that's what your drawing ability has given you, and you know what you now want. It's a matter of practice. Copying is one way, looking at nature is another.'

'I can walk out here on my own, can't I? Position my easel and there . . .' She was thrilled at the possibilities ahead of her.

*

As their lessons progressed over the following weeks, the clouds, pastures, savannahs and mountain ranges, the very reality of distant palms, the foreground of shrubs, small trees, and even bamboos, proved not to be the main difficulty, not even the Maraval River in flood. Elizabeth Prowder improved, excelled with each lesson. Building on her drawing ability, she began to paint freely, and, more importantly, draw in watercolour. It was heavy-handed at times, but at other times she achieved the required delicacy. This was the same delicacy Michel Jean heard in her recitation of one of her poems to Lavington:

> The purple woods on distant hills,
> The perfume of the passing breeze.
> That o'er my tranced senses steal . . .

He had arrived earlier than expected and had stood at the door and listened.

The guards were now accustomed to his arrival. He was still looked at with suspicion, but allowed to enter without any undue interrogation. The riots of the previous year had been successfully quelled and were showing no sign of repetition. The subsequent trial, which he had sketched for *The Illustrated London News*, had resulted in clemency from the Governor for the agitators.

As he was about to knock on the porch door, he heard Lavington's and Elizabeth Prowder's voices. He was arrested by their talk, which followed upon her recitation, the phrase 'tranced senses steal' still echoing in his mind. Elizabeth Prowder was in full flow on quite a different subject, in a quite different tone. 'I do really want to laugh at those women in church with their gold chains, earrings and rings. Sometimes, a Negro girl can look well in these if she wears her Madras handkerchief tied round her head. But when they wear white bonnets and dresses they are quite ugly.'

'But, ma'am . . .'

'No, Lavington, even you can't possibly appreciate, or defend such tastes. For instance, the other day I saw a jet-black girl in a funny straw hat trimmed with white satin. Can you imagine?'

'You do realize the economy at the moment, ma'am? A year ago the Treasury was empty. What kind of money do you imagine people have?'

'Nonsense. The economy has nothing to do with how these women dress. There's very little poverty.'

'No poverty?'

'The men spend their money on liquor and the women on showy clothes.'

'Would you have them walk around in rags? These are minor indulgences to cheer up their wretched lives. These are morsels of dignity, clothes, cheap frills.'

'I think that's very dangerous talk, Lavington. You'll be supporting what happened in Haiti next, or more recently in St Lucia. Or, what happened right here last year. There should've been no clemency. Harris is quite weak, really. This is not economy, Lavington. It's simply a matter of taste, that refinement we find in civilized people. It's not knowing what to do, how to look – you know the old women with their straw hats over their Madras, quite frightful, as if they've bandaged their heads after a cut.'

Michel Jean turned his back to the door and stood on the porch looking out into the yard, but he could still hear quite clearly the argument that had ensued as he was on the threshold of his arrival. Not again, he thought. Surely she cannot still be obsessed with these issues.

'You must admit to a beauty . . .'

'Yes, I do. Some of the coloured women are beautiful. I have not seen prettier faces, the reddish coloured women are handsome, the high coloureds. But, you know, they do look bold and vulgar.'

Michel Jean wondered how he would announce his arrival. How would he continue with their lessons? Her blue eyes, her black hair, her fiery tongue, keen intelligence and sensitive verses seduced some part of him more than might be proper for a tutor, but these attacks on coloured and black people, especially on the women, at a time like this, confused his commitment to lessons with her, and at the same time any other admiration he possessed for her beauty and her talent.

'I must stop this talk, Lavington. I had not intended to enter upon this subject,' Elizabeth Prowder said decisively.

Michel Jean wondered, as the rain then came down to drown the voices of the women, as it pelted down on the low roofs and created an instant flood in the yard, where Esther Murray and Amalie Devillias, the new cook and maid, had put themselves in the small house so that they might be out of earshot of their mistress. They, too, would be unable to listen to this talk.

He could now hear the children making their different demands for their mother's and their governess's attention. Their loud screams competed with the thunder and the shock of the lightning. Michel Jean knocked on the door, wondering whether he would be heard.

It was Lavington who opened the door. 'Monsieur Cazabon! You must come out of that awful storm.' As she spoke, the rain lashed against the walls of the porch, driven by a strong wind off the gulf and the near shore of mangroves.

Lavington looked embarrassed, he thought. He wondered if his face revealed that he had overheard the recent argument between her and her mistress. He was entering from one storm into another.

The rain turned out to be interminable, keeping them at the barracks. At first they thought to cancel the lessons for that week. But then, Michel Jean, not wanting to lose his pay, and not wanting to run the risk of cancellation altogether, suggested they use the time on figure drawing and painting.

'How on earth are we going to do that?' Elizabeth Prowder exclaimed. 'Who will be our models? Should I use the children? I don't think they could stand still for a moment. Lavington? No. She has to be with the children; they will go for a walk around the barracks, ready to dash for it if there's another downpour.'

'There's your cook. And there's the woman I've sometimes noticed, helping with the cleaning.'

'The servants? Do you think they'll agree? How will they combine this modelling with their work? We can try, I suppose.' Elizabeth Prowder began to look a little anxious. She obviously had not thought of her servants as suitable subjects for her art, for her sketches to take home.

Lavington was very pleased with the idea and said she would make sure the children did not interrupt. She was the one to talk to Esther Murray, the cook, and Amalie Devillias, both of whom had come from the nearby Peru Estate. Lucia, the Portuguese girl, had left the employment. 'She said she was going to work in a shop her father was opening in Couva,' Elizabeth Prowder announced. 'I thought that was quite astonishing. They've hardly arrived on the island, and these people are already opening shops and making something of their lives. The Negroes should take example, is what I say.'

Elizabeth Prowder's little speech created a silence that had Amalie and Esther turning their backs and attending to their chores. 'Cheups. That woman is something, *oui*,' Michel Jean heard Amalie say to Esther. They were no longer inclined to humour their madam and her governess. Amalie, the younger of the two, began to giggle at first, and then looked less pleased at the prospect. But with Michel Jean trying to cheer things up with a little teasing, she came round to the idea. She had never seen a portrait of anyone. It was an entirely new concept for her. Lavington showed the two women a daguerreotype to suggest the kind of thing, explaining that it would be a painting. Esther Murray said she would see how it went with Amalie, before she committed herself. 'Let me see what Amalie do, nuh.'

Michel Jean smiled sympathetically, understanding the women's uncertainty.

The rain continued unabated. There had been fine mornings and then stormy afternoons, but now the clouds hung low in the valley, even lower over the plains and the gulf. St James, close to the mangrove, had become a damp, mosquito-ridden hole. There was the danger that caimans might walk out of the swamp into the garden.

However, they were able to work out on the veranda once the rain had let up, while Lavington could read to the children in the small nursery. Amalie stood patiently. Michel Jean and Elizabeth Prowder drew. He stopped intermittently to look at her progress. 'Let us now draw with brushes not with our pencils.' She watched while he painted, dipping his brush into the browns and ochres, the red sienna and the cobalt blue. She was learning how to paint the colour she found so difficult to appreciate. Amalie, a *chabine*, was mixed.

'Amalie, you're doing splendidly,' her mistress said. Michel Jean felt exasperated at Elizabeth Prowder's hypocrisy; her voice was so patronizing. She could have been an actress. The conversation he had overheard from the porch was distracting his concentration.

He countered with: 'Amalie, girl, you want something to drink?'

He noticed Elizabeth Prowder wince at his easy familiarity with the young girl and the smile which Amalie gave him. He knew that he was ganging up on her, leaving her out. This was not the way to create a successful lesson. It was not what he wanted to do. He had to rid himself of his anger against her. He tried instead to concentrate on her talent. 'Your mistress is doing very well.' He knew that, too, sounded patronizing on his part now. 'Let's take a break.'

Amalie looked to see how her mistress had taken this reference to herself in front of one of her servants.

'Amalie, you can bring us some orange juice. Esther has squeezed gallons. Yes, you must have some too. And there's ice, remember. Just a small bit left. The man has not yet arrived. Must be the rain.'

'Thanks, madam.'

A new peace reigned.

'Is this going well?'

'It's a start. Not easy working with instruction given in this way.'

Michel Jean felt that they were both working for the same end. He noticed her smile, with satisfaction.

After the break, Esther joined the lesson in the second half, the two women making a joint study that their mistress proclaimed she was going to call, *Two Fisherwomen*. They looked doubtful. Michel Jean smiled encouragingly. They, too, were irritated with their mistress. 'And you does sell fish for your mother down in Carenage,' Esther joked with Amalie, who giggled at the idea.

A simple wash of blue created the sea as the foreground with the women leaning against the rocks on a fictional shore.

Michel Jean stayed behind on his own at the end of the lesson to examine his student's work. Heavy-handed, he thought; she had made of the women ugly creatures. He supposed he should be sympathetic as it was her first attempt. He looked at his own. He had captured the contrast between the pretty young girl and the older Esther. He had noticed how Esther, in eventually volunteering to sit, or stand, had made an effort with her dress and the foulard around her shoulders, which gave her a pleasing dignity. Amalie could have worn rags; nothing would have disguised her beauty. How different to Mr Bridgens' work, he thought; his student's unnecessarily crude portraits reminding him now of that English artist, his diminishment of Negro characters to caricature.

A week later, a dry spell had descended upon the valley. The grass was now scorched. Michel Jean arrived for his lesson with the hope that he and his student might venture out from the barracks.

Amalie and Esther were in the patch of garden beyond the gate. He stopped to listen and to join in their conversation. He was surprised that they were still talking about the last lesson.

'I ent find she paint we pretty, you know,' Amalie announced.

'Child, what is the point with this painting?' Esther agreed.

'Better get Miss Lavington to take out we picture with that thing, what she say it call?'

'There was a white fella by the square when they had the wedding, showing people what he could do. That look like the portrait Miss Lavington show we.'

'That is what we want. I ent find Madam do we good.'

'Good morning, ladies. What am I hearing?' Michel Jean said, joking with the servants.

'I say, Madam ent paint we good, you know. You yourself I find ent get we like we is, sir.'

'So you're not going to model for us again?' Michel Jean broke in.

'Well, I might give it one more try,' Amalie volunteered. 'Better than doing housework. Better than this blasted slavery, *oui*.'

'Slavery, child, what you know about that?' Esther, the older woman, looked sharply at the younger woman.

Then the two women joked and laughed again.

'I ent think so.' Esther was more decisive. She preferred to get on with her cooking. 'Is guava jelly today, you know. Plenty work. You see when she start . . .'

'What, no painting? Look at the day.'

'She up from early with her boiling. When she in this thing she not giving up. I say that for her.'

The women were both older than Elizabeth Prowder and were intrigued by this young Englishwoman, a girl, the two servants thought, but with a mature determination when it came to her tasks.

'Miss Lavington is the real madam, though.'

'But she have Miss Lavington under her thumb.'

'Boiling since early, and with this talk about this child in Chaguaramas.'

'*Mon Dieu!* She still with that? Since last night when I putting down the mosquito net, she with that. The child that loss in the forest.' Amalie began to laugh. 'You hear what they say, the man chop up the child and cook he in a pot.' Both women laughed at the ludicrous scene they had painted, based on the gossip they had heard.

'Telling Miss Lavington all kind of thing.'

'Miss Lavington don't agree with she, you know.'

As Amalie and Esther had intimated, yet another argument was in full flow as he entered the house.

Michel Jean composed himself.

'Mr Cazabon. You're so punctual.'

Lavington did not interrupt her speech. 'Ma'am, you have taken this to quite an extreme. I can't believe your fear has got the better of you to this extent.' Lavington was again speaking in a moderating tone, though gently upbraiding her mistress.

'Mr Cazabon, do excuse us. Lavington, I can't believe you can take things so lightly. I have two children of my own, little mites. Do you think I want to risk them as dainty morsels for some cannibalistic appetite?' She almost giggled at her own appetite for description.

'Ma'am. But I must speak my mind. It is to counsel you, not to disrespect you.'

'The child was seen to have disappeared and from all accounts there is this man in the forest at Chaguaramas. And, as you know, they were brought out of savagery.' After this comment, she looked at Michel Jean. 'I do exaggerate. Have you heard this story, Mr Cazabon?'

'What story is that?'

'The one of the disappearing child in Chaguaramas.'

'Ma'am, you must read. You must read accounts of the advanced civilizations and developed societies that were discovered. You must temper some of your views with more information, information of a contrary kind from that peddled by Mr Carlyle and his friends, with their inflammatory statements on Negro character. There are other accounts which are well documented, based on empirical observation.'

'What's this got to do with anything, Lavington? I must get to my painting. You do sound very superior at times, Lavington, if I may say so.' Elizabeth Prowder wiped her hands on her apron. 'But, I do, I do beg of you to be very careful on walks outside the barracks. You know I have heard that some have their teeth filed to a fine point in order better to manage their cannibalistic eating. There I go again. My little ones! I can't imagine it.'

'Nor I, ma'am. You must trust me, ma'am, on this matter. It's dangerous and wrongful talk. It's tittle-tattle. I can't believe this darkness that you're imagining. Mr Cazabon, I'm so glad you're here and that the painting lesson can commence.'

'Sounds quite a story,' he said.

The kitchen steamed with the fragrance of guavas being boiled for jelly and jam.

'Will I be safe, though? Will someone be nibbling at my ankles?' she asked.

'Ma'am! At least you still have your sense of humour.'

Michel Jean did not join in the laughter, though he noticed Lavington look at him with apology on her face. He saw again the older woman's affection for her mistress, as well as her confidence in her own opinion. He saw her protective nature and her influence on Elizabeth Prowder.

'The newspapers love these stories,' he concluded, before going off to the veranda to set up for the lesson.

'Aren't we going out? I feel quite safe with you, Mr Cazabon.'

She had gone too far, and he could see that she knew it. Lavington was right about her, he thought.

They found an ideal spot near the Maraval River. This was where the bridge crosses to the de Boissière estate of Champs-Elysées situated at the entrance to the valley beyond the Rookery.

The subject this morning, once they had set up their easels, was to be the great house and the *usine*.

'This will make a wonderful view to take back!' Elizabeth Prowder remarked.

'Yes, there's great variety here. You've got the mountains, the river and the broad samaans in the pastures and, of course, the industry of the factory itself. Quite a view to take back, as you say. There are people working on the estate.'

'Negroes, I see, and some of the new coolies. Yes, I'm never very good at people.'

He wanted to be angry with her, to tell her she'd be better with people artistically if she viewed them as people, if she was respectful of their humanity. But he knew that if he were to teach her, then he had to enter her imagination. He needed to indulge her a little after the last lesson. She knew she had not done well with the figures of Esther and Amalie; she had tried them again, but to no avail. He felt that he needed to rescue the best part of her as he watched her move around animatedly, arranging her paper on her easel and getting out her box of paints. She had begun without instruction and he let her go ahead, pursuing his own painting alongside hers. He would intervene eventually.

'Why don't you start me off?' She turned to him pleadingly.

He knew that there was still a great deal of nervousness. He put it down to her alarm over the disappearance of the child in Chaguaramas and the outlandish stories she had allowed herself to believe. But she had agreed to be escorted here by him, so he felt some confidence in their relationship. Maybe the spark lit on the causeway at Caledonia had been rekindled?

'Not many trees for me to fail at, are there?'

'Oh, you mustn't be pessimistic about your endeavours.'

'I know, but . . . . and there're the bamboos. I will have to tackle those. You're so good at them. You'll have to start me off on those as well.'

'I grew up with them. Probably the first foliage that I ever painted, under the tuition of my aunt.'

'Yes, I forget your childhood here. Where was that?'

'In the south. Naparima. At Corynth Estate. And also in the town of San Fernando.'

'My husband means to take me there on the steamer some time, across the gulf. Maybe I can paint there as well. Get those views. I understand that it's a quaint town clustered around an extraordinary hill.'

'Yes, the hill is very special. My playground as a child.'

They chatted intermittently as they worked. He was being very careful not to be too intrusive. He could feel her bristle when he remarked on the pencil drawing she was employing. 'I do not require tuition in drawing. I thought I told you that.'

'I realize. I was commenting on the pencil drawing in relation to the watercolour.' He had to be patient.

'The trouble is that your style is very different to my tutor's on the Isle of Wight and to my master's in London. And I might say . . .' She stopped herself. He wondered what it was that had made her bite her fiery tongue.

'Yes?'

'Well, I think you're quite . . .'

'Maybe, different?'

'Well maybe, but I must be allowed to develop . . .'

'Of course.'

He thought he would drop his brushes, put away his paints and walk away, leaving her to herself. But he knew that he could not do that at this point.

Something really was upsetting her, he could see. These outbursts. These dragons which she constantly challenged were indeed illusions of her own making: coloured women, black women, lost children in Chaguaramas, cannibals in the forest, and, he thought, even himself. He did not react. But he felt it was not acceptable that she should speak to him in this way. She went silent, kept with her painting, and then he saw that she had given up sketching with her pencil and was drawing with her brush.

'That's excellent,' he said.

She turned towards him, smiled and then looked at him pensively. She then returned with concentration to her painting. The Champs-Elysées house with its factory was taking shape; the mountains beyond, the river in the foreground. It was all coming together. 'Yes, you have helped me here,' she said, putting down her brush, and leaning away from her easel to judge her own work.

They rested in the shade of one of the samaans. 'Do you know the story of this great house? Champs-Elysées, is it? Belonging to a French family?'

'Yes. Like many of the great sugar and cocoa estates.'

'But this one has had quite a history?'

'Well, I have acquaintance with the present family, but I also have the story from my mother.'

'A good story?'

He noticed that she was much more relaxed than she had been earlier. Maybe, she had needed to be frank with him about her drawing. She had removed her sun hat and strands of her black hair had fallen out of her bun onto her shoulders.

'Your mother's story?'

'Well, a bit of it. Then we must get back to work and return in time for lunch, otherwise Lavington will be fretting.'

'Lavington frets, though she thinks that's what I do.'

She was now quite a different person, he thought. He continued with his story. 'Her name was Madame de Charras. She was born Rosa de Gannes de la Chancellerie. She came from Grenada. Her son, the famous Philippe Roume de Saint-Laurent, by a previous marriage, persuaded her to come here and to leave one island for the other. Some say she was escaping debts and debt collectors.'

'So, not a noble history?'

'Well. In those days, Port of Spain was a mud fort, a church and some eighty tapia houses. A desperate place, I expect.'

'Tapia?'

'What you would call wattle.'

'What a splendid town it is now.'

'*Oui, la belle des Antilles.*'

'Governor Woodford's creation, I understand.'

'Hmm.'

'You didn't like Woodford?'

'No. Not good for the coloureds.'

'I see.' She blushed a little at the directness of the conversation. She looked over at him and he could see a change in her demeanour, and he wondered whether it had to do with what Lavington had been saying earlier, as if something was clicking into place. She was beginning to understand. 'Tell me more about the house.' She held her painting away from her. 'When I show the painting at home I can tell the story to go with it.'

'Woodford had wanted to buy it for Government House, but never managed to get the funds for that transaction.'

'It's sugar now.'

'Some. Always been some. There's always been a mix of crops: cocoa trees, lemon groves, coffee bushes, plantains and guinea grass.'

'What a list! I've ridden up to the Saddle on horseback with Charles, or I attempted to, and then he had to call a trap.'

'That's a good ride.'

'What do you call them, those trees with reddish flowers in the cocoa?'

'Immortelles.'

'A beautiful name. And from the Saddle I looked down into that other valley.'

'Santa Cruz.'

'Charles has promised to take me there one day to visit Señor Gomez . . .'

'And his beautiful house.'

'I was drunk with the beauty of the island on my return that day to the barracks, as we descended the valley in the late afternoon. There seemed to be mountains upon mountains going east, a sense of distance I had not quite experienced before. They say the island is really quite small. But your copies make it seem larger and allow me to travel without actually going anywhere.' She was flushed with excitement at her memory.

Michel Jean continued with the story. 'When the estate went over to the de Boissière family they knocked down Madame de Charras's house. Well, the termites had already eaten their way through it. John de Boissière built another beautiful one, open to the breeze. It breathed through its jalousies; its hot air funnelled through those chimney-like domes you can see.'

'Does it have a garden?'

'Famous. And a marble bath-house, with black and white tiles. The garden descends in terraces. The baths and the fountains are watered from the Dibé valley beyond where we're looking.'

'A very calm story.'

'I think there was a fire once.'

'And . . .?'

'Well, the bit my mother liked to tell about is the story of Zuzule.'

'Who was Zuzule? Your mother is not alive?'

'No, she died a couple of years ago.'

'I see. I'm sorry. But Zuzule?'

Michel Jean wondered whether he should carry on. He decided to leap in.

'She was John de Boissière's mistress.'

'I'm not sure I want to hear any more.'

'It's not as salacious as that observation might suggest.'

'Well. It's surely quite disreputable really.' She looked at him and he looked at her as she said this.

'That infidelity . . .'

She let him interrupt her. 'Well, you know I might not be here if there had not been infidelity by my grandfather.'

'Really?'

'But the bit my mother likes is that, not only was Zuzule a mistress, but she had been once enslaved. She was given her freedom and she had a house all to herself. Madame de Boissière went to see her and they came to an arrangement that she stay in her house and Madame de Boissière in hers. So there was a second family as it were.'

'Why did your mother like the story?'

'She liked the spirit of Zuzule, she said. But then she . . .'

'What were you going to say?'

'She in her turn had to cope with a similar situation with my father.'

'He had a Zuzule?'

'Yes, he had his own Zuzule. She is called Ernestine.'

'I can't imagine it. I'm going to return to the painting of the house, Madame de Boissière's house. And Zuzule's house?'

'It's in town, a special gingerbread house he built for her, full of filigree and lattice-work jalousies with awnings over the windows. At the back there are Demerara windows.'

'I think they built with a certain nostalgia for their past in Europe. Wouldn't you say? They mixed that with local influences. Peasant influences?'

'Yes. I would say so.'

'My husband knows about building. I draw for him.'

It sounded like a challenge she was delivering yet again.

'You paint for me.'

'I paint for myself.' She laughed.

'Of course.' He felt rebuffed. But he felt that they were talking honestly and that honesty between them mattered.

They put the last touches to their paintings. 'Can't really do much more.' Michel Jean began packing up his equipment, looking over his shoulder at her trying to alter what was already fixed in watercolour. She kept on.

'No, you can't alter it now. You'll ruin it. Start another next time. Catch another moment,' he said, as he began to pack up his satchel.

'Here, let's catch this before the light changes.'

They were returning to the barracks through the Rookery.

She looked to where he was pointing, the fisherman and the encompassing light and shade.

Everything that he had ever learned came together to inspire his craft. But, it was her presence, above all, being there with him at this moment, which had him unpacking, without waiting for her answer. She followed where he led and began setting up her own easel and arranging her paper and box of watercolours to paint the fisherman at the dyke. They worked together under the bamboo as the light fell on the river with the dry leaves on its surface. All the while there was the single call of a bird, sounding like a bell.

They painted without interruption. They each, in their own way, with scratching-out and white pigment rendered the wet rocks around which the fast-running water made channels to the wider river. They sat dipping their brushes. The fisherman sat quite still with his rod and baited line held out in front of him, lowered into the churning water.

Michel Jean could never be sure whether what he felt was shared with his student. Their common silence, their mutual act, led him to believe, maybe wrongly, that it was shared. Only once did they turn towards each other and smile while saying nothing. At no time did she stamp her foot in irritation at not finding her way with the sweep and delicacy of the bamboos. She did not complain that she could not achieve their grandeur. She drew with her brush, a brush almost as slender as a pencil.

They handed each other their work to judge. They looked at each other's paintings in silence, examining them. Then she said, 'I would like to give you mine.'

Michel Jean answered immediately. 'And mine is yours now, too.'

'I wanted to offer you something as your pupil, a thank you. I couldn't have done it without you.'

Michel Jean knew that this was an enormous admission for her.

'Would you not like to show it to your husband? I'm sure Lavington would like to see it as well.'

She looked disappointed in what he was saying. He wanted her to know that he treasured her gift. 'No. I can do other paintings for them. This one is for you.'

'And mine.' He reached out to touch his painting, as if to offer it to her again where it lay upon her lap. His fingers brushed against hers. The moment passed. Their eyes had met and then were immediately averted.

How easily, he thought, he would have got close to her and run his fingers all along the nape of her neck if she had been Augusta. How easily he would have drawn her round to kiss her on her mouth. He was thankful that the lesson was coming to an end. He could not allow his fantasies to stray, could not tread beyond the admiration of a tutor for an outstanding student.

Michel Jean arrived back home just in time to see Jean Pierre from Orange Grove about to leave the yard. He announced proudly that Augusta had had a baby girl. 'She looking good, boy. She send me with this letter for you.' Michel Jean detained the young fella while he wrote a note in reply. He remembered the tip he had thrown him in the past when he had come to collect Augusta, coins which were not her worth. Jean Pierre had made a mocking claim to her then. Michel Jean liked him even less now. Her letter had said very little apart from what he had just learned. He wrote back, formally expressing his best wishes for the health of her baby and herself. He then added that he would be coming to visit her at Orange Grove. As Jean Pierre swung his trap out of the yard with bravado, Michel Jean wondered whether this was the action of a proud father, or of someone who had made his claim to fatherhood and was determined to show him who was man.

Later that week, as he drew close to the familiar house, feeling hot and thirsty, he became a little apprehensive about this reunion.

The place was deserted.

As he was about to depart, there was the 'Heigh, heigh' of a rider's high-pitched command to his horses. A buggy came racing round the corner, fast, the carriage swaying, the wheels dangerously close to overturning and pitching its sole occupant from the comfort of her seat. Michel Jean recognized the rider as Jean Pierre. Augusta was clutching on for her own dear life and for that of the baby she was holding close to her bosom. The sight indicated that some kind of anarchy or new rule had come to Orange Grove. Was this the new master and mistress of the house?

The buggy came to a halt in front of him. Jean Pierre was clearly delighted to have shown off his racing prowess. Augusta looked aghast, as if she had seen an apparition. She and her baby were in no condition to be transported in such a terrifying and dangerous fashion, he thought.

'You see, I taking she where she want to go.' Jean Pierre was the first to speak, eager to lay down his claim again. While Michel Jean knew that a part of him was happy not to claim anything at all, another part wanted to take responsibility.

Augusta descended from the buggy. Jean Pierre was gallantly there to assist her. His smirking bravado appeared to confirm that he thought he was the child's father. Maybe the old ram Burnley hadn't been able to manage it. He was certainly on his last legs now.

This New York frock was too tight to cope with Augusta's newly maternal body. As she stood in front of him, smiling with clear delight, she cradled her baby in her arms. 'Monsieur Cazabon,' she said breathlessly. She glanced at Jean Pierre as if to say, You can take your leave. He looked rebuffed and reluctant, but eventually his horses forced his attention for feed and water after their sweaty gallop.

'Augusta.'

'Things change here now. Master sick. I gone back to Tacarigua by my father.'

'Yes . . .'

'See how big she is. Look, nuh.' She unwrapped the baby girl to show him.

'Beautiful as ever. Like you.' Her fecundity had made her bloom even more spectacularly.

'You was always one for the sweet-talk . . .'

'*Non*, not sweet-talk. It's always been about your beauty. And now your beautiful child.' He felt he was truthful in that last remark. He wanted to make it up to her, but did not know how.

'Well, life have a way . . . Master . . .' She didn't conclude her speech, couldn't finish what she was going to say. Master, he certainly had been. Not any more, it seemed. Michel Jean looked around at the yard and the acres beyond of sugarcane fields. He wondered what had been going on at Orange Grove. He noticed that the pastures and yard looked neglected.

'What you mean?'

'The child? You don't want it to be yours?'

'I didn't say that.' He was playing again. 'We don't know, do we?'

'As she grow we go see who she is.'

'*Oui, oui* . . .'

'That day by you I feel it was yours . . .'

'But now?'

'How I go know, for truth. As I say, as she grow. Now she look like me.'

He saw the tears welling up in her bright eyes.

'True . . .'

'You see what happen to me? You see what does happen? You see what I tell you. It not easy in this house.' She lowered her voice. 'They all think they have a right.' She looked across the yard to where Jean Pierre had taken the horses to water them.

'I'm sorry.'

'You have your own wife and children.'

'Yes.'

'Why you didn't tell me from the start? Have me dreaming. Portrait for posterity.'

'Well, there is a portrait.'

'What? That washerwoman? That's me? That's me now, for truth.'

'An empress . . .'

'What you say?'

'Something from the past . . .'

'I tell you, from the past, in truth.'

'So, you with your mother?'

'Yes, you don't have to worry. My father take she back. Master let we go. People in Tacarigua laugh. But he's a good man. Jean Pierre treating me good, too. He bring me to get some things I

299

leave behind. Master nephew coming soon to see to his uncle and to manage the estate. Work go pick up. You see how quiet it is. So it is, since he sick. He go leave me comfortable. Me and Mama.'

'I hope to go away soon but I'll be back.'

'That sound like you.'

'I go ask about you. Anything I could do? Here, something for both of you.' He gave her his contribution in a small purse.

'Thanks. I go put it aside for she, for later, for she education.' She fixed her eyes on him. 'Well, as you see, I go be busy.'

'*Au revoir.*'

'Bye-bye. You walking out?'

'Yes.'

'Is come-you-really-come, to find me? You lucky I forget some things. I doesn't be here now.' She smiled as she went up the back stairs to the house.

'Before I go, I thirsty.' He felt that she, too, wanted to hold the moment for longer.

'It hot for so. Come, let me give you some water to drink.'

As he drank, he took another look at the baby girl. How could he be sure she was not his daughter?

'Hold she, nuh.'

He took the baby in his arms. 'Pretty like you,' he said, gazing at her face.

'I bet you have nice children.'

'*Oui.*' He smiled.

Once he had quenched his thirst, he took his leave.

'I go come and find you, you know. When she grow.'

'That's what you tell me last time.'

He waved as he turned to leave the yard.

He kept wondering about the child as he returned to Port of Spain. Jean Pierre might want to boast it was his, and then, if the child was the old ram's they would all know. Augusta would know soon enough when the child sucked on her breasts and looked up at her face in the dead of night. She would have time to decipher the features as they formed and re-formed and told their truth.

Things were happening too quickly. He had heard that Excellency would also be travelling to Europe. Could that be an advantage to him? Wildman thought that he should get a cabin on the *HMS Wellesley*. He thought that he could secure his berth. They had just returned from a trip down south with new paintings. It had been like their early friendship. The awkwardness that he had felt when he had met him with Charlotte Bushe was no longer there.

The Earl of Dundonald, who had commissioned an earlier album, and had been managing the beginning of the asphalt enterprise at La Brea, wanted a painting of the famous Pitch Lake with the Earl and his wife standing on the expanse of bitumen. He also suggested that he should illustrate the grand ball, which was to take place on the *Wellesley* and which he was now in command of, the ship being due to depart some days after the festivity. Wildman told Michel Jean that he thought the coincidence was made in heaven.

He now had something quite definite to tell Louise about his departure. He caught the packet just in time with a letter.

When he told his father of his latest commission, he again warned him. They had taken to meeting at the Planters' Club on Marine Square, that his father had gained access to through St Luce. 'This is more work for patrons,' his father said. 'Still their view of things.' But he needed the money and the work for *The Illustrated London News* gave him further strings to his bow. He felt like he was putting the island of Trinidad on the map. It was also a useful advertisement for his talent that might yield further commissions. His paintings might be seen as his *Free Mulatto*, his text for the freedom of the artist, as Jean Baptiste Philippe had earlier written for the rights of the coloured people.

There were times when he felt at the very centre of things, just as there were times when he felt right out on the fringes.

It was impossible, what with the race question, the narrowness of society, and his inability to see how he could advance himself while maintaining the necessary self-respect. How could he paint what he wanted to paint and at the same time make a living? He knew that there was still his share of the sale of the Belle Plaine Estate at Aricagua. He had reassured Louise that there was still this last bit of inheritance to come. Though that would not see them through for ever. He had to work. He had to earn money. But, at this moment, he had more work than he could cope with, given his impending departure.

Michel Jean and Elizabeth Prowder kept to the arrangements that they had made for their last lesson. It was possible that they might be accompanied by Wildman, who had been wanting to fit in a last lesson himself. '*Tempus fugit*,' he had said. He had invited them to break the journey at the Cottage, and after some refreshment to continue together into the hills. Michel Jean had not seen a way to avoid Wildman accompanying them. His presence was not what he had planned for his last lesson with Elizabeth Prowder.

They were detained while Elizabeth Prowder completed a letter to her *dearest mama* that she wanted to go by the packet that evening. Lavington was busy with trying to get the children dressed and equipped for a longer morning than usual away from home. Kate would go to school as usual and Eddie would stay with Lavington at the Warners' with the younger Warner children.

He witnessed the family in transition. He had arrived before Charles Prowder had left home for his work.

'Mr Cazabon, we meet again in passing.'

'Good morning, sir. Yes, you're earlier than even I am and I'm usually out into the country before the dawn breaks.'

'Yes, you to paint pictures and me to build roads and bridges.'

'Where's it this morning?' Michel Jean asked, trying his best with the gentleman.

'Couva, by steamer. That's if I don't miss it, and then by horseback to Gran Couva where we are building a number of bridges in the cocoa hills near Montserrat.'

'Wonderful, the central hills. A morning in Tortuga. The views from there on a fine day are expansive and allow you to see how the archipelago links the northern cordillera to the continent.'

'Also one of my favourite places out of town.'

Their small chat broke the ice between them. 'How would you measure her progress? Would you say that she's doing pretty well?'

'Oh, yes, exceedingly so.'

'She was very accomplished before she came out here, you know?'

'Certainly, I could see that.'

'I mean in drawing. I could not do without her assistance in my work. She's proved quite an asset in that regard, helping me with intricate plans for my bridges and piers. The one at La Brea, for instance, which was ordered by the Earl of Dundonald for the shipment of pitch.'

'I can imagine her competence in draughtsmanship.'

'So, she does not need any lessons in drawing.'

Michel Jean wondered why Mr Prowder was going over ground already covered by his wife many moons ago. They had progressed so far since he had heard the same from her.

'Needs very few lessons altogether, I would say,' he replied. 'She needs practice. She's got the fundamentals.' Better to agree with this husband, he thought.

'Exactly. But she does appreciate your tips on the painting side.'

'*Oui*. I give her a few tips. She's coming along.' Tips! Was that all these protracted lessons were? He had a nerve, this husband of hers. Who this blasted man think he is? Michel Jean fumed, but kept his mask in place.

'And I understand that you're going off on quite an expedition today.'

'Well, not too far. Tortuga would be an expedition.'

'I would have to accompany you if you were going that far. I don't think she could manage that sort of thing.'

'Oh, I don't know . . .'

'Well, I do.'

Michel Jean noticed the irritation in Charles Prowder's tone and the way the gentleman did not look at him. He, too, found it difficult to keep eye contact with this rather gauche man.

He wondered what kind of jokes the soldiers made about Charles Prowder and his wife, who was going into the bush with that coloured man. Given the cannibal stories, which Elizabeth Prowder herself seemed to relish, he wondered what lurid episodes they might imagine taking place. But, of course, it was not really those outlandish fantasies, but more the fact that the coloured artist had witnessed one of the most private events in his wife's life. At that moment, when he had lost his baby, Charles Prowder was not there. It was the coloured artist, Cazabon, who was there to get help for her. Not him, her husband and father of her children. He would also torment himself with the soldiers' crude imputations. And, the idea of his wife with her art teacher, however groundless, had been released into the fertile imaginations of all those men cooped up together in the barracks. Michel Jean could feel it when he passed the soldiers' searching eyes and heard sniggers behind his back, heard the word 'nigger', stifled by laughter. It was perhaps not so very different for Charles Prowder.

'Anyway, Mr Wildman is with you today, I understand.'

'Yes, stalwart James will be there.'

Charles Prowder caught his eye at that point, caught the familiarity of his relationship with the Governor's cousin and secretary. He could see that he was eager at that point to take his leave and make for the steamer at King's Wharf.

The children were dressed now and brought by Lavington to say goodbye to their father. Michel Jean noticed that they were much less exuberant with him than with their mother and Lavington. In fact, they were noticeably excited to find Monsieur Cazabon so early on their veranda, and were far more interested in the workings of his easel than in paying attention to their father's daily advice and admonishments.

'Now, Eddie, you're not to give Lavington any trouble today.'

'Oh, he's no trouble, sir. Are you?' It took Lavington to get the boy to listen to his father.

Kate, on the other hand, had learned from her mother to be dutiful. 'Have a good day, Papa.'

Charles Prowder was then out on the porch, leaving with a perfunctory kiss on his wife's cheek. Elizabeth Prowder was flustered, busy sealing her letter to be carried to the wharf to catch the packet to Barbados for its onward voyage to Falmouth.

Just when they thought they might set off, there was an almighty crash of thunder, with fork lightning fracturing the sky. Nature was certainly delaying events. The sun disappeared and rain suddenly came down from the heavy black and purple clouds which were stacked above the Maraval valley, hitting the ground with force, creating an instant flood in the low-lying garden. The nearby Maraval River on the boundary of the St James savannah could be heard rushing on to the coast at Mucurapo.

'Well, that's our day gone,' sighed Elizabeth Prowder. 'We'll never get out of here. Managing the climb into the St Ann's valley after this will be impossible.'

Kate and Eddie were shrieking with delight at the drama of the rain, the thunder and the lightning that continued above in the hills of Dibé and had disappeared into low cloud. It was such a sudden transformation from the bright yellow light of the morning into a world of water and wind. Lavington calmed the children down with reading one of the Mother Goose books that had come in their grandmother's box from the Isle of Wight. Elizabeth Prowder set about copying one of Michel Jean's bamboo scenes. He used the time to look through her extensive portfolio.

The children were absorbed in their story. Lavington's voice came through from the other room in gentle modulations, expressing the tensions and resolutions of the tale. The rain continued to fall, but then the drumming had given way to the *drip drip* from the trees on the shingle and the gargle from the roofs along the guttering. On the veranda there was the sound of the scratching of pencils and the swish of paintbrushes being washed.

The settled quality of the domestic scene took Michel Jean back to his home. The Prowder family was not like his family. Nevertheless, the early morning rising and familiar activity of the household conjured a scene with Louise together with his own children in rue de la Rochefoucauld.

The mood changed. As the clouds lifted off the hills, there was a burst of sunshine lighting up the lawn at the back. Light was streaming through the samaans. A gentle wind was moving the plumes of the palms. The humidity had lifted.

'Look, the green, the yellowest green!' It was one of Elizabeth Prowder's favourite expressions. 'Do you think we might actually be able to venture out?'

'Of course. We've had our morning shower and now we can go out into the sunshine, up into the hills. We need parasols and galoshes. Is that what the English call them?'

'We've got galoshes.'

'Lavington! We must get Kate off to school and I think you can get to the Warners'. Both will understand the delay the rain has forced upon us.'

Elizabeth Prowder got her equipment together and Michel Jean stole a moment for a cigarette on the porch as he waited for both parties to set off on their different expeditions for the day.

The buggy was called for Lavington and the children, and the trap was brought for the expedition to St Ann's. Elizabeth Prowder took the reins. There was a great deal of waving and cries of goodbye and *au revoir* to Monsieur Cazabon as the children and Lavington separated at the crossroads leading away from the barracks.

Michel Jean noticed the exhilaration with which his student managed the reins and the trot of the horse, avoiding the puddles that were threatening to splash them with muddy water. In no time at all, they had sped along the traces between the cane fields of the St Clair Estate and were on the well-gravelled road heading around the savannah to the Paradise Estate.

On their arrival, they were met by Wildman's man who informed them that, because of the delay caused by the rain, his master could not accompany them to St Ann's valley, as he had to assist Excellency on important business. Michel Jean realized that it had never been his intention to spend the whole day with them, but simply to go into the foothills, and then return for his appointment with Excellency. The rain had thrown his schedule out. He had left instructions that they stop and take refreshment before continuing, and that his man would see to their every need. They decided, however, that they should not delay any longer. Esther had packed them a picnic and there really was no need to have refreshments at this stage.

As they left the Cottage, they were both nervous. He guessed it was because of Wildman's absence. While this was what he had originally desired for their last lesson, he was surprised that Elizabeth Prowder had not immediately cancelled the outing. He wondered if the anxiety he sensed was in part about what she felt her husband would have wanted her to do, which would surely have been to cancel immediately and return poste-haste to the barracks.

They continued on their way. In no time they had arrived at one of the small cocoa estates in the St Ann's hills. They had passed Coblentz and the Marryats' estate and were headed for La Cascade. They left the trap at the overseer's *ajoupa* on the cocoa estate and continued on with a donkey, which Elizabeth Prowder rode side-saddle, led at the bridle by Michel Jean with their equipment in panniers. The weather had improved and the shade of the immortelle in the cocoa made it an altogether quite pleasant temperature in which to make the climb.

'I'm so excited to have another chance at the sublime, as you might say.' She tilted back her head to view the tall mountains above the valley, remembering their visit to the Maracas waterfall with the family and Lavington.

'This one is not as high. There's a lot more water and a larger pool. So there'll be much play of light and shadow. Great scope for your palette.'

'I cannot wait. And this track through the cocoa, such verdure and colour.' Her anxiety had given way to expectation. She was now focused on the expedition.

The cocoa pods hung like yellow and purple lanterns amid the dark green shade of their branches. They both quenched their thirst. He collected water from the fast-running stream, offering the drink first to her.

They heard the waterfall before they saw it. The roar of the volume of water drowned out the birds and the quieter sounds of the wind in the trees.

They were out of the shade and into a dome of open cobalt sky. Rising out of the spume and spray, was *le saut d'eau*, La Cascade. Michel Jean pointed out details of the little wonder, as he was accustomed to call this waterfall in comparison with the grandeur of the Maracas waterfall or the falls in Diego Martin at Le Bassin Bleu.

They lost no time in dismounting and setting up their easels for their lesson, tethering the donkey with enough rope to graze with ease.

Elizabeth Prowder made no reference to time, or to the disappointment of Wildman not being with them. But Michel Jean was well aware of the horror with which their secluded and prolonged stay would be greeted back at the barracks.

He supervised the choice of her palette, the amount of white that was needed for the volume of water, the need for scratching-out and the use of pigment.

The falls began partially hidden among the low-hanging angelin trees and cocorite palms. The crimson leaves of the wild crotons dotted the banks on either side. From the summit of the fall to the rim of the pool, the breadth of the fall grew as it descended from its forty to sixty feet of plummeting water over a staircase of rocks.

From time to time, she paused and looked across at her tutor.

He was ever ready to return her gaze. They were both drugged by the sound, the colour and their intense desire to get their paintings as well executed as they could manage.

He had paused and was looking intently at his student poised over her easel. She seemed not to notice this time and kept on working her brush. Each act of her absorption moved him: her concentration, the movement of her wrist, the journey of her arm from palette to her jar of water, her choosing of paints. They were no longer divided by race, colour of skin or culture.

He spoke her name without thinking. 'Elizabeth.' He had never called her Elizabeth before. He had always kept to the obligatory formality around names and titles in previous conversation.

She paused and turned to him. 'Yes.'

'Are you happy with your progress?'

'Yes, yes, I am for the moment.' She resumed her brushstrokes, her speckling. He did likewise.

'Michel Jean.'

He heard his name and could not believe it. He let her call him again. 'Michel Jean.' He could have sat all day to the sound of her voice calling his name.

He turned to return her gaze. 'Yes, Elizabeth.'

'That's wonderful. I know you're not finished, but I think it's splendid.' This compliment was spontaneous, a generous gift.

'Yours has come on.' She accepted the sober comment. Then, he said, 'It's your best work.'

They sat back on their stools and breathed in the mountain air.

'I'm starving.'

'Me too!'

She went off to the panniers and fetched their picnic of cold chicken and salad. They drank cool water from the stream.

'It's just occurred to me that this will be our last lesson.'

He did not say anything immediately, nor did he believe that the thought had just occurred to her. That was a kind of guard she put up. But the remark had the effect of indicating that this last hour of painting had had a special quality about it.

'Yes, now that you say it.' He followed suit. 'I'll soon be leaving for Paris.'

'Of course. How time flies. I would not have missed this for the world.'

For the world, he thought. The well-known phrase made him wonder what the world would be to her. What would she sacrifice for the world, and for this to happen again?

'I'm glad the weather permitted it in the end.' The restraint of his response was a measure of his intensity of feeling. Not now, not here, could he risk any misunderstanding which might frighten her off and result in another debacle at the barracks.

There was no easy permission to make a move, no joking flirtation as he might have indulged in with Augusta. He knew his career depended on honourable behaviour. He knew he could not have their relationship end dishonourably. He had to keep the memory of their time together intact. That, at least, would last.

'I have learned a great deal today and learning it here like this could not have happened without you. I won't get this chance again.' She paused for an instant and then continued. 'I know the barriers which exist between us, Michel Jean. I have learned more than I can describe about that sort of thing. I could have turned back at the Cottage. I would have been so disappointed to have done that, though. Lavington would have been so annoyed and, in her way, disappointed too, if I had lost this opportunity.'

'Lavington?'

'Yes. Lavington has been my other tutor. My tutor in life. She's a dear.'

Michel Jean thought back to his lunch with Lavington after the wedding. He could definitely see the attachment the governess had to her mistress and the care that she took with her welfare.

'Yes, she's quite a remarkable woman,' Elizabeth Prowder continued, 'and her background has allowed her to grow in a very different way from myself. I've benefited from her wisdom and her solicitude for myself and my children. She delights in my poetry.'

'Yes, I can see that she does have a certain wisdom about life.'

'But now,' Elizabeth Prowder said, suddenly changing the subject, 'I want to shake your hand. I want to acknowledge here, in the seclusion of this beautiful spot, something I would not be able to do in the glare of society. You have been a gentleman. I cannot imagine what you must have suffered at that time of my miscarriage and the wrongful accusations that were implied and made. I learned of how prejudice can mislead the judgement of the mind.'

Michel Jean stood and listened. There was nothing in the shaking of her hand that allowed him to go further, or allowed him to draw her into his embrace. There was nothing in her demeanour that invited him to believe that he could have sealed their eventual openness with a kiss.

He saw now that duty to her husband and children was paramount. He saw something else about her relationship with Lavington, which he had not noticed at first, something of their mutual attachment that he had not understood. He learned from her the restraint he knew that he would feel better about once he was on the *Wellesley*, heading for Europe, heading to Paris, to Louise and the children. But he also knew that if she had given him the slightest amorous signal he would have ventured further. And, as if to witness their unspoken regard for each other, more than qualities of tutor and student, they stood side by side in silence, in awe of the natural beauty of the place, absorbed into the drumming, crashing waterfall which they had painted together, the paintings still on their easels, the colours still as fresh as the drizzle, which had started to fall through the light and which made them pack their equipment away quickly and shelter beneath their umbrellas.

As they said farewell back at St James Barracks, it remained unclear when and where he would see her again. Their series of lessons was now completed. There would have to be a farewell meeting.

He was detained by Lavington and the children in the yard, who wished him well on his voyage. The children expressed their disappointment, and Lavington again spoke for herself and her mistress. 'We'll miss you at the house, Monsieur Cazabon.'

'*Au revoir*, Monsieur Cazabon.' Kate and Eddie waved goodbye.

'Thank you, Miss Lavington.'

Michel Jean wondered whether he would see the family and their governess again, as he looked back at the grey cottage and went through the gate of the white picket fence. They came and went these people, he thought.

So much had been experienced of an intimate nature, so much had been exchanged, yet there was no assurance of how any of these memories might be cherished or even remembered. It was as if no one knew how to look after what had been exchanged, what had been learned, so instead kept to the conventions of departures and farewells. What kind of future could they guarantee themselves?

Michel Jean now had his passage booked on the *Wellesley*. It was in part-payment for his work commissioned by the Earl of Dundonald. It emphasized his eventual separation from Elizabeth Prowder. There was still a couple of weeks before the actual departure. It also meant that he was now finally returning to Louise and the children in Paris. This emotional dilemma was underlined by a letter he saw was from Louise and which Josie had brought in with his coffee that morning. 'Packet bring this for you.'

Michel Jean let the letter rest there on the breakfast table without immediately opening it. Instead, he studied the watercolour he had painted at dawn on the beach at Corbeaux Town.

'You not going and read the letter? You want more coffee?'

'Josie, sweetheart. Leave it, nuh. Just put it down, nuh.' He had not stopped examining his watercolour.

The letter carried the Luc-sur-Mer postmark. Josie had not recognized it the way she did his letters from Paris and Vire. Why had he not taught Josie to read? he wondered. True, she could read a little, but she did not consider herself a reader. He had thought of this many times before. But this morning it struck him how peculiar it was that she had not recognized the postmark. Such a little thing in life could fool her, could bring her illiteracy into sharp focus. After all these years, he reflected on how, as a boy, he went off to his tutor, Mr Woodford, and she stayed at home to work in the house or in the yard. All these years and he had not really thought about it.

Darling . . . *Mon chéri*, I must write to you immediately. As you can see, I'm on the coast. The children and I took the train to Rouen. You remember how we so loved it back in '43? Looking at the landscape framed in the window of the moving train.

His eyes filled with tears at the sound of her voice.

There's been a crisis of sorts. You know how well Rose Alexandrine has developed. So bright, creeping so quickly, then beginning to walk in no time and the words coming so clearly from her little rose-mouth. You must remember those delights? She's grown so. You won't know her when you get back.

He fingered the paper of the painting. Then the pages of the letter were beginning to turn in the breeze. He continued reading. Louise's voice so clear in the letter he thought he could hear her in the room.

He could feel himself becoming a father with responsibilities. His heart felt torn apart at the thought that his children would forget him, that they would not know him just as he was able to be a father again with them in Paris.

The boy is not the same and what I thought was just his own little personality expressing itself differently has now begun to alarm me. His consumption is much better. But you remember how quiet he was when he was a baby? He was so passive, so easy to care for. Slept all the time, rarely woke, seldom cried. We thought we were so lucky being able to get a night's sleep, you working so hard to complete your paintings. I remember once when we talked about him in comparison with Rose Alexandrine, we thought it might have been unnatural that he was so good. Was there a little devil lurking inside which would come out later? We laughed at our suggestion. Sometimes when I lay awake on my own, you so fast asleep, so quickly, I used to hear him scratching the lace of his cradle. His little fingers working away like an engine quite separate from his sleeping form. I wondered that he did not wake himself. And then he seemed to grow pretty well. It's too long, my love, since you've seen him, since you've seen us. I had not wanted to alarm you at the time when you first arrived back in Paris with all the demands on you. I feared that he would suddenly have a screaming fit that I could not control. They told me babies can have this at this early age and it passes. It would pass for a while and then come again and more violent, screams then obsessions about little things as he grew into a toddler. There has been so little help with this, so little understanding. I've told you some of these things before. At five years old, all these symptoms are more exaggerated. I hate that you have missed being there for the children's birthdays.

One day recently, while throwing himself to the floor, he cried out, 'Papa! Papa!' It so alarmed me because he has spoken so few words. I thought he would've forgotten you. Thank the Lord you came to Paris on that short trip. By the age of three Rose Alexandrine had an entire vocabulary, it seems. But even at five it is very difficult to understand Louis Michel's wishes, except when he demands and throws a tantrum and then he will eventually find some comfort in pretending to suckle, even at his age. I prefer the tantrums to his silence and remoteness. I have been worn down with this and so have decided to come to my parents in Vire. I am hoping that with a new place and with his grandparents our son may settle and that our trips to the coast will do him good. He gets comfort from drawing. When Rose Alexandrine was showing him how to mix his paints and was pointing out colours he grabbed the brush from her and exclaimed, 'I know. I know,' and pushed her away.

I wish you were here. Your children need you. But I know that you are preparing to return soon.

Josie had brought in another pot of coffee and then disappeared downstairs. The sorrow of Louise's letter had disturbed him. He took up his pen and began to write a reply.

Ma chérie, What you say about our son, Louis Michel, has saddened me. But I don't mean that you should not have written about this matter. I miss you. I sometimes forget how much I miss you. I will be with you soon.

There was a watermark staining the edge of the painting, the watercolour he was still examining, where the seawater had splashed on the paper.

My affairs are pretty settled here. I am booked on the *Wellesley* to return in September. I dread the winter, but the autumn I remember as colourful. I'm very excited to show you my work. I am returning with a new album to present to Lemercier.

He wanted to start over, his last visit had been so short; he longed to be with her again like when they had stayed at Luc-sur-Mer and had taken a room at the one place on the front that offered accommodation, a place with windows which opened onto the wide beaches and to the sea beyond with the endless line of the horizon. Most of the fishermen's cottages had their windows facing the flat land of the inland coast. Only further inland did they have the beauty of the rolling countryside with the streams and the hedges of the bocage. Then the children had come so quickly. Louise was transformed from that girl in the studio near his rooms into a woman, a wife and a mother.

There was so much that he had made Louise believe would happen before he could return. They were like a lifetime these separations, with an ocean and those long journeys by steamer between them. He took down the box where he kept her letters. He read them over again, as if he had not read them before, the minute detail of the children's lives, her life, and her work to keep the family together. He needed to hear her voice. The passing seasons unfolded in her words. He saw the sacrifice she had been making. Her letters were testimony to her continuing love. But then he wondered, if like himself, she had ever taken a lover. Did she have that need? Was there a life she did not speak of?

'I gone in town.' He heard Josie's voice in the yard. Distracted, he had thought she had already left.

The house settled around him. There were the smells of salt and fish on the breeze from Corbeaux Town. There was rain in the hills and a squall out on the gulf. There was the stench from the mangrove.

Michel Jean felt sure that the response of people to the first three albums was a basis for him to advertise for subscribers for this album of his own. He would call it simply, *Views of Trinidad from Drawings by M. J. Cazabon, 1851.* Excellency had let Wildman know that he would certainly subscribe and take five copies. Wildman himself would take two and had already begun to persuade some of the top people from the important families in the island to subscribe.

While chatting at the Planters' Club, François Cazabon began to laugh, mocking his son's enthusiasm. He repeated his disapproval. 'Of course they want to buy, boy. You paint what they want you to paint. You paint their large pretty houses on their estates. You paint the colony as they want to see it, a settled place. They can boast back home of how they have civilized the niggers and pacified the coloureds. Your paintings will be one of the ways they can show their success.'

'Father, you don't understand.'

'We're an unsettled place! I tell you! You paint their enterprises, their ports and their cathedrals. You paint their military barracks, you paint their engineering exploits, how they dam rivers to create reservoirs and build bridges, evidence of how well the colony is secured and governed. The Governor's house will tell them back home, how like England it all looks. All is peaceful on earth and happy with God in his heaven and the Queen on her throne. That's what they buy and support.'

'You don't understand art, *Papa*. You say I paint what they want me to paint, and that is partly true. They commission and I give them what they ask for, so in that sense, yes. But you must look at the quality of what I paint. I don't paint what Mr Bridgens painted, that Englishman who used to paint our landscape for them, a parody of itself, our people like savages jumping around, doing a gig or slaving in their sugar fields like their coolies are now doing all over the island.'

'Well, you've one less powerful so-called friend now. You hear Hardin Burnley died?'

'Died? When?' Michel Jean's mind raced to Augusta and Mrs Farquhar.

'It's in the papers this morning. He had not been well since he had been attacked in his carriage.'

'That was a while ago. I'm so caught up with the album I'd not thought of him since.'

'Well, he might've bought one or two. You lose a patron.'

'Father, you have to understand my work. I paint people with dignity and beauty. As they are. Not hideous caricatures. My paintings will infiltrate their drawing rooms and their minds with a subtlety that is about quiet revolution. It will take time.'

Michel Jean had never wanted to paint with such anger, but he had not thought that he had such conscious ideas about his painting until he gave his little speech to his father.

'So, why you? Will we become a republic of artists? You'll have pleased your mother. Though, I don't know. She may have preferred you to be Fedon or Toussaint or even Schoelcher in her own Guadeloupe, just now bringing his people to freedom a couple of years ago.'

'I leave the politics to you, Father. Joseph wants to be a planter like a white man, taking his compensation. I think you want change. But there's something I want to talk to you about. Look at where Josie and Ernestine still are. I, too, am at fault there. You must settle something on them before you kick the bucket, as them English say.'

His father never liked being reminded of Ernestine and Josie, though in his own way he thought he did his best for them. That best had been their eventual freedom, but not the giving of his name. He had never agreed to legitimize his union with Ernestine or to legally recognize Josie.

'You're right about Ernestine and Josie. I'll attend to that matter soon.'

Michel Jean felt better about his speech to his father. He had learned how to speak to him and be heard.

'You know, you must see that my work is different. I love this landscape. I love these people. Yes, my patrons, when they look, yes, they will see something pleasant. No, my art will not show them the squalor of their barrack rooms, the lash of their whips, which still continue. It will not show them their contraptions to encase the head, the bits to weigh down and entrap the tongue. These things have gone, but not the thinking that perpetrated them. A landscape and people in servitude has not completely passed. We must make it pass. My art in a subtle way can do that. Though I must admit that all of this is not uppermost in my mind when I paint. I work from my honest labour, from my craft.'

By the end of the conversation, François Cazabon had signed up to buy one of his son's albums, and he later encouraged a Miss Escalier and one of the coloured Boissières to place orders themselves. When he noticed that Mr Numa Dessources, the radical editor of *The Trinidadian*, was also subscribing, he was pleased to be in such company.

There was another long letter from Louise. Michel Jean had rushed on over the opening pages. The nuns at the local convent had reported that, having been slow in starting to speak, Louis Michel was now talking much more. They had helped with his nursing. Louise and Rose Alexandrine were not able to humour him. His only spark of life was when he was given watercolours to play with and Louise said that she was encouraging him to paint a picture for *Papa*. And there it was. The front of the house at rue Blanche was well drawn and painted in a child's bright colours. She and the children would await his arrival there before moving to rue du Four, where he had planned to move in with money from the album.

His little son was now five, going on six. He wept as he turned the pages of Louise's letter and the creased paper with the watercolour of the house on rue Blanche. It struck him that the child had a curiously developed sense of composition and perspective. How odd, he thought, at such a young age without any formal training. There was the façade of the house with the linden trees that were customary in that part of Montmartre making an avenue of the street that led into the square at Pigalle. He remembered the heart-shaped leaves in the spring, the great rushing sound of the wind among their branches in the summer, their dying in the autumn. In the winter their brittle, iron-hard skeletons of trunks and branches stood out in the grey, metallic winter light. His son had painted his picture on a bright summer's day.

It was the only way to survive, he thought. Never to stop painting.

Hardin Burnley was buried with pomp and ceremony at the Trinity Church. Michel Jean made an appearance at the funeral service. Afterwards, Augusta was there, standing to the side of the grave in Lapeyrouse cemetery with her mother. He expressed the briefest formal words of condolence to her and Mrs Farquhar. When he had a further opportunity, as the funeral party began to disperse, he asked about her baby. 'She doing good,' she said, smiling.

'That's good. Take care of yourself.' He pressed into her hand all the notes that were in his pocket.

'I ent ask for this, you know.'

'I know. Buy she a present.'

'You still with the manners and the sweet-talk. Thank you.'

Mrs Farquhar came and drew her daughter away.

Augusta was looking over her shoulder and waving as she let her mother guide her out of the cemetery. Michel Jean stood among the tombs of Lapeyrouse, waving back at her diminishing figure. Once the crowds had left, he visited his mother's grave.

They had had a brief moment at the grand ball on the *HMS Wellesley*. He had spotted her at once among the swirling dancers. Then she was at his side. 'Monsieur Cazabon.' He noticed the title, noticed that she had not called him Michel Jean like at La Cascade.

But, as if still in the aura of that moment at the waterfall, he broke from convention and replied with her name. 'Elizabeth.'

'I spied you from a distance. We may not see each other again. The *Wellesley* sails in a day or two. You'll be gone.'

'Yes,' he said, becoming monosyllabic with the thought of his loss.

'I will not write.'

'No,' he replied, meaning that he agreed with what she was saying. He imagined catching her up in his arms and taking her out of this public glare into the darkness of some corner of this grand ship, where he could make love to her. Impossible.

'I will remember you.'

He wondered at her own thoughts, whether they were wild like his. 'I will always remember you.'

It was as if they were exchanging vows. Failing to find some of his own words, he echoed her sentiments and hoped. Hoped for what? he asked himself. Then he added, 'You were a very special student. We were artists together.'

There was no need, in the din and bustle of the great ballroom that had been erected on the deck, to pursue her any longer. He concentrated instead on his commission for *The Illustrated London News* in the knowledge that the woman he saw swirling off into the dance did know him and had at last fully acknowledged the nature of their relationship. They had recognized that to go any further in this society at this time would have destroyed them both.

He could not help wondering as he watched the dancers, in the midst of that reflection, how the same society would allow his white wife, Louise, and his two coloured children, to be received.

The *HMS Wellesley* sailed two days later.

Michel Jean wondered, as they steamed through the small archipelago between Trinidad and Venezuela, how he might find the island on his return.

BOOK FOUR

1851

BOOK FOUR

1852–1854

I

On the arrival of the Cazabon family at King's Wharf, Louis
Michel took at once to Josie, who was there to meet the steamer
as it berthed. Josie clasped him to her bosom and lifted him
up. Louis Michel was all smiles, though a little bemused by
the extravagant attention of this black woman.

'Oh, God, Master Michel, look at him. Look at our boy!
Garçon!' Her expression of ownership did not escape Michel
Jean. Only after that claim was made did Josie, at her most
diplomatic, make her curtsey to Louise, who stood at a
short distance from the drama, holding the baby, Jeanne
Camille, in her arms with Rose Alexandrine hanging onto
her mother's skirts. '*Madame*, welcome to Trinidad.' Then
she turned her attention to Rose Alexandrine. 'And she, so
pretty! *Très jolie!* Oh God, Jeansie! And the baby; so many
children!' The formality of her earlier curtsey was immediately
undermined by her smiling intimacies. 'He does make pretty
children, eh?'

This last comment was made to Louise, who smiled. Michel
Jean could see that she was taking these songs of praise to be
expressions of a faithful retainer's admiration and affection.
He did not dispel these generous impressions that Louise
seemed to have formed. Josie had refused to accept any
responsibility that she might have had for the procreation
of the children or for any features that they might have
inherited from their mother. When Josie was taken up with
Louis Michel he leaned over and whispered to his wife, 'She

can be excitable. She's been in the family house all her life. So, you can imagine . . .'

When they were alone, back at no. 9 Edward Street, Louise exclaimed, 'Jeansie!' imitating Josie. 'Well, well. You're the apple of her heart.'

Michel Jean now played down Josie's enthusiasm, wondering to himself how the history would unravel and whether it would allow him to save himself in the eyes of his wife. How would he be able to retain the affection of his sister? How would his wife, himself and his sister learn to live together? He should have prepared Louise when he was in Paris for the inextricable family secrets that would now inevitably be revealed.

These were his thoughts as he rose early the following morning, escaping the house for a walk down Edward Street to Corbeaux Town. He had to trust Josie. He had to trust Louise.

He ventured forth with Louis Michel as the dawn began to tint the water in the bay pink and light up the sand on the beach at Corbeaux Town with ochre. The little boy held his hand as they walked past Miss Melville's sugar factory. They had grown close on the voyage. It was not the intimacy he had with his daughter, Rose Alexandrine, but on this last visit to Paris they had renewed their bond. The small palm which held his had been firmly entrusted on their walks up on deck to spy whales and view the dolphins which followed the steamer.

Louis Michel broke from his father's clasp and ran towards the shallows. Michel Jean watched with delight. Here was a freedom greater than Paris. He would thrive here, the little fella. That was his hope as he watched him stoop at the sea's edge and reach out to cup the water in his hands, looking around to draw his father's attention, crying out, '*Papa, Papa! Regarde! La mer!*' He waved back at his son. He hoped that this spontaneity would continue and develop.

The light was changing fast, beginning to pick up the red on the roofs of the boat-builders' houses and workshops, the ochres on the scarred hills above the Diego Martin valley. The sky was thinning out into a tint of cobalt, strung with floating wisps of white cirrus clouds. Was that Pompey and his daughter he could see at the end of the beach? A dash of red for the bright dress on the little girl caught her exactly. A splash of denim blue worked for her father's breeches and the scratch-out of the white of the paper was his gleaming white shirt and cap. The man carried a rolled up fishing net over his shoulders. Yes, the sky did govern all. Michel Jean was glad to be back home.

Louis Michel had set the paints open and the brushes stood in sea water he had fetched in a jar. Michel Jean had started this ritual on their walks in the Bois de Boulogne, where he had taken him over the last year to make up for all the time he had lost with him. This was more than school would give the boy, where they had failed to understand his nature. He would give him his own freedom, those green days that he and Josie had stolen in the foothills of Morne Jaillet.

'Your *papa* has done a new painting,' he declared to his son, who was sitting in the sand at his feet building a castle. The boy's eyes stared back, large green pools of intelligence he struggled so hard to express. He had his mother's eyes, but they had turned with the green of a *chabine*. Michel Jean broke from building the body colour for the foreshore of rocks and the jutting out timber of a broken-down jetty, to rake his fingers through his son's hair. 'You is real little sugar-head, you know.' He then continued to draw in the hulls of pirogues. Gouache was best. The boy looked on, standing by his side. He drew the hogsheads and panniers lying abandoned on the beach; the tall silk-cotton tree and the coconut palms.

'Pompey!' he shouted across the length of the beach. 'Pompey!'

'Eh, eh, Monsieur Cazabon. You come back. You reach.' Pompey hurried towards him. 'And this is your son? This is the boy you leave for so long. He look like you. You bring your wife?'

Michel Jean presented his son and talked of his two daughters.

'Three! You working hard when you away. Eh eh! And I must see this wife you bring from Paris! Is a white woman? Town talking, you know.'

He put out his hand to shake the boat-builder's rough hand. 'Come, Pompey, and this is your daughter.' He clasped the child, blessing the girl with his hand on her head.

'Yes, is Marguerite.'

'*Oui*, she grow big.'

Pompey smiled proudly at the shy girl. 'Go and play.' Marguerite joined Louis Michel building sandcastles.

'I reach home, boy. I tell you, I feel like I went to the end of the world and come back.'

'You did them journey before, man.'

'Yes, I know, but this time was different. This time I really back.'

'I go believe you when I see it.'

'Where else I going, Pompey?'

'Is you that does go. You asking me?'

'You find everything here, Pompey?'

'Everything?'

'What a man needs.'

'What a man needs? Them is big questions. I go be here. A trip to Five Islands. You know where to find me.'

'I can always depend on you, Pompey. Come, son, let we go. Married business.'

'Yes, you is a husband now. You is a father. Watch yourself, eh.'

'Boy, I tell you.'

Pompey's daughter claimed the sandcastle as her own, as Louis Michel abandoned his creation.

The bright morning had changed everything; immense skies with caravans of clouds drifting out over the gulf. There would be rain in the afternoon.

Michel Jean stopped to buy his son some sweets from a *marchande* at the corner of Prince Street. 'Here, try the *touloum*. *Non?* Sugar cake? Is coconut. It nice. *N'est pas?* Nice?' The boy was fussy.

The sweets were different from the ones he was accustomed to in Paris. Michel Jean bought himself some *pistache*.

As they approached no. 9 Edward Street, Louis Michel began running ahead of his father. '*Maman! Maman!*' He had recognized the house and was running up the street. Michel Jean lingered behind watching, the play of light and shadow on the pavement from the palms swaying in the wind.

Josie greeted them at the gate. Michel Jean held back. She kneeled to speak to Louis Michel. 'Eh, eh! So you gone down town and you ent take me with you? You buy sweetie?' He stared up at her, bewildered, his eyes getting larger and larger, like he was seeing Josie for the first time. It was not the mutual attraction of yesterday. 'Eh, eh? You ent know me?' Michel Jean saw how she would have to get accustomed to the boy's unpredictable, changing moods.

Louis Michel escaped into the house. '*Maman! Maman!*'

Josie stood aside as the child broke from her. She then turned her attention to Michel Jean. 'I ent know how this thing go work out, you know. Your way is to go out and leave us to it. First morning she here and you just gone out and leave she to look for things, coming in my kitchen as if this is . . . how this go work out?' She lowered her voice, looking behind her into the yard and the open front door. 'What you tell her? I think she think I is some kind of servant. That I in the house as some kind of servant.'

'Lower your voice, Josie. No need to make this thing bigger than it is.'

She lowered her voice to an agonized whisper. 'Bigger than it is? This could be any bigger? Eh!' She pressed each syllable from her clenched teeth.

'Josie, sweetheart.'

'*Non, non, non.* Don't do that. Don't sweetheart me here this morning. You mad. Your wife inside.'

'Josie, what you want me to do?'

'What I want you to do? What we could do? What we ever could do? Tell me, nuh. You see anything we could do?' Her

329

eyes filled with tears. So long, and all her feelings were still so intense, always at the very surface.

'You want me to tell her the whole story?' He stood looking at her. He felt helpless. 'The best we can do is to live together.'

'So, you ent tell she nothing? All this time? Nothing. Three children. Nothing. Why that surprise me?'

'Josie, understand me.'

'I understand you. I understand you better than you understand yourself all your life. Is whether you understand me. You think the best thing is for we to live together. But how? That is what I ask myself. But how? What it is that you go have she thinking?'

'Josie, how I could tell her everything?'

'What? Is shame you shame?'

'That you are my half-sister. That we have the same father.'

'That would be a start. It true. I ent know why you couldn't tell she that before. So when Madame Congnet and Madame Fabien, your full sisters, arrive to meet your white French wife. When she meet your sisters, where I go be? In the kitchen? Outside with the children? Magdeleine and Clotilde, they never want to see my black face that look like their father. If I cut my wrist the blood is the same. You know that? If I chop my foot . . .'

'Josie!'

'Come, let we go in. You see people watching. People ent stupid, you know. They know I is family. If you don't tell she, she go find out sooner or later and she bound to ask you if it true. And she go want to know why you never tell she. Like is shame you shame.'

'But, what about the other, Josie? What about us? About *our* past?'

She turned away from him. Then she looked at him again. 'You come and go. You leave me and you gone. I live without you for years. As my mother say again and again, we not children now. No. I don't expect you to tell the woman that, to tell she that, Jeansie . . . to tell she . . .' Josie turned from him again and looked behind her to see if anyone was looking or listening. 'But, that don't mean she not going to wonder and she not going to find out.'

'Josie, I could . . .'

'*Non*, you couldn't. *Non*, you won't, not while I living in this house. Because I can see what will happen now. This will be she house. You bring your wife and children home to their house, Jeansie. You have to take responsibility for that . . .'

'But, Josie . . .'

'No. You want to put me in another house? You want to put me in a house with Mama and that is where we is and you can come and visit we there . . .'

'Josie, what you saying? That's a dream. You mother would never like that. You mother right. We not children no more. But, Josie . . .' He went to touch her arm, to stand close so that he smelled the ginger on her tongue. 'Josie, you will always . . .'

'Stand back. Don't touch me here. You mad? Don't say nothing you can't mean. Too long we live with an impossibility.'

'We can have a secret, Josie.'

'From who? Because the world don't speak loud each day, don't mean the world don't know. You go keep that from she and let she lie awake at night thinking. I have to live here in the same house, Jeansie, with she. We have to live like we live together. We have to respect each other otherwise what kind of life you bring she to, eh? To leave she place in Fwance, for what?'

They stood, silenced, at the gate for what seemed like an eternity.

Rose Alexandrine came to the front steps and called out. '*Papa, Papa, vini mangé!*' Michel Jean noted how she was picking up the patois.

He felt how he and Josie were both cut to the bone, so that the blood of their feelings flowed freely. They felt exposed, standing by the gate out in the street in the hot sun, brother and sister baring their souls, speaking so loud that even the walls could hear. The palms scratched themselves to say that they were keeping watch. The frangipani, smelling like a courtesan's bosom, hung over the wall to catch the talk.

Michel Jean found Louise out on the veranda with the children. Rose Alexandrine sat in a rocker that had been in the house since his childhood. Louis Michel was sitting close to his mother on her chair. He was trying to tell her about his walk to the sea with *Papa*, how he had built a sandcastle with a little girl and how *Papa* had painted a picture.

'Let me see. Let me see.' Rose Alexandrine did not want to be left out.

'Later, *chérie*.'

'What was all that at the gate? Is everything all right?' Louise silenced the children's excitement. 'Josie has been so good showing me everything around the house. Explaining how everything works. We had fruit and bread and wonderful coffee from Montserrat; Gran Couva, she said.'

'And guava jelly,' piped in Rose Alexandrine.

'Let me get you something.'

'I'll manage. Remember I've been a bachelor.'

'Not any more, darling.' She kissed him on his forehead. 'Josie said she was going to shop. She wouldn't take any money. Was that what all the quarrelling at the gate was about?'

'Quarrelling? There was no quarrelling. You must realize that I've known Josie since I was a very little boy.'

'You told me. And she was telling me her story.'

'What story?'

Louis Michel was sharing his newly bought sweets with Rose Alexandrine. 'That's good, sweetheart, you share with your sister.'

'I don't think he likes them. This is called *touloum*,' Rose Alexandrine added.

'Then you try them. You don't have to eat them, Louis. *Papa* won't mind. What story?' Michel Jean insisted.

'The house at Corynth? You'll have to take me there,' Louise continued.

'I'll take you everywhere. There's the whole island to discover. I want to rediscover it with you.'

'I met her mother. You didn't tell me that she was also living here.'

'Didn't I? I must've mentioned Ernestine. She came with my parents' marriage. She's as old as the island for me.'

'What do you mean?'

'She nursed me. That was how it was. That is why Josie and I are close. We were nursed at the same time. We were like brother and sister.' He could hear himself start to tell her the story. He had found a beginning. 'And that was the story my sisters always told me. They heard these things from my mother.'

'What did they hear from your mother? You should've brought me here in '48, so I could've met your mother. So she could've seen the children. So she could've met me. I'm very sorry to have missed seeing her.'

'I'm sorry too, but, Louise, don't let's go over that again. You know we didn't have the money. Anyway, Ernestine was one of my father's wedding gifts to my mother. She came from Martinique. He eventually gave her her freedom.'

'*Mon Dieu!*'

'It's how things were.'

'I know, but . . . you read about these things. You hear about them. Then it's here. *En famille*. Is that why she lives downstairs? Why can't she have a room upstairs?'

'That's how it's always been. She would find it strange.'

'Would she? Yes, I see. She was your nurse.'

'Like a mother.'

'A *mother* who lives under the house?'

'Louise. You know it was the same in France. Where you think we get it from?'

'Why are you so angry?'

'I'm not angry. She and Josie have always had their separate quarters.'

The children had ventured into the garden and were now in the yard looking into the busy street. '*Maman!* Come and see!' Rose Alexandrine was calling excitedly. 'They're selling pretty things, ribbons and buttons. Windmills! Can we buy something?'

Louise kept her eyes on the children. 'I see.'

'You will find many things different.'

'I know. I love the house. The light. I love the hills over there and the sea right at the end of the street. I heard it last night breaking on the shore. And the ships coming in from the world. My letters will arrive at the wharf.'

'I'll take you everywhere.'

'You have your work to do.'

'We'll take the ferry to San Fernando to see the family. I want to do that with you and the children.'

'I thought they would be here to greet us. There are things you haven't told me.'

'Of course there are things I haven't told you.'

'I need to understand the world to which you've brought me.'

'They're very busy and the journey into town is not that easy for my father. My brother can hardly ever leave the estate, and my sisters . . . They have their children. They want to see you. And the children.'

'Well, we must go soon. But you must start working. There is the album to show, the patrons to be given their copies. Josie and I will be fine together. And she's so good with the children. Did she never have children herself? She didn't want to marry?'

Michel Jean left that question hanging in the air. He looked away. Then he thought of the impression that he might be giving. 'No, she chose to stay with her mother. To look after her mother.'

'I see.'

'There's a lot to understand. Buying and selling. Property.'

'Property?'

'Yes. You won't understand everything at once.'

There had been so many hiding places in the past, Michel Jean thought.

334

'*Non.*'

'*Café?*'

'*Oui.*'

The dawn on the beach at Corbeaux Town had exhilarated him. But now there was a kind of inertia. He should be out, as Louise suggested. He should be trying to contact Wildman. His young friend was now married. The wedding had taken place when he was in Paris. He wondered if he would have been invited. He must see Excellency. There was the album to show and the copies to be distributed. It was what he so wanted, to return with the lithographs by Eugene Ciceri and the magnificent printing done by Lemercier in Paris. This would show the family. This would show Port of Spain who he was. But there was so much to protect Louise from, or so much to make her understand. He would have to take it slowly.

He lay in the hammock on the back veranda, looking out to sea where he could just catch a view of the Five Islands. There was a squall developing down south. His meeting with Elizabeth Prowder on the causeway between Craig and Caledonia came back to him. What had happened to her over the last year? They had agreed not to write to each other and they had kept to that decision.

The children's voices came from the backyard. His children with Louise here, at last, in Port of Spain! Then, voices of the women. Ernestine was sitting by her door, rocking Jeanne Camille in her perambulator and Louise was being entertained with stories. How was he going to manage to unravel, to confess? Was he going to allow events to take their course or would he act to bring the truth about? What would happen if Augusta came to the house? Should he go to her or wait for her to get in touch?

He could hear the talk down in the yard. Louise was asking Ernestine who her husband was. He heard the old woman's laughter. Her answer was laughter. Louise would soon be able to read the whole story. He would not have to say anything himself. All would soon be out. It would be best to let things unravel themselves.

'*Papa, Papa!*' It was Rose Alexandrine. 'Come and play! Come and play in the rain!' It was the rain falling on the shingle that had woken him and then his daughter's voice. The wind swept the drizzle into the veranda. He got out of the hammock and looked down into the backyard to see his son and daughter running about naked in the yard, screaming with delight, while Louise sheltered with Jeanne Camille in the doorway of Ernestine's room. He noticed that Josie was not there. Then she entered the yard from under the house. Her clothes were soaked. It had been raining hard. Of course it was Josie who had got the children out into the warm rain. It would be Josie. No one else would be so extravagant. There was a sudden glimpse of himself as a small boy with Josie playing in the rain on the Café in San Fernando.

'*Papa, Papa!* Come and play in the rain. See, *Tante Josie* is playing in the rain. *Maman* must look after Jeanne Camille. Come down, come down, please!' She had Louis Michel shouting with her, shrieking at the tops of their voices. He liked to see his son taken from his solitude into such spontaneous play. The sight brought joy to his heart.

He waved. *Tante Josie?* Where did that come from? Children will intuit without knowing what they say. Out of the mouth of babes and sucklings, he thought. He returned to the hammock. He felt threatened by Josie's familiarity with the children. He was happy for them, but afraid for himself. The gulf had disappeared. Change was so sudden. He had forgotten what it was like; this rain without warning blowing in waves off the Atlantic, or coming up from the Orinoco delta in squalls on the gulf.

'Darling! *Mon chéri*, are you all right? The children have had such a wonderful morning. You've had a very long sleep. You must've been exhausted. All those nights you didn't manage to sleep at sea.'

'I'm fine. Just resting.'

'I must see to Jeanne Camille. Ernestine has had her most of the morning. There'll be lunch soon. I've been learning about plantains and breadfruits. You rest till we call you. Oh, by the way, a letter was delivered. A liveried man brought it from the Cottage.'

'Must be Wildman.'

'Wildman?'

'The Governor's secretary. I told you about him. He was my student for a time.'

'I know . . .'

'What?'

'And Elizabeth Prowder? You mentioned her. An Englishwoman?'

'Yes, another student. I must've told you about her as well. I think she may have returned to England by now. You know when you are far away and you don't know the context. It can be difficult to imagine. And you were coping with so much at the time.'

'Ah, well. I must return to the yard. The letter is in the drawing room. I think it was Rose Alexandrine who received it at the door.'

'Wildman. He's quick off the mark. Must want to see the album. They'll all want to see it.' There was a crate with all the printed volumes for the subscribers stacked in his studio.

He could hear the noise in the kitchen downstairs, the preparations for lunch, the children's screams of delight, Josie's instructions, Louise's soft voice of inquiry and acquiescence.

So Wildman had not forgotten his arrival. He'd have to go there this afternoon. He would arrive unannounced after a walk across the savannah. Surprise him.

The hot midday sun was at its zenith. The bell like the one at his mother's dining-room table was being rung. The old institutions were being set in place again. This would be Josie's doing, trained from childhood, there would be nothing that she did not remember from the fluted napkins standing in glasses to the salt and pepper cellars, which looked like the steeples

337

of Mr Wren's churches dotted around London. Their silver shone so that the filigree and engravings picked up the light and glittered. The linen was laid, the soup tureen brought steaming to the table, and the entrée dishes got out of the cabinet for the serving of vegetables, meat and fish. There was a new madam in the house.

After lunch, he read Wildman's letter. Excellency and Lady Sarah had had a son in the last year, and she was now pregnant again. Wildman's own wife was also pregnant. They would have more in common once his child arrived, Michel Jean thought. Was he being presumptuous? How would Mrs Wildman feel? Wildman wanted to see him. He had some news for him. Wildman always had news. But what of Excellency? Was his commission still good? When he saw the new album, surely, surely then, he would be more committed than ever. There would be more work.

He decided to put off his visit to the Wildmans' for the time being. It would be fine if he could be sure that he would find his old friend on his own.

'Monsieur Cazabon?'

He had not been able to resist returning to the little grey cottage with the white picket fence at St James Barracks. It was odd how easily they had let him enter at the gates. He turned to the voice, feeling silly to be caught staring into the house. How long had he been standing there? How long had he been noticed?

'*Oui. Bonjour.*'

'Is Amalie. You remember you paint me.'

He had been so far away that he hesitated. Then he recognized her. 'Of course, that day we worked in the house when it was raining. Yes, two fisherwomen.'

'You come to see her?'

Michel Jean felt embarrassed and pretended stupidly at first that he did not understand to whom Amalie was referring. 'Who?'

'Madam. Mrs Prowder.'

'Yes, I suppose so.' He wondered at his odd reply.

'They gone away, you know. We all went down by the wharf to wave goodbye.'

'When was that?'

'Not long. A couple of months now.'

The loss of Elizabeth suddenly felt more complicated than when they had been together, with the opportunity to see each other. Now their time during all their lessons came to represent failure, and he now realized it made him angry.

That he had only just missed her filled him with dismay. She would be back on the Isle of Wight, not yet in India or some other colony. Maybe there would be something here, perhaps something she had left in the house. In leaving, she must have felt as if she were abandoning some part of herself. He wanted to believe that. He still had her painting, the one that she had given him.

He took his leave from Amalie. 'Maybe I'll paint you again someday. Get you to look pretty like you are.'

She laughed. He could still hear her laughing as he closed the gate of the white picket fence.

On his way out of the barracks he could not resist standing under the bamboos that Elizabeth had tried so hard to paint well. He stood and stared, wanting to touch the hand which had held her brushes, the wrist that moved with his in the paintings of the hills, and of these very bamboos which creaked and knocked in the wind in recognition of those times.

She had left, taking with her her views of the island to show to those back home.

The rain came and continued without stopping, leaving the savannahs and low waterfront streets in Port of Spain, which were beneath sea level, swamped. Marine Square was flooded.

Louise read stories to the children, pulling them in close to her on the couch in the drawing room. When they got bored, the children asked to make something and Josie, who had come upstairs, suggested making a kite. She got old *Gazette* paper and showed them how to make paste from flour and water and how to build the kite with cocoyea and thread.

'What is cocoyea?' Rose Alexandrine asked.

Josie explained how you had to strip the leaf of the coconut palm. She showed them the spine that was left and promised on a fine day to show the children how the stripping was done. 'When we go down by the beach I go show you.'

Michel Jean stayed in his studio. He listened to the household growing accustomed to each other. This domestic rhythm was new to him. It felt particularly strange in Port of Spain, though he had grown accustomed to it in Paris. He noticed that Josie had stayed downstairs earlier with Ernestine, who was unwell and had not been out for days. She was nursing her mother in her room.

Because of the heavy rains, everyone anticipated a plague of mosquitoes. The children were excited by the idea of sleeping under nets. But the adults felt the threat of yellow fever and malaria. The scent of citronella was overpowering.

As the months of the rainy season went by, Michel Jean found he could not work in his studio. The rains had kept him in. He was aware of every movement in the house and in the yard. The albums to be delivered to their patrons were still stacked in the studio. It had not been the weather to go about the town delivering. He needed to escape by engrossing himself in something new. There was so little light. Everything was gloom and shadow. It fed a depression growing in him.

With the Indian summer, as the English called it, or the *petit Carême*, that little Lent, as the dry season in the midst of the rainy season was known, Michel Jean stepped out into the late afternoon light with Louis Michel. It was his birthday. He was seven years old. His son took his hand, clutching his newly made kite with the other, as they headed up Edward Street towards the Queen's Savannah. As they approached the vast open green, encircled by the still-dark blue hills, there was a constant change of light from indigo into lilac. The sunset, which formed over the gulf as a result of the heavy rains clearing at the coincidence of the failing light, began to alchemize into a stunning orange and vermilion, which bled into each other in streaks across the sky. On the far horizon, where the Venezuelan coast dipped from the highest peaks in the cordillera, the Andean foothills, the sunset lit the coastal lowlands and the port at Guaira where there was scrub land at Araya, the bare vegetation of cacti, acacias and agaves. Michel Jean was glad that he had remembered his paints. Louis Michel helped with his easel.

The boy had insisted on the kite. 'Is not real kite season, you know. But let we see if we get a wind.' He had not the heart to refuse his son's birthday wish. They stood close together, the boy struggling with the string, the father reaching ahead to give deliberate, guiding tugs, as high above them the kite took the breeze in swirls and swoops. 'Though is a chickichong you have, it flying like a real mad-bull.' Michel Jean was lost in the play with his son, lost in his own childhood, wanting his father. Louis Michel stared at his father, not understanding 'chickichong' and 'mad-bull'.

'Chickichong is them little kites like yours. It singing like a finch in a cage. But a mad-bull is a real fighter. I go get you some zwill to tie to the tail. When we come out on the savannah in the real dry season with the high wind, you go fight them fellas with their big kites and you go go so.' Michel Jean pulled on the string to make the kite swoop and then ascend rapidly. 'You go cut their tail.' The kite became a white moon in the growing dark, father and son tugging and guiding. 'Here, you take the string. Hold it tight, eh! Good.'

The boy was given a strong wind for his first kite-flying on the savannah. Michel Jean settled down to catch the fast-changing light and his small son flying-kite with his father, sketching in his own attendant figure. He used white pigment and scratching-out to achieve the delicacy of white ribbon for the tail in the breeze.

'*Papa, Papa! Regarde. Le cerf-volant.*'

'*La lune.*' The father offered the boy a metaphor and smiled.

He ran after his kite, almost being lifted off the ground, his small frame tumbling. As he ran, he cried out, '*La lune, la lune!*'

As Michel Jean packed up his paints he felt distracted. Looking up, he could not see the boy in the gloom. He began calling aloud, 'Louis Michel, Louis Michel!' There was no reply. The darkness was increasing. Fireflies were flickering on and off. 'Louis Michel,' he called again. Still no reply. Then he stumbled upon the boy lying on the ground on his back, looking up into the dark sky with the first stars, the kite on his chest, the string and long tail in a confusion of knots.

'*Papa, regarde, les étoiles,*' he kept repeating. '*Les étoiles.*' He had forgotten the excitement of the kite and the moon. Then Michel Jean saw that his son was pointing at the fireflies all around him. '*Les étoiles. Ils tombent.*' Stunned, he walked back home alongside his father, repeating at intervals, '*Les étoiles, les étoiles.*' The constellations were transformed by the boy's imagination into stars, fallen to the ground, flickering on and off.

At last, Michel Jean possessed the necessary optimism about his work to visit Wildman with the albums for himself and Excellency. His young friend had been taken up with the new domestic life of his marriage and the birth of his first child.

'Why have you stayed away so long? I wrote to you.'

'Settling the family in,' he explained, trying to hide his embarrassment.

'These are stunning,' proclaimed Wildman. 'This will be the making of you, Cazabon. The production is far superior to either the Burnley, Lamont or Dundonald albums, even with those splendid nautical paintings of the *SS Venezuela* and the *HMS Wellesley*, all decked for her departure through the Bocas.'

'You think Excellency will be pleased, and Lady Sarah? I know she liked the wedding views.'

'Charlotte, what do you think?' He turned to his wife. 'Cazabon! You haven't seen each other since Excellency's wedding; such a pity you had to miss ours, and now there's my son. Charlotte, dear, can the nurse bring him in?' Wildman was his old enthusiastic self. His wife was more reserved.

Michel Jean understood so much more now about English class in the colony. The English Creole woman smiled her self-contained smile. After all, she was Charlotte Bushe of the Bushes of Port of Spain. 'I think they're very fine,' she said, turning the pages of the album that was laid out on a table on the veranda of the Cottage. 'Very fine, indeed. You must improve, James.'

Wildman looked a little subdued and Michel Jean did not want to gloat with the compliment, or rub salt into his friend's wound.

'Maybe the lithography has improved the watercolours, do you think?' she remarked with a feigning nonchalance, as she closed the covers of the album. The two friends looked at each other, taking in the barbed compliment.

Michel Jean kept up his civility. 'Thank you. I hope Excellency will be pleased.'

'Oh, I'm sure . . .'

'Charlotte, dear, the baby . . . and you know I think the watercolours, if you've ever seen them, and the lithography, are both fine in their different ways. The subtle effects of each are quite different and bring out distinctly different aspects of Monsieur Cazabon's art.' Wildman looked at Cazabon as if to say, I'll not have her talk about your paintings in this way.

'James, there's no hurry, and Nurse will bring the boy in after his bath.' She ignored her husband's comment about the paintings and the lithographs. She ignored Michel Jean, too. 'Let us wait for Nurse. I'm trying to train her. If *I* then do what I've asked *her* to do, she won't ever learn.'

'Cazabon, you'll soon see him.' Wildman turned back to the album of lithographs. 'This is excellent. Your achievement is astounding.' He was again turning carefully the large pages. 'So well executed.'

Michel Jean smiled at Wildman, who was trying to be mature and to save them all from embarrassment.

'And your wife and children are here now?'

'Yes, the whole family is here now.'

'That's capital.'

Charlotte Wildman sat and watched. Wildman paced about the veranda while Michel Jean stood again near his albums. There were five for Excellency stacked on the table.

'Will I leave these here?'

'Yes. But I'm sure Ping will want to congratulate you himself. I need to pay you for his and mine. I have it right here. He reached for the draft in the drawer of his desk. 'Ping is mortified that he and Lady Sarah, who is indisposed at the moment, can't be here. She sends messages of congratulation. You know she's suffered quite a bit of bother with a recurring condition.'

Michel Jean noticed Charlotte Wildman adjust her seating position, bracing herself at her husband's reference to the Governor by the family's familiar name. Or, was it the financial transaction that had peeved her, or the mention of Lady Sarah's condition? But Wildman remained in full flow, not quite getting the hint. So, she interrupted him in a subdued tone. 'James, I don't think we use . . .'

Wildman noted the tone of censure in his wife's voice, but did not heed it. 'Charlotte, my dear, Cazabon knows all about Ping. Don't you, Cazabon?' Wildman risked sounding like a petulant schoolboy proving a point to a parent. 'Here, let me give you this.' He handed Michel Jean the draft.

Michel Jean felt put on the spot by his friend and caught within the quibble between the wife and the husband. But this was more than chatter for him. This was work. He was glad to have his payment of forty-two dollars. He was not accustomed to the presence of Wildman's wife as a witness to the familiarity between himself and Wildman, but he was beginning to learn the different postures he had to adopt. He pretended not to notice the signs of a marital tussle, while thinking that perhaps they were signs that he might lose his friend sooner than he thought. Charlotte Bushe, now Mrs Wildman, had the upper hand.

With six dollars for each album, Excellency taking five albums and Wildman two, he was feeling particularly gratified. There had been one hundred and forty-eight subscriptions. Louise had said that she wanted to help with the delivering of the albums. Michel Jean was not sure of the etiquette. It certainly would be an opportunity to introduce Louise to some of the people with whom she would have interests in common. She needed to enter the wider society. He remembered, as he planned, advice from Uncle St Luce. 'It's almost as difficult as if I had married a black woman. You are despised on both sides. The whites think you've moved above your station and the blacks think you have betrayed them, and say, "Who you think you is, white nigger?"'

Wildman had also said that he would help with the delivery. 'It would be a pleasure, old man. Anyway, I need to get out more on my own. I'm far too domesticated. I miss our trips around the island. Oh, for the smell of paint and salt and the wind in our faces, *en plein air*!' The two men had smiled, understanding each other. Wildman had reassured him that the albums would be delivered to all the patrons.

The house was dark when he entered the yard, with just Josie's lamp burning low in her room. In the past he would have sought her out on a night like this. She had a way to massage away his torments. He could lose himself in her scent and the smell of his childhood. Hers was an intimacy that had never needed negotiation. But they were no longer children, her playing his bride in his sisters' wedding dresses in the yard on the Café. He could not do that to her now. He would not face her with that choice. He had to respect her dignity and her loss, her vulnerability. He had to accept his own loss, a child's loss.

Michel Jean lit a lamp as he entered the house. He climbed the stairs to the upper floor where the children were asleep. He looked in on them, their forms below their tucked-in-tight mosquito nets, the baby Jeanne Camille in her cradle. He wondered about their futures, his Creole children, his little 'white niggers'. How he hated the thought of them being described as such.

'Darling?' Louise's voice stopped him in the corridor. He eased the door of Rose's bedroom shut.

'*Oui.*' His voice was hardly audible. Charlotte Wildman grew into a monster in his mind, her smug words hammering on his brain.

In the lamplight he could see Louise standing in the doorway. 'You're late.'

'*Oui.*'

'Is something the matter?'

He stared at her without knowing what to say. After their long separation, they had salvaged and remade their marriage, sealing it with their new baby girl, Jeanne Camille, sleeping peacefully in her cradle, just there on the other side of the corridor. He put down the lamp.

They were sitting on the side of their bed next to each other. Louise took his hand in hers. '*Mon chéri*, tell me what it is that worries you.'

He thought that she looked afraid of the answer to her own question. At first, he did not speak, but turned towards her to hold her face in his hands. He remembered so clearly the first time he saw her face. He drew back her hair, which she had loosened for the night, brushing it out before bed. He could see a subdued reflection of himself in her blue eyes. Drawing her closer to him he kissed her on the mouth, preferring this language of their senses to the inadequacy of words. She let him take her into the bed for them to find their love, to find their young passion for each other. This reunion was what would save them, save him from the darkness which crowded his mind with the world of prejudice. Where had his newfound optimism gone? They slept and woke in each other's arms before dawn. The children were still asleep. Life was whole again.

It was down on the beach at Corbeaux Town before the sunrise, before even Pompey had emerged from his boat-builder's yard and Miss Melville's factory still quiet, that he found the fuller solution to his disenchantment with Charlotte Wildman and her kind. He settled down to paint. All the details of the bay that he had known so well were imperceptibly being lit by the touch of an invisible hand. The months had flown by since returning from Paris.

Light, which was not yet real light, but a gradual visibility, rolled in with the gently moving sea hardly breaking on the beach, leaving a ruffle of lace skirting the shore that was gathered in by an embroidering hand. Above, the sky began to be tinged with an increasing light, throwing rose tints upon the white cirrus clouds. Then, sharper light, like from a pen dipped in ink, picked out the bow of a pirogue and wrote its name: *A Few Good Men*. Michel Jean's doubts vanished as imperceptibly as the light changed to increasing brightness, as he wondered about the crew of that boat.

While he painted, the dawn at Corbeaux Town beckoned Pompey out from his hut. 'Eh, Monsieur Cazabon, is you, boy. Like you painting in the dark.' This was his signal to cease, and to go and ole talk with Pompey before the sun got too hot for the walk back to Edward Street.

Pompey was a friend he would not lose. He had cherished his freedom all these years. He had been one of those to desert estate work and make something of his own in boat-building and fishing. Michel Jean liked to think of his craft as an art. He watched him now saw and shave a plank of wood for the side of a pirogue.

'Coffee on the coal-pot. Help yourself.'

'*Merci bien. Oui*, I here since foreday morn.'

'You like that, eh? You like to catch the light as it turn.'

'Who this for?' Michel Jean watched the shavings curl and fall like rays of light onto the ground.

'I making this for Etienne. He going and start to fish. He say he finish with the sugar. He have garden up in the valley, but is fish he want to fish.'

The *bois canot* took shape under Pompey's eye.

'How long this taking you?'

'He go get this month end.'

347

Everything had its time: a painting, a pirogue, fishing and boat-building. They all took it out of you. None of it was easy and it always required you each day to start over again.

'You looking a little troubled. What happen?'

'I could live here with you, you know, Pompey.'

'You could live here with me! What you saying?'

'I tell you, I could live here with you and eat fish and paint.'

'You go paint. But you go fish?'

'I want something simple. I want that now.'

'But you have small children. And you tell me you does work for the Governor and thing.'

'That's not everything. Small children and a wife.'

'The little boy, how he going? And the baby? She must be bigger now.'

'He going good. If you see him fly kite. The baby beginning to walk.'

'Is so? I find the boy does look . . .'

'Well, you know. He wap. You see like that *bois canot* you have there and you can't get it straight, You say it wap. The water does warp it. And you can't get it back straight. So he is. But he go do good.'

'Well, you go have to care for him. He looking bright, but seeming slow. Not like his sister. She sharp and bright as a star.'

'Look where the sun reach and I ent have parasol self. I go see you, boy.'

The house was unusually quiet. As he entered the yard, Ernestine emerged from her room to say that they, Louise and Josie, had together taken the children for a walk. 'They gone in town. Your wife say, breakfast in the pantry.' Then, as he made to mount the stairs, she held onto his arm. 'Jeansie, is your son.'

'What happen?'

'Go and see.'

'What?'

'He need to quieten down. Is so, his mother say.'

'What happen?'

'I ent see nothing. When you go upstairs, you go see. Josie say they go clear up later.'

Michel Jean could not imagine what had taken place. 'Okay, Ernestine. Let me go and see.' He thought how old Ernestine looked as she talked to him.

As he entered the drawing room it was very evident that something extraordinary had taken place. He stood and stared. Everywhere, strewn upon the floor and on the tabletops were copies of the same painting, *Sunset on the Savannah*: the cows grazing, the samaans and *palmiste* palms silhouetted against the great crackling cane fire of a sunset, the boy with his father, the kite high in the sky, the white of the moon. Each painting was identical to the one he had done and left in his studio. The boy had painted it over and over. He could not imagine how. What had actually happened? Why were they strewn all over the floor? He remembered the painting of the house at rue Blanche sent from Paris. But Louis Michel had not painted since then. There was something both macabre and amazing, he thought, sitting there staring at the repeated copies of the same painting. Then the fear that thought provoked transformed itself into a sadness, which overwhelmed him. Louis Michel must have painted these at an extraordinary speed. Seeing the young boy caught up in his obsession must have filled everyone with terror. Michel Jean kept looking at the painting of himself and his son flying kite. He found that he was weeping as he sat there staring. There was a wonder about it all, but also something quite disturbing. How was he to explain the skill and the untaught ability at such an early age? How to explain the compulsion? Flying kite, he said, smiling to himself.

Louise returned to the house alone. The children had lingered longer in Brunswick Square with Josie to view the carnival. They stared at each other across the drawing room as she entered. She put down her hat on the back of the couch. She looked weary. Michel Jean went towards her. He held her against his body in his embrace.

'He would not stop,' she said. 'He just would not stop. I doubt you have any paper left.'

'That's the least of it.'

'I'm afraid for him. Who will help us to understand him?'

'We must keep him at home.'

'Yes. Josie understands that. We talked. I like her.'

'Good.'

'She managed to calm him. It had become a frenzy. She sat with him on the floor, talking to him all the while, trying to collect up the paintings. In the end he listened to her. It was her voice, I think.'

Louise was worn down.

As they spoke, they heard the others arriving. Louis Michel entered the room, ignored the paintings completely and went to his room. Rose Alexandrine went in with him and soon they could be heard playing as children should play.

The following day, Louise came to stand behind Michel Jean as he worked. The studio overlooked the lanes that spread into a maze of destinations, which got lost in Miss Melville's factory yard behind Corbeaux Town, together with the wandering goats, the barking dogs which punctuated the night, and the cockerels which now heralded the break of day.

Emancipated Africans had set up shacks along these lanes for commerce. On this dawn, joy and pain came up to the windows of the studio from their carnival, to remind him of his mother's ambitions for him and their republic. The skin drums and the masquerade were just passing in the street below and the children had run out into the yard with Josie.

Louise stroked his neck. He imagined now her loss of him when she had been preoccupied with Louis Michel and all alone with the children in Paris. There was so much that they had not shared over the last three years; so much that he had shared with others, Josie, Augusta, Elizabeth Prowder, Wildman and even Excellency. The irony was that their separation had furthered his career.

His wife had become a kind of memory to him. Again they were having to recover their lives. He felt that this was happening as she stood enfolding him in her arms, claiming him again here, where he had brought her to live on this island with its impossible conundrums. He vowed to himself that there would be no more separations.

Prodigal, he was coming home to her in himself, to the new life they would make here. He vowed in the silence of the stroking of his neck, her soft fingers kneading the lobes of his ears, as if massaging them for the entry of some secret promise of her own, that he would not leave her, not even if tempted to by one of his brief liaisons. His brush hovered over a lilac sky, drying. He paused, allowing her to bend and kiss the nape of his neck, dragging her fingers through his hair.

As they looked down into the street with the carnival, he wondered where the new republic would come from. How would his art write its story?

He had brought Louise and the children here and would now take that responsibility for what had been missed and that he now needed to make up. He did not want to count, not add and subtract, not balance emotions and affections as in a ledger, as he had seen Wildman counting his albums and pricing them for Excellency and the other subscribers. He wanted to give his all to his wife and children. But his thought brought Augusta to mind, with her child. She had not yet come to tell him whether she believed that child was his.

'*Ma chérie.*' He broke the silence as he turned to her face and they kissed as their mouths found each other. '*Chérie.*' He hoped that she knew in the tone of his voice, in the touch of that kiss, that they still had time to repair their lives.

'*Chéri.*' She put her fingers to his lips. She did not want a conference. She did not want to go over again what they should do with Louis Michel, whether he should go to the nuns, or whether a private tutor should be employed, or whether he should be left to the love and care of Josie, with herself managing and supervising, as she did so well. She did not want to discuss whether maybe in Paris they might have got one of the new doctors of the mind to help them understand their son.

'You're homesick for Paris, for Vire, for the coast, for the countryside of the *bocage*.'

'*Non, non, non*. This is home now, my darling,' she protested.

'I know, but . . .'

'Maybe Saint Pierre would be a little like Paris.' They had once been thinking of Martinique as a destination and eventual place of settlement.

'Sweetheart.' He could feel her passion.

'I think of you and how long you can take this, how long it can be good for your work. Who are going to be your patrons? There won't be many like that governor. You say that Wildman will continue to help; but for how long? Let's see. Maybe in Saint Pierre there will be more of a chance and we'll feel more part of France. Six years after Emancipation there, it should be better. Who is there to talk to here?'

He let her talk.

'Saint Pierre is like having something of both worlds. We're in the Antilles and we're in touch with France. There is a bit of both of us.'

He listened to his wife while he looked out onto the gulf and the swifts darting and swirling in great flights of instantaneous change, the carnival music fading at the end of the street, the children's voices calling for more, for the carnival masquerade to come back.

He was not ready for another change. They had been back a year. The 1851 album had become eventually a grand success. He could not leave now. There was work to do. There was still the island to show her. As he sat there, staring out onto the gulf, he felt a resolve, and then a sense of elation. He would do another album, more along the lines of the views in the 1851 one. *Grand Races* had not been for a wide public and had not worked. It was not his best work; though there was humour and observation. He was in the process of selling his best work to Harris. He was bereft, though richer. 'Let our son stay with me. Let him hang around the studio. That's what he wants to do.'

'But he needs other children.'

Louis Michel was always on both their minds. His future was just beneath the surface of most of their considerations. Rose Alexandrine was settled with the nuns. She walked to school with her friends. Jeanne Camille, now a toddler, was more than enough for Josie to help with.

'Yes. Maybe the nuns would let him come for a couple of hours in the morning.'

'*Oui*, and Josie makes too much of a claim on him. I don't think that's good for him.'

Michel Jean looked at Louise. 'What do you mean, a claim?'

'I expect she fills up her own loss. She's not had a child. Her emptiness, maybe. Though she seems to have found her fulfilment in this house and this family. Is that a consequence of the past?'

'What do you mean?'

'Surely you've seen this? Her devotion to you. No one does this if they've always been free.'

'It's as if she's been free.'

Louise stood at the window with her back to him, talking, as she looked down into the lanes still loud with the carnival, puzzling on what he had just said. 'I feel there are things I don't understand. You need to explain them to me.'

'What can I tell you?'

'You can tell me your story of Josie.'

Michel Jean came to stand next to his wife at the window and looked down into the lanes and out to the gulf. They could see the southern peninsular of the island curling like it does from San Fernando towards the Serpent's Mouth and the Orinoco delta. The day was a fine blue and not the usual dry season haze clogged with Sahara dust. Soon it would be Lent and the same carnival town would become penitent. Would he be penitent?

'We must go south. We'll take the ferry, go with the children and visit the family at last. I will take you to Corynth.'

*

353

It was the ferry, *Lady Macleod*, that morning and again it was a fine day with a little more haze obscuring the Montserrat hills as they passed Couva along the coast. Michel Jean pointed out Gran Couva, where the cocoa was the richest in the world. Louise, excited to get away from Port of Spain, felt like one of those travellers out of Europe. She kept a close eye on Jeanne Camille. Rose Alexandrine looked after Louis Michel at the railing of the deck as they passed fishermen and oyster-catchers along the mangrove shore. They were followed by a flock of pelicans feeding in the wake of the ferry, while over the mangrove they caught glimpses of the white egrets and the flame of ibis and flamingos.

They had to wait for a while before being allowed to disembark and Michel Jean had sketched and painted on deck, looking at the San Fernando hill. 'Morne Jaillet, we always called it,' he said, happy to see it again. Louis Michel was at his elbow measuring every move and quite spontaneously producing about ten sketches as they waited to disembark. Louise had to scramble up the sheets of paper as they fluttered about the deck, threatening to be blown out to sea.

'Like father like son,' one of the travellers looking on said. 'He's a little genius.'

Louise pulled her son towards her to protect him from prying eyes. She did not want anyone seeing him like an act in a circus. Louis Michel had become agitated with the delay, exhausted in his production. His sister was learning ways to keep him still. 'Look, Louis, the pelicans.' The flight and plummet of the birds held the boy's attention. Eventually, they berthed and alighted at the quay. Rose Clotilde met them at the San Fernando wharf.

They went first to the Fabiens at Mon Chagrin where Louise was at last formally introduced to the family. She met François Cazabon, old and dignified in his white linen suit. 'What a handsome old man,' she said to Michel Jean. Her presence helped to heal those estrangements Michel Jean had experienced with his family. They ignored the fact that a year had passed since their arrival.

'Welcome to the Cazabon family, *madame*,' François Cazabon said, showing his charming side. Everyone was on their best behaviour to welcome Jeansie's wife from Paris.

In the afternoon, the children stayed with their cousins. Rose Alexandrine was given strict instructions as to the care of Louis Michel, while Jeanne Camille was left with the nurse. Louise and Michel Jean took a buggy to Corynth, travelling alongside the Cipero River past the Union Hall and Retrench estates and turning up to Corynth's *usine* just before reaching the boundaries of Golconda. Michel Jean pointed everything out in detail. He was so excited to be here with his wife. Every scent was smelled anew, the air was filled with the fragrances of crop-time, the nearby fields burned before harvesting, the trash blown by the wind and the sweet taste of molasses in the air coming from the factory yard; the more intoxicating aromas from the small rum distillery. 'This is where I was born and grew up.'

She smiled. 'As if I do not know. You've spoken of it since I met you, but I had so little with which to imagine it.' He knew that she could see the emotion in his eyes and hear it in his voice, and would be wondering what had happened here, wondering what she was going to hear about his origins.

They had climbed the hill above the *usine*, the wind coming across the fields from Savanna Grande and the estates as far as Malgretoute and Cedar Hill in the distance, nearly blowing her bonnet off. They trotted along the bamboo grove to where he had been taken to paint by his aunt Marie Lucille, and on turning the bend in the road they came upon the first view of the house. 'The house where I was born.'

'*Oui.* You described it so well.'

He brought the horse to a walking pace and then he drew the reins in tightly to a halt. 'Whoa, whoa,' he said, like he had heard the men on the estate do.

'When I first met you in Paris you could not have been further from your home. And now, I'm here.'

'So this is where it all began. Where Josie and I began.'

'Why we're here.'

'It's a story which I myself had to be told. I did not know it from the start. How could I?'

'Tell me.'

They had stopped in the shade of a samaan, which was growing in the pasture and whose branches spread beyond the fence over the muddy trace. The horse had settled into grazing on the fresh grass on the verge, the horseflies buzzed in the heat, hovering on the fresh dung.

A group of workers, Africans and some of the new Indians, passed them, coming along the gully, black as the soot from the fields of burned cane which they had been cutting and loading onto carts. Michel Jean thought of how he had erased the cruelty of this labour from his paintings.

He had to decide where to begin and where to take his story. Which conclusion would he leave Louise with, which conclusion would be satisfactory to her to quell her concerns about what she judged to be the situation of Josie in the household? How far into adulthood would he take the story, what details might help and which might be sure to create greater problems? The truth was that he was not sure he knew how to tell Louise the bit of the story, which in the end would explain everything, everything which she had been noticing since her arrival but did not know how to interpret.

'Josie said she too was a child here. She too was born here.'

'*Oui.*'

'You were children together. But she would've been a slave?'

'I'll tell you everything, Louise. You know all the simple bits.'

'Being a slave? Nothing simple in that. I can't imagine it.'

'No. But that isn't what I'm talking about.'

'What could've been harder for this child? You free, she a slave? She said you played together.'

'Louise, shhh. Let me speak. Josie *is* my sister, Louise.'

'*Mon Dieu!* Why did you not tell me before? Your sister? What do you mean? You've said in the past that you grew like brother and sister. I took that to mean that you were very close as children. That she was one of the most faithful retainers.'

'No, she is my real sister, Well, my half-sister. My father's child as I am my father's child.'

'She must think I'm terrible. You should have told me. It must be awful for her. What will I say to her? And Ernestine, that old woman downstairs, dying, her mother, your father's mistress? They must think I have no respect.'

'No, they don't think that. They know you don't know the truth of the household.'

'How could you have kept this from me? Why have you done this to me?'

'Josie wanted me to tell you.'

'Well, she is right. I should've known. She's like Rose Clotilde, your full sister.'

'Well, she's not.'

'What do you mean, she's not?'

'Don't be naive, Louise. I'm not saying it's right. But she's illegitimate.'

'And you?'

'Legitimate, of course.'

'I can't measure these things.'

'But they're measured. Frenchmen, you know this, white Frenchmen measured it down to the infinitesimally smallest percentage. There were one hundred and twenty-eight divisions.'

'But who knows the proportions? What proportions are we talking about between your mother and father? What proportions with your father and Ernestine? And Josie is not black in their terms.'

'There are things you have to accept that have happened here. Europe is more than complicit in this creation. In fact, it is not a matter of complicity; it is what was part of their trade and enslavement. You know this. You don't need to be shocked. I don't have to spell this out to you. Or, should I? The true true mulatto was the child of the pure black and the pure white. You like the word pure? Who is pure? What is purity? The child of the white and the mulatto was the *quateron*, ninety-six parts white and thirty-two parts black. But there's another way to bring this miracle about. The *quateron* can be produced by the white and the *marabou*? *Oui*? The proportions? Eighty-eight to forty. That's pretty marvellous, *quateron*, *marabou*, don't you think?'

'I understand.'

'Do you? But I bet you've not heard of the *sacatra*. Eh heh!'

'I understand. No more.'

'The proportions there are a little different, seventy-two to fifty-six. Imagine an empire; imagine empires with their clerks at their ledgers, which have calculated these measurements, because you know these facts and figures are linked inextricably to employment, to profits and losses, to who can own what property, who can inherit property, this very property. That was the difference, those who were property, and those who owned property. Those with property received justice, those without did not.'

'Stop.'

'You asked me to tell you the story of Josie. My sister, my father's daughter with a woman who was his property, who was indeed, as I've told you before, the wedding gift to my mother. That beautiful piece of ebony, he used to say. He owned her and he owned her progeny.'

'I've never seen you so upset.'

'*Oui*, yes, because they never told me. As we grew up, they never told me that she was my sister. She was there with her mother in and out of the house, eating the food that we ate, sleeping downstairs, yes, but in the house, making the beds, pulling down the mosquito nets. Like we were twins, ironic, *oui*. You know our birthdays are almost the same day. It was that neat. My father was a wizard at this thing.'

He stopped, brought up sharp by the thought of Augusta. Was it a matter of like father like son? Was it an example of how the sins of the fathers are visited upon the children? He thought that others might think this way if they knew.

Michel Jean looked at Louise and he thought he could see in her frown the dawning realization that he did not want ever to have to confirm. Leave her with her imagination, the preposterous thoughts she might be thinking, and the horror of possibilities. Was she thinking, even now, at least there isn't a child? And then, to leap from that place as to why Josie was making these claims on her own son, Louis Michel. Had she ever imagined what she was taking on in this marriage, what secrets, what conundrums of nature lay beneath the seemingly placid surface of an adventure into a new world? Had any of this been in the questions and warnings of her parents when she brought them a black man to be her husband, her Othello, as an uncle had once called him? '*Mais, oui, il est Otello.*'

They sat for a moment in silence and heard the wind whistle across the serrated fields of sugarcane, knock and whisper in the bamboo grove, lift the grand branches of the samaans and then lift their shadows in that shade which mottled the bright gravel trace which led to the ancestral house. What an ancestry for her children he had offered her. He could see her calculating. What proportions were they? How much white did Michel Jean have? Louis Michel? Rose Alexandrine? Jeanne Camille? How did that disturb the calculations in the ledgers, the price of the property, their claim to justice? How would this affect her own children and their children?

She put her hand in his. When she spoke of her love, he guessed that she had tucked her doubts, her frightening imaginings, into some dark corner of her mind into which she would never pry. She asked no more questions about Josie's story. She began to say something about François Cazabon. 'Your father . . .' Then she stopped, unable to voice the horror of her thoughts.

'He's an older man now,' Michel Jean said, hoping to diminish any fears provoked by his recent revelations.

Michel Jean hoped that Josie, as an aunt, and Ernestine, as a kind of grandmother to replace the grandmother their children had missed having, would strengthen the family they now were. All Cazabons.

The *Lady Macleod* got them back safely to Port of Spain that evening, though they had suffered a squall near the coast at Chaguanas, where there was the pretty village of Felicité, and had to go below deck for the remainder of the journey, coming into King's Wharf as the last light of dusk faded. 'What a family, *mon chéri. C'est formidable.*' Louise kissed him on the cheek, while at the same time drawing her children close to them, as they strolled to Edward Street.

Louise wasted no time with her acts of reparation. Michel Jean heard her and Josie talking down in the yard by the kitchen door. Later, he saw them both open the door into Ernestine's room. He guessed that Josie would realize that he had only done the least that he could do.

'At least that you do,' Josie said to him the following morning by the gate, as he was leaving to escape into a painting on Belmont Hill. 'Don't worry, I ent let out we secret. And Mama so old now, I think she forget what she know.'

'Give it time, Josie. Give it time.'

'Is time we give it, *oui*. And you know is time we give it.'

He left her looking at him as he made his way up Edward Street, across Park Street, the town fading behind him as he finally disappeared into the green expanse of the Queen's Savannah and the circle of the blue hills.

Many things seemed to suggest reasons for optimism with the new year 1853: the arrival of Chinese immigrants on the *Australia* from Amoy and the *Lady Flora Hastings* from Fukien. There were Lord Harris's reforms from town councils to borough councils to enlarge and improve representation. There was the two-mile road built across the Grand Lagoon of Oropouche. All of these should have given Michel Jean a sense of achievement, now that he was so publicly identified with recording the Governor's projects.

The response to the 1851 album had been, on the whole, favourable. He wondered again at the audiences for his work. Charlotte Wildman's past comments came back to irritate him; hers was an educated voice without education. It was fine work, he kept saying to himself. I know my work, and Lemercier and Ciceri are some of the finest lithographers and printers in Paris. Yes, but it was the watercolours! She had questioned his talent without even having seen them. Her voice had come to represent a whole society's prejudices drumming away inside his head with a persistence he sometimes found difficult to quell.

But apart from his demons, the private grief of Excellency was deeply felt. Lady Sarah's sudden death while she was in Barbados, from the recurring condition of thrush and further complications was announced in *The Gazette*. The Governor, with his little girl and boy, portrayed a melancholic sight to Michel Jean whenever he saw the trio on walks along the new paths in the Botanic Gardens with the children's governess in attendance. The gardens had recently become again another of Excellency's personal projects.

They had become a refuge and a solace, as he strolled along the avenue of palms near the Queen's Savannah and ventured further in among the walks of nutmegs. The orchid and bromeliad collections were a particular delight and distraction. They would be a fitting legacy of his term in the colony.

The small children ran ahead of their father towards the Cottage, where the Wildmans were still in residence. Wildman was always a distraction and an entertainment.

Michel Jean and Excellency chose to have one of their last conferences as the year neared its end and it was certain that Excellency would be taking up an appointment in India. The certainty of his appointment to the Government of the Presidency of Madras put a stop to the first rumours that he was heading for Sydney.

'London wants me to make immediate preparations for departure.' He wanted to take his leave with as little ceremony and pomp as possible out of respect for his late wife, the mother of his children.

The conversation turned to the choice of paintings which he would take away with him. It was strange to think of his views of Tamana and Cotton Hill hanging in an English drawing room, possibly detaining some viewer for a moment, provoking a remark about an old Creole drawing master, a comment on the unfinished watercolours sketched as they had rambled through the exquisite scenery of the lovely island. Is that how Excellency might remember him?

The collection was to be extensive. He chose and Michel Jean made a list, hoping that he would find the required paintings stacked in his studio at Edward Street, half wondering what might have happened to some of them while he was in Paris. He was sure that Josie would not have removed any of the work, but there were always misunderstandings and errors.

George, the Governor's boy, had run ahead and his nurse had followed him among the clumps of bamboos, with the toddler holding her hand. Excellency was suddenly anxious about his children. 'Where has Nurse got to? They're only little.'

Michel Jean recognized the man whose sensitivities he had learned. There was the man who would under no circumstances allow the coloureds representation on his councils, would not even trust blacks to be competent gardeners, no matter how he saw reform, and yet he had drawn him, Michel Jean, into intimate confidences by way of his work with the paintings he had done for him. Beneath the stoic schoolboy at Eton, the Merton scholar, there was the young man who had had to go south in search of a warmer climate to attend to his delicate health. As he grew up, he had become more and more alone, with his sister dying when she was six and he was eight, two baby brothers in infancy when he was just five and six, and then his surviving brother, William, had died at twenty-six. And now the man who had experienced his mother dying when he was seven years old was compelled to be a protective guardian for his own two children, who had just lost their mother in early childhood.

'He has been marked by death,' Wildman had commented one day.

Excellency had dropped confidences along the way, and together with pieces of family history from Wildman, these had allowed Michel Jean to build a much more complex portrait of his patron than the society around him might have done.

They had arrived at the cultivation of imported flowering plants, which Excellency had arranged to be sent from Belmont. Michel Jean became a student of the botany of Belmont, learning how the plants had been sent out by James Moneylawe, the gardener, to Mr Purdie to propagate in the soil of Trinidad. He had sent thirty sorts of annuals, perennials and flowering plant seeds and twenty sorts of vegetable seeds, including melons and cucumbers.

'These are dahlias, and those are fuchsias. Roses you will be familiar with and the pinks. These are less well known, Liliums and Calceolarias. Carnations, they are less extraordinary.'

Michel Jean listened to the lists of plants. They seemed to comfort Excellency. 'So, it's all settled, your departure?'

'Well, there's not a date set. It will depend upon the schedules of the steamers. And there is the weather to consider, but January is spoken of. I must also think of the children, who will accompany me as far as England in the first instance. I may have to take the nurse, so that there is some continuity in their life. They don't know their English relatives.'

The impending departure of Excellency saddened Michel Jean. He saw his life changing. He was leaving with his views to take home. Just when he was getting established, his principal patron would no longer be there. 'We must get the rest of the list sorted. There is the one of your house.'

'Yes, let us go this way by the new bougainvillaea walk. The plants are originally from Hawaii, I believe.'

They had now listed a substantial representation of Excellency's projects and favourite prospects. 'A fair collection of oils.'

'Yes, I think the remaining choices must be watercolours, landscapes . . .'

'And some portraits . . .'

'Who would you like? There are, of course, the paintings of your wedding.'

'Well, I did commission one or two in particular, but there was that girl at Beau Séjour, a mulatto. In fact, I remember quite a few girls at Beau Séjour.' Excellency smiled wistfully. This was another side to his character. Michel Jean remembered his trips with the Governor to the east coast to stay in the cottage on the Ganteaume Estate.

He now felt embarrassed. It did not seem appropriate that, soon after Lady Harris's death, he should discuss the portraits of the Beau Séjour *belles* he remembered painting at the cottage on the estate. Excellency had had the cottage built to stay in while he spent his time there riding and supervising the breeding of the thoroughbreds. Being a guest of the planter, Monsieur Ganteaume, would not have afforded him the same freedom.

'But, Madame Erzulie from Beau Séjour . . .?'

'Is that the one you would like, in her best white gown?'

'Was that on the occasion of the feast of St Joseph?'

'She's quite splendid on her throne of rocks I had specially constructed for her pose. The dress was magnificent as I remember, damask and embroidered, both the border of the skirt and the foulard around her shoulders exhibited the finest embroidery.'

'Yes, Madame Erzulie. And whatever happened to that young mulatto, or was she a *quadroon*, at Orange Grove? You must have a portrait of her, I would expect.'

Michel Jean did not want to dwell on their times at Orange Grove. 'Her own and her mother's lives have been radically altered since Mr Burnley's death, I hear. They have been well provided for.'

Michel Jean caught Excellency looking at him, as if expecting some more information, possibly of a quite different kind.

'You're not in touch, then? I remember James being quite smitten that night we got back from Tamana. I thought you were both game. And you were brave to have designs on her, what with Burnley, the old codger, being there.'

'She was called Augusta. I did do a portrait once. No idea now what happened to it.' He knew exactly where the nude was lodged. And there was the last bust.

'Well, you must search it out. Quite a beauty, as I recall.'

Excellency's request disappointed and unsettled him. The idea of him searching out a portrait of Augusta to give to him to hang at Belmont, and possibly to boast and joke about with his gentlemen friends as they moved from dining room to drawing room to rejoin their ladies after Havanas, coffee and cognac, left a bad taste in his mouth. An old thought about his work being property, the property of planters, much like how their chattels, their bartered slaves and exported hogsheads of sugar had been, disturbed him now as he drew up his register, his list of paintings to go with the other items on the inventory which Excellency had accumulated during his stay on the island.

'Where's Nurse got to now? She's gone way beyond the mahoganies.'

'The children will be fine.'

'You've been reunited with your wife and children. That must be very rewarding.'

'It is.'

'Yes. So, sunsets and sunrises. We'll need some of those. I've not forgotten the *belles* of Beau Séjour, though. Nor Augusta. Is that what you said she was called?'

'Yes. I'll put the sunsets and sunrises on the list. I'll look out the portraits.'

'There's one you did of Wildman's cottage, which I quite liked.'

'Your memory is extraordinary.'

'Well. I'll need a full record of this time. My wife loved the island. I know some people thought I should not have entangled myself with a Creole. This was her home. She's borne me two strong children. They'll be the memory of her, but I'll need some views to take me back, probably when I retire to Belmont after this stint in Madras.'

'I'll do my best.'

'Of course you must not forget one of the St James Barracks. One of the parades.'

Michel Jean was pleased that Excellency had moved away from the women of the island, his *belles* of Beau Séjour.

'We must go in soon. But you know I've been very partial to your marine and nautical sketches, the HMS *Wellesley*, of course.'

Michel Jean made a note to himself to remember sunsets and to look out for the *belles* of Beau Séjour. He would conveniently forget the portrait of Augusta. Not even Louise had discovered it. And Josie had never seen the nude.

They had arrived at the house. 'You must not be anxious about your work after I've left. I shall be recommending you most highly to my successor.' Excellency stopped to deliver his assurance before entering the house from the west wing. 'Run on, children. Nurse. As I was saying, my successor will be told about your work. Wildman will be staying on to clear the decks and get things ready for the handover. He'll make the necessary introductions, I've no doubt.'

'Thank you, sir.'

'We'll see each other again when you deliver the paintings. There's just one more thought on the collection. You once did a still life, a sewing basket and a smaller basket with threads, two items of clothing and a terracotta bowl; ochres and greens and that startling white chemise. I would value that. If you remember, it was at Beau Séjour and you were sitting on the veranda of the cottage. She had left these items casually strewn there as she strolled out on to the beach.'

'That is who, sir?'

'Madame Erzulie.'

'I see. I'll have a look. Must be there if you say so.'

'Good; thank you, my man.'

*

366

Michel Jean handed over the inventory of forty paintings. Wildman looked after the drawing up of a money note to cover his fee: twenty-four thousand francs. Excellency seemed distracted. The children were running in and out of the reception room that looked out onto the front lawn. It had been six years. He did not know what to expect from this farewell.

'What do you make of this talk of cholera?'

'We all hope it won't take hold here as it has done in Venezuela.'

Wildman was displaying the oils and untying the portfolios, allowing some of the watercolours to fall out onto the table. Councillors came in and out. Excellency glanced at the oils and watercolours, letting his eye travel over the inventory. There was the still life: the sewing basket, the red foulard and the white chemise belonging to Madame Erzulie prominently displayed.

What fictions paintings were, Michel Jean thought. But also, what a record they were if one knew how to read them as an imagined life. When he took his leave, they shook hands, each of the men promising to remain in touch. Michel Jean did not believe that he would see the Governor and his cousin again. He did not see how that could happen. The Governor had grown more distant with his grief at his wife's death, and Wildman had been changed by marriage, entering the narrow English set with his ambitious, Creole wife. After all this time, Michel Jean's relationship with the Governor and his cousin would, he was sure, seem a mere moment in a life.

The brief sunset vanished over Patos as he left the Botanic Gardens and strolled across the Queen's Savannah. He remembered the first meeting with Wildman and his introduction to the Governor. They were leaving with what they were taking. He felt angry about how they could come and go. He could still return to Paris, he thought. He and the family could go with the last of their money, with the money from Excellency's commission. He could force the family to sell Belle Plaine at Aricagua. He could take his mess of pottage from those acres. If they thought he had to stay here and disappear in this colony they had made, into which they would still not allow him, they were wrong. They should know that he had a reputation. It was not money and position that made him an artist.

As he left the savannah, the swifts flitted like bats in the dusk. The parrots were already roosting.

Michel Jean sat on the steps of the Governor's cottage at the edge of the Beau Séjour Estate. He had travelled east with Louis Michel, leaving the family in Port of Spain. He had come back for the purpose of finding the young women, whom he had painted for Excellency, and in particular to trace Madame Erzulie. He asked for one of the mulatto girls, whom he had painted on the request of the Governor. He was told that she had gone to St Mary's at Guayaguayare, because her mother was there. 'She mother go look after she baby,' he was told. Michel Jean had not thought anything of it until inquiring about the other girls. He was told similar stories of the girls having to find work elsewhere, so that their mothers could look after their babies.

He thought of his portraits returning to England with their fictions, their imagined lives, and the real lives hidden here in the coconut grove of Bande-de-l'Est. No one at Belmont would know how to read the texts and understand the story of the *belles* of Beau Séjour and the Governor.

Madame Erzulie had also left Beau Séjour and had taken her trade to the new town of Sangre Grande.

Michel Jean pondered the stories of the *belles* and the Governor while he watched his son running down the beach, trailing a little behind the others. He had heard one of the other boys calling him Hop-Along. 'Come on, nuh, Hop-Along.' It quickly caught on with the chorus of other children in the yard, each echoing the other. 'Come on, nuh, Hop-Along!' He had found an acceptance here that he had not in the *école* in Port of Spain with the high browns and *grands blancs*, taught by the nuns. But Louis Michel was afraid of venturing into the mango groves behind the bridge beyond Dry River, the eastern side of George Street with the black boys he had befriended. The children had gone so far down the beach he could not see him.

'They does look after themselves. The big one mind the little ones,' Miss Marianne from the estate house said, noticing Michel Jean's anxiety.

As the children arrived back, the rain was sweeping in off the sea in swathes. Louis Michel was now fully initiated into the yard, playing in the rain. Hop-Along was one of the brood, mothered by whichever mother was present in the yard. He waved at his father, but was far too preoccupied with his play to come over to him or to need his care. This was what he missed in Port of Spain, in the tight streets of the town. His father had not seen him so uninhibited before.

'You see him playing,' Miss Marianne said, 'but days we don't see him. He down by the sea among the coconuts, painting what he see. The other children say he must teach in the school. Even Father Peschier say he must come and teach the children. Look, I collect up all the paintings he do.'

Michel Jean looked amazed at the collection of watercolours of coconut groves and the creeks where the fresh water met the sea. He noticed the bright colours and how Louis Michel had used the gouache as he had taught him.

'Thank you, Miss Marianne.'

'He not go want to leave, you know.'

As they prepared to return to Port of Spain Louis Michel pleaded, 'I want to stay, *Papa*. I want to stay.' His tears and the salt of the sea blast stained his face while standing on deck with his father, as he looked back at the coast with which he had made a bond. The children on the jetty were waving goodbye and shouting. 'Come back, Hop-Along. Come back, Hop-Along.'

On returning home, he was met by Louise on the doorstep with the news of Rose Clotilde's sudden death. It had been impossible to get in touch with him at Bande-de-l'Est. It was just Joseph, Magdeleine Alexandrine and himself with his father now.

*

Back in Port of Spain, the cholera was spreading as fast as the news itself and, as the year galloped on, the deaths were mounting up in the morgue on Charlotte Street. The coffins were piling up on the gravesides in Lapeyrouse. Governor Elliot, after his recent arrival, was finding it difficult to instil a sense of calm into the population that was close to having a death in each household.

Louise suggested a trip to Martinique. 'Let us take the family to Saint Pierre.' But the news there and on the other islands was not encouraging. The disease was taking hold. 'Maybe we should go to the country, move away from Port of Spain,' she suggested to Michel Jean. The town was fast degenerating into the squalor that increased the risk of the disease spreading. Ever since a dead ox had floated into Corbeaux Town from across the gulf and some of the fishermen had become ill from the roasted meat, people were convinced that cholera was coming over the gulf from Venezuela.

The *marchandes* with their sparse trays were neglected. Their cries went unheeded. Their faint calls of '*Pistache, touloum,* sugar-cake' were melancholic in their tone. The disease stalked where poverty led.

Dr Lange visited the house at no. 9 Edward Street to attend to Ernestine, whom everyone was worried about. Jeanne Camille had a fever. Panic had come right into the Cazabon home. Rose Alexandrine was kept away from school. The nuns of Cluny had eventually closed the convent. It was a grim scourge, everyone said. It was indeed as the newspapers were proclaiming: *En temps Cholera.* There was a letter from a Dr de Montbrun in the Port of Spain *Gazette* warning people of the dangers that he and his family were experiencing in Caracas and on the east coast inland from Guaira just across the Gulf of Paria. People were saying they needed a fire like that in 1850 to burn out and cleanse the town of the disease. Michel Jean left his home each day to paint in the countryside.

*

Josie looked weary with caring for Ernestine. At the end of September there was still no let up. In fact, quite the contrary; the deaths had trebled. The sanitation of the yard was a prime duty to be conducted by Josie and every other member of the household. Rose Alexandrine was given her jobs to help sweep and clean. Louise had made it known that the days were over when all the household duties were performed by Josie alone. The family would share. 'After all, we're all one family,' she announced.

François Cazabon wrote to his son that it would be fine for the family to move to Belle Plaine out at Aricagua during the epidemic that was still showing no signs of abating. He had not extended the invitation to Josie and Ernestine, however.

'I've no intention of moving anywhere without Josie and Ernestine,' proclaimed Louise at the dining-room table, taking the letter from Michel Jean's hand and then folding it decisively, as much as to say that was that.

'*Ah, mais oui!* You must tell your father that action needs to follow his words to include his common-law wife and daughter in the invitation.' She knew that Josie was listening to the bacchanal from the backyard.

Ernestine and Josie were still not fully accustomed to Louise's new dispensation and could sometimes be shocked by how the white woman reprimanded Jeansie. They ended up chuckling. 'Jeansie, boy, what you bring upon yourself now with this white woman. Poor boy.'

Mother and daughter began eventually to look quite comfortable with the new state of affairs, though. Ernestine seemed to have a new lease of life. 'She good for sheself, *oui*.' She began to enjoy her new room upstairs and the children coming in to see her, bringing her their gifts; even Louis Michel, who had little to give, but yet another copy of one of his father's paintings. They were always appreciated by the old woman, who saw them as her own grandchildren.

Louise had found her voice. The truth, or at least some of the truth, of the household and the family ancestry had liberated her and allowed her to find an allegiance with the women of the house. Michel Jean's reaction was to leave the women to it and depart with his paints as early as possible in the morning.

'Cholera or no cholera, coolies, niggers, or Haiti, art must continue,' he said. He left the house in high spirits.

'Darling, what are you saying?' Louise had never quite caught the irony in his tongue.

Everyone who came to the house at no. 9 Edward Street marvelled at Louis Michel's gifts, as they called his obsessive drawing and painting. 'You'll soon be learning from him yourself, Cazabon.' That was the joke among Michel Jean's friends.

But after the guests had taken their leave they were left with the reality, the burden, of a child who seemed not to have any of the usual social habits of children. Mostly it was Josie and Louise who sat with the boy as the obsessions took hold. Rose Alexandrine had stopped being the attentive sister. She was getting on with her own childhood, playing with her girlfriends at the convent, or now that school was closed, with her friends in the street. Jeanne Camille was still too small to be fully aware of her brother's condition.

It was after one of those evenings of visitors commiserating over the death of a cousin from the cholera that Michel Jean lost his control. The boy had not stopped all evening, copying over and over a view of the St James Barracks with the parading soldiers in their reds and blues. 'God, Wap, when you going and stop this thing?' He had picked up all the paintings and flung them into a pile upon the sofa. 'Clean this up, right now.' He was almost about to hit the boy, he was so frustrated.

Louise took hold of his arm. 'Michel! *Non.* You know he can't help it. And don't call him Wap.'

'Can't help it? He wap, *oui.*' He was about to break from her, but she held on to him.

'You'll never forgive yourself, if you hit him. Look at him.'

Louis Michel, a boy of nine, was sitting among the pile of his paintings and drawings on the sofa, looking up at his father, clearly not understanding what was happening. He stared, unconcerned with the paintings or with his father's temper. He was unaware of his own skill and seldom commented on the paintings except sometimes to say, 'They nice, eh.' He seemed to have very little understanding of what he was doing.

Michel Jean stood and looked at the boy. Then he turned away and went off into his studio, leaving the debris of paintings and injured feelings to Louise and Josie, who now had the room next to Rose Alexandrine's. The disturbance had caused Jeanne Camille to cry. Josie was at hand to pick her up and to give her a comforting shoulder.

From the studio he heard Louise saying to Josie, 'He'll be better when we get out to the country. It's this town. It's the cholera.'

He overheard them as the two women sat with the boy. 'Is the father, you know, François. He find it difficult to discipline Jeansie when he was a boy. Is his mother's son. Always. Maybe he see Louis Michel like that. Things used to happen to Jeansie we don't like to talk about, we ent even like to think about them things. Boy, François, he was something.'

'I think it's the hurt he feels. It comes out as frustration and anger.'

'Is so with he father too.'

'How was he with you?' Louise asked.

'Me? Who? François? Monsieur? He have few words, you know. I sure you notice that when you gone San Fernando. He have few words; he don't deal with words so much, except to give orders.'

Michel Jean listened to Josie and Louise exchanging intimacies. He thought of how much Louise still did not know. He was glad Josie had not said any more. There were secrets, too many for a lifetime to unravel.

A messenger boy came from the ferry with a letter from Mon Chagrin. It was his brother, Joseph, informing him that his father had been taken ill. He had noticeably weakened since Rose Clotilde's death. He was with himself and Jeanne, at their home on the estate. René, Rose Clotilde's widower, was also with them. There was a sense of the grim reaper taking his toll, a fear of the dreaded cholera. Dr Philippe had visited. Joseph advised that Michel Jean should take the next ferry and be prepared to stay. There was an afternoon ferry soon after lunch.

Louise stayed behind with the children.

Josie and Ernestine seemed to have retreated into their own sense of what was beginning to unfold, a sense of being excluded from the real emotions of the moment. It was on these occasions that the awkwardness of the outside family, the second family, was most sorely felt. Josie sat with her mother, who was herself on her last legs. Everyone was preoccupied with their own thoughts. The children were looking on as the adults seemed to be sleep-walking. The house had become very quiet.

The scratching of Louis Michel's pencils could be heard distinctly in the silence.

Outside, there was the continual sound of the carts that had been employed to convey the dead to the cemeteries. There were processions up and down the streets all day until after the ringing of the Angelus, a natural curfew that came to settle over the town with the darkness. There was a stench that would not go away. The women in particular walked about the streets with a sachet of vetiver held up to their noses. But gentlemen were seen to make a distinct flourish with their handkerchiefs, a gesture of etiquette, while they were in fact blocking the awful stench as they made their way about town.

François Cazabon was taking shallow breaths. He was ashen. He had lost the lustre of his brown skin. Michel Jean stood by the side of the bed and watched his chest, its gentle rise and fall. He watched his eyes, barely open, seem to acknowledge him and then close again. He leaned towards him and whispered in his ear, 'Father, *Père*, is Michel Jean.'

His lips moved, but there was no sound. What had not been said would not be said now. It was too late, too late.

Michel Jean surveyed the room. There was his father's pith hat for the sun, with its rim of sweat. There was the gourd he carried for drinking water. There was his whip. There was the cane for his horse. Behind the door hung his white linen suit.

His father's hand lying by his side tugged at his shirt sleeve. He was astonished at how much strength there was in the grip of his fingers. But his arms and hands were grey. Then he slipped his hand into his and said again, '*Père*.'

'*Mon fils*.' The sibilance was in the whisper. '*Mon fils*.' His eyes opened wider as he claimed him.

'*Papa*.'

'I leave instructions for you to make sure Ernestine and Josie get look after. It in writing.'

'You want me to handle that?'

François Cazabon nodded, then closed his eyes. Michel Jean heard a movement at the door to the room. He turned to look. It was his brother and his wife. He turned back again to his father. He had gone. It was the last breath that he had heard, which had made him turn to look. It was his last exertion. Michel Jean took his father's hand and laid it on his chest. He closed his eyelids with the tips of his fingers. Then he left the room.

He stayed for the funeral at Notre Dame de Bon Secours. They processed together to the Paradise Cemetery. With the mounting dead from the cholera, the funeral procession was delayed. Eventually the sods of earth were beaten down and the wreaths placed to create a mound of flowers. The free-coloureds of the Naparimas had come out in their numbers for one of their elders. It was a political as well as a friendly gesture that they performed. They were still defending their rights, won from the British, the right to assemble in public.

It was only when he was out on the gulf, on the way back to Port of Spain, that Michel Jean allowed the tears to come as he stared out to sea, the spray in his eyes, the island emerging and fading in the changing light and haze. The mangrove coast was a dark shadow. He felt as if there was a fight going on inside of him, between an anger he had felt towards his father's distance while he was growing up, and a new-found respect for him in recent years. He had come to value his advice. He allowed the battle to rage, the tears alone allowing the calm to eventually descend as the ferry pulled into King's Wharf.

He walked through the town with the last of the carts bearing the dead, making their way to the mortuary or to Lapeyrouse. The Angelus announced the curfew. Darkness descended on Port of Spain.

Michel Jean began to think again of how much time he should spend with his own son, while reflecting on the death of his own father and how much he had missed in that relationship. Louis Michel needed him and he needed his son.

Louise was out in town. Rose Alexandrine was at school. He had to go and fetch Louis Michel from the convent. Mother Philomena had offered to supervise him in a small group when it was seen that he could not learn in a full class. She had decided to take him with the Metivier boy, who was deaf, and the little Laurent girl, who was dumb. 'They're all so gifted,' she said. 'They're like angels, messengers. We must listen to them in their actions.' Michel Jean listened sceptically to the old nun.

'Each of them displays aptitudes in very particular skills.' Mother Philomena continued her instruction. Michel Jean stood at the door of the classroom and looked on.

Pierre Metivier did carpentry like a craftsman, and Annette Laurent sewed the hems of elaborate wedding dresses as if she were a designer of *haute couture*. Mother Philomena was sitting and reassuring the children in what they were doing. 'Very good, Annette. Excellent, Pierre. Ah, Louis, you're a genius.' When silence prevailed she sat and muttered her rosary from the long string of beads hanging at her waist.

The room which she had been given by the Mother Superior was soon too small to hold Pierre's tables and cabinets, Annette's elaborate trains and veils of tulle for her wedding dresses and

Louis Michel's sheaves of paintings scattered among the gowns and shavings of cedar and pitch pine. Mother Philomena was just trying to find spaces on the walls between the other paintings that the boy had done. She often joked with the parents when they came to collect their children that they might not be able to find them beneath the paper, the tulle and the satin and the shavings of wood.

Michel Jean extricated his son from the room that was filled with the sound of the rustle of satin, the delicate hammering of a small boy and the scratching of pencils.

Louise was grateful to have Louis Michel out of the house for some of the morning, though Josie had offered to take him completely into her charge. This was the scene that Michel Jean saw from his window overlooking the backyard, after he had settled Louis Michel down with paper and paints in a corner of his studio.

Louise and Josie were folding the sheets that they had just taken off the line. The tone of their conversation rose with the emotion of the subject.

'But I can look after the boy the whole day, Louise.'

'Josie, you know what I feel about that. I want him to meet other children to try and have some conversation, though I do admit I'm not sure what can be done with a deaf boy and a dumb girl.'

'Well, that is what I telling you.'

'*Oui*, but he can at least see other children who have problems like himself. He can relate. And Mother Philomena is very kind and understanding.'

'You know I think you just don't want me to grow close to Louis Michel.'

'Josie, how can you say that? We have never come between you, not myself nor Michel Jean.'

Michel Jean looked at his son. He was oblivious of the voices in the yard.

'He wouldn't come between us. But I feel you jealous.'

'Of what, Josie?'

'That he go love me more.'

'Why should he do that? He does love you . . .'

'Yes, *oui*, but like a mother, I mean.'

'I'm his mother.'

'That is what I mean. You frighten you lose him.'

'Why should I lose him? What are you suggesting, Josie?'

Michel Jean had stopped working. He could not help moving closer to the window to hear them better. The painting on his easel was drying fast. He was all ears.

The women were continuing with their chore of lifting down the sheets from the line and then together stretching and folding them.

'You can't lose him.'

'No. We can both love him. He can love us both.'

'What you saying?'

'I am his mother. He knows that, but you can also love him. Louis Michel is fond of you.'

The argument went back and forth as they approached each other and then retreated to begin the stretching and folding of each new sheet.

'Cheups. Well, what I know about this?' Josie asked herself, sucking her teeth.

'You would have liked to have had children, *oui*?'

'You know how that feel?'

'Well, I had my children.'

'Yes, you had my children.'

'What did you say?'

'I say, you had your children.'

'No, you said, you had *my* children. What do you mean by that?'

'How I could say that? What that mean?'

'You tell me,' demanded Louise. 'You tell me.'

There was then a long silence, so that Michel Jean went to the window to look down into the backyard. The two women were now sitting in silence, not looking at each other, folding smaller linens on their laps.

'Tell you? You want me to tell you what it mean?'

'You sacrificed husband and children to look after Ernestine?'

'Who tell you that? How you could know that? You just come.' Josie looked at Louise in a challenging way. 'How you could know that? Is that what he tell you? Is so he explain that part of it to you?' Josie's voice was getting louder. 'Is so he explain it?'

'Josie. I did not mean . . .'

'You did not mean what? You just come, you not live here . . . you . . .'

'Josie.'

'You want me to tell you what I give up, what we had to give up?'

'*Non, non, non* . . .' Louise screamed.

That was when Michel Jean saw her getting up and dropping the linen on the ground and running away from Josie towards the tamarind tree.

He had heard Josie's last challenging question and saw in Louise's refusal to wait for an answer the realization of what their conversation had brought Josie to say. The smile on Josie's face was the smile of the girl he had fallen in love with as a boy. He knew that smile of Josie's when she had decided to defy the world. He went down into the yard to Louise. By which time, Josie had climbed the stairs to her room.

Michel Jean felt useless in attending to Louise where he kneeled next to her in the shade of the tamarind tree. 'Not now,' she whispered. 'Not now. *Je comprends tout.* Now I know what has been worrying me since I entered this house.' She looked at him and the pain he saw there was unbearable. He turned away from her to look at the house. The house could not speak. It had learned to let things be. All the houses had learned to let things be, except those that the enslaved had burned down.

Michel Jean knew that there was no way to repair this. He could not undo a life. He could not rearrange his childhood, his youth. He could not rearrange history. Josie was never going to give up her best chance and he could not give it to her. How could they, how could they say to the world what they were and what they had done?

Time did not heal anything; it just moved them all on to a different place. Josie never continued with her explanation. She did not have to say any more. In time she became responsible for collecting Louis Michel from the convent. There had been an unspoken compromise.

'The boy looks to her like you must've looked at that age,' Louise said to Michel Jean, as an explanation for this new state of affairs. 'What children can become!'

Michel Jean listened to his wife, but had not the words to reply.

Michel Jean and Louise chose their trip by ferry to San Fernando then on to Cedros, to see parts of the island she had not seen before. Josie was entrusted with the supervision of the children. He found himself developing a series of views that would make a new album. This was the album he had been promising himself. He would proceed in the same way with patrons. This time he would have to do the proposals himself and in some instances it was Louise who managed to get a commitment from some of the white Creoles.

Travelling by ferry all along the west coast gave them the time they needed. It took six hours from Port of Spain. They felt like the couple they had been in Paris, or the couple who had wandered the Calvados coast. When they anchored in Cedros Bay they had to take a rowing boat to the shore and be borne to dry ground on the shoulders of stout men employed for this purpose. They felt like explorers. They walked the beach from Bonasse to Fullarton. These were fishing villages at the end of the world, on an island on the edge of a continent, barely eight miles away. 'Where are we?' Louise kept asking.

They stayed first at Monsieur Peschier's estate at Constance and then in an overseer's house loaned by Monsieur Agostini, situated among the criss-crossing coconut palms on his vast estate at the end of the peninsular.

It was on this long trip that Louise and Michel Jean learned to talk again. She was intent on rebuilding their old intimacy, and he responded to this intent. He learned again about the mole in the centre of her back, the small bump along her thigh. He let his hand travel along her arms and over her shoulders. He had always loved her shoulders and the nape of her neck, the way the sun reached there beneath her muslin until it became dun, the way her sweat was a crystal drop between her breasts. These rituals were renewed as he lifted her damp hair; these ceremonies of courtship were rediscovered by the middle-aged couple.

'Louise.'

'*Mon chéri.*'

'I need to explain.'

'I can imagine, you know.'

'How can you imagine?'

'Well, I know you; I know Josie. And I see now this world. You've been a family of secrets.'

'Are not all families? Don't they all have their secrets?'

'*Peut-être.*'

'I need to tell some of those secrets.'

'I'm not your confessor, Michel. Find that priest, Father Violette. Maybe he can help you. Listen to your secrets.'

'But it's you who needs to know them.'

'*Non.* You need to tell me them. I understand. But I don't need the details. I don't need to hear, *chéri.*'

'How can you be so understanding? Why aren't you angry with me?'

'What can I do now? You want me to leave you? Go with my three children? Where to? Nothing dramatic is called for. I love you.'

'It is not the childhood part. It's . . . I love you too.'

'Michel, I know. Can I be jealous of childhood, the liberty of childhood? The ignorance and innocence of childhood? But what? Can I be jealous of history? There's anger. But see how people live. They have to live. They can't eat themselves up with anger and regret. You want me to sit and listen to what? To those things which are hardly spoken of among lovers? There are things we do, but don't need words to describe them. They're just felt. They're done. We do them.'

As they spoke together beneath a parasol on the beach under Monsieur Agostini's coconuts, they spoke of something else, of a bond, of a friendship mixed with their passion; an amplified relationship. They spoke of their children, the hope for their daughters, and above all their hope for Louis Michel. He spoke to her again of his mother's hope for the republic, somewhere for them to have their equality.

There were sloops in Cedros Bay and he painted them against the red dirt of the hills with collapsed sails, those Dutch sails he was so fond of. The business of boats on the coast always drew his attention, the arrivals and departures. He walked along the shore in the dawn and painted himself walking along the beach at Los Gallos, Monsieur Courbet style: *Bonjour, Monsieur Courbet*; *Bonjour, Monsieur Cazabon*. He would get a new album of his work out this year.

Back in town, their newly found idyll was fractured by the old reminders of the past when they actually saw Josie with the children. Louise had to go to her room to compose herself. She missed now her own mother to talk to, her father to whom she could go to for advice. She felt keenly that she was not among her own people. Again she asked whether they could not go to Martinique. 'There's so much more for us there. Maybe you would feel more in touch with what is happening in Paris. The talk is of new paintings, a new idea of painting.'

'What about Josie and the children? We've just arrived at some kind of understanding,' Michel Jean protested.

'Understanding? What understanding? How can she be a reason to stay here? She's not their mother. I am their mother.'

'Louise, of course. I know who their mother is. But . . .'

'But nothing. I let her as an aunt have some part of their life. That's correct. Remember, it is me who has pressed for this *rapprochement* in the family.'

'I know.'

'Well.' She relented. 'It's maybe not the right moment and you have to get your new album completed here. But after that I think we need to give my suggestion serious consideration. We can accustom Josie to our plans gradually.'

He watched her in her maturity. He could still see the beautiful girl on the Calvados coast. Still see that girl he had first encountered in a Paris studio.

'That's better. I'm going into town.'

'I keep trying, Michel. I keep trying. You must realize the enormity of what you've asked me to accept.'

He looked at her as she spoke. There was so much she did not know. The weight of all that truth was a burden that he could not put down. At that moment, he thought of Augusta and her child. That girl was surely not his. She must be the old planter's or Jean Pierre's, who had driven his gig at such a speed into the yard when he had last seen Augusta. Imagine, another daughter running around! The truth of that might be something to unite both Louise and Josie in their adversity, in their disappointment with him. His worry reminded him to send some money to an address in Tacarigua, where he had discovered Augusta now lived in a new marriage with a coloured planter, Monsieur de Gannes. Michel Jean deduced from her silence that Augusta did not want to disturb her own family life or his.

Some months later, Michel Jean had noticed a new closeness in the relationship between Louise and Josie. He had not said anything that might disturb what they seemed to have achieved. He did not know how it had come about. Had they had some more explicit confessions of feelings? What had made Louise seem so much more tolerant, and Josie so much less combative?

Then, one morning, when he had returned earlier than usual from one of his painting expeditions in the Maraval valley, as far as the Saddle, still remembering Elizabeth Prowder, he caught a glimpse of something he had not seen before. Quite clearly this was something that was conducted when he was out of the house, and it was his early return that now allowed him to see and hear it.

He had gone straight to his studio, and it was there, while unpacking his portfolio of the morning's work, that he heard the women under the tamarind tree in the backyard.

What had caught his attention was the voice of Josie. It was not her usual way of talking. And, at intervals, he heard her voice repeat what Louise had just said. It sounded familiar. When he went to the window and looked down into the backyard he had his explanation. It was not a speaking voice. It was a reading voice. Josie was reading. She was sitting next to Louise, who was looking over her shoulder at the book that Josie held on her lap. He stood transfixed, watched and listened. Josie's head was bent towards the book, Louise towards Josie, the pose catching the women in an intimacy of extraordinary concentration. This obviously was the outcome of weeks and months of endeavour.

Louise had taught Josie how to read! Why had she never said anything to him? Michel Jean could not take himself away from the window, except that he did not want to be caught watching, and so stepped back a couple of feet to where he could just see them, but still hear them distinctly. All the children were out. Ernestine was completely bedridden. Josie's voice read the tale that Michel Jean then recognized from school.

'*The Crow and the Pitcher*. A Crow, half-dead with thirst, came upon a Pitcher which had once been full of water; but when the Crow put its beak into the mouth of the Pitcher he found that only very little water was left in it, and that he could not reach far enough down to get at it. He tried, and he tried, but at last had to give up in despair. Then a thought came to him, and he took a pebble and dropped it into the Pitcher. Then he took another pebble and dropped it into the Pitcher. Then he took another pebble and dropped that into the Pitcher. Then he took another pebble and dropped that into the Pitcher. Then he took another pebble and dropped that into the Pitcher. Then he took another pebble and dropped that into the Pitcher. At last, he saw the water mount up near him, and

384

after casting in a few more pebbles he was able to quench his thirst and save his life.'

'Excellent, Josie. You read that very well.'

Josie looked at Louise and smiled. 'You think so?'

'The most fluent you've been.'

'You want me to read it again?'

'If you would like.'

Josie read the tale once more, adding the concluding moral of the tale: 'Little by little does the trick.'

This was how it must have been with Josie's learning to read. Little by little had done the trick and now she could quench her thirst for knowledge at the pitcher of this book, and any other book she might now choose in the future.

Louise had won through and allowed Josie her true emancipation. While Michel Jean was thrilled at this, both for Josie but also for their relationship, he could not help feeling regret and guilt at his family's prolonged negligence. What an extraordinary omission. He remembered now the separation that he and Josie had experienced when he started going to Mr Woodford for lessons and Josie was left at home to do the housework and the cleaning in the yard. Once he remembered Josie asking why she could not have lessons also. It was Ernestine who had reprimanded her with, 'Know your position, girl.' He knew that Josie had not been happy with that, but it became more and more settled and then he went away to school at thirteen. When he arrived back at seventeen they allowed themselves the pleasures of lovers to take over from their childhood discoveries.

Josie was reading. Truly astonishing. It brought tears to his eyes.

When he mentioned to Louise that he had overheard the reading of *The Crow and the Pitcher*, she smiled and put her hand in his where they were standing by the window, looking into the street at the children coming back from school. With her love, she had brought to him insights he had not understood before with regard to Josie, Ernestine and the past. These insights entered his paintings, not that anyone would notice, as he searched out some of his old haunts on Belmont Hill, in St Ann's and Maraval. He was feeling liberated to tentatively try some other styles. Little by little does the trick, he thought, as he moved his brush over the paper.

He returned to what he had first seen in Bonington's skies, water and foliage. His figures grew naturally as he drew with his brush. He knew that he had to do something. He needed this change. But at the same time he had not realized that he could fall in love all over again. This time, he felt it was a truer love than that he had felt as a young man in Paris or on the Calvados coast. Younger, love had felt like so many other things.

He wondered if this newly felt love was something that Louise felt. She was so taken up with the children, with Josie's reading, and with her plans to go and live in Martinique.

One morning, as he returned from an early painting session at Corbeaux Town, he met Josie returning from market and said, 'So you reading now, girl.'

'Boy, that is something, *oui*.'

'I should've taught you to read, you know.'

She looked at him and smiled. She looked at him and laughed. 'You! We didn't have time for that, Jeansie. Is so we go have to leave it, *oui*, we didn't have time for that. We was young and didn't know nothing.'

'Josie . . .'

'*Oui* . . .'

'Josie . . .'

'I like she, you know. I get to like she. And she teach me good. So much . . .'

'So much . . .'

'In reading. I going on, you know . . .'

'Bit by bit . . .'

'Pebble by pebble . . .'

'Pebble by pebble . . .'

'I thirsty too bad, *oui*. Boy . . .'

They both laughed and laughed.

'Josie, you good for yourself.'

'Boy, is time, *oui*.'

'And Ernestine, how she doing?'

'She going down fast, you know. Just now so, she gone. You must go and see her.'

'Is so? I must visit.'

It was two nights later that Josie called Louise and Michel Jean from their bed in the middle of the night.

'Is Ernestine. She calling all you.'

They followed Josie, trying not to disturb the girls and Louis Michel as they went to the room at the end of the corridor, which Louise had made Ernestine's room at no. 9 Edward Street.

'She calling everybody, you know. She say, call all of them.'

Louise and Michel Jean looked at each other. How would Louis Michel react to this?

'You wake the girls,' she said to Louise. 'Jeansie, come, is you and me go bring the boy.'

And so, as a family, they sat around Ernestine's bed, where she sat up looking stronger than she had for weeks.

Louis Michel sat at the end of the bed.

'Come, *mon garçon, vini*.'

The boy responded to her gentleness and edged up the bed a little more.

'I call all you. Because I tell Josie I ent want to go without telling all you. I so long here and is all kind of thing I see.' She smiled at Rose Alexandrine and Jeanne Camille. 'I glad all you come from away and living here. All you get to grow up here where you father born. So long I know him. Now is something all you must know. The way all you find things, is not so things must stay. Things have to change. Things change, a little.'

'Hmm, hmm!' Josie breathed her agreement, her breathing entering into an ancestral Yoruba chant.

Louise and Michel Jean nodded. The girls looked at their parents for their cue. Louis Michel stared and sat quietly, listening.

'Yes, Ernestine. Should I bring you something hot to drink?' Louise asked, wanting to comfort the old woman.

'Keep the drink for later. Maybe I take something strong later.'

They all smiled, but for Louis Michel, who stared without smiling.

'I was your grandfather wedding present, *oui*. He give me to his wife, Madame Rose. Is from she you get your name, you know.' Ernestine looked at Rose Alexandrine. 'You know that? He wanted to give she something beautiful and something useful. He buy me in Martinique and he bring me to Trinidad. You didn't think I was beautiful?' She looked at Jeanne Camille with her question. 'You didn't think so, eh? Well, I was more than beautiful when I was young. Watch you *Tante Josie*. You will see some of that beauty there.'

Everyone looked at Josie and smiled their approval.

'She getting some years, but you could see the beauty I talking about. When I leave all you, you go see me in she. My only child. And, she is a Cazabon, eh.'

The children looked at their parents with questions of interest and some shock on their faces.

'She is a true Cazabon. Not because François ent give she the name she's not a Cazabon. She's a Cazabon. He knew that. François gone. I go meet up with he. And they say there's no difference where he is now, you know. If I give him a son it might've be worse. He might not even have call it he child. Is a girl with no threat, but still he not give the name. Is so things go change.'

'Hmm, hmm!' Josie breathed her agreement again, her chant seeking the words to accompany her mother's speech.

'See you father. He on one breast, *Tante Josie* on the other one. Is so it was. Both of you is my children. Cazabon children. Madame Rose know, you know, that is why in time she bring me in she house. No way she giving up the boy. But she know is me who nurse him. Is as two mothers we understand we self. Both of we forget François, like François forget we. He come round in the end, but really he forget we.'

The family listened. The children held their questions for later. Rose Alexandrine knew something of the world. She drew close to her mother.

Ernestine's voice began to falter. 'I go take that drink now. Always take a shot of rum, you know, when I have something important to do.'

Michel Jean brought her a little of the rum.

'Spill some on the floor for the ancestors.'

Michel Jean poured the libation.

Ernestine took a drink and lay back. The family stood and watched as the moths played around the flame of the lamp. Somewhere, some foolish cock was crowing long before its time, and down the street the dogs were barking and still the room seemed so quiet they could hear each other breathing, till they could see that Ernestine's chest was still. There was not a breath of life left in her.

'Swing low sweet chariot . . .' Josie sang for her mother, finding her words from a chant that a sailor from New Orleans had been singing down by the wharf one day.

'She's already in heaven,' Father Didier from the Rosary Church said, blessing her early the next morning after mass, anointing her body for burial, which took place that afternoon at Lapeyrouse where she was buried in Rose Debonne Cazabon's grave.

'Is right,' Louise said. 'The two Cazabon madams in the same grave.'

The family listened, but Josie and Michel Jean shared memories of a darker time.

Maybe it was all the thoughts and talk that came after Ernestine's death, and the fact that she had originally come from Martinique, which meant that Louise's desire for the family to move to Martinique began to become a practical plan. Louise did not need to rehearse her reasons, and with Michel Jean's commissions an increasingly dwindling prospect with the departure of Lord Harris and Wildman, the idea of transporting the family to

Martinique was seized upon again. It would not be easy. Leaving Josie in Port of Spain would not be easy. She was adamant that she could not travel. 'Who go tend Mama grave? Who go look after the house?'

She would keep Edward Street open for the family. Therefore, for the time being, it was decided that they would be going on a prolonged visit. This helped with the farewells. 'Anyway, Martinique just there, up the islands. I just have to jump on a sloop and I down here in no time.'

'You full of talk, *oui*, Jeansie.'

Michel Jean remained unconvinced about the move, though he was excited by any idea that there might be new work. He wanted to move for Louise and the children. That was what they wanted. After all, Saint Pierre was the Paris of the Antilles. Life there would offer the possibility of having both worlds at the same time.

BOOK FIVE

1870

I

Louise was homesick for Saint Pierre a month after arriving back in Port of Spain. She had had to wait patiently for eight years before they had, in the end, left for Saint Pierre in 1862. The new governor had become a patron and his son a student. But it was the itinerant photographer, A. A. Hartmann, who had detained Michel Jean with a trip to Demerara as a subject for a new album, which had also persuaded them to postpone their departure.

Michel Jean could see that look of homesickness on Louise's face, as she sat at the side of his bed trying to be a good nurse. Bad luck had struck and he had gone down with what was probably yellow fever. There was talk that there might be one of those epidemics. Michel Jean took this as a sign that he should never have decided that the best plan for his family's present fortune was to return to Trinidad from Martinique. His hopes, eight years later, had foundered in the frequent melancholic moods he was inclined to as the years went by. Now, a fever stalked him in the streets of Port of Spain.

They could hear Josie in the backyard speaking to a passing *marchande*. 'Eh eh! What you say? I can't hear you. You know, is them bells at Trinity, them like an infliction self on the air. Girl, Mistress Espinet! Pappy! That go be a funeral!'

'So, your brother sick?'

'Nah. They just come back from Martinique. Must be *mal de mer*.'

'*Mal de mer*? Hmm! I see . . .'

'I must go, *oui* . . .'

'Girl . . .'

The voice of the *marchande* faded with the bells in the surrounding hills.

A flock of pigeons fluttered off the eaves of the veranda and circled, so that Michel Jean caught their swoop, and then again, after a pause, like an interval in music, another swoop through the blue air as if he were looking at a shoal of fish in some gigantic aquarium among the palms. 'Look.' He pointed out the peripatetic repetitions of the pigeons to his wife.

'Rest, darling, rest.' Louise soothed his brow with a pad sprinkled with eau de Cologne. 'Here, suck this ice. Your fever is still too high.'

The house at Edward Street was turned into a hospital. The marital bedroom became a ward. Josie relieved Louise at the bedside. Jeanne Camille helped with the washing.

'You still here, Josie?' Michel Jean asked through his fever.

'Where I going?'

After eight years, Josie was still there in the yard and busy in the house, keeping the family home.

'You keep the house good. Louise say you keep it good.'

Josie had been mistress, awaiting Louise's return from Martinique. 'Like the freedom never come, eh?' Josie said aloud to herself.

'Someone there?' Michel Jean called out. Voices were sometimes real and then sometimes part of his fevered delusion.

'Is me, Josie. I say, like freedom never come, eh?'

'What's that you say, Josie? I've hardly seen you since our return. This illness.'

She said it again with emphasis. 'I say, like freedom never come, eh?'

'Freedom come and gone. Is that what you say, Josie? You not leaving eh, Josie?'

'Leaving? *Non*. I miss all yuh.'

'Josie, I thought we had settled things before we went to Martinique. We leave you happy.'

'Yes, you leave and go. Josie will keep house. Everything fine. Well, everything not fine.'

'Josie, what has brought this on? What's not fine?'

'No one write to say, *Dear Josie, how you keeping?*'

'We write, Josie. You forget. How's the reading? You keep up the reading all these years? Now Louise back you must keep up the reading.'

Josie went silent.

'Josie, what's the matter?'

'Is a long time all you gone away, you know.'

'We back now. Tell me what happen.'

'Joseph coming to make *commesse*, always pushing his nose into business not his, but he think is his own. Maybe he want to take the house when his brother away.'

'Joseph? What he could do?'

'And, Monsieur Saturnin Congnet. I ask him if he not shame. Magdeleine son. Young boy wanting to take advantage of a woman twice his age.'

'Josie, what you saying?'

'He say he's family and he want to stay in the house when he come in town. You didn't know the perils to get away from that young man. He imagine he is lord and master of all he survey when he come into the yard. Like he don't know we blood mix.'

'Josie, when I better, I go talk with Joseph and the Saturnin boy. They still with this thing.'

'Yes, like is blasted slavery all over again.'

While the family were away she had been madam. Michel Jean could see what she described. She cleaned and kept the house at her own pace. She cooked for herself. In the evenings, she sat right there and watched the sunset over the gulf. She could even forget the family as she dozed into the night and then locked up. She was alone in the house with Ernestine gone. But she had been lonely and vulnerable.

The order they had achieved before they had left for Martinique seemed to have been shattered. 'But, Josie, we did write to you. Louise wrote letters. We sent things. You don't remember? The girls sent mementoes, and Louis Michel sent his paintings. What have you done with these things? What has happened?'

'*Oui, oui.* I have them in my room. I can't read them so good.'

Michel Jean saw that they had underestimated the extent to which Josie would miss them.

'I miss all you. Look, Jeanne Camille grow up now. Rose Alexandrine not come back. Louis Michel is a man now.'

'See what a view I bring you.' Opening the shutters near his bed, Louise greeted her husband.

It had been a night of long, hot sweats and remedies to bring down his temperature. Louise commented on the dark circles under his eyes. He had not slept a wink. She had been on the chaise-longue outside his room on the veranda.

'Let Josie help.'

'She does help me. Don't bother yourself.'

'Your eyes are still the colour of the ocean.' He pointed, as he leaned over to her, directing her gaze to one of his frequently painted views in the crack under the Demerara shutters, of the islands and the blue channel between the mainland and the archipelago.

'Feel the air; the sea breeze will do you good.'

His heart was heavy with her pain and her loss of their home on rue Longchamp that she did not complain about. 'I make you leave Saint Pierre?'

She rested her hand on his, smiling at the paint engrained in his fingernails. '*Ma jen peti neg,*' she joked in his patois.

Louis Michel hung by the door with a bouquet of pink and white anthurium lilies, not wanting to pester his father and mother or burden them with his needs, those needs which were always there, though he was now a young man of twenty-five.

'Come and sit by *Papa*. Let me get a vase of fresh water for these. Look at the flowers he's brought you.' She invited him to sit at the end of the bed, inquiring whether he was doing his work in the studio, getting his father's colours ready. 'Sit with your father. You're his colour-man. You need to talk with him. He'll be well soon.'

Michel Jean smiled at his son. He had picked up skills in Martinique. He worked for his father and slowly he was being persuaded to sell his own paintings. 'Bring me you last painting. Let me see what you doing now. When I better, we go go Macqueripe to paint.'

Louis Michel sat by the bed and held his father's hand. But soon Josie was hurrying him from the room, as if he was still a boy. 'Come, boy, let you father rest. When he good, you go come and sit by he and talk all the painting you want to talk. And you is an artist now?'

Michel Jean looked at Louise watching her son leave the room. He could see the effort she made with Josie. An old jealousy lingered, but she let it go. They heard Josie teasing Louis Michel outside. 'You is a real saga boy now. You is a man, and so you good looking like your father.'

'You do miss your home in rue Longchamp.' Michel Jean had seen that it broke Louise's heart to leave. Martinique had been good for the children. 'You did it for me.'

Saint Pierre had held a promise it did not keep for him. They remained outsiders to the coloureds, despite the family connections, she being white and French. And despite her marriage to him, she was more often than not identified as *béké*.

'We must not regret. We mustn't go over this matter again and again.'

He knew Louise would not go against his wishes. He knew that she had found Saint Pierre better for the completion of the girls' education. They had gone to the *école* run by the nuns right there in rue Longchamp at the corner with rue du Petit Versailles. She had found help from Dr Lefebvre for Louis Michel at the hospital. He had diagnosed and prescribed a mixture of herbal and homeopathic remedies to quieten his continual agitation. Over the eight years of his stay Louis Michel had increased his capacities for learning and above all for painting, beginning with his accomplished expertise of mixing colours for his father. His obsessive behaviour was now supported by a craft. He was being skilled. 'They're now proper French children,' Louise used to say. 'None of them is English, you know.'

Louis Michel had returned with his mortar and pestle, mixing his father's favourite cobalt green. 'You painting today?'

'You want me to paint. I'll sketch a little from here. I can catch the Five Islands from here.' Michel Jean had lain awake on the chaise-longue out on the veranda. He preferred to be there than always in his bedroom. He stayed there now till the light faded, till the watchmen lowered the lamps. He was also there early in the morning when the sewage collectors passed with their buckets in the street below. He heard the bell toll for the five o'clock mass at the cathedral.

The following day, Louise came to sit with him after lunch. An increase in his fever had created delirium. He was wandering the streets of Saint Pierre, the pearl of the West Indies, the Paris of the Antilles. 'Louise, Louise. Where am I? It's these miasmas from the swamp. I feel sure. You smell it on the wind? Shut the window. Is that stink from the mangrove at Caroni.'

The quinine Dr Lange had prescribed brought the fever down in the early morning. But then, as the hot afternoon came, the fever rose and he was again on one of his delirious journeys. He trudged over the black sand of the beach through the quartier du Mouillage into la Place Bertin, where the sugar was landed. Then he lost his way off the rue Victor Hugo and could not get home to rue Longchamp. He was lost in a maze that terrified him. He climbed from the pit of the rue d'Enfer to the heights of rue Monte au Ciel. From rue du Precipice he saw the *anse noire* and the blue harbour below with the sloops and steamers entering and leaving, some finishing one voyage and others beginning another.

'Where am I?'

'Port of Spain, darling.'

'It's what the light does with the sky and the water and the wide sands.'

'Rest, sweetheart.' Louise soothed his brow with eau de Cologne.

Josie entered the room with a basin of water and fresh linen. He had sweated out the fever and the sheets were soaked. Jeanne Camille remade the bed.

'Drink some water. Here, and some fresh lime juice Josie has made.'

There was some respite, but by afternoon the fever had begun to rise again. He was on the *plages* along the coast from Fort-de-France to Saint Pierre, beneath the high, cloud-capped mountains and the deep gulches with the dark green enamel of their flanks into which he used to climb to paint for the owners of the different *habitación*s, like he had painted at the Habitación Sucrerie Fond Chamomile and Habitación Pecoul near Saint Pierre.

'Michel, try and sleep, darling.'

'Do you remember when we were in Carbet?'

'Many times, sweetheart.'

'Yes, but that time at Carbet . . .'

He described the day they were sitting there in the shade of the palms and the *gommiers*. 'Hartmann, that photographer, was photographing us together. I can see the scene near the drying seines hanging on bamboo poles while the fishermen mended their nets. You were in your white muslin and you wore a straw hat from one of the *marchandes*.'

'I think we have the photograph somewhere.'

'You looked perfect.'

'Not what I used to be. We're growing old.'

'Not you.'

'Sweetheart.'

'Hartmann cried out for another and another. *Louise, un autre, un autre!* Do you remember him shouting at the top of his voice? That confounded man.'

'Why all these memories?'

'We were having lunch at Bourg de Case Pilote, where the painter, Carpenter, had a studio. "As you know, *mon ami*, it's the light, it's all in the light." I remember him saying that. Do you remember him saying that?'

The fever was running so high that Louise called for Dr Lange again, who visited in the afternoon. He sat and talked a while.

'Saint Pierre was like Marseilles at the port.'

'Yes, I know both towns, Monsieur Cazabon.'

'I'm lost in the maze of streets. It's Paris now, rue Victor Hugo with its shops. At the Douane and fish market, the smells and the noises are like Marseilles.'

'You must try and rest, Monsieur Cazabon.'

'The loud applause at the theatre . . . Augusta!'

'Try and rest, Monsieur Cazabon.'

Dr Lange turned to Louise. 'I've given him a remedy to calm him,' he said as he left the room.

'The surf is breaking on the black sand. It's night in the harbour below. Louise, Louise . . .'

'Rest, darling.'

'Louise, you want to return to Paris?'

'Calm yourself, darling.'

He asked this, but in reality the money was not what it had been; the children could not be left behind and it was too expensive to find the money for all their passages. The wealth of Corynth and Belle Plaine was finished.

'Louise, Louise, where am I?' He had woken suddenly and could not recognize where he was. He had been strolling in the Jardins des Plantes on the slopes of Morne Parnasse, descending along a gravelled avenue with arches of bamboos and palms, branches festooned with bromeliads. 'Louise, Louise!' He thought he had seen Louise leaving the veranda with Josie. He thought he had seen them standing there and then they turned towards each other and Louise escorted Josie down the stairs. He thought he had seen that before. He wanted to call out, but he could not raise his voice. He had told her that he wanted to tell her something about Josie, but then he had not, and she wondered what it was that he would want to tell her about Josie that she did not already know.

The next morning his temperature had fallen.

'Darling, who is Augusta?'

'Why Augusta?'

'I thought I heard you crying out the name Augusta yesterday.'

'What?'

'It was just before we went to Martinique, I think. This woman came to the gate asking for you. Josie said she had been a model. She had a little girl with her. I never told you. She said her name was Augusta.'

'Augusta. Yes, she lived at Orange Grove. You say she had a child with her? What was she called?'

'What? The young girl . . .'

'Nothing . . .'

After more liquids and soothing bed-baths, his temperature came right down. But this was a false hope; it rose again in the night. Josie and Jeanne Camille continued to attend with fresh linen. Then Michel Jean returned to the Jardins des Plantes. He was hearing his own voice loud in the room, telling Louise of the cascade which he had painted for the *Album Martiniquais*, using that German's, Hartmann's, photographs to prepare for the lithographs. It was so vivid. They were standing for the camera that morning. They had gone with Hartmann to the garden. Louise and Hartmann were standing under the powerful fall of the water, the *saut d'eau*, from the cascade plummeting down before them, over and over. They seemed mesmerized by the force of the falling water that drummed in the hollow enclosure, which collected the water and directed it through sluices into an ornamental stream which flowed through the gardens. He remembered the percussion he had heard in the hills above Saint Pierre. 'It was the drums of Africa. The people were crying: *Liberté!*'

The image of Louise and Hartmann returned to haunt him.

'*Papa*. Don't excite yourself.' Jeanne Camille was keeping vigil.

'Louise, is that you?'

Louise entered the room to relieve Jeanne Camille. 'Darling, what is it?' Here, lime juice.' She held the glass to his lips.

'Did you have an affair with Hartmann?'

'What are you taking about? Of course not. This fever has really caught you.'

The album of Martinique lay open by the window. The breeze was turning the leaves. They sounded like almond leaves in the wind in the dry season. Then he was again looking down into great bay of Saint Pierre. The heights of Mont Pelée looked down onto the bay. The Habitación Pecoul, where he had liked to go and paint, was just outside the town. He had rejected Hartmann's photograph in the Jardins des Plantes and painted his own sketch in preparation for the album of lithographs the two men had embarked upon. Mr Hartmann had entered the shade, leaving his camera standing. Suddenly they are not in Saint Pierre, but standing in the streets of Georgetown with its tall lighthouse at the end of Water Street and the boats crowding the rickety stelling jutting out at the mouth of the Demerara River.

'Those lithographs are so stilted.'

'What are you talking about, darling?' Louise was patting his forehead with eau de Cologne.

'That man, Hartmann, made me do such ugly work.'

'All that's over now, darling. Who was he anyway? He suddenly arrived and then disappeared without trace. You don't have to work with him any more. That was a long time ago. Why let these demons persecute you?'

'Daguerreotypes, ambrotypes, tintypes, forever with that blasted photography. Telling me that painting was finished.'

'Darling, you must rest.'

He was much better the following morning when Josie came in with a cup of coffee.

Louise rose from his bedside and went out of the room. Then he heard her on the piano that the men had brought from the wharf that morning. 'What are you playing?' he shouted down to her. He was surprised how strong his voice was.

'Herr Bach, Herr Bach . . .'

The notes were like heavy drops of rainwater that fall from trees a long time after the rains have passed, limpid with the light. He remembered the piano on the deck of the *Anemone* as they set sail for Martinique. They had taken it there and brought it back. He had finally forced himself to make a booking for the fifteenth of August, 1862, the Feast of the Assumption. He even remembered the name of Captain John Remy. Where had time gone?

Michel Jean felt better than he had for weeks. He dressed slowly and then went down to the drawing room. He stopped at the foot of the stairs, hearing a voice he recognized.

'Yes, they supported my husband in those days. You think they'll support him now? I don't see that happening. He feels more and more deserted.'

'But he had the best production team! Ciceri to do the lithography and Lemercier to execute the printing. You could not do better.'

'Ah, *oui*! It is not the quality of the work that I doubt, monsieur. I've never doubted the quality of my husband's work. I'm talking about the support. And you know even the support for the albums I've mentioned and I'm sure you've seen. Of course, you've seen. That is not enough to live on . . . it was never enough to live on with three children to educate. I knew that my daughters would marry, but they must bring something, they must have something of their own. And my son, my dear son. So much, so much I must make sure that he has. He has so little in this bewildering world.'

'Madame, I understand, but maybe Monsieur Cazabon should branch out into photography.'

Michel Jean, standing at the foot of the stairs, recognized his friend, Fabien, talking to Louise. He crept closer and recognized his other friend, Johnson. He had painted both their houses. What were they going on about? He listened, keeping himself hidden behind the half-open door.

'He's a painter. He doesn't want to be a photographer. They don't have anybody else doing painting here. He's on his own. He's the first one to go into that jungle and paint. To go where they have their estates and paint. He is the first one. He made a choice between there and here and he chose here. It's difficult to understand. He could be in Paris. I met him in Paris. You should've seen him in Paris. He was unusual, you know, in the studios, the salons and the soirées. It's there I first saw him. Then, you can imagine, in the Louvre. Not many black men in the Louvre. Of course, you know, French landscape. They refused anything else. No landscape from here. One at the beginning, and then, *non*!'

'Madame, you speak out of passion. That's wonderful.'

'I speak of what I know. You call it passion and it sounds as if you thus seek to diminish what I say, to dismiss it as mere passion.'

Louise was becoming upset, he could tell. He wondered why his two old friends were here this morning.

'Madame, how could you think . . .?'

He watched them through the crack in the door, getting ready to leave.

'Your husband is a most delicate painter. His watercolours have the lightness of clouds, the fragility of a breeze in a bamboo grove. But our age is the age of photography. It is going to transform our perception of our world. He must take photography into account. What we record and how we record is changing rapidly. As you know, and your husband must know, in Paris painting is no longer like the painting we have known. Painters are doing such different things with reality. The relationship to light and how we represent light is changing.'

'You should be saying all of this to my husband, monsieur. Or not. It would make him very angry. He's not well at the moment. He has a fever. I must attend to him now. I must excuse myself.'

'Of course,' the two old friends said at once.

Michel Jean felt weak with emotion. He retreated upstairs to his room before he could be seen, as Louise ushered Fabien and Johnson to the front door.

The house was quiet. The fishermen's shouts and cries from Corbeaux Town were far away, filtered as it were through swathes of cotton as Louise came up the stairs. She found Michel Jean on the chaise-longue, painting the white cirrus clouds strung out across the blue sky over the gulf.

'You feeling better, darling?'

'*Oui.*'

'Those were your old friends. Did they disturb you?'

'Yes, I heard them.'

'When?'

'Yes. I came downstairs and when I recognized their voices I did not come into the room. I hurried up here as they were leaving. You spoke well. I could not argue again about photography versus painting. So wearying.'

'They were beginning to irritate me. I could have lost my temper. But they are good friends. They had your welfare at heart.'

'I'm glad to be home.'

'Yes. And you have your award from the Savanne du Fort for your new painting.'

'*Oui.* And Rose Alexandrine found her husband.'

'Yes, there's a letter today from the new *Monsieur et Madame Deymier*. Our daughter is pregnant. We've a lot to be thankful for, *chéri*. Martinique had its rewards.'

'Wonderful. Stand there. No, sit. Let me paint you. Let your hair fall loose.' He could see the streaks of silver. 'That's it, darling. Look out to the sea.' She sat by the door and relaxed as he painted her. He painted what he saw and each time he painted her she was different. There was so much to see in her. 'You're just as you always were.'

'Sweetheart.'

'You don't look at all like a grandmother.' He saw in her all the different Louises that he had loved, and he felt sad that he had ever betrayed her. Not any more, he thought to himself.

*

'What has happened to time?' Michel Jean asked, expressing the hurt he felt for his son and his condition, as well as their own disappeared youth. He and Louise sat at the breakfast table after Josie had gone downstairs. Augusta was on his mind. 'You mentioned a young woman, Augusta, and her child.'

'That was a while ago. What's worrying you?' Louise put her hand on his.

'Time, my dear?'

Time had passed and his fever had gone.

Louise, ignoring the rhetorical nature of his frequent exclamations, tried to answer this repeated question about time in as philosophical a way as possible. He could see that she tried to attend to the practicalities of their life. His melancholia had continued to punctuate the long days of his inactivity. 'Time? You keep asking about time, sweetheart. This time is the time we must cherish.'

He looked at her, then turned and stared out of the window at the sea emerging from the haze over the gulf. He would have to go and find out the truth about Augusta's child. He did not want to speak about this to Louise. Why raise it now, if the child was not his? Augusta was married, she sounded settled. Perhaps she just wanted to show him how her daughter had grown, for old times' sake.

'There's so much we must be thankful for, Michel. You're now well established. We cannot change how photography has affected the reception of your art.' She knew that this was his anxiety, started by Hartmann's gauche declarations on the new science, the new art form. 'Your albums remain the definitive work of the time here. No one else has achieved as much as you in that regard. That's the general view. There was your special reward at the Agricultural Show back in 1866 at the Savanne du Fort. That showed how much you were appreciated. You must remember that.'

He tried to smile at her little affections, to reciprocate her efforts to cheer him up. But he was not able to sustain such a good mood. He looked at his wife, bewildered at how she could pluck from the past these crumbs of recognition as they now seemed to him, though he had to admit that he was grateful for that small reward for his watercolour of the Habitación Pecoul and the whole *Album Martiniquais* at the time.

'The photograph has usurped the prospect, a notable artist in Paris has proclaimed.' There was now a new realism, something people were calling Impressionism. 'What on earth do they mean? What, just an impression? What the arse is this?' He finally lost his patience altogether with the reports from Paris.

'Darling, you must not react. You have to find out more. It's something that has grown out of the kind of work you and the artists in Normandy were doing, if you remember. Remember Boudin's work . . .'

'Why didn't we stay in Paris? I would've been at the very centre of the revolution.'

'Michel, we can't think like this now, sweetheart. Revolution? There was a revolution and you escaped it in '48. I was there with the children. Then you argued to me that you had to be here. Here was where you would make your name. There was the work with the English set, for the English Governor. I heard nothing but Harris and Wildman in your letters, when there were letters. You were obsessed with your students Elizabeth Prowder and Wildman. You had planned it all and it succeeded. You would come back equipped to paint their prospects in watercolours.'

'Louise? Why are you continuing with this . . .?'

'You captured their homes and municipal projects. You made their empire seem benign and just, as your critics have indicated. Is that what you now regret? You had your patrons.'

'I know.'

'Then you had the idea you would be painting your republic, you would be subversive, you would be a cryptic critic of the regime. That was to fulfil your mother's dreams of her republic. You would be a West Indian artist. Not a planter, but a painter. You remember?'

'Why are you telling me all of this now?'

'You said you would go unrecognized in Paris amidst the great number of artists who were flocking to the salons. Your colour and your race, you argued, would exclude you there. And you know how many have excluded you here. But, you would make your name here.' With her husband being so maudlin, Louise could not resist these reminders of the choices he had made.

'I should have listened to Pissarro and Melbye when I met them in Caracas with Hartmann. I should've listened to Camille when he was preparing to embark from Charlotte Amalie for Europe. I could see myself at his age. It disappears. So quickly you have your moment and then it's gone . . .'

'Maybe you should've and I would've been able to bring up my children as French and not have them educated in this half-baked English-French backwater. Neither fish nor fowl. Isn't that how they put it?' She tried her best to imitate one of the English accents she had heard.

'Is that how you feel?'

'That is how you make me feel, Michel, when you go on like a spoilt child. You did what you thought was best at the time and it has had its rewards. Okay, so things have changed. Things change. Science gallops ahead. Who is it, Darwin? Who would've thought? The world isn't what we knew. You can paint what you like now. There're no patrons any more, a few commissions from the Creoles and then nothing more. Your friends, Johnson and Fabien . . .'

'Thank God for friends . . .'

'But how often can you paint the same view, the same house for an English governor? Go out and paint what you want to paint. See what happens. I know some of those paintings that you do which are not for governors and English ladies to take home to *dearest mama*.' She sounded scathing and she looked at him for a reaction.

'And money? How will we put bread on the table?' He talked with his back to her, still looking out onto the gulf and Corbeaux Town.

'Don't be dramatic, Michel. Look at us. Anyway, there are your two teaching positions to continue with. You should be grateful that educational institutions value your work, your gift, and your craft. A Creole schoolmaster. Those salaries combined will put enough bread on the table, as you describe it. I am planting lettuce and tomatoes in the backyard. Josie is making cakes. Jeanne Camille is sewing. We won't starve.'

He hated it when he knew she was right.

Josie came in with the laundry. Her face revealed that she had heard the fracas from downstairs. She looked at each in turn and raised her eyebrows. 'Is true, you know. He too harden. Is so he stop since he small. Not so, Jeansie?'

Michel Jean ignored Josie's teasing smile. What a trio they had made of their life, he thought. He still did not know how Louise dealt with the truth. All that seemed such a long way away now, yet he knew that it could resurface as part of another past which he had more regrets about.

Out on the veranda, he escaped the two women going on about what he should do and what he should not do. He returned to his studio. The truth was that he hated teaching schoolchildren. They had not the slightest interest in his art. At the Roman Catholic College on Frederick Street and at the new Government School in the Princes Building he struggled with discipline in order to impart the rudiments of drawing and painting. The boys ragged him mercilessly because of the way he spoke, the way he dressed. The man with the *chapeau* they called him. 'Look, the man with *chapeau* coming!' They could not see the point of the subject as they did with the mathematics and composition. Thankfully, in each class there were one or two boys who asked for special lessons. In a small group, he could be heard and he could instruct.

He would have to persuade the headmasters to allow him smaller groups, rather than throw him to the wolves in an overcrowded classroom with children who did not want to learn his subject. It was even worse when he thought to give them an experience of painting *en plein air* and have them strung out over the Queen's Savannah playing at games, anything other than painting. A boy even flew a kite one day, which at least was a subject for the others to attempt. Only in smaller groups would he be able to continue, he argued to himself. He was ashamed that he could not cope. He had lost his confidence. A young student, Leon Wehekind, had emerged. He had agreed to give him lessons at his home on the Santa Barbara Estate in Santa Cruz. They sat and painted light coming through bamboos by the river. There was something different happening in his paintings. At the same time, Michel Jean was painting the planter, Stollmeyer, and his wife at Mon Valmont further down the valley.

It was predictable. If he were to start again he would have to return to Belmont Hill, his old haunt. After he scrambled through the ruins of the old Government House he found a suitable place to set up his easel, giving him a view of the Queen's Savannah, and beyond that the barracks at St James. He found himself hardly able to control his emotions, moved by the memory of himself and the young Elizabeth Prowder caught on the causeway between Craig Island and Caledonia. It was unreal, after so long, the effect on him of that time.

He began to set up his palette. He did as Louise suggested. Paint what you want to paint, she had said. She had not said paint how you want to paint. He did not know how he wanted to paint. Was there any other way than the one he knew? He drew on his learning, on his practice. He drew on a tradition. Where else was there to go?

They were telling him constantly that Louis Michel was going somewhere else. They were telling it like a joke. 'Boy, that fella could paint, *oui*!' But, was it a joke? When he looked at his son's paintings, he truly wondered. They were something new. He had seen some of that newness in Pissarro's work in Charlotte Amalie. Surely, he too could be confident in his own style.

And then there was the confounded photography at every turn. One of Joseph's sons was setting himself up as a photographer in San Fernando. 'Uncle Michel,' he had said politely the other day. 'This kind of painting passé now, you know. Why you don't come and do some photography with me? We could do well together. You have an eye for composition.' This was the kind of talk he had to listen to when he met with his family. 'Young Joseph is doing so well with his photographs,' they said.

Louise was right. It was here that he wanted to be. It was here that he wanted to paint. It was this world that he wanted to paint. He did not have to think about who would buy the paintings now. He had got carried away with Harris and Wildman filling his head with all kinds of ideas. Albums, albums, albums, views to take back home.

That was the trap in which he had been kept prisoner on his return from Paris in '48. Yes, Louise was correct again. There had been an achievement. He had put down some work. Where it was now he did not know. Views to take away. The paintings had gone with their patrons; they had all been bought from him. 'They're gone, all gone now.'

He was not going anywhere. And photography? Let it be.

The haze accumulated in the distance. This was no French or English summer. This was not summer at all. This was the dry season.

Nostalgia for Port of Spain or Paris was no good to him now. The streets, the visits to the little cafés in the Mouffetard, which had become habitual and were associated with assignations, with gifts of flowers and strolls by the Seine, could not help him now; the anticipated excitement of their entrance to maybe hers or his apartment. He forgot now, the youth, or some *mademoiselle*, some Laurent or Marie-Therese. Nearly every part of the city held some moment like that, some memory of an anonymous rendezvous which could be smelled or tasted or touched, as he, *flâneur par excellence*, found himself addicted to pursuing his quarry, no matter the season or the inclemency of the weather. It was always romantic and, if not romantic, erotic. Sometimes, the dirtier the streets, the more dangerous the alleyways, the more exciting the adventure. '*Mademoiselle . . .*' Where was he?

At least he had survived those adventures; better men had gone mad with some *maladie*.

Nostalgia would make him sick in the end, he thought. There would have to be some more robust resolve to motivate his work now, here in the present with Louise, his children and grandchildren.

Louise and Josie were back at the house. He liked it when Jeanne Camille and Louis Michel brought their lives into the house, when they entered with their clatter and their voices. '*Papa et Maman, ou êtes-vous?*' They shattered his present melancholy with their very different selves. Though, settling down into the rhythms of family life would not save him either, he thought. Is that what he was to become, some bourgeois painter?

Jeanne Camille's suitor, Edmund Basilon, came on afternoons to sit with her and talk out on the front veranda. Then they went for a stroll towards the Queen's Savannah and the Hollows. He looked at them and envied their lives just beginning. He heard Louise's voice with a tone of caution: 'Don't be back late, *mes enfants*.' He wanted to shout after them: 'Lose yourself, have an adventure.' He knew that he needed something dangerous to happen, to extricate him from his lassitude.

But it was his son, Louis Michel, who really absorbed him and took him out of himself as he observed again and again his obsessive way of working. The copying of his father's paintings was now something of the past. He was doing his own work. Since the years in Martinique and his time spent with the young artist from Paris, who lived at Carbet, he was painting his own watercolours and even some oils.

There was very little conversation about his work as they stood together in his son's studio that afternoon. But there was an exchange in the way he brought out a painting and rested it on the windowsill for his father to look at it. It was the way he looked at him and then looked away again, the way he went up to the canvas and touched it, or hesitated, hovering with his brush, wanting to ask his father a question, gesturing, but seldom finding the words. Michel Jean had learned those codes, reading the language of the painting. He, too, used few words. He dabbed a brush in his son's palette, trying out the colour on a bit of paper. They studied the effect. Their raised eyebrows, the shrug of their shoulders, their exchange of ironic smiles, spoke their opinions and feelings. Michel Jean hated to intervene, but Louis Michel drew him in, like in a game, quietly saying, almost to himself, '*Papa, Papa, dis moi* . . . Tell me how you do it.'

'*Mon fils*, what can I tell you?' He patted him on the shoulder and then had to excuse himself from his son's studio and return to the solitude of his own with some of the old watercolours hanging on the walls and peeping out of ragged-edged portfolios stacked on the shelves. Did he want to live in an archive?

He stood, overcome with the years he had missed of his son's very early childhood, when his remoteness had begun, when his obsessions were made manifest. These things could not be undone. They still tied him up in knots. That was when the boy had needed to hear his voice, have his example, feel his touch. He had tried to make it up in '51 when he returned to the family. But even then it was too late. It was only now that he understood what he had missed, what he had given up for his painting and the life he had lived away from the family, that hectic time with governors and planters; his escapades with Augusta and his fantasy about Elizabeth. Could you gain the world and lose your soul? Could you regret everything in a life? Maybe he had lost both, the world and his soul.

He stood at the window, looking out into the backyards, noticing the blossom of the dry season sprinkling their petals on to the streets. Such a riot of colour, such optimism in nature, in its yellows and purples, was contrasted with such pessimism in himself. He allowed his welling tears to fall, to wet his cheeks. He allowed the paradox to hurt him. He had to stifle deeper emotions rising in his chest. He heard himself gasp for air.

He was startled by the sound of the door opening. It was Louis Michel. He had not knocked. He stood in the open doorway holding a watercolour in his hand. His eyes were beseeching his father to talk to him. Michel Jean took the painting from his son. 'It's very fine. I like it.'

Louis Michel looked doubtful.

'No, you have . . . Yes, you see here, the water, the way you have lit the water. The way the sky is in the water. Where were you when you did this?'

'Carbet.'

'*La plage au Carbet?*'

'*Oui.*'

They both smiled and laughed gently at the memory of the beach and the fishing village down the coast from Saint Pierre. There were always the doves and their melancholic moans in the hot sun amid the acacias and agave on the dry hillsides, the detonating screams of the *cigales* calling for the rain. Out over the cliffs the wide ocean went on and on between the islands, burning and crinkling, the colour of mercury.

'You were painting with . . .'

'Simon.'

'Ah.'

'Where you get the tubes? Expensive.'

'Simon.'

'Generous.' Michel Jean found himself feeling jealous of his son's relationship with the young Parisian artist, Simon Blandin, who had taken him under his wing.

Why had he not done more, always obsessed with his own struggles, to find his way in Martinique, leaving his son to Louise, and to the fussing of his sisters? In the last years the work had fallen off almost completely. He had lost his son again. Now he was a man, young for his age, but even more talented than he was as a child. Being tutored had combined with nature's gifts to produce a sort of prodigy. Who would notice? Would the world learn of him? Would it matter?

They both looked at the painting that Michel Jean was holding in his hands, holding it away from him and then resting it on the windowsill to gain the light. He thought how proud his mother, Madame Debonne Cazabon, would have been to see the work of her grandson. Maybe here was another chance, another opportunity for her progeny to realize her dreams of a republic.

Louis Michel was a natural. He had not spent his afternoons drawing the masters in the Louvre. How had he come by the compositional ideas and devices? Then he thought, *Ah non!* Not through him, transmitted through those obsessive copies? So he did have a hand in his son's gift. Perhaps.

The pouis and petrea, carpeting the streets with their yellow and purple blooms, were suddenly enriched by this thought. The flamboyante flamed even more riotously, its red not now discordant, but proclaiming its reality.

La plage au Carbet possessed nuances, new tones. '*Oui*, and the white.' Michel Jean spoke his thoughts aloud now, having them become a conversation with his son. '*Le blanc*, that you add, has increased the luminosity, so much, so thick.' Michel Jean ran his finger over his son's painting. It was as if he had painted with a trowel.

The boy stared at his own painting, hearing in his father's words effects that he had not been able to articulate as words. The words, spoken by his father, gave some authority to his endeavour. A smile played at the edge of his mouth. Maybe he was reminded of Simon Blandin.

'*Papa, Papa, continue.*'

'There's something immediate about the scene. It's there.'

'*Alla prima.*' He laughed, conscious that he was quoting his tutor.

'*Alla prima? Ah, oui.*'

'*Un étude. Rapide.* Simon *dit . . .*'

'Simon . . .'

'*Oui.*'

'And the light . . .?'

'*Oui . . .*'

'No chiaroscuro.'

The boy's face lit up. He knew that word. Simon Blandin had taught him that word.

'*Non!* Chiaroscuro, *n'est pas! Jamais.*'

'*Oui.*'

'*C'est un impression.*'

'Impression?'

'*Oui.*'

Louis Michel suddenly dashed from the room, leaving Michel Jean wondering. He returned as suddenly with an oil painting in bright colours: reds, purples and yellows.

'*Mon dieu!*' his father exclaimed.

Louis Michel smiled. He had become more courageous with his showing and his few words of conversation.

'Very bright!'

'*Papa?* You don't like?'

'*Non. Oui.* I like it. It's different. How did you mix these colours?'

Louis Michel left the room again and came back with the tubes that Simon Blandin had given him. Michel Jean read the labels. 'Windsor and Newton, the best. And stoppers. *Bien.*' The boy was already using the most up-to-date paints.

'I become your colour-man.'

Michel Jean smiled. Indeed, he wondered how he might continue to afford paints.

He woke the next morning with that sense of approaching dawn and felt the draw of what might be a firm decision, once he began to make preparations in his mind, lying in the dark. He felt a strong sense of elation. It had begun after speaking to Louis Michel in his studio. Yesterday, a flame had been lit.

'You out today?' He heard Louise's sleepy question as she turned over in bed.

'Hmm. Back this evening.' She would understand. He knew that she had been waiting for him to resume what she called his monastic call; like a monk rising for Matins, she would tease.

He could hear a cart, its wheels crunching on the gravel, approaching in the distance. 'This is my place, self,' Michel Jean said, laughing to himself. He spoke aloud in the darkness as he jumped on to the back of the sugarcane cart. 'Let them paint the

Seine. You think I playing the arse, I go keep on painting this place no matter what they think, no matter whether they want to buy painting or no painting. Photography! To hell with that. Whether they know where this is or not. You think I joking? I go keep on painting you, *doudou*!'

A stray dog barked in reply to his talking aloud so early, so absurdly, snapping at the wheels of the cart. He pulled his hat down more firmly over his forehead against the dew. He took a little nip of rum from the flask in his back pocket. 'Haul your arse.' He kicked at the snapping dog. 'What is this now, a man can't talk to himself in his own sweet country? You ent hear about freedom, or what!'

Michel Jean thought of what his son had said, his self-appointed colour-man, mixing his father's pigments, arranging his gums and oils, washing his brushes, stretching his canvasses. He remembered when he had heard him say to some caller at the house, 'My father is an artist from Paris. You come to sit for Monsieur Cazabon, the artist? Wait one minute. Take a seat on the veranda.' His little Wap. He just Wap, you know. He smiled to himself.

To get out into the bush he had to be up at this time, walking fast, propelled faster with a good poui *bois*, hitching lifts in the chill of morning with his easel, brushes and paints packed on his back, and arriving at his predetermined destination in order to be ready for the light. He had to catch the light in its very beginnings of the foreday morning. He was remembering and planning it all out in his mind. He was becoming the painter again.

He had to get back to seeing and feeling the light right here, this light that he had always wanted to paint, now in the early morning; get the first sketch, the first watercolour, let it flood his imagination, maybe start an oil. Let it dictate the pigments and the washes. This was what made the whole enterprise true. He had to forget what was going on in Paris.

Did they think that he could paint Augusta how he had painted her, all dressed up standing in the studio, if he had not first painted her in the pasture at Orange Grove? He knew what she was like in her real element. It was like when he painted the young *blanchisseuse* with her arms deep in the water, wringing out her skirts and sheets, lashing the rocks with the tight knot of her *fesse*. Did they think he could paint her without smelling her sweat, without smelling her saltfish? He laughed to himself: '*Doudou*, darling!' He knew he might not get there with them now; these young girls too bad now. Like when he pinched their bottom and they screamed out to their friends.

Michel Jean walked, intoxicated by memories of his youth. It was him, his son, who looked like him. He would get him painting again. He had another nip of the good rum from the distillery at the St Clair Estate. He swigged it down. Soon, he was feeling light in the head. 'Like they think them is the only ones with Gothic arches. They ent know the beauty of bamboo. This is our Chartres.'

'Mister Cazabon, where it is you say you want to get drop?' The sugarcane driver called from the front of the cart. Michel Jean had fallen asleep on a bundle of grass. Where was he? He had forgotten even that he had caught a ride.

'You reach River? I going Bagatelle, up so, to North Post. But I go walk this last couple of mile. I go take a coffee and eat some bake at the kitchen of Mister Huggins before I make the climb. I need to wake up, man. Here take a nip and God go with you. *Bonjour. Merci.*'

There was a fresh sea breeze coming from the mangrove shore. He could smell the salt in the air, the gutted fish from the foreshore where the fishermen prepared their catch for market.

The sun was burning itself through the scrim of haze in the distance along the north coast towards La Fillette. The road above River was loud with parakeets. In the early morning the fresh smell of the wild deer and quenk were close to the forest path. He crushed the wild thyme and mint on the verge. He tugged at the wild chadon beni, the smell of coriander he remembered in the alleys of the Mouffetard. Michel Jean gazed into the distance. The sea! This was in his mind when he first woke this morning. He would come to North Post, where above him the gulls soared and the pelicans hung in the air beneath the cliffs.

In his work he saw Louise and their son where he had left them in the house on Edward Street, two beats of his own heart.

Later, that evening, Michel Jean had to listen to Louis Michel's story of what had happened that day when he was away. '*Papa, Papa, écoutes* . . .' Still like a child, this young man, this prodigy. Louise lay on her bed inside, wishing her son would stop talking. This was the other extreme. Either he did not talk at all, or he would never stop. It was something about two women coming to the gate and asking for Mister Cazabon. 'She would not leave,' said Louis Michel, insistently. 'She say she will wait till Mister Cazabon reach.' Sometimes one was not always sure that what was being said bore any resemblance to reality. It might just be a script adopted for the moment, repeated again and again until it felt like the truth.

'They reach right up here on the veranda, you know. I catch them peeping into the drawing room. She say her name is Augusta de Gannes. The young girl with her pretty, but I ent catch she name. Madame de Gannes leave this.'

Michel Jean read Augusta's note, which informed him of her daughter's marriage.

Later, in his studio, Michel Jean could see her exactly as she had been that last time in the studio, pregnant with her baby. Then he remembered her at Orange Grove. The conclusion of her note told him what he already knew, that she had eventually married and she, with her daughter, now adopted by Monsieur de Gannes, were comfortable in their Tacarigua home. What in truth had happened to time? he asked himself. Things turned out the way they turned out.

The following morning he wrote to Augusta at her Tacarigua address. He enclosed a gift of money for her daughter on her wedding day. He directed the messenger carefully for a safe delivery. He felt that Augusta did not want the past to be dug up by his presence. She had not invited him to the wedding. Yet, she had come to his home with her daughter. As she had come before in his absence. What did any of this tell him? He didn't know what it was that she wanted to tell him, and now it seemed he would have to live with his doubt.

The impulse the following week was to go to Corbeaux Town and employ Pompey to row him out to Craig Island, another of his old haunts.

'You still going there, man? I say you done with that, so long now . . .'

'I need to just go there and see what going on.'

'You must have painting like peas of them islands. What it is about them islands. And the water choppy this morning, you know.'

Pompey was right, not exactly like peas, but there were a lot of paintings of the islands and the channels between the islands. He could see those blue chasms between the islands and the coast at Carenage.

'But you know I go take you. Let me just finish off planing this wood. This fella in my tail to get this pirogue finish.'

'So, work good?'

'Come and go. People will always fish. And more and more people need transport down to Chac and Monos. But now some people going back to the land, cocoa opening up again in Montserrat, you know. I myself thinking of getting a little holding up there. Them peon people and them from down Venezuela does work the cocoa good, *oui*. Get a fella up there to hold on for you. So I could then keep the boat-building going and also try a little thing on the land.'

'I see.' Michel Jean had his sketchpad and his watercolours out, yet another of Corbeaux Town, as Pompey shaved the *bois canot*. His bent figure over the bow of the pirogue entered the sketch as did the sweep of the bay and the grey rifling smoke out of Miss Melville's factory. Wap should come down here and paint, he thought. He should get to know Pompey and the fellas of Corbeaux Town now that he was a young man. He should come and take a nip now and then. He must bring him, as he used to bring him as a boy.

At the water's edge, two *blanchisseuses* beat their clothes on the rocks and wrung them out where a stream, a tributary of the Maraval River, entered over the rough beach to the sea. As the women sang their old song of abandonment and chattered among themselves, Michel Jean wondered why he had ever thought of leaving the island. The natural rhythm of the waves, the song of the women in alternating couplets, the lazy trails of smoke joining the scarves of cloud from the chimney of the factory held his attention as he painted. Pompey's hammering, the voices in the distance as fishermen hung out their seines, were all harmonized in the heat of the day into an ordinary beauty that he felt under his skin. He smelled and tasted both the bittersweet of the sea-grape and the salt of the sea; the water's ripple and wash in gentle waves heard since the womb. He sat back on the rock and took in his sketch, the painting hardly dry, the wind threatening to rip the paper.

Coming through the channel along the coast of Gasparee was a tall ship. 'See the name, *Ganges*, from Calcutta. They heading for Nelson Island.' They were still delivering their cargo there, entering the long line of men and women into quarantine. The tall ship bore down on them. Beneath the high masts and sails in full flood, they could begin to make out the people standing on the decks. Pompey waved. One figure waved back. Michel Jean followed suit and waved. A small group waved.

'Them still coming.'

'Is bring-they-bringing them.'

Pompey weighed anchor between Craig and Caledonia. In the shelter of the bay there was a calm. Intermittent swells would break upon the rocks and then the pirogue found its equilibrium again. Pompey threw a line and almost immediately caught some carites. Michel Jean sat in the bow and sketched. They both from time to time watched the *Ganges* anchored off the islands, offloading the new arrivals.

'Boy, that's some distance they come, *oui*.'

Michel Jean listened but did not reply.

They were using Lennegan Island for the women. He watched while some women with babies clambered onto the jetty.

He thought he saw an image of Elizabeth Prowder on the causeway. His reverie, his pilgrimage, was interrupted by a new reality. What was the point of returning there? A decade and a half later, they were living in another time.

'Pompey, I done, *oui*. Let we go.'

'Yes, boy.' Pompey lifted the anchor dripping over the side of the pirogue.

As they returned to Corbeaux Town, Michel Jean sat in the bow and watched the receding islands and the *Ganges* with the pirogues plying back and forth, delivering the passengers to the islands.

'That's work if you want it.'

'Not me. I can't hardly watch them people. To look into their faces it too sad when they first arrive. And they sick, you know. They does arrive sick, sick too bad.'

'Must be a relief to arrive, to step onto land.'

'Is true.'

They arrived at Corbeaux Town. 'Pompey, I go bring my son to meet you. He's a big man now, you know.' They pulled the pirogue up onto the beach.

'Bring him. Take a nip. He's a painter like you?'

'For his sins.'

'What you does do with all them painting, boy?'

'Good question, Pompey.'

'When you come to think of it, for true, people hardly have house, some of we. The big people and them, they does like to have them, I suppose, pay you for that.'

Michel Jean listened. 'You have a point, Pompey. How many pirogues can you make?'

'As many as people want.'

'Painting is different. Is like people don't know if they want till they see it.'

'But you can't stop painting. You need to paint, not so?'

Michel Jean looked at his friend and smiled. 'Since long you wise, you know, Pompey. I can't stop the thing.'

'But who you does really paint for, in truth?'

'I paint for myself.'

'That's a privilege, boy.'

Pompey ran his hand along the planks of wood he was planing for the bow of the new pirogue.

'I go see you, Pompey.'

'Bring the young fella.'

'And what about Marguerite?'

'You remember she? She making baby.'

'She get catch.'

'Boy . . .'

As Michel Jean made his way home, he thought of Pompey's question: 'But who you does really paint for, in truth?'

BOOK SIX

1885–1888

I

'*Papa?*' Michel Jean had a way of ignoring his son's attempts to interrupt his work. In fact, Louis Michel knew that he should not enter the studio when his father was painting in the afternoon, trying to catch the last of the bright light before the sun ducked away behind the islands of Caledonia and Gasparee. '*Papa, Papa!*' Louis Michel's voice was accompanied by a tremulous knocking on the door. Being ignored would not deter him. His voice was no longer inflected. It was insistent in its repetition.

'Wap, I tell you . . .' his father called out with irritation.

'Yes. *Oui*, but, *Papa* . . .'

'But what?'

The paintings that he was collecting, for what he did not know, were taking up all the space in the studio. He had decided to revisit some of his old sites and paint them again. There was one of Craig Island and another of the First Boca. Josie had brought up some mangoes from the Julie mango tree in the yard. He had completed a still life yesterday: Julie mangoes and pommeracs; ripening yellows, ochres and reds.

He had now lost the moment with Louis Michel's insistent knocking. He could not see to paint. The young Indian woman on the easel stared back at him forlornly. He was losing her, losing the young girl by the side of the cane field who had spoken to him in that half-Hindi, half-English way, a transformation of words; virtually a new language, he thought. She had not yet come alive. He had not yet been able to work his old charm. Maybe all the attention was in her clothes, in her jewellery, not in her. Who was she? Who was he painting her for? He felt that stab of melancholia as he felt for her, so politely allowing him to intrude. He could see fires burning on the beach from the window of his studio, like one of those pyres you saw now on the sides of rivers where the Hindus were performing their pujas. She was the new figure on the landscape. He looked into her face on the easel. Who are you? he asked himself, looking at the portrait.

Josie had already put down the mosquito nets in the adjoining bedrooms. He thought how ordinary life went on. Josie was still here. That was good.

He did not want to leave the studio. He did not want to pay attention to Louis Michel's calling. 'Papa! You ent hear what I saying?' How long had Louis Michel been calling? He found that this was happening to him more often now, losing himself in his own thoughts, time drifting away.

This was the moment that she had chosen to leave him. His son was tentatively announcing her departure without knowing what to immediately do. He had usually followed his mother on her journeys, but this afternoon he was standing outside his father's studio, lost and perplexed, unequipped for this journey his mother was embarking upon. 'Papa, is Maman, you know.'

Michel Jean wondered how he himself would start again. It had been getting harder and harder each time. At the end of each day he wondered if he would ever paint again. And, now, she was leaving him to struggle on his own.

Michel Jean opened the door. 'Wap, boy, come take a nip with your papa.' He lifted the rum bottle, tilting it into the glass on the table with the tubes of paint. 'Take a nip, boy, it go help you to sleep tonight. Here, take a nip. You mother not go see.' He smiled at his son and then laughed a little. He lit the oil lamp. He looked up to see his son standing in the doorway between the studio and the corridor to the bedrooms, his twisted form casting a crooked shadow along the floor with the lamplight illuminating his fallen face. Chiaroscuro? Yes. He had never forgotten when they had lifted him from between his mother's legs and the midwife had handed his son to him. He heard himself then: 'He wap, eh?', cradling the small warped body of his son in his arms, leaning in to kiss him on his creased forehead, noticing how a baby can look like a wise old man.

He could see now beyond his son's shape the long corridor to the bedrooms and heard there the rustle of the women further in the depths of the house, already dressed in bombazine. The poor had collected, women she had befriended, from the street, dressed in white cotton with heads tied in white, already into their humming and low chanting of Africa's memory. They were sitting on the stairs with their naked children in their arms.

Louis Michel moved aside to let his father pass into the corridor, refusing his nip of rum. The lamplight lit up the faces of the women standing and looking with a mixture of resignation and shock, before the grief descended. '*Papa*.' It was Jeanne Camille. They moved their lips to speak, but neither uttered a word, leaving the faltering story of the end to his son, the women accompanying him with their humming of a hymn. It was Josie leading them with: 'Swing low sweet chariot coming for to carry me home. Swing low sweet chariot . . .'

'*Papa*, come and see.' Louis Michel tugged at his sleeve. 'Come and see.'

He allowed himself to be led by his son, as if he were a blind man, walking ahead of him, grasping his father's hand and pulling him along to come and see the sight upon the bed. It struck him then how like a small child he could still seem, his forty-year-old son, excitedly pulling his father along by the arm to come and look at some wonder.

He had decided the night before to wait out the time in his studio, trying to paint rather than sitting at her bedside. The demonstrations of public grief and the ministering of the nurses over the last few days had made him want to be on his own at his easel with his own thoughts about the Frenchwoman, Louise Rosalie Trolard, his Rosie, as he used to call her at first, the name her own father called her; his wife, who was preparing to depart from him. He was never too good with departures.

He felt that they had said their farewells some days ago, before she had lost consciousness. Old Dr Lange had put it to him: 'You can sit and watch if you care to, but she may never stir again. We'll know when the breathing stops completely, very shallow now, and the pulse is slow slow. But you may still care to be here rather than anywhere else.' Doctors sometimes possessed a wisdom about these kinds of events, these deathbed situations.

He had tried sitting by her with his hand in hers for a day, but then he found that with the women coming in and out, and Louis Michel himself, and Jeanne Camille, performing their own ceremonies of farewell, his son constantly testing his mother's breathing by going close up to her face and then resting his ear to her heart, that his place by the bedside of his wife was being usurped.

Rose Alexandrine had arrived from Martinique with her son, Pierre Deymier, a youth that looked like him when he was that sweet age of sixteen. This was the family that Louise Rosalie Trolard, white Frenchwoman from Vire had looked over with a wisdom she had not known she possessed. Josie, the woman she had taught to read, was kneeling at the foot of the bed.

He entered the bedroom, following his son, to find that she whom he wanted to see more than anyone else in the world had now made her final departure. He noticed how the face had changed completely. She had left the room as imperceptibly as the sun had sunk down in the gulf. The radiance without contradicted the darkness within.

'Leave me here a while. Wap, ask your sisters to go downstairs, give the guests something to drink and eat. Josie, give me some time.' She rose, resting her hand on his shoulders.

He could already hear the drone of the rosary being recited by the plaintive voices, like the waves breaking on the beach at Corbeaux Town; antiphons breaking on the shore of death was how he had thought of them at his mother's funeral. She would not want any of this confusion, but she was not here to control any matter in this world now. She had crossed the ocean to a new world and it had become her world. She had learned its ways and had taken them into her understanding of life.

Once the bustle in the corridor had subsided and Louis Michel had successfully performed this duty for his father by saying in his subdued voice, '*Papa* want quiet now,' urging on his sisters and promising that they would be allowed to return with the other women to prepare their mother's body for burial, Michel Jean allowed himself to experience his grief to the full. He leaned over and kissed his wife. He was aware that there was a sweet smell on her lips; that taste of death they always called it, like communion bread on the tongue after Sunday Mass.

As he sat on the chair he had vacated some days ago, holding her hand in his and letting his mind drift without worrying about any immediate preparations for her dead body, he noticed that the paint he had been working with was engrained in his fingernails and his jacket smelled of turpentine and he had smudged the broderie anglaise trimming of the sheets with charcoal. None of this mattered, though he could still hear her voice, 'Michel, *mon chéri*, wash your hands, darling.' That was the last thing she had said to him. How long would the sound of her voice last in his mind? He got up and stared into her face. Would he forget how she looked at this moment or would that always be the face that he remembered? He saw her running against the wind on the beach at Calvados, running into the light, disappearing with her white muslin, lifting her skirts to run. Yes, he would still see her that way, always that beauty.

'How long it is since you pass near Corynth?' Jeanne Camille coaxed her father. 'And I don't think you see the *grande usine* at Sainte Madeleine recently?'

His younger daughter tried to paint a picture of the sites for her father that she thought he might enjoy. She conjured the journey as a distraction for him in his melancholic mood; what she thought of as the prolonged grief since the death of her mother. 'You'll enjoy the countryside from the window

431

of a moving train. All them beautiful cane fields in the rolling Naparimas. You don't have to ride donkey again, go on foot, is train now, you know. Take your sketchpad. When you last do a painting down south?'

Michel Jean watched his daughter busy herself around the studio. Since Louise's death she was regularly at no. 9 Edward Street to check up on his welfare. Rose Alexandrine had returned to Martinique with his grandson. He let Jeanne Camille talk as he put the finishing touches to *A Bridge at St James*. The area around the barracks and the outskirts of Peru Estate were changing into a little Indian village along the Diego Martin Road. A small white temple had risen among the cane fields and the wide pastures. Some of the early indentured workers were making the island their home, no longer praying in their shrines, the small *kutiyaas*, but being bold enough to build a temple. Later, not allowed by the authorities and the estate manager, it was in ruins.

'*Papa*, you hearing me? Where you?'

'In India.'

'India?'

'India in St James.'

'*Papa*, sometimes I really wonder, you know.'

'Jeanne Camille, what happen? You must not stop laughing. And you must take a good look at what happening around you. You think I is an old man?'

'*Papa. Papa.* I think . . .'

'What you think?'

She looked like her mother, though she was more African than French. Her green eyes, her crinkling long hair twisted into a knot and held on top of her head, gave her the look of Louise. 'You was our love child, you know.'

'You never tell me that before.'

'When I go tell you. Things have their right moment.'

He told her the story of returning to Paris after his early years in Port of Spain, after that long separation, then his reunion with Louise: 'You were that reunion.'

'*Papa*, you good for yourself, you know.'

'We love each other too bad, *oui*. You wouldn't know them kind of love.'

She laughed. 'I miss her, *Papa*. I miss her so much.'

He looked at his daughter, looking like his wife, and smiled knowingly.

'Anyway. Is down south I want you to go. And is down there you start to do your thing. Who it was, Wildman, your student, that English fella, who used to work for the Governor in them days? You remember you tell me them things when I was small, painting the island for me when I was a little girl in the perambulator in the Bois de Boulogne. Maybe is afterwards that you tell me these things and I remember it so, remember how *Maman* tell the story. Perhaps that was *Maman*'s idea of how it happened.'

Jeanne Camille was moving about the studio, trying to keep some semblance of order.

'Sweetheart. Don't tidy up too much.'

'But, *Papa* . . .'

'No buts. Is my studio, you know.'

He could see that his daughter was beginning to understand what her mother had had to put up with: the dirty trousers and shirt on the back of a chair, the unwashed brushes, a rum bottle under the table. Those things were the least of it.

'You don't believe we love each other?'

'*Papa*, what I know.'

At that moment Josie was coming in from the backyard. He saw his daughter looking at her aunt and smiling. Josie was still here, ready to look after Jeanne Camille's baby when it arrived. They were family.

'*Papa*, I going now. Think about the train. I'll organize how to pay for you and Louis Michel. They tell me the train does pass near Corynth on its way from San Fernando to Savanna Grande. They say the views are stunning. Is like us when I was small and we take the train to Rouen. Of course, I was only a baby then. *Maman* tell me the story.'

Michel Jean listened to his daughter and kissed her once on each cheek before she left the room. 'I not sure about that train journey.' Stunning, he thought. For a fleeting moment the cane fields of his childhood opened up in his mind, then the small, ordinary scenes that he painted. He had no other language for them. *Un paysage.*

'I not going. I tidying up in here.' Jeanne Camille had moved into the bedroom now. He heard her reprimanding Josie. '*Tante Josie*, if I don't come here all you will bury yourself under all kind of confusion.'

'Child, we burying soon anyway. You ent see how old your father and me is. Don't fuss yourself. Is so you father like it. When he young he used to tidy up. Especially when things worry him. And I ent able. You see me, I ent able with some things now.'

Michel Jean shouted from his studio. 'Jeanne Camille, leave you *Tante Josie*. Josie, don't listen to them young people.'

He heard Jeanne Camille laughing. 'All you like a real old couple now.'

Josie laughed. 'You hear what she say, Jeansie? You hear? These young people good for themselves, *oui*.' Josie's laughter continued.

Jeanne Camille put her head round the door of the studio once more, smiled and waved *au revoir*.

There seemed to be no place where he was at ease now, except in the old sea-beaten, sun-stricken, salt-ridden studio in Edward Street. He hardly even went to Corbeaux Town. Pompey had died. Louis Michel came back from Corbeaux Town with the news one day. The studio smelled of the years, the layers of memory in the shelves of dust. It smelled of turpentine, gum arabic and paint.

Sometimes he saw Louise standing by the door the way he had painted her with her hair streaked with silver tumbling from on top of her head and her eyes so bright. He never let that portrait leave him. They had just come back from Martinique. Pack up somewhere down there, under the counter, he thought, or up there in the attic. Must give it to the children, was another thought. 'You have eyes like the colour of the ocean.' He spoke the words aloud. He had told her that when he had first met her, meaning the ocean between the islands which she had never seen and which he told her was near to the colour of the Midi. He would paint it for her one day. He would take her there, he had told her.

He could still hear Jeanne Camille busying herself with papers. Everything depended on having the papers in order; her mother's will, documents of her mother's family in Normandy, her parents' marriage certificate, and their birth certificates.

'Papa, look at this.' It was the Hartmann daguerreotype that the German had taken of Louise in Saint Pierre standing on the steps of the rue Monte au Ciel where the young girls loved to play, running up the steps with the drain cascading down the centre. They liked to run right to the top where the palm trees grew in a courtyard. Jeanne Camille and Rose Alexandrine had liked it when Hartmann came strolling with them, with his camera that made everyone in the street stop to look.

'And this one, Papa.' Jeanne Camille sat on a low stool beside him and stared at the photograph. Then he noticed just how pregnant she was.

'Sweetheart, you want to keep that? You can take that, you know. You can take these things, all of these things. For you and your children. The less that is left here the better. She gone now,' he said, holding the photograph.

In the evening he was alone with his son.

'Papa.'

Louis Michel was like his father's shadow now that his mother had died, and there were no longer those eyes as blue as the ocean in which to drown his frustrations.

He had noticed that Louis Michel liked to be near him more now than he had in the past. He had always liked to be near him in the studio, mixing the paints, but this nearness that his son now sought was different. He had begun to sleep in his room on a cot put at the foot of his bed. He wondered how precisely he imagined his mother's disappearance. He woke immediately on hearing his father stumble onto the veranda. '*Papa*.'

Michel Jean had to stay awake to listen to his son's excited speech about what he was doing and to show *Papa* what colours he had mixed, which palette he had laid out.

'And look, *Papa*, see what Wap do for you.'

'Boy, you drinking?'

'*Papa*, just a nip. I take a nip for *Maman*. Nightcap?' He tilted the rum bottle in his father's direction.

His son had collected all the candles and lamps to the centre of the room and had heaped them on the table with the tubes of paints to form a giant candelabra to gain the most light. The street lamps were already lowered into nothing. He showed his father his painting of a *case nègre* in a yard looking like something behind the bridge, beyond Dry River, one of his own favourite spots to paint bridges, and the steep gully with the trickle of white chalk for the river.

'Wap, boy, I go have to see this in the morning, because I can see what you painting here is light. Is light you painting, boy, and them candle not letting me see what you doing.'

'*Oui*, *Papa*, and is rum you want, a ti-rum like when we in Martinique with *Maman*. Eh? I've some limes, you know.'

'Come, boy, come. *Mama* not here now and we have to sleep.'

It struck Michel Jean, that night, the way his mother lingered in his son's mind as *Maman* and not the patois, *Mama*. Sometimes he himself would call out her name. 'Louise, that's you?' And, then, he would catch himself.

He heard the boy talking as he worked in his studio. '*Maman*, come and see,' inviting her to view some new painting he had done for her.

The son and the father scared each other with the intensity of their grief.

The next morning, Michel Jean sat among his portraits and oils, the portfolios of watercolours, the unsold albums of lithographs, the achievements of a younger artist stacked in the corner, accumulating dust. He could see the names on the spines of the 1851 and the 1857 albums.

He sat and stared at them as Jeanne Camille came in to get Louis Michel some breakfast. The M. J. Cazabon was fading, but he could read Eugene Ciceri, the lithographer, on the spine of the 1851 album and Levilly on the 1857. Termites had got at the covers and spines of the *Demerara Album*, like the woodlice in the eaves of his room. But, he could still read A. A. Hartmann, Photographer.

'Wonder what happen to Hartmann, boy?'

'You say something?' Josie had entered the room looking for Louis Michel.

'I thinking back, girl. Hartmann? He was that photographer. You ent remember him coming to the house? We went Demerara together. That was a journey. By sloop, you know. Down the coast, down the main. In the Orinoco delta and then further down the coast to Georgetown. Your boy was sailor in them days, you know.'

'You was a real saga boy, you know, a smart dresser.' Josie was trying to cheer him up this morning.

'Josie, you must remember Hartmann. He was good for himself. He must at least have pinch your bottom.' They laughed together.

'What with you this morning, Jeansie? Is them things that you does remember in your old age?'

'How you mean, Josie? Come give your fella a squeeze, nuh. You was good for yourself in them days, you know.'

She laughed. 'Jeansie, keep yourself still, eh. You daughter doing she business.' Then she looked about the room and at him among his paintings. 'These little things, Jeansie! You want to keep these little things?'

'What little things is that you talking about, Josie?' He looked at where she was among the stacks of portfolios, watercolours falling out, and the oil canvasses. 'Leave them for the moment, nuh. You never know. You does never know . . .'

'Knows what, Jeansie?' She was still intent upon sorting through what she called these little things.

'You know. You never know, nuh . . .' His voice faded with the wind off the gulf entering the studio and blowing the recent watercolours of dawn and sunset at Carenage off the table. 'Pick them up for me. I just finish them. They fresh. I send some like that to exhibition, you know.'

'Exhibition? I ent know you does still send things to exhibition. Them still want these things? Cheups. What I know, boy. You see me, what I know, boy? I say you want to throw these little things away.'

'I ent feel you really think so, you know, Josie.' He laughed. He knew his Josie so well. 'You didn't see when Louis Michel take the parcel that morning last month, up to Princes Building? Is nearly twenty paintings, *oui*. I send to them people for exhibition. What they call them? Trinidad Agricultural Exhibition, something like that. I ent know what it have to do with any agriculture thing, but I get the receipt the other day. They going and show them. At least it ent loss. Where it is?'

He was intent upon showing Josie the evidence of this exhibition that was going to happen in Port of Spain. He was sorting through the drawers of his worktable till he found the bit of paper.

'Here it is. Read what it say, nuh. I know I had it. You see these little things, Josie, how they come in useful. Is about sixteen watercolours I send and twelve pen and ink drawings. Not so it say?'

'Cheups. What I know?'

'And you does read now. Read it, nuh.' He found himself sounding harsh.

Josie toyed with the bit of paper and then continued with her dusting and sorting, careful to put the receipt back in the drawer of the worktable. 'Yes, sixteen watercolour.'

He was beginning to get upset. Not with Josie. He did not know with what.

It felt like he was upset with the neglect that he saw all around him, right here in Edward Street, but more with these lanes he saw climbing the hill behind Dry River. He knew that there was a connection between what he was doing, what he had been doing all these years and how people lived. It was something that grew out of his mother's ideal of a republic of free people. He did not understand it fully. He did not get into the politics like his father and Joseph. He would just paint, paint his way to freedom. He did not understand it rightly. He said again, hurt now, and still sounding harsh, 'Read it, nuh.'

Josie continued to busy herself as if she had not heard what he had said.

The word *little* echoed in his mind. Was that what Josie had always thought, or was it what she had come to think over the last years? He felt that he almost understood her this morning as she busied herself, trying to impress Jeanne Camille with her usefulness about the house.

His painting must have often seemed a little thing to Josie, who had battled her way through her life with very little to show for her efforts; very little reward. There was no house, no husband and no children. She had stayed with her mother. She had stayed with hope in her heart for him, for Jeansie. She had stayed for their thwarted love. That seemed like the largest freedom that she could seek. Though she had known it a long while and taken her mother's advice years ago, to be the sister she indeed was.

Her pleasure was to imagine that things could have been different. That they had had the same father had meant very little to them since he was so absent from both their lives. Yes, Josie was still there, after a long life and a long resignation that she would stay by him as a sister and be the nurse to his grandchildren as she had been to his children; children with that white woman, who had taught her to read. She had come to love Louise. Her small exasperations about his paintings, these little things, while they questioned his whole existence, his *raison d'être*, was how she expressed her anger and her sadness. He knew that what was most precious to her, in spite of everything, was her unconditional love for him.

'Jeansie, boy, let we leave them for now.'

'Yes, Josie. Leave them for now.'

Jeanne Camille still showed up weeks later, each morning, to make sure that Louis Michel had not allowed things to get on top of him.

'But, Jeanne Camille, who it is you think doing this all the time, for years before you get it in your head that you must come here and look after your brother? And you need to watch yourself and that baby.' Michel Jean listened to Josie's challenge and praised her in his heart.

'*Tante Josie*, you and *Papa* getting old now.'

'Your father and me, as you put it, here from the start, you know. We getting old, is true. But we know how we like things. Louis Michel need his father and is me who look out for him. I look out for you when you small. Like you forget.'

'*Tante Josie* . . .'

'Go ahead.'

'*Tante Josie*, I ent know why I does bother. You're right, you know . . .'

'Good. Trust yourself, don't listen to them voices from the past like Uncle Joseph. He done. We bury him. We have to see this thing through. Come when you ready. Girl, is your father, your brother, but don't forget that me is your real family too. It ent get make up so, you know. Me is your father half-sister. Your grandfather is my father. That's how it is.'

'You're right, *Tante Josie*. You talking like Ernestine now.'

'You remember what she say? We is all Cazabon. And she was like grandmother to you. Good. Let we leave it so for now.'

The voices of the women travelled through the house. Michel Jean heard the conversation.

Louis Michel accompanied his father into town to buy paints. They were just coming out of Brunswick Square when Michel Jean said, 'Wait here, son. Wait on the corner.'

'What it is, *Papa*?'

'You just wait here.'

Louis Michel watched his father walking too fast and almost running. He waited on the corner.

Michel Jean doubted himself at first, but, no, he could not forget her figure, her face and her posture. Though, of course, she was older, she had the same air about her as she strolled and stopped to look into shop fronts. Augusta of Orange Grove. He was sure. She was now outside Glendinning's. But then he stopped. There was a stab in his chest that made him give up the attempt to reach her. Louis Michel came running up behind to hold him before he fell over.

'Sit, *Papa*.' They were almost at Marine Square. 'Here, *Papa*, in the cool.'

She had stopped and looked behind her, conscious of the commotion. She was accompanied by a younger woman, who looked like her daughter. Their eyes had met when the younger woman had become aware of his attempt to catch up with them and had turned back to see why an elderly gentleman was pursuing them. He saw her tug at her mother's sleeve. Then she was there standing over him. 'Can I help?' She was speaking to Louis Michel. 'Are you his son?'

Louis Michel looked up from his attendance on his father. '*Oui*, he not feeling well.'

'Monsieur Cazabon,' she said, leaning towards him.

When he looked up she was smiling and bending down to take his hand. She could not be that young, there was silver in her hair, but still so smartly dressed, like she used to be in frocks from New York.

'Augusta,' she said, close to his ear. 'You remember me?'

When he looked up he took the hand of the younger woman next to her. 'Augusta.' She, too, was fashionably dressed.

'No. That's my mother, sir.'

He then looked back at Augusta. 'She's the image of you.'

'Michelle Jeanne. We call her Michelle.'

'I see.' He took her hand. 'Michel Jean Cazabon.'

The daughter looked at her mother.

'Monsieur Cazabon used to come to the house at Orange Grove when I was a young girl. He came to paint. Remember I pointed out that painting to you, the one in the drawing room, of the house with the hundred and one windows.'

'Yes, I remember.'

Michel Jean kept looking at the younger woman. He could see the mix, particularly with Louis Michel next to her. He could see the family that they were, the children, half-brother and sister.

'Your son?' she asked.

'Louis Michel.'

'I see. Your wife was Louise. I saw the announcement in *The Gazette*. I'm sorry.'

'So, this is your daughter. You never bring her.'

'You were going away, remember? Then one day I thought to come, the day she make First Communion, but they said you was away. A woman called Josie at the house in Edward Street. She told me you went away. Then one birthday I come again, but your wife tell me you was out. She didn't tell you I call? Then time pass, years. I come with her when she marrying, but you son here say, you out painting. Then I say it too long now. But I get your messages and gifts.' Augusta had relaxed now, the way she was talking.

'You look well.'

'I keeping good.'

He looked at Louis Michel and Michelle Jeanne. They both looked puzzled.

She smiled. 'Better to let things rest now. Things settle a long time now. I comfortable. We comfortable.'

'Yes, I suppose. If there's anything . . .'

'She's a big woman now with her own children.'

'Yes, of course . . .'

'We must go. Look after yourself.'

They began to walk away. He lost his voice. He sat and watched them walk into Marine Square. The daughter turned around before they disappeared in the crowd. Yes, things had been settled a long time ago. Augusta was right.

'You feeling better, *Papa*?' Louis Michel attended on his father.

'Take me home.'

'People you know? Is them that come to the house?'

'I knew her a long time ago. Look at what time do . . .'

'Is in *The Gazette*!' Josie shouted.

'What? What happen to all yuh?'

'Come and read!'

When they all got back to the house, Jeanne Camille went and got the paper to show her father the announcement that he had won the first prize in the Trinidad Agricultural Exhibition. 'Twenty dollars! *Mon Dieu! Papa!*'

Louis Michel rose to the occasion and shook his father's hand formally. '*Papa*,' he said and embraced him.

The women were ecstatic. 'They say they giving prizes in March.'

'*Maman* would've been so proud.' Jeanne Camille was crying.

'And is only the other day you telling me how you send them painting to make exhibition. You ent even self tell we so we could go and look. Where it was? Princes Building?'

Josie was fussing to see what they could drink as a toast.

'*Papa* and I went. Not so?' Louis Michel found his voice again for the occasion.

'Yes, Wap and I went. Next time is Wap turn.'

'Them little things? You was teasing me.'

'Not teasing, Josie. You didn't know I was vex?'

'You not vex now?'

'Well. I still vex.'

'*Papa*, what you talking about?'

'You ent see the state of the place we living in?'

'*Papa*, what you talking about?'

The prize giving came in March, as had been announced. They all went to the ceremony. Later, Michel Jean was called into the mayor's office to discuss the export of his paintings to London to represent Trinidad at the Colonial and Indian Exhibition.

When he got back to his studio he thought to himself, Things are picking up.

'London?' Josie was astounded.

'They want the paintings from the exhibition to represent Trinidad in London.'

'In London?'

'Yes, Josie. Colonial and Indian Exhibition, something like that. I ent know what it have to do with any Indian thing, but they sending the lot by packet. They must go soon. Here is what it say. "Trinidad: Class 9 Arts and Manufacturers!" Is the same sixteen watercolours and the twelve pen and ink drawings.'

'Jeansie. I happy for you. After all these years. Things quiet since you come back from Martinique. Is a long time. Things used to be wild when you was young.'

'You remember, Josie?'

'You ent want to go up there with the paintings? Why they don't send for you?'

'Send me? Where I go find the money to go?'

'Is true, but they could send you. They will provide. Is your paintings. Is you self that represent Trinidad.'

'That would be something, eh, Josie.'

He had a vision of his paintings hanging in a hall in London like they did at the Princes Building. His mind went back to the times that he was hung at the Salon du Louvre. But what would he do in London? Imagine his old art-master, Mr Barnaby, coming to London. Barnaby must be long dead, though. He wondered who else might see his paintings in London, those men of power who had copied and taken away their views of his island.

Michel Jean stood in his studio, alone, looking out onto the gulf. He could hardly see San Fernando Hill for the haze. The sea was blue and there was the terracotta colour of the sandbanks beyond the harbour, silt from the Caroni. He lost himself staring and thinking of London with his paintings. He stood there gazing at so many of his views that were his paintings; his island, and he its painter.

He turned back into the studio and was looking at his still life of tropical fruit, the mangoes and pommeracs Josie had brought up from the yard one day. Hanging in London, he thought. And there, he looked out of the window once more, Craig Island, hanging in London. The harbour of Port of Spain, the bamboos by Dry River, they too were hanging in London. He started to laugh. He did not want to go. He preferred to stay here and imagine them in London. He did not want to make that voyage.

'*Papa*, *Papa* . . .' It was Louis Michel.

'Show me what you catch today. Where you was?'

'I went up St Ann's. Immortelles in bloom. And pouis catching fire in the hills.'

'Is so?'

'*Oui*.'

'They sending the paintings up to London, you know.'

'What you say, *Papa*?'

'The paintings, for a big exhibition in London.' He thought of his landscapes, Josie's little things, the past they had recorded. How would people view them, what would they understand by them? He thought of the portraits of Indian women. He had sent two paintings, one of a family and the other of a young girl, both done at the old Peru Estate. They had labelled them: *Coolie Woman* and *Coolie Group*. India transported to the West Indies, hanging in London.

'*Papa. Papa*. I know you is the best, you know.'

'Boy, you know what it is to just keep on painting?'

'*Oui. Oui*. You like this one?'

'Immortelles in bloom. Pouis catching fire.'

Towards the end of '86, Josie brought in a letter that had gone to the mayor's office. A messenger boy had brought it over to no. 9 Edward Street.

My Dear Cazabon, I hope this manages to get to you. They told me I could post it to the Mayor of Port of Spain. You must be very important. My old friend, my old travelling companion, what I'm writing about is that this afternoon I was so surprised to find myself standing in front of your watercolours and pen and ink drawings here in London. A whole world opening in front of me, your world, the world you returned to. I have not seen you since '42. How are you? From the looks of things, very well indeed. But above all, I want to say how fine your work is, how very fine, how exceedingly fine. You can write to me at the Grosvenor Hotel in Victoria where I stay when I'm in London. Just a few words. Just to hear your voice, fella, so to speak.

Your very dear friend,
James Fitzwilliam.

Michel Jean put the letter down on his worktable and anchored it with a tube of paint.

'*Papa.*' Louis Michel was at the door.

'Not now, Wap, later. *Papa* need to do something.'

Fitzwilliam seeing his paintings. He would have liked to have been there with him, standing next to him wherever it was that his paintings were hanging, then gone out into the London streets like they used to do when Barnaby sent them off to the Royal Academy, talking and finding an inn, drinking ale and talking and talking. A whole world came back which he had known and lost, his friendship with Fitzwilliam. He did not allow himself to become lost in memories like he had done in the past to revive the boy who was his best friend at school. What he wanted now was a contemporary friend, someone who had known that part of his life, their shared times in Italy and North Africa and during that last visit to the Highlands in '42. He remembered their visit to Nice. Where were all those paintings, were they also among the little things Josie was going to throw out? He saw him at the open window in their rooms on the Spanish Steps in Rome, his best friend, and his protector. There in London looking at his paintings. He found them fine, exceedingly fine! He let himself savour the moment. He would send a letter by the next packet to the Grosvenor Hotel in Victoria. He would write the letter tonight.

My dear James, Fitzwilliam old boy, your few words have made it all worthwhile. No, I'm not important; it is just the colonial government who decided to send the paintings up to London. I don't know what their intentions were. But they've raised you. Like you, I'm an old man now. What you saw are some of my last paintings. The earlier ones are of many of the same places; the difference is in how they are painted. That you find them fine makes my heart sing. That I could be standing with you in London would make my heart sing even louder for our old friendship. My wife died last year, my daughters are married, and my son is one of the new painters. I'm sure you've seen the new style of painting in Paris. What about you? We were the Barnaby boys, remember? I don't think there is time left for all the talk we could do, old friend.

I remain, your friend with fondest memories, Cazabon.

Louis Michel got the letter to the packet with a painting, *Dawn at Carenage*.

'Is the one with the heron, *Papa*?'

'*Oui.*'

In another dawn he was out at Carenage again. He was up long before Josie and Louis Michel had risen. He needed to do another painting down on the coast, now that he had given his most recent one away.

His old friend the heron was there again, crouching at the water's edge. He set up his easel. He fixed it firmly in the sand. His small stool sank into the sand when he sat down, crouched like the heron. He mixed his paints. There was the wash and then he began. It had rained in the night and the yellow flowers of the seaside mahoe glistened as the sun began to burn its way through the clouds into a pinkish dun haze, erasing the town

447

ahead. He balanced his palette on his knee. He was looking back at Port of Spain and not out to the Five Islands, his usual obsession. The small stream took him into the sea and into the perspective of the painting. It flowed with the brackish brown of the fresh water to mix with the faint blue of the sea. In the foreground were the driftwood, small cocorites and vines with purple flowers. There was the lilac of the sky. Three gulls came in to land on the shore and out in the bay was a single sloop with white sails. The coastline emerged, shimmering like a mirage, the tall *palmistes* picked out in feathery plumes. The heron remained crouched and still all of the time as he worked. He sat back and examined the painting.

He let the painting dry. In the shade, he ate the bread and cheese he had brought with him and had a nip of the rum from Miss Melville's distillery. He had brought Fitzwilliam's letter with him and read it again. His friend had thought the paintings exceedingly fine.

2

Now that the train made travel easier, Michel Jean found himself returning to that place where his aunt, Marie Lucille Debonne, his mother's sister, had first introduced him to a sense of what landscape possessed. Jeanne Camille had at last persuaded him to travel south again. The Cipero to Mission train stopped at Corynth Junction. From there into the sugarcane estate was the memorable road: *Sugar Plantation or Estate called the Corynth Estate situated, lying and being in the quarter of North Naparima*. He was drawn to that road like to no other place that he knew.

The language of his parents' 'Deed of Separation' was playing its music. It entered and re-entered his mind like a musical fugue. It had once been a punishment to copy out the hundred and four pages when he was a boy of twelve, and to learn them by heart. It was hardly a road compared to some of the new roads now. It was a gravel trace that led from the junction into the estate with the house, the yard, the barracks and the *usine* in the gully: *Buildings Cultivations live and dead stock and appurtenances* . . .

Very little had changed on the estate, but then he saw the *jhandis*, the Hindu prayer flags flying from their bamboo poles. He had not walked here for a long time. The Indian workers passed him, greeting him in Hindi. *Salaam*. He stopped and talked to a young man from Golconda. 'I is Mohur Singh. They shoot me you know, them fellas in '84. Baker and them English fellas. They shoot me arse!'

'Like is Lucknow or Cawnpore they fear here?' Michel Jean had read the accounts.

'I tell you. They shoot me arse. I is twenty at the time. I just arrive from Calcutta and they shoot me arse.'

Michel Jean sat and sketched Mohur Singh standing by his house with his wife, Seeta. They talked about the Muharram riots and how the English soldiers had shot dead those who were coming with their *tadjahs* from the estates into San Fernando. Now they had been confined to the estate ponds and rivers for the throwing of the *tadjahs* at the celebration of Hosay. The English feared the massing of the people. The south was becoming a new country. Further east at Savanna Grande there had been the recent Carnival Riots. His mother's republic was taking a new shape.

Mohur Singh and Seeta looked and wondered at the Negro painting them. '*Salaam.*'

Then, he left them, carrying his easel and paints on his shoulders. '*Merci bien*,' he called out.

Undulating away from the house, which stood on a small promontory, surveying all beneath, were the cane fields: *eighty and one fifth quarres of land and butted and bounded as follows: North by the Ne Plus Ultra Estate, South by the River Cipero, East by Sainte Madeleine Estate and by the River Cipero and West by the Concord Estate . . .*

He had pored over the deed with his mother when he was twenty-three in 1836, the year before he left for Paris. He had never forgotten the details. The phrases returned like mantras of family history, memories of punishment, to haunt his present journey.

When he conjured this road in his head the colour was almost ochre and the stones were sharp. The music of the road, besides the strong Atlantic wind over the serrated fields, was the crunch and rattle of carriage wheels; a music which had so disturbed his sleep as a child and well into adult life, a music which could still wake him from a nightmare.

He worried about the walk into the estate under the hot morning sun. The guard at the station had enquired if he would be okay: 'Is Monsieur Cazabon? Eh, sir? Long time, long time. You be all right? Is painting you come to paint?'

Times had changed. Michel Jean answered, 'I've got my *chapeau*, man. I go be okay. And watch, parasol and all. You could tell I is an old man now. Painting, you say? They don't want painting now, boy.'

'Remember one you do. San Fernando Hill.'

'Morne Jaillet, you mean.'

'Long time they call it so, *oui*, for truth.'

Michel Jean let his parasol open wide. 'What time it is, you say, the train returning to San Fernando?'

'Twelve o'clock. Sharp.'

'I go be there. Don't let the train go without me, eh.'

He noted that he had a period of three hours if he was to get the next returning train. He thanked the guard. He would make the time do. Make the time do, he said to himself. It had become a recurring phrase this last year, make the time do.

The road held so many memories. The one which possessed him, now that he had walked a bit further, and which could return with such frequent force no matter where he was on the island, or elsewhere in the world at the time, was the place where he had been brought by his aunt, Marie Lucille. It had seemed so ordinary then where she took him on one of her walks in search of a good place to settle down to paint, until his aunt suddenly said, 'Look, sweetheart, see, the light falling on the bamboo. Do you see?' She had dropped to her knees to be at his height and pointed with her arm outstretched before her. He had followed the arrow of her aim. He remembered her statement, her exclamation and then her question which he now felt his entire life had been trying to answer. 'Yes, I see. *Oui, oui*,' he had said in a small boy's voice, unsure of what he was seeing, but not wanting to disappoint her, or to embarrass himself.

He had been trying ever since to see the light falling on bamboos in the way that his aunt had meant when she so excitedly pointed it out to him when he was a boy of ten. His aunt's seeing was the seeing he wanted his paintings to possess. How to paint that seeing had been his life's task.

It had been along a certain stretch of that ochre trace when he fell under the spell of moving shadows and mottled patches as he entered a bamboo grove. Bamboo patch, he knew well, that place where the clumps grew thickly together but separate. Josie, Ignace and himself would hide in the bamboo patch when playing hide-and-seek, or sometimes it was him and his cousins. But, grove, that was a new word, one he thought he had learned from his aunt as she talked and walked along and he listened. This was when the bamboo clumps grew thick and close to each other and the high branches arched over to meet the other thick, close clumps on the other side of the road. These extraordinary grasses, transported from India into the Antilles, as he had learned as a young man from Mr Lockhart, possessed that wonderful combination of lightness and strength.

To see them, to catch them in paint, watercolour or oil, had been the challenge of his life. He had seen that look on the faces of foreigners when they looked at the effect which his lithographs had created with their peculiar light and shadow as the feathery branches made their arches in that print of the *Maraval Dyke* in his 1851 album. Only two years ago, he had sent off to the Colonial and Indian Exhibition in London *Bamboos at Dry River* and *Bamboos at St Ann's*, those well-loved haunts of his, not far from town.

He had, he thought, just about enough time to complete the journey to the old estate house, have a look around, and then get back along the road to catch the train returning from Mission. Whether it was the hot sun, despite his hat and parasol, or the exhilaration of being in the bamboo grove, he arrived at the house more agitated than he liked to be these days. He paused at the end of the gap to catch his breath and to still his nerves. He did not like these palpitations that were more and more frequent now. He did not like the stab in his chest.

The house seemed to be locked up. As he got closer, he noticed that it looked abandoned. He stood now at the bottom of the steps leading up to the veranda. He worried again that he had not enough time to go into the house, have a look, and then to return along the road.

The wooden house was two-storeyed, with a veranda at the top of the front steps. It stood on the edge of the sugarcane fields. These fields fell away from all sides of the house beyond the tall hibiscus hedge into folds in the low hills, which stretched towards Petit Morne and Golconda. He knew that part of the estate by the teak trees on the brow of the hill and the tall *palmistes* near the overseer's house, which was just visible from this distance.

He had reached the top of the steps and stepped onto the pitch pine floor of the veranda. It creaked and he could feel the old boards sinking beneath his feet. He wondered now whether he was up to this visit.

From the front of the house, he looked out over the cane fields, the barrack yards and the *usine* in the gully. *All dwelling houses, boiling houses, Negro houses, curing houses, out houses . . . mill houses.*

Over the fields, towards Petit Morne, there was a dairy and the avenue of mango trees they called Hang-Man-Alley.

He had got his breath back and he stood and stared at the mango trees and the stories attached to those trees flooded his mind; men's bodies had swung from nooses in the past from despair, punishment and murder. He remembered the one time he had come upon the body of a young man. He had stood and stared at the limp hanging body, the face encrusted with buzzing flies. He had run back to the house between the traces in the fields, calling on Ernestine to come and meet him.

Why was he on this pilgrimage? The breeze was strong. He tried the front door. It was unlocked and he entered, calling out, 'Anyone there?' There was, of course, no answer. It was stifling hot inside and dismal in the still, stale air. He opened up the windows of the drawing room and inhaled the fresh air and the world that had formed him. He remembered the high

453

breezes from the east off the Atlantic and the savannahs near Mission. The open windows sucked the wind into the belly of the house, up the well of the mahogany staircase which ascended from the hall and the welcoming front door off the veranda through which he had just entered, climbing to the second floor with the four bedrooms and a bathroom off the top landing. The windows rattled. Banisters sagged. He had caught the place just in time.

It had not been a good idea to climb the stairs to the bedrooms; luckily there was a chair just there on the landing outside the room that had once been his parents' bedroom. He could hear Jeanne Camille's voice, '*Papa*, don't overexert yourself.' He sat down and gradually recovered his breath, heeding his daughter's advice this morning before he had left home. He had had enough. It had not been a good idea, he kept saying to himself. He should have known better.

It was only as he was about to leave the house out of the front door that he saw the small door to the room under the stairs. He steadied himself. He moved towards it and stood there wondering whether or not to open it, whether he should enter the darkness of the cupboard he liked to hide in as a child.

Why was he doing this?

The idea had been the train journey to see the views again, as Jeanne Camille had suggested he would enjoy them, not to come to the house and subject himself to these memories, which were now becoming an ordeal. It struck him as he looked at the closed door to under the stairs that it was lower and narrower than he had remembered.

But he stood outside the door, as if rooted to the spot. The memories of his aunt Marie Lucille disappeared with the dark mood of a small child waiting for his father to reach into that small, dark room and draw out his favourite cane, the one he called Justice, or the leather strap, which he called Master. Which was it to be? He continued to stand there, forgetting everything, but the sharp, cracking sound of a whip being administered. Each stroke echoed through the now-empty house.

Then his rebellion came as clear as it had done then, with as strong a voice as he had had as a boy. He was astonished to hear his voice travelling through the house. He stood and spoke to the closed door. He had not wanted to open it. 'You cannot beat me. I'm not a slave.'

He realized the time was running out and that he had absent-mindedly wandered down to the estate yard. He found that he had to stop to catch his breath. Quite spontaneously, he was beginning to weep. He noticed workers on their way from the fields staring. He carried on walking down the road to the yard towards the estate, reciting a child's punishment: *usine . . . and other edifices, erections and buildings thereon and all boilers, coolers, coppers, skimmers, ladles, carts, waggons, lamps and other plantation Implements and utensils thereto belonging and all Plantation and cultivations of Sugar Canes, provisions and pastures thereon . . .*

The list went on and on. The memory of that punishment.

Even now, like the young boy that he once was, he recalled the dreadful details of that Deed: *and all mules and horses . . . bulls cows, heifers, steers, yearlings and calves and all other live and dead stock therein now or belonging thereto and woods, underwoods, way rights, of way paths, passages, roads, commons and rights of commons and pasturage, waters, watercourses, drains, canals, cisterns, uses, services, enjoyments, servitudes . . . rights of privileges and appurtenances to the said Sugar Estate called Corynth belonging or in any manner or wise appertaining and also the several and respective services for the remainder of the periods of their apprenticeship of the thirty apprenticed Labourers who were formerly slaves belonging to the said Estate and duly registered in the Registrar of slaves office of the said island by the respective names.*

And, when he came to the names, they were the names of people he knew: *Lucien la Bonne, Marie Claire Guime, Marie Esther Lubin, Will Williams, Marie Susanne . . .* He had wondered where the rest of her name had gone . . . *Marie Louise*

Guime, Marie Jeanne Susanne Lubin, Marie Julie Susanne, Marie Rosette, Jean Rosette, Jean Antoine Engelle Muturin Cazabon . . . Jean had collected so many names . . . *Scipion Hilaire, Louis Cezard, Marie Claire Erine Erinette, Gloria Sonomine, Jean Louis Rosette, Marie Catherine Rosette, William Williams Nesbitts, Patty Williams, Success Williams, Martha Williams, Iain Williams, Hannah Williams, Cato Williams, Brice Williams, Billy Williams and George Williams and all the Estate rights, titles, Interest, Inheritances, uses, trusts, property claims, dominion and demand whatsoever both at Law and in Equity of the said François Cazabon and Rose Debonne Cazabon his wife* . . .

Michel Jean called, '*Maman.*' He whispered her name, his dearest mother.

It was only as he stood on the empty platform of the small station at Corynth Junction, inhaling the Atlantic breeze, exhausted by his hurried return along the road, that his father's words again entered his consciousness. 'I'll beat you and then put you in the stocks.'

Then he remembered again the door he had been staring at, thinking that it looked like the lid of a coffin. He could no longer remember why this threat and punishment had happened. He thought how his whole life had been one of trying to make sense both of the light falling on bamboos, which his aunt had pointed out to him, that ordinary beauty, and the context in which he had become a painter, and in which his father beat him as if he were a slave, and threatened to place him in the stocks in the middle of the estate yard, the way Ignace, his childhood friend whom he had betrayed, had been beaten and placed in the stocks.

As the train rattled back along the rails into Cipero Street in San Fernando, Michel Jean reflected upon the time he still had with which to make do. He pulled his flask of rum from his pocket and, raising it to his mouth, he took a swig.

BEAU SÉJOUR

1900 . . .

They knew him along the coast; the slight limp, the crooked shadow cast upon the ochre beach beneath the criss-crossing coconuts at late afternoon around five o'clock, coming back from his trek with his easel and paints on his back. The older villagers, as old as him now, remembered how his father called to him, 'Wap', a sugar-head among the other boys splashing in the surf; white, like sprinkled salt, in their own hair now. They knew to leave him alone in the place where he had moved soon after his father's death, coming here from town.

It was the time of day when the fishermen sat in groups with their pirogues tied up on the beach after pulling seine. Their nets were strung out between bamboo poles. The pirogues were painted in their bright colours. Their names, prayers for safety, *Ave Stella Maris*, were written along their hulls. So many fishermen could not swim. The bows were directed towards the horizon and their morning's destination.

Madame de la Borde had told him that there was a room there for him. She asked no questions. It was the paintings that had drawn her to the slight figure standing in the middle of the room, lost among the viewers, as if he had nothing to do with the paintings hanging on the walls of the Victoria Institute in Port of Spain.

She had heard of his sojourns to Beau Séjour, and recognized the source of his landscapes in the paintings, the long road through Manzanilla to the Cocal. Another was of a country road taking you to somewhere through the bush and scrub, following the light. These were not mere representations of a place, but paintings beyond photography. He had gone much further than his father, whom she had admired, had dared. 'I was at the Trinidad Agricultural Exhibition in 1886 as a young girl, when your father won the first prize. The exhibition went on to London.'

Louis Michel stared at her. 'Ah, *oui*.'

'There's a room for you on the coast if that is where you would like to live and work. The estate is dying with the red-ring disease. I would be only too willing for you to make use of the rooms at the back of the house.'

He said he would be grateful for the accommodation. He had wanted to leave no. 9 Edward Street. Josie had died a month after his father. Jeanne Camille wanted the house sold so that she and her husband could get some money for their family. He, too, could do with some money himself.

He had taken the room at the back of the coconut estate house, sunk down among the low dunes and the young palm trees. He might have preferred a room facing the sea, the relentless noise of the waves. But it was almost a blessing that on mornings in his studio he stared out of the back-room window into the coconut grove with the greens and yellows. He was able to see the way the light pierced like shafts, or was filtered through clouds casting gloom and moving shadows. It was a changing landscape, which trained his eye to see the creek along the side of the house in ways he might never have seen it if she had given him a room at the front. Turning his easel this way he could see the river flowing out to the sea, to where the mouth was channelled by the shifting sands; the fresh water flowing over a shoal mixed with the salt.

Painting most days *en plein air* like his father, he walked with watercolours and with oils. He remembered sites he had known as a boy. He sought out lagoons where the sea rushed under a bridge meeting the mouth of the river Ortoire. He clambered over rocks at Point Radix. He worked at night in moonlight at

Manzanilla. And, like his father, he caught the dawn at Mayaro, like he had done at Carenage.

'You are the master of coconut trees, the way your father was a wizard with bamboos,' Madame de la Borde said to him when she came to see him in his new studio in the back room. She had come all the way from Port of Spain through Sangre Grande and the forest beyond.

They stood together and stared at the daring use of cobalt and aquamarine, the trunks of the coconuts, as slender as pencils, bent in their eagerness for water with their crowns sculpted by the wind, twisted and shaken out. All along the wide beach with the chip-chip gatherers, the palms settled down only in the darkness of the hot nights for which the coast was famous. The paintings were broken open, all frames gone, the eye moving with the direct light of photography, playing with perspectives, nuances and subtleties, the wrist moving over palette and canvas directed by an eye that painted what it saw and not what it imagined.

'You see it so? You see that blue like that? And the lilac?' Madame de la Borde asked. She toyed with the watercolour on the easel.

'*Oui.*'

'Is carite or redfish you want?' a fisherman's wife called from the beach. The front of her dress bled with the colours of the painter's palette.

All the while, the engine of the surf, the white noise of breaking combers, coming in as far up as the house in high tide, set among the low dunes and coconuts, did not cease in this small corner of the world.

AUTHOR'S NOTES

Historical Note

This work of fiction was inspired by the life and times of Michel Jean Cazabon, 1813–1888, Trinidad's most important nineteenth-century painter, whom the French place among the Barbizon school of artists. While a skeletal biography of the artist has been established, very little is known about the man himself beyond that which can be read in his many paintings. In this regard, I am deeply indebted to the historian and art critic, Geoffrey Maclean's two books, *The Illustrated Biography of Michel Jean Cazabon* and *Cazabon: The Harris Collection*. These introductions to the biography of the artist and his paintings were an invaluable springboard into *Light Falling on Bamboo*.

While the truth of the age that is sought here is the truth of the story, I have made extensive use of historical sources mentioned in my acknowledgements. I use the names of some nineteenth-century historical figures, including the artist himself and his family, and also the Governor of the time, Lord Harris, and his secretary, James Wildman. There are other historical figures, for example, the well-known planter, William Hardin Burnley. I was influenced in the writing of Elizabeth Prowder's character by the 1847-1851 correspondence of Margaret Mann, an Englishwoman from Guernsey, who was resident in Trinidad with her husband and wrote extensive letters to her mother describing her life during her stay on the island, the originals of which are in the Bodleian Library, Oxford. The character of Flora Lavington, the Prowder family's governess of the novel, was inspired by Mrs Fitton of the same letters. I wish to acknowledge some direct quotation from these letters and the use of two verses of Margaret Mann's poetry. However, in all these instances, and others, it is not my purpose to give a historical account. These are, properly speaking, fictional characters. The detail and real substance of the novel is entirely fictional.

A significant collection of Michel Jean Cazabon's paintings in Britain exists at Belmont House in the village of Throwley near Faversham in Kent. Belmont is the seat of the Harris family, and the third Lord Harris was Governor of Trinidad in the mid-nineteenth century and a principal patron of the artist. Cazabon's paintings also exist in private collections and are frequently sold at Christie's, Sotheby's and Bonham's. Another major collection is in the National Museum of Trinidad and Tobago. Martiniquans also claim Cazabon because of his family history and his residence there in the second half of the nineteenth century. There is continuing interest in Cazabon's work as an artist, particularly because of the historical record that his paintings represent.

A Note on Language

French Creole or patois was considered the true lingua franca of Trinidad in the nineteenth century. English was spoken from 1797 after the capitulation of the Spanish to the British. With the significant settlement of French planters in 1783, French had a dominant effect on the language. These European languages were mixed with the West African languages, Yoruba and Kikongo, from the eighteenth century onwards as a result of the retention of African culture among slave populations. Hindi and Bhojpuri entered the linguistic mix from 1845, with the arrival of indentured labourers from the Indian subcontinent.

I have tried to give a sense of this linguistic diversity of Trinidad in the nineteenth century by using standard English and English

Creole with a sprinkling of French and patois phrases. It would have been, and remains the case, that speakers can move easily between standard English or French and Creole within the same moment of conversation. The landscape of Trinidad is defined by names from all of these languages, and these are a record in themselves of the diverse linguistic history of the island.

ACKNOWLEDGEMENTS

I wish to acknowledge the support of many people in the researching and writing of this novel. Firstly, I am grateful to Professor Kenneth Ramchand, Associate Provost, for supporting my application for a Senior Research Fellowship at The Academy for The Arts, Letters, Culture and Public Affairs, The University of Trinidad and Tobago.

I wish to acknowledge Professor Bridget Brereton of the University of the West Indies for her *A History of Modern Trinidad 1783-1962* and to thank her for her insights and warm encouragement. I wish to thank Professor Brinsley Samaroo of the University of the West Indies and The University of Trinidad and Tobago who introduced me to The Cottage of Lord Harris and organised a memorable visit to Nelson Island and The Five Islands. I am indebted to Dr Amar Wahab's *Colonial Inventions: Landscape, Power and Representation in the Nineteenth-Century Trinidad,* Anthony de Verteuil's *Great Estates of Trinidad,* Carl Campbell's *Cedulants and Capitulants: The Politics of Coloured Opposition in the Slave Society of Trinidad 1783-1838,* Lise Winer's *Dictionary of English/Creole of Trinidad & Tobago: On Historical Principles.* I wish also to acknowledge Jean-Baptiste Phillipe's *Free Mulatto,* Lafcadio Hearn's *Two Years in the French West Indies,* E.L. Joseph's *History of Trinidad 1838,* C.L.R. James' *The Black Jacobins: Toussaint l'Ouverture and the San Domingo Revolution,* Gerard Besson's monograph on the de Boissière family, *A Tale of Two Families: The de Boissières & the Ciprianis of Trinidad,* and many other historians, particularly from the school of Caribbean History, as well as art critics and commentators who were extensively acknowledged at the time of my Cazabon lectures at the National Library in Port of Spain, 2007-2009.

I have used quotes from the *Deed of Separation and Articles of Agreement, Francois and Rose Debonne Cazabon*. I also acknowledge Derek Walcott's *Tiepolo's Hound* (Farrar, Straus and Giroux, Faber & Faber, 2000) and Earl Lovelace's *Salt* (Faber & Faber, 1996, Persea Books, 1997) for the quotes which are used as epigraphs and thank the authors and publishers for the use of those quotes.

There were many people who offered me assistance in tracking down valuable texts. I wish to thank: Mr Adrian Camps-Campins for the use of his personal library, his hospitality, and the gift of a set of his unique historical cards; the archivist Margaret Woodall at Belmont House and the administration of Belmont House for their generous attention in allowing me to visit and view Cazabon's paintings; the staff of the Bodleian Library in Oxford in allowing me to read and grant me copies of the Margaret Mann Letters, part of the Dame Kathleen Courtney Collection; the family of Margaret Mann: John and Nancy Furlong, and Bridget Brice who allowed me to have examples of Margaret Mann's poetry and to use two verses.

I wish to thank the following institutions and their staff: St Edmund's College, Ware; the Roman Catholic Archives of the Archdiocese of Westminster; the Library at the St Augustine Campus of the University of the West Indies and the West Indiana & Special Collections; National Museum of Trinidad and Tobago; The President's House, Trinidad and Tobago; the National Archives of Trinidad and Tobago; Kew Gardens Archive; the National Archives of Britain; the British Library, the Bureau du Patrimoine Conseil Regional de la Martinique; the Carnegie Library in Georgetown Guyana; the Department of Literature, Film & Theatre Studies at the University of Essex.

Many friends and people who have become friends offered help with documents, assistance and the viewing of paintings.

I wish to thank: Nick Addison, Frances St Clair Miller, John Stewart, Kathleen Helenese-Paul, Professor Funso Aiyejina, Mario Lewis, Leon Wainwright, Bunty O'Connor, Joseph Fernandes, Lady Simone Warner, Vickie Downie, Michael Maniloff, Angelo Bissessarsingh, Mark Perreira, Anne Walmsley Lennox Honychurch, Bruce Huggins, John Gransaull, Jak Peake and Peter Hulme; Martine Vuillard and Sylvain Tamar who were generous with the loan of an apartment in Paris and their gift of Philippe Roy's *Memoire Des Rues* in helping me to imagine Cazabon's Paris; Joanne Mendes for the loan of her beautiful apartment at Coblentz House in Port of Spain in the last stages of editing.

Throughout my research I was helped by the practical and thoughtful assistance of the office staff of The Academy UTT: Lana Allard, Ghansham Mohammed, Nekeisha Nelson and Joy Gibbings. Mandy Isaacs, Professor Alison Donnell and Patricia Murray have been sensitive and encouraging readers of my draft manuscripts at different stages, giving valuable assistance. Marjorie Thorpe offered me generous hospitality, moral support and advice through long and sometimes difficult periods of research and writing. I will always be grateful. Jenny Green has been a collaborator in this whole enterprise: planning research trips, transcribing letters, reading drafts and endlessly discussing and being there in every possible way, not least crossing and re-crossing the Atlantic several times.

I must thank my agent Andrew Hewson of Johnson & Alcock for his encouragement and sound judgement as well as for that seminal discussion on savants in the work of Oliver Sacks. Alan Mahar of Tindal Street Press has been such an understanding, thoughtful and sensitive editor; my warmest thanks to him and the rest of the Tindal Street Press team: Luke Brown, Melissa Baker, and not least, Emma Baker, such a thorough and involved copy editor.